I KNEW THEN that I had very little time left on this earth. This pretty, decaying little room would be my last sight on earth—that, and the beautiful face of my murderer, who was looking down at me with such a closed, angry expression. He was all everyone suspected, a vampire, the ghoul of Venice, and I would be his final victim before Mark deciphered those damning papers and had him arrested. But by then it would be too late for me.

"No," I said, and my voice came out in a croak. I couldn't move; I was frozen in place with his hand on my neck, his golden eyes capturing my helpless ones.

"It is only what you deserve, little one," he murmured, and his mouth moved down and brushed my lips, very lightly. He kissed my eyes, my cheeks, my chin, soft hurried little kisses that made me feel dizzy and dreaming. This must be death, I thought, not minding one bit.

"Look at me, Carlotta," he commanded, and, startled out of my reverie, I looked up. It seemed to me I had never seen a face so evil or so sad, so beautiful or so death-like. Without further warning his head moved down and I felt his teeth on my neck, sharp and painful, felt the blood come just before the blackness closed in.

Other Anne Stuart novels from Bell Bridge Books

Historical Romances

Lady Fortune

Barrett's Hill

Prince of Magic

Romantic Suspense

Nightfall

Shadow Lover

The Demon Count Novels

by

Anne Stuart

Bell Bridge Books

Bell Bridge Books
PO BOX 300921
Memphis, TN 38130
Print ISBN: 978-1-61194-547-8

Bell Bridge Books is an Imprint of BelleBooks, Inc.

We at BelleBooks enjoy hearing from readers.
Visit our websites
BelleBooks.com
BellBridgeBooks.com
ImaJinnBooks.com

10 9 8 7 6 5 4 3 2 1

Cover design: Debra Dixon
Interior design: Hank Smith
Photo/Art credits:
Woman in gondola (manipulated) © Nejron | Dreamstime.com
Woman (manipulated) © Olga Ekaterincheva | Dreamstime.com
Texture (manipulated) © Natis76 | Dreamstime.com

:Lcdn:01:

The Demon Count

For Frank, of course, and vampires everywhere

Chapter One

I'VE NEVER BEEN one to give way to hysterics with great frequency, but I knew that if this wretchedly sprung carriage hit one more bump I would scream at the top of my lungs. It seemed like months since I'd first climbed into this vehicle of the devil, and my poor, tired body was a mass of bruises and aches since we started on this rocky and ill-kept road across the plains of Italy. As the miles passed, each turn of the wheel was torture. Once more I was flung against my unwilling fellow traveler, a stout and surly banker, and without further hesitation I shrieked.

The coach pulled to a halt far quicker than I could have imagined possible, and the cheerful Swiss driver appeared at the window, creases of worry in his ruddy face. "What's the matter?" he demanded anxiously in German.

The banker gave me a look of withering disdain. His opinion of womanhood was obviously not very high, and his opinion of a young lady who traveled unaccompanied on a public coach through the strife-torn Italy of 1840 was even less. And when that same young lady chose to scream for no reason . . . All this he communicated to the driver in a few short German words, while the comfortable-looking grandmother across from me nodded in weary agreement. It had been a long day, and the May weather was unseasonably warm.

I had the grace to look abashed, while the spotty young clerk on the lady's left tried to catch my eye with a speaking glance of sympathy. I ignored him.

"I'm terribly sorry," I said in my clear English voice. "I don't know what came over me. I'm perfectly all right now."

The banker, after giving me one last look of helpless dislike, turned and translated my gentle speech into German, adding a few distinctly uncomplimentary remarks about the English in general and this one in particular. I smiled at them all apologetically, bland incomprehension written on my face, settled back against the rough seat, and sighed.

For not the first time I wondered whether I had been incredibly foolish in taking off like this. Without question my reputation was in shreds, my meager finances almost gone, and my spirits at low ebb. I couldn't help but wonder how my new guardian would react when his detested and despised young charge arrived at his palazzo. The thought cheered me.

As the coach began to bounce once more along the potholed highway, I let my mind drift back to the England I had left, the home in an uproar, the rage and disapproval of my mother's family, providing a momentary diversion from the tedium of travel.

"You cannot, you absolutely cannot travel alone to Italy at this time!" Great-aunt Matilda stormed.

"Those wretched foreigners are about to erupt into war again!" Cousin Horace announced. "Not that they aren't always in that state. I don't know what could have gotten into your father, to have left you in the care of some damned Spaniard!"

"He's Italian, Cousin Horace," I corrected gently, my soft voice a reproval for his swearing. "And for that matter, he's half British and a cousin by marriage. Father traveled widely . . . he knew many men and many places. I trust him to have chosen the best of them for me."

"But to travel alone, Charlotte!" Aunt Isabel reproached. "So soon after your poor mother's funeral."

"I won't be traveling alone. I'll have my maid with me at all times, and luckily a friend of Mother's is planning a trip to Venice. She has graciously offered to bear me company. So you can see I couldn't possibly wait . . . Mrs. Hartmann is leaving in a week, and I'll have to be ready. Count del Zaglia insists I come as soon as possible."

"Damned impertinence, if you ask me!" Cousin Horace snorted, his jowls quivering with indignation. "Still, he's your legal guardian for another year. There's not much to be done about it. Now, if only your father had had the sense to talk to me about this, he would have seen that I was a much better person to take charge of your well-being." *Not to mention my comfortable fortune,* I thought cynically. "We'll have to meet this Mrs. Hartmann." He snorted again, a distressing habit of his.

I had brightened at this sign of capitulation. "Of course, cousin."

But they had never met, for the simple reason that Mrs. Hartmann, like my guardian's summons to Italy, was a fabrication or, to put it more frankly, a lie. Two days after that fateful conversation in the cold and dreary library of my mother's rented house in Brighton I was safely on board a small ship making its leisurely way along the coast of Europe to the Mediterranean Sea and the Italian port of Genoa

I received not one word on my mother's death, not one note of condolence from my appointed guardian, merely a cold communication from his agent in England that I was on no account to even think of venturing to join him. I was to continue my schooling (schooling I had completed two years ago at the age of seventeen), and when the situation in Italy calmed a bit, Count del Zaglia would arrange something for me.

Arrange something for me! The very thought turned me livid with rage. I had at that moment decided I would instead arrange something for the dear count. A trip to the continent would be just the thing to help me over the shock of my mother's unexpected passing. Within a day the tickets were purchased, two small bags were packed with my mother's cast-off mourning clothes, and I was ready to depart.

As the carriage rumbled along at a painfully brisk pace, I thought back to my mother's sulky, delicate face, and wondered what she would think of me now. She probably wouldn't care that her only daughter was traveling alone and unchaperoned. She never had much maternal feeling for me.

I had often wondered what had possessed my father to marry her. Theresa Brunwood was pretty enough in her youth, indeed, even till her untimely death, but there were others with as much beauty. She had quite a frightening intellect, a curse she had passed on to me, which perhaps accounted for poor Charles Morrow's initial enchantment, so accustomed was he to brainless society belles. As a rising young diplomat perhaps he thought the lovely creature would be an impetus to his burgeoning career. If so, he had reckoned without Theresa's intrinsic coldness and self-absorption. One year after their only child was born my father took up residence at the embassy in Rome. Theresa remained behind, victim of a conveniently failing constitution.

To say my mother enjoyed ill-health would be to put it mildly. Every day I would be brought before her chaise longue to kiss her artfully pale cheek and recite to her my lessons. Each day I would look for some sign of affection, some gesture of maternal love. I never found one, and by the age of twelve I had given up looking.

Theresa had taught me many things, however. She taught me to revere learning, to be self-sufficient, to smile prettily and play the fool when gentlemen were about.

"But my dear Charlotte," she would say softly when I was older and more romantic and would dare to mention an attractive would-be beau, "he has the mind of a well-bred horse. Surely you couldn't really be interested in one such as he?" And I would blush before her gentle mockery and agree miserably that no, of course I could not be interested.

All in all, I grew up totally unsuited for the one profession open to me, that of marriage and motherhood. I could speak seven languages, five fluently. I could cipher, discuss politics, literature, and history, outrun, outtalk, and outthink any man of my limited acquaintance. And if I did have a weakness every now and then for a pair of broad shoulders or clear blue eyes I would catch my mother's faintly superior smile and turn away with great resolution and only the faintest trace of lingering regret.

"It won't be much longer, signorina," the spotty young clerk opposite me broke into my none-too-pleasant thoughts, and the banker frowned warningly at him. "Another hour or two and we'll stop for the night."

"And none too soon," the banker harrumphed, casting a steely glance in my innocent direction, placing the blame for our delays squarely on my delicate shoulders.

I considered the two of them for a moment, then offered the younger one my sweetest smile. "Thank you," I murmured gently, and then deliberately directed my attention to the gently sloping countryside below me, leaving the crestfallen clerk to stare moodily at my averted profile.

I couldn't blame the fellow. Every time I looked in a mirror I experienced a start of surprise that the fairyland creature should be me, Charlotte Theresa Sabina Morrow. A perfect English rose, a smitten young man had once told me, and I could unconcernedly see the truth in that. I had guinea-gold hair that fell in delightful, soft curls around my face, a retroussé nose, rosebud mouth, and china-blue eyes as big as saucers. My complexion was touched with a healthy pink, my eyelashes were thick and curly, and my natural expression was one of charming innocence. My body lacked the perfect, insipid beauty of my face, but it was well enough. A bit over average height and not quite as plump as was the current style. In all I was considered to be a beauty, and it interested me not one whit. In my soul I fancied myself a dark, tragic figure, with melting dark eyes, hair black as night, and an alabaster complexion that was both pale and interesting. The porcelain English beauty that stared at me was a bland and uninteresting stranger, and my recognition of its attractive qualities had nothing to do with vanity. It simply existed.

I had learned swiftly in the last two years since I left school that I had only to smile and some nice young man would rush to do my bidding. Even motherly ladies would respond to my gentle requests, a fact that amused my own mother no end. "You should do splendidly, my dear," she had chortled one evening with uncharacteristic glee. "Everything that should have been mine will be at your fingertips. You need only to perfect your use of your natural gifts, and the world will be yours."

I had watched her amusement with somber doubt. I had no idea what great future my mother had in store for me, but somehow I doubted it was something that would appeal to me. In truth, I would have been far happier if I had been able to succumb to just one of those stalwart young men that flocked around our rented mansion in the seaside resort town. But I was far too much my mother's daughter to do that.

In the end I had broken free . . . only by her sudden death, but free I was, and reveling in it. I had abandoned my maid in Southampton with a fatter purse than my limited pocket money could truly have afforded. Dressed in one of Mother's cast-off black wool dresses, I knew I made a pathetic and appealing picture to my fellow travelers. I had exchanged my set of shipboard protectors for equally vigilant champions, and never once had I been forced to suffer importunate suggestions. Indeed, it was a source of disappointment to me that my trip had been so tame, even boring.

But I counted on the rage of my unknown guardian, the excitement of living in a new country, and the turbulent political situation to change all that. I had no doubt I could bring Count del Zaglia around my finger in short order . . . I had seldom failed when I wanted an elderly gentleman to succumb to my feminine wiles.

I remembered my mother's exclamations of anger and disdain when my father's will was read. "How dare he!" she had fumed, looking temporarily quite healthy in her rage. "Leaving you in the care of that . . . that foreigner! And a Catholic at that! The man never had any sense." For an educated woman Theresa was surprisingly narrow-minded about what she stigmatized as "dirty foreigners."

"But, Mama," I had ventured with the usual timidity she alone had inspired in me, "he was Father's dearest friend!"

"He was no such thing," she snapped. "Luc del Zaglia has to be years younger than your father—closer to my age than to his. And totally disreputable if half of what I hear is true. It is highly fortunate that I am not quite as sickly as your father hoped. If I were in my grave I shudder to think what would become of you at the hands of such a one as he!"

All this was just the sort of thing to appeal to an over-imaginative young woman. My one act of rebellion against Theresa's strict rule was my love of lurid novels. I was amazingly gullible, and I took to daydreaming all sorts of melodramatic fantasies about the demon count, as I had dubbed him. Deep down I knew well enough he must be harmless—my father had loved me too dearly to have risked placing me in any but the best of care. It had always grieved him deeply that my mother had kept such a tight hold on my company.

I had always wondered what had prompted Theresa to deny my companionship to my lonely father, and decided long ago that it could only be spite. Theresa certainly had never cared for me, nor for anyone but herself. And I couldn't help wondering if my father, knowing full well the specious nature of my mother's illnesses, hadn't placed my care in the hands of the most dissolute person he could find, simply to irritate her.

"Well, there's no helping it," Theresa had lamented bitterly. "There is no way I can fight this infamous will—in English law women are less than nothing. I will simply have to live until you are twenty-one."

I had never doubted that she would. But two years later, fourteen months to the day before I would be free of Luc del Zaglia's onerous control, my mother had dropped dead at the age of forty of a sudden heart attack, leaving me at the mercy of my father's appointed guardian.

I had been entirely ready to resist any suggestion that I might change my way of life when that terse, authoritarian message had arrived from the count's lawyer. My mourning for my cold-hearted mother had been surprisingly painful, but now I found myself filled with a new, life-giving rage. Even as I was bounced and jounced across Italy, I could remember the message and my own reaction to it. Well, the count was about to be repaid in full for his bland assumption that his little charge would mindlessly obey his instructions. He was about to find out he had gotten far more than he bargained for.

The coach pulled to a sudden halt quite a full hour before our usual evening stop. The banker stuck his head out the window and then drew back in with a snort. "A detachment of soldiers," he muttered. "As if we were not late enough."

"Papers ready!" A voice called from the driver's seat, and I continued to smile blankly until the banker repeated the words in English, pointing to my reticule and swearing savagely under his breath.

"Your papers, miss," he grumbled. "These Austrian soldiers haven't the best tempers in the world, and when they want to see your papers you'd better have them ready!" He was busy rustling for his own identification. "They'd as soon clap you in irons as look at you, the way things are now."

"Oooh," I let out a little squeal of dismay, the brainless young English girl to perfection. "They wouldn't do that to me, would they?"

"No, of course not," the spotty young man reassured me, glaring at the banker. "They would never harm such a beautiful young lady as yourself. Signorina . . ."

A ham-like hand appeared at the door. "Passengers dismount!" a voice demanded in German, then repeated in French, Italian, and English with acute boredom. We all stared at each other with sudden nervousness, and the grandmotherly figure across from me crossed herself with abrupt piety. "Now!" The guttural voice grew testier, and, tiring of my cowardly companions, I climbed out over the portly form of the banker and scrambled down from the coach, eager to be on solid ground once more.

Chapter Two

THE FEEL OF the rocky turf beneath my sturdy traveling boots after so long in the bouncing carriage was unexpected, and my knees gave way beneath me in a most undignified manner, plummeting me into a pair of manly arms. I allowed myself the unfamiliar luxury of a pretended swoon for a moment, so welcome were those strong, protective arms, and then pulled myself together.

I righted myself abruptly, shaking my head to clear the mists. I smiled up at my noble protector and almost swooned all over again. Looking down at me were the bluest eyes I had ever seen, set in a sternly handsome face that could scarcely have come closer to my romantic musings had it been planned. He was very elegant in his white and gold uniform, his blond curls peeping out from beneath his cap, his shoulders quite the broadest I had ever seen. And I did have such a weakness for broad shoulders.

"I beg your pardon, Captain," I murmured helplessly, batting my thick eyelashes at the man beguilingly. "A momentary dizziness . . . I'm quite all right now."

He stared down at me with a stunned expression on his face, swallowed once, and quickly doffed his cap. "My pleasure, fräulein," he stammered, suddenly a smitten little boy. "Perhaps you might like to sit . . . ?"

He gestured to the coach, and I gently shook my head.

"No, thank you, Captain. I believe you wanted my papers?" I questioned, rummaging in my reticule like a helpless female before offering them.

He stared at them stupidly for a moment, and the grumble of the other passengers came to my ears. Our conversation had been in English, and I had no idea how fluent my fellow travelers were. Flirtation, however, is the same in any language, and no one was particularly anxious to be held up longer than necessary on that windy border. As I have said, it had been a long day . . .

Suddenly the captain seemed to pull himself together, standing upright so that he was even taller, well over six feet, with a stern look in his ice-blue eyes and a grim expression around his full lips. "That will be enough!" he said sharply to the querulous travelers. "Your papers will be checked, and then you may proceed. Where is your destination?"

No one spoke for a moment, obviously expecting me to do the honors. I, however, remained silent. Finally the driver spoke up in broken English.

"Eventually to Venice, Captain," he ventured. "We are already a day behind schedule . . ."

"The problems with your timetable are none of my concern, driver," he said abruptly, barely glancing at the papers handed him. "You will have another passenger."

"There's just enough room as it is," the banker protested, speaking up for the first time. "We can't fit another person."

The captain stared at him with mild disdain. "There are four of you, no? And the carriage usually holds six. I expect no more objections."

"Who will be accompanying us, Captain?" The grandmother spoke up then, not one to be cowed by an Austrian upstart.

He allowed himself a stiff little smile that in no way diminished his rather heavy attractiveness. I could feel my heart melt a little, and his blue eyes met mine. "I will, Madame."

I MUST ADMIT that the rest of the trip passed far too quickly for me. Captain Holger von Wolfram, once he recovered from his initial stupefaction, was both sophisticated and charming, with a hint of steel beneath his perfect manners. He was civil enough to the other passengers once he had made it perfectly clear who was in charge, but it was obvious he had chosen to take our carriage for the sake of flirting with a silly young English girl. I couldn't help but be flattered—Holger was the image of the man I thought I would someday marry. Handsome, strong, ruthless, and perhaps not terribly bright. I flirted oh-so-gently with him as we traveled into Italy, and he responded with satisfying ardor.

"But where are you going, Fräulein Morrow?" A question I had been carefully avoiding finally could be avoided no longer. The lagoon surrounding the ancient city of Venice was only hours away, and there was no distracting the good captain. Why I wanted to distract him I had no idea. For some instinctive reason I had carefully parried all his surprisingly personal questions during the remainder of the trip.

"To stay with my guardian," I replied after a long moment. "Oh, look at those lovely cypresses!"

The captain ignored the cypresses. "But you must tell me his name, *liebchen*. I wish to call on you when we reach Venice. This will be the first time I have been stationed there, but the Venetians are notoriously unfriendly to the Imperial Army. There is little enough decent company around, I hear. I would be desolate to lose you so soon after we have met."

I eyed him speculatively. I could imagine he would have little decent company. Occupying armies were never popular, and the uneasy state of Europe certainly didn't help matters. I doubted the Italian families approved of consorting with the Austrian powers-that-be, and the French, in their zeal to regain possession of northern Italy, would hardly be likely to cuddle up with their enemy. No, Holger would undoubtedly lead a lonely life in the ancient republic, and if it were up to me I would ease that loneliness a trifle. However, I had no idea how the illustrious Count del Zaglia would react to that.

I met Holger's gaze limpidly, not liking the petulant insistence in his pale blue eyes. "I doubt you'd have heard of him."

My swain didn't like being thwarted. "His name!" he demanded.

I sighed, my warmer feelings for him abating rapidly. "Count del Zaglia," I replied shortly. "I believe his palazzo is on . . ."

"On the Grand Canal," Holger supplied, a curious expression nearly akin to satisfaction sitting on his heavy features. "Count del Zaglia is not unknown to me. By reputation, that is. He has been most helpful to the Austrian government, and to the French government, I am sure. I had no idea *he* was your guardian."

"Would it have made a difference?"

"Yes," he replied bluntly, if ungallantly. But for some reason I couldn't quite believe him. "One does not trifle with Count del Zaglia's possessions lightly. He is a man greatly to be feared in Venice and, indeed, in all of northern Italy. How came he to be your guardian?"

I didn't like this conversation, not one bit. However, I was anxious to find out anything I could concerning the man who would attempt to have control over me, so I controlled the flutter of annoyance and answered Holger with far more courtesy than he deserved. "I believe he was a friend of my late father's, and a distant cousin besides. If my father trusted him I'm sure I can do the same."

"You've never met the man?"

"No," I confessed uneasily. "But it makes no difference. It is my duty to obey my father's wishes." This was a blatant lie . . . I rarely did anything I didn't want to do, but Holger nodded pompously.

"Have you no family back in England? No one you could turn to?"

"None," I lied.

He sighed gustily. "Then may God have mercy on your soul, fräulein. You have a dark and dangerous road ahead of you." He shut his mouth firmly, obviously determined to say no more, and I wouldn't lower myself to plead. I turned away and met the frightened eyes of the old grandmother. She and the other passengers had obviously been listening to our conversation with the same rapt absorption they had given all of our previous conversations, and at my sudden attention the old crone quickly crossed herself and made an odd gesture in my direction.

"Don't cast those evil eyes on me, witch," she hissed in Italian. "Keep it for your master, the Devil! *Strega!*"

A chill ran through me, despite the warm and welcoming May afternoon. "What does she mean?" I whispered. "Why does she call me a witch?"

That much Italian even a cloddish English girl could be expected to understand. The banker stared at me solemnly for a moment. "Pay no attention to the old one," he said finally. "Count del Zaglia has a . . . a certain reputation in Venice. Not a very pleasant one, to be sure. It is said that he sold his soul to the Devil many years ago. Absurd, of course, but then, he has done nothing to dispel the notion. One would think he enjoys being thought of as a prince of darkness."

"But what of the contessa? Surely his wife would help to stop such absurdity!"

"The Contessa del Zaglia has been dead for many years, Fräulein Morrow. It was perhaps her tragic and untimely death that started the foul rumors that have grown and spread over the last few years."

I was suddenly very frightened. "How did she die?" I whispered, not sure I really wanted to know.

"I do not know the details, fräulein," the banker said, and his cold gray eyes told me he was lying. "All I know is the official report, which was that the young woman died a suicide. But there was little doubt at the time that the poor lady was murdered. And no question at all who was responsible." He leaned back against the slightly threadbare seats and blew his bulbous nose in a fine linen handkerchief. "How long until you are free of his protection?"

"Fourteen months," I replied, shaken.

"Fourteen months," he echoed soberly. "Not such a long time, then. I suggest, fräulein, that you say your prayers every night, attend Mass, and keep out of Count del Zaglia's way as much as possible. And leave Venice as soon as you are legally able."

I turned back to Holger, my eyes pleading with him to refute the absurd statements of the heretofore seemingly rational banker. But his blue eyes looked down on me with infinite sadness, and he patted my gloved hand in a paternal gesture.

"It will be all right, *liebchen,*" he intoned. "If you do as Herr Seitz says. And I will be there to watch over you."

For some reason I failed to find this as comforting as it was meant to be. "Will you, Captain?" I carefully kept my skepticism out of my voice. I didn't know what use a straightforward Holger von Wolfram would be against the powers of darkness, but I had just as soon not fight them alone. I could have kicked myself for being fool enough to abandon everything in England for this mad dash across a war-torn continent, straight into the lair of one of Satan's henchmen. If my small fortune of pocket money was not almost depleted I would have turned around and headed straight back to Calais, but the tiny amount of French money in my reticule would get me several yards past the border, not more. I had effectively burnt my bridges, and the sudden smell of sulphur was not reassuring.

"I'm sure it cannot be so bad," I said bravely, not sure at all. "There is no such thing as the Devil." I dearly wished I believed my brave words.

The old woman crossed herself once more and began a mumbled Ave Maria in her distant corner of the carriage, all the while keeping her aged, basilisk eyes on me as if daring me to make a move in her direction. Gone was the comfortable, motherly attitude. In her mind I had obviously become linked with the evil master himself, and my most innocent smile did nothing to dispel her fear of me.

Even Holger had a wary look in his eyes, tinged with a faint expression I could only identify as speculation. I leaned back against the squabs, trying to look blissfully unconcerned by the superstitious terror my guardian's name had inspired. At least my destination was only a few long hours away. If I had to live with this suspicion and nerve-wracking uncertainty for much longer my courage would fail me altogether. I managed a convincing yawn and pretended to fall asleep.

Chapter Three

MY FIRST SIGHT of *La Serenissima,* the most serene republic of Venice, temporarily banished my misgivings. A light rain was falling, more a mist than actual precipitation, and a fog almost enshrouded the mysterious roofline. As our boat moved slowly across the lagoon, drawing closer and closer to the historic city, I was conscious of the first stirrings of a deep enchantment. Venice seemed to float just above the water, a magic place where anything might happen.

My involuntary intake of breath, my initial awe and wonder as we drew nearer seemed to signal a more negative reaction in Holger. He had been morosely silent since my startling disclosures in the carriage, but apparently my fascination with the rapidly approaching city was enough to stir him out of his torpor.

He snorted loudly. "You like Venice, fräulein?" Disapproval was strong in his heavily accented voice.

I eyed him speculatively for a moment, then turned back to the twilight glory ahead of me. "Yes, I do, Captain. I doubt I've ever seen such a lovely place."

"Ha!" He laughed without humor. "You will find, my dear young woman, that it is cold and damp and miserable. The natives are rude and unfriendly, the food is indigestible, the lodgings highly conducive to inflammation of the lungs. Epidemics ravage the population, buildings lean in every direction, the weather . . . ," he broke off his grumbling tirade before my interested gaze.

"I hadn't realized you had been to Venice before, Captain," I said silkily. As a matter of fact, I was certain he had announced to us all that this was his first visit.

In the dim light I could still see the flush that suffused his fair features. "I . . . I was stationed here previously," he replied stiffly.

"And now you are returning, poor man. To such a place!" I mocked gently.

The spotty young clerk looked up then, and spoke with more conviction than I had heard from him in the past two weeks. "If the Imperial Army finds Venice so inhospitable, perhaps they would be happier elsewhere." He spoke slowly and distinctly, so that even someone with as rudimentary a grasp of Italian as Holger obviously had could understand.

But for once the good captain seemed unwilling to rise to the bait. He continued to stare at the approaching quayside with an abstracted, brooding gaze.

I scrambled onto the *fondamento* and looked around me with unabashed curiosity. I knew from Holger's reluctant descriptions that we were in the Piazzetta San Marco, just off the famous piazza. The place was a beehive of activity even at such a normally restful time of day, and two giant columns, one on either side of me, seemed to look down at all the bustle with quiet reproach.

"That's where they used to hang felons," Holger said cheerfully, coming up behind me and pointing at the tall columns.

"What's on top of them?" I questioned, straining my vision through the twilight.

Holger shrugged contemptuously. "I have no idea."

"Pardon me, signorina," the young clerk bashfully interrupted. "On one side is Saint Theodore, former patron saint of Venice. On the other is the lion of Saint Mark. We have a saying in Venice, signorina. That to be *'fra Marco e Todaro'* is to be . . . how you say . . . caught in the middle? In a state of perplexity."

I had to laugh. "Then truly, I am standing in the proper place."

Holger harrumphed, not liking this one bit. "In a few short years, fräulein, when you arrive in Venice, you will do so by railway. The Imperial Army is overseeing the construction of a railway line between here and the mainland. Very modern, very civilized."

I was busy watching the young clerk disappear into the night. "Ah, but I like arriving by boat, Captain," I chided gently. "It's so much more fitting for a place such as this."

"I won't quarrel with you on that, Fräulein Morrow. A leaky boat, preferably, for a leaky city. I wish you joy of both."

I didn't bother to reply, and in a moment he was gone, with my other companions of the last few weeks, gone into the night with only a few frightened, pitying glances at my lonely figure. Even Holger, forgetting momentarily his promise of protection, found it necessary to report to his commanding officer at once.

"But I will call on you as soon as I can," he vowed, obviously anxious to disappear with the others before my Faustian protector materialized from out of the darkness. I had neglected to inform him that the count had no notion of my impending arrival.

"But you need my address," I reminded him, not for one moment expecting him to keep his promise.

"The Palazzo Edentide is well known all over Venice," he replied. "On the Grand Canal, as I have said. God protect you," he added in German, and strode off into the night, leaving me alone on the rain-drenched cobblestones, suddenly feeling very frightened and unsure of myself. I looked above me at the two saints and offered a little prayer that I might survive my own rash stupidity.

"Is someone meeting the signorina?" The gondolier, a swarthy Italian who had replaced the ruddy Swiss when we switched transports, approached me hesitantly.

I shrugged with what I hoped was charming helplessness. "It appears not. Perhaps you could help me arrange transport. I need to go to the palazzo of Count del Zaglia. On the Grand Canal."

An expression of horror crossed the man's dark face. "Why would you want to go there, signorina? That is a place of the Devil."

"The Devil," I replied with some asperity, tired of all this fuss, "is my guardian. And he would not like it if I were kept out in the rain on an evening like this." I was taking unfair advantage of the poor man's superstitions, but I needed to see my new home before my courage failed me.

"No, signorina. I mean, yes, signorina. I would deem it an honor if you would allow me to convey you there," he said hastily, terror showing plainly in his wide brown eyes, "If you would consider climbing back in the gondola, it will take but a few short minutes."

My relief and sudden nervousness nearly overwhelmed me. *Just a few short minutes, my girl*, I told myself grimly. *A few more minutes, and you and the count will be laughing at the gullibility of the crazy Venetians. And the crazy Swiss, the crazy Austrians, and the crazy French*, I thought, suddenly not liking the odds. And the crazy English girl, too.

The palazzo was indeed only a few short minutes away. To be sure, the boatman moved through the still waters like a bat out of hell, obviously eager to be rid of his unwelcome passenger as soon as he could without further antagonizing the powers of darkness.

Edentide, the incongruously named palazzo of Count del Zaglia, was hardly reassuring. With great haste the gondolier dumped my bandboxes out, helped me onto the slippery quay, and took off before I could reach for my last few coins to pay him. I watched his rapidly receding boat until it turned off the wide canal and was out of sight before I turned to face what would be my new home for the next fourteen months.

A weaker woman would have sat down on her luggage in the light rain and wept. It was full darkness now, and not a light shone from the crumbling facade of the building, not a curtain stirred. Dark, narrow alleyways led from the canal on either side of the house, and I wondered whether a possible front entrance might not prove more welcoming. I stood hesitating for a moment, wondering whether I should investigate further, or whether I should save myself a great deal of trouble and throw myself into the dark, still depths of the canal. And then I caught a strong whiff of the unmistakable odor of the waters, squared my shoulders, gathered up my luggage, and marched to the nearest door.

It opened before I had a chance to rap. A very tall, very thin, very English butler appeared, eyeing me with disfavour out of gimlet eyes. Without a doubt he had been watching me from some secret place behind that peeling green door, and I shivered slightly.

Before I could get over my uneasiness and sheer astonishment at seeing such a piece of England in such an unexpected place, he spoke, and his tones could hardly have been less welcoming.

"Yes?"

His blatant discourtesy put me on my mettle, all the while I was regaining my faltering courage. An English butler would hardly buttle for the powers of darkness.

I threw my head back, unfortunately spraying my inquisitor with rain water. He didn't blink. "I am Miss Charlotte Morrow," I answered haughtily. "Count del Zaglia's distant cousin from England."

The butler was unmoved. "Is he expecting you, miss?"

I hesitated for only a moment. "Not exactly. But as he is my guardian I am sure he'll be delighted to see me."

"No one enters Edentide without the count's permission," he intoned.

I stared up at the man in astonishment. "Well, then, get his permission, man! It's raining cats and dogs." I tried to move past him, but he remained inexorably in the way.

"The count is not at home this evening," he informed me. "If you would return tomorrow perhaps he may have left instructions."

"But I can't return tomorrow!" I wailed. "Where will I go tonight?"

"There are a number of suitable hotels in Venice, Miss Morrow."

"I don't have any money!" I was becoming frightened. I had foolishly assumed that once I reached my guardian's home all would be taken care of, and I could retire, temporarily of course, to my proper role as dependent young lady. My self-reliance had just about been depleted.

"That is too bad, miss. Now if you'll excuse me." He moved to shut the door in my face.

"But you must let me in!" I demanded shrilly.

"No one enters without the count's permission," he repeated. "If he really is your guardian," and the butler's expression took leave to doubt it, "you could seek him out at the French embassy. He's attending a party there."

"But how will I get there?" I was close to tears now.

A brief flash of human pity must have stirred in his marble face, though I couldn't be sure. "If Miss will wait here, I will arrange for a gondolier to take you there. That is the limit of what I can do for you." He vanished inside the tomb-like palazzo before I had a chance to thank him.

It was just as well. I didn't feel very grateful at that point. I dumped my luggage in front of the door and turned to face the gloomy, rain-spattered depths of the canal, ignoring the pouring rain while I awaited my deliverer.

Fortunately I didn't have to wait long.

My first ride in one of the smaller, private gondolas on the still waters of Venice could certainly have been accomplished under more pleasant circumstances. Even in the dim light I could tell the boat had seen better days, and there was a rank smell of sour wine clinging to the frayed cushions. I rode the waves with my hands clutching nervously at the side of the small, teetery boat, keeping a sharp eye on the villainous-looking boatman who had sullenly introduced himself as Gianni and then proceeded to glower like a fiend from hell. With such an evil countenance, the man would certainly find it difficult to contrive a living, ferrying about the myriad tourists. If I'd had any choice I certainly would have chosen a more cheerful sort.

As I tried to control the nervous shivers that wracked my rain-drenched body, I couldn't help wondering how the villainous Count del Zaglia would react to being presented with a sopping young lady in the middle of a dinner party.

Well, there was no help for it, and he had only his own pigheadedness, rudeness, and distrustfulness to thank for it, I told myself virtuously, and sneezed, drawing my soaked cloak closer around my thinly clad shoulders. He could rant, he could rave, but he could not turn his poor distant cousin and ward out into the Venice night. There was nothing he could do but take me in, and before long I would bring him around. I was very good with elderly gentlemen.

Unlike the dark and crumbling exteriors of Edentide, the French embassy was a pink and gold palace, ablaze with light. Laughing voices in several languages and loud music echoed forth over the rain-drenched canals. Gianni steered the gondola over to the brightly lit mooring, grudgingly helping me to alight before pushing off into the night.

"You won't wait?" I asked plaintively, hating my weakness.

"There is no need, signorina," he replied from over the water. "Either the count will escort you back to the palazzo, or he will send you about your business. Either way, my services will not be required."

I had to concede the logic of this, much as I disliked being stranded in the middle of this strange and magical city. I mounted the slippery marble steps past the loudly admiring French and Austrian soldiers, keeping my eyes demurely lowered.

After the cold, drenching rain the deserted foyer of the embassy was blessedly warm. I put back the hood of my cloak and looked about me with great interest. I had been in some of the great houses of Britain, of course, and admired them. But I could immediately appreciate the delicate, almost frivolous style of this elegantly proportioned hallway, with its fanciful gilt trim and warm pastel shades.

"May I help you, mademoiselle?" A warm French voice inquired from behind me, and I jumped nervously, nearly answering in the same language before I had a chance to gather my wits about me.

"I beg your pardon," I said in a firmly British voice as I turned to face my inquisitor. "Do you speak English?"

The small, elegantly clad young man bowed gracefully. "I do indeed, mademoiselle. How may I assist you? Jean-Baptiste Perrier, *à votre service.*"

I gave him a brief smile, trying to hide my uncertainty. "I am seeking Count del Zaglia. His manservant said he might be found here."

A well-shaped eyebrow rose on the young man's face, and an almost indiscernible familiarity crept into his manner. "And may one ask what your business is with the count?"

I hesitated, then decided frankness was best. "I am his ward. I have just arrived from England, and his butler refused to let me in until he had permission from the count." I felt very foolish recounting this absurd problem, but the Frenchman nodded sagely.

"Ah, yes, the good Thornton. How very like him to refuse shelter to such a charming young female." I took note of the fact that he did not call me a charming young *lady*. One hand reached under my elbow, and I was steered in the direction of one of the inlaid doors. "If you would be so good as to wait in one of these rooms I will send someone to attend to you." He spoke smoothly as he led me into a comfortable little salon, and I decided to trust him.

"You will find the count?" I inquired anxiously, settling myself down on a brocade sofa.

"All will be attended to, mademoiselle," he replied, closing the door behind him, leaving me alone with my thoughts and fears.

I hadn't long to wait. I was staring into the welcome fire when I heard the door open behind me, and I rose and turned to face the man I supposed to be my guardian, Count Luc del Zaglia.

My first feeling was acute disappointment, yet I refused to fathom why. The man before me was well-dressed, though his waistcoat was stained with food and wine. He was well into middle-age, with grizzled hair and tiny, pig-like eyes that glistened with what seemed amazingly close to lust. He licked his thick pink lips and stumbled forward.

"May I help you, mademoiselle?" he asked in a slurred voice.

"Count del Zaglia?" I questioned, and was relieved to see him shake his head. A smirk spread across those thick lips as he moved closer to me, and the heat of the fire brought out the sour smell of him, that of old wine and unwashed bodies. It took all my self-control not to step back.

"Now what would you be wanting with that dago?" he leered. "He's here all right, but I doubt if he'd want to be disturbed for the likes of you. Deep in a card game and winning as usual. Why don't you come with me somewhere private where we can discuss your business. I'm sure I can help you." He put a too-familiar hand on my arm, and angrily I shrugged it off, moving away this time.

"Count del Zaglia is my guardian," I informed him in a furious voice. "And I wish to see him at once."

"Of course he is, *ma petite*. And Louis Napoleon is my uncle. Now come with me and make no more trouble, and I will see you are more handsomely rewarded than Luc del Zaglia would. A man who gambles as rashly as he does must always have his pockets to let. Not that I've ever seen the bastard lose," he added morosely. He gave me a little yank. "Come along with Georges, my little pigeon. Let's have no more reluctance."

His hand was like iron on my arm, and struggle as I might, I couldn't break free of his grip. I reached out to slap him, but his arms came around me like a vice, and I felt myself being dragged across the floor as I kicked and screamed imprecations worthy of an English dockworker. My assailant shouldered open the door at the far side of the room and dragged my struggling body through, and a fresh wave of fury and terror engulfed me. In desperation I sank my good strong teeth into his arm; and he flung me away with an incredibly foul oath, raising one of his meaty arms to strike me when a hand reached out and stopped him while a soft, menacing voice spoke in excellent French.

"I wouldn't do that, Georges."

Chapter Four

MY ENEMY STOPPED, motionless, his blotchy face blanching in an expression akin to absolute terror. "A thousand pardons, milord," he babbled, stumbling backwards. "I had no idea . . . what was I to think? He said . . . you can see for yourself . . ."

Dazedly I rose from my ignominious position on the floor where Georges had flung me, feeling bruised and battered and very angry now that my initial danger was over. All my attention was for the suddenly cowering Georges, and I failed to notice my soft-spoken deliverer at all for the moment.

"Son of a pig," I hissed at him in Arabic. "Brother of four thousand camels!" I advanced upon the quaking figure, my eyes flashing, as I added an extremely pungent and quite pornographic curse I had learned from one of Theresa's military admirers. A small, low laugh escaped from Georges's adversary, who released the poor man.

A flush mounted to my pale cheeks as I realized he must have understood every word. I turned and for the first time gave my full attention to my savior. For once in my talkative life I was astounded into silence. I was later to learn that certain creatures of the undead are reputed to have that effect on people.

Georges took advantage of my astonishment to make a fast exit, babbling apologies in French, Italian, and English. Neither of us paid any attention, my rescuer looking down on me with cold, quiet amusement, while I took in the full glory of what could only be my guardian, the prince of darkness himself, Count Luc del Zaglia. There could scarcely be two such as he in Venice.

He was extraordinarily tall, even taller than my mountainous Holger, though without the Austrian's breadth of shoulder. The man who stood before me was a lean, graceful aristocrat, dressed exquisitely in black evening dress, not a speck of color anywhere around his remarkable person. His brown-black hair curled off a high, sensitive forehead, his hypnotizing topaz eyes watched me with a quiet cynicism. An aquiline nose, high cheekbones, and a surprisingly sensuous mouth completed his unforgettable face, and I could see why superstitious and uneducated people might think he was a spawn of the Devil. His beauty was deeply disturbing—an unnerving mixture of the spiritual and the sexual that seemed to bespeak the powers of darkness. I swallowed once, twice, determined not to show the absolute irrational terror

I felt at being confronted by such a creature.

Suddenly he bowed, a courtly gesture that mocked even as it honored me. "Luc del Zaglia, at your service, signorina. I was told you wanted to see me?"

I presumed Jean-Baptiste had belatedly come to my rescue, and I sent up a silent prayer of thanks. I cleared my throat, but my voice still came out oddly shaken. "I am Charlotte Theresa Sabina Morrow," I announced bravely.

There was no change in expression on that pale, handsome face, just the same mocking courtesy. "Do I offer my felicitations or condolences?"

"Your condolences," I snapped, nettled. "I am a newly-made orphan, with the doubtful honor of being your ward."

This did happen to move him, but not in the direction I could have wished. Mild annoyance crossed his face, followed swiftly by an unholy amusement that did little to reassure me. Suddenly I felt very small and powerless indeed, and I wondered why I had ever been such a fool as to leave England to place myself in the hands of a man such as this. If, indeed, he was a man, and not something of the night.

He smiled then, but I was not reassured. "Ah, yes. You must be Charles's daughter. Someone told me your mother had died, but I took no notice." He waved one slim, elegant hand, unadorned except for a large, ornate gold ring set with what I grimly recognized as an unusually fine bloodstone. "So you have come to Venice to join your devoted guardian? Perhaps to lighten my declining years? How thoughtful of you. And yet somehow it seems that I must have misplaced your letter signifying your intention. The mails are so unreliable nowadays. And no doubt you failed to receive my orders that you were to stay put in whatever dreary little girls' school you were attending?" There was only the slightest hint of menace in his soft voice, but I found myself trembling nonetheless.

I have never lacked for courage, however. I tried to look him squarely in the eye, but he towered so far above me that I gave up the effort. "I received your letter," I replied bravely. "And I chose to ignore it."

"Really?" He sounded no more than casually interested. "Did you also choose to ignore the courtesy of letting me know of your impending arrival?"

I swallowed again, determined to stand my ground. "Yes. I knew if I told you I was coming you would try to stop me. And I wasn't to be stopped."

"How perspicacious of you, Charlotte Theresa Sabina. I would indeed have stopped you." He moved across the room gracefully, and as his attention left me I could feel my tightened nerves relax slightly. But only slightly.

When he turned back he was holding two glasses of ruby wine. I had seldom been allowed to partake of wine in England, and I viewed the liquid with misgivings.

Apparently I wasn't to be given the chance of refusing. He placed the thin crystal glass in my unwilling hand, looking down at me from those tawny, unreadable tiger's eyes. "A toast, Charlotte. To your stay in Venice. May it profit us both."

He tossed the wine down lightly, then lowered his gaze to me. I had no choice but to follow suit. It was very bitter, and I could barely manage to control the shudder of distaste that swept over me. I met my guardian's eyes, and saw from their cynical depths that he hadn't been fooled.

He held out an arm, and there was nothing I could do but take it, my hand trembling slightly as it rested on the surprisingly steely strength of his silk-clad forearm. "Your first lesson, my dear, will be not to disobey my orders," he said gently as he led me from the room. It was a gentleness that was not at all reassuring. "I will deliver you to my palazzo and into the welcoming arms of Maddelena, my housekeeper. She is reputed to be a witch." He felt my start of fear and smiled down at me. "Nonsense, of course. I do hope you aren't superstitious, my little ward. You won't be very happy at Edentide if you are."

I accompanied him in silence, scarcely aware of my surroundings, of the curious and uneasy glances of the people around us, of the immediate appearance of the count's elegant gondola, aware of nothing but my companion and a peculiar heaviness in my limbs. "Perhaps . . . perhaps it would be best if I returned to England," I suggested, unable to keep a quiver of nervousness from my voice. The sour wine, while making my stomach churn, was beginning to have a numbing effect that couldn't quite calm my unusual agitation.

"Oh, I couldn't allow you to do that," he murmured as he helped me into the boat. "Not after you traveled so far to be with me! It will be most . . . entertaining to have someone like you around. Someone young and . . . innocent." He stepped in beside me, the boat barely moving under his weight. "Once you have learned to obey me, it should be very amusing indeed."

I moved as far away from him as possible in the gondola, wondering vaguely whether my wisest move might not be to jump overboard. Even Venice's dark canals might be preferable to the horrors my overtired brain was busy imagining. I stared at him in the darkness, fighting against the tide of exhaustion that threatened to overwhelm me. I had been a great fool, I thought, not for the first or last time. And then, quite suddenly, I slept.

IT COULDN'T HAVE been the light that awoke me the next day. The murky green shadows that seemed to ooze from beneath the shuttered windows turned my dark, cavernous bedroom into an underwater tomb. I opened my eyes warily, for the moment afraid of what exactly I might find. The last thing I could remember was riding in the gondola with my guardian's strange golden eyes upon me. I must have been more tired than I had guessed. I stretched, yawned, and sat up with more energy than I would have thought possible twenty-four hours ago.

Any suspicions I might have held about the count's possible interest in my comfortable little English fortune vanished at the sight of the almost oppressive luxury of my bedroom. The walls were hung with dark green damask, green velvet drapes surrounded the massive bed, the sheets were of the purest, finest white linen trimmed with lace, and the marble floors were covered with oriental carpets of a wondrously complicated design. Each piece of furniture was intricately carved, a craftman's joy, and the ewer and tray beside me were of solid silver.

I scrambled out of my massive bed to the chill marble floors. My first move was to fling open the heavy velvet curtains and the louvered shutters and take in my first sight of Venice in the daylight.

And what a glorious sight it was, with golden sunlight pouring down on the massive buildings, gilding them with a splendid afternoon glow. Even the noisome canal was transformed into a magical waterway; the gondolas sailing back and forth like fairy boats. My depression and doubts abated as I stared at my new city, and I wondered how I could have been so foolish the night before. Count del Zaglia must have thought me a perfect ninny, I decided ruefully. I still couldn't imagine what had possessed me to fall asleep like that. And then I quickly shrugged off my mind's unfortunate choice of words.

But today was a heavenly day, and I would start afresh with my saturnine guardian. I turned to look for my portmanteau, so that I could dress and face the wicked count in proper style.

My luggage was nowhere to be seen, and my determination vanished. For the first time I allowed myself to wonder how I had come to be in this sumptuous room, whose strong arms had carried me from the gondola and placed me in that comfortable bed. I looked down at my thin chemise. And whose hands had stripped off most of my clothing while I slept with such uncharacteristic soundness?

I stood stock still, trying to stem the tide of anger and uneasiness that threatened to overwhelm me. I had never been a coward. Indeed, Theresa had often wished I could show just a trifle more restraint. But this city, this palazzo, these people were totally beyond my ken, and I felt most unpleasantly helpless and out of my depth. I was still considering this novel experience when the gilded door knob began to turn with a sinister slowness.

I bit back a nervous scream, and with barely a tremor in my voice called out, "Come in!"

There was a hesitation, and then the door opened, revealing not the supposed demon count but a small, hunched old woman dressed in the heavy black that was a uniform for Italian women of a certain age. She moved into the sunlight, and my reassurance dimmed. Beneath her oily black hair was a face incredibly old and incredibly evil to my impressionable young eyes, wise in the ways of the world and the fools that inhabited it. When she spoke it was in a rasping, guttural voice, using a slurred dialect I found just barely comprehensible. My perfect Italian was almost useless, and I wished she would slow down just a trifle. After a moment I began to comprehend.

"Can you speak English?" I requested when she paused for breath. I had been taught by Theresa to keep all signs of intellect well hidden, as a woman with any sort of brain was considered a freak of nature by the superior male of the species. Keeping my knowledge of Italian and French a secret might prove a very useful advantage in the fourteen months that were to come, and I had an uneasy feeling I would need every advantage I could find.

The woman snorted. "I am Maddelena," she said in broken English that I found almost more difficult to understand than her dialect. "I am the house-keeper here. You wish to take a bath?"

Such words could turn any monster into a saint in my eyes, and I nodded with heartfelt gratitude. "Above all things," I said fervently.

"It will be brought. The count will see you at five."

"At five? That must be hours away!" I don't know why the wait distressed me so. I told myself that I wanted reassurance that the demon count of last night was merely a figment of my overtired brain.

"Compose yourself, signorina," the old witch said cynically, a smile showing several gaps in her teeth. "It is past three now. You have slept a long time."

"Who . . . who brought me here last night?" I questioned hesitantly, and then blushed. I should have pretended disinterest.

"Who else but Antonio, the gondolier? Do you think *he* would soil his hands with such as you?" the little crone demanded fiercely. I didn't know whether to be relieved or disappointed.

"And who undressed me?"

Once more she smiled, and her little currant-like eyes shone in the afternoon sunlight. "I did, signorina. But be patient. You are not bad looking, though not in his usual style. I'm sure he will come to your bed eventually."

Unfortunately during the last part of that speech she lapsed into Italian, and I could neither refute it nor upbraid her for her insulting suggestions. I could simply stare at her in mute frustration while she went off, cackling, and repeating over and over in Italian that my time would come.

I stared after her. "Damn!" I said finally, finding more relief in the good solid British word than in all my repertoire of obscene foreign curses. All this absurd melodrama and rampant lechery was both unnerving and highly contagious. I would have to be careful not to be seduced into reacting as the old witch no doubt wanted me to.

But the bath was heavenly. Two sturdy and obviously very silly maids carried in an ornate silver tub, much tarnished, filling it with steaming and scented water carried in equally ornate and unclean silver buckets. The wealth of the place seemed unbelievable, and I wondered what the demon count had done to own such splendor. Perhaps he had simply been born to it. Or perhaps, the evil thought intruded, he had traded something, like his immortal soul, for such Croesian riches.

And there you go again, I chided myself, sinking into the scented luxury of the first bath I'd had in many long weeks. This place seemed to breed such absurd fancies. A good English stiff upper lip was what was needed, and a stern no-nonsense attitude. After all, I had always prided myself on my level-headedness and lack of sentimentality. Now was a fine time to lose it.

With the bathwater appeared my missing luggage, and I dressed carefully for my interview with Luc del Zaglia. My heavy blond hair was scarcely dry, and I arranged it as best I could. The cool spring air in the palazzo would no doubt give me pneumonia, but I did not doubt that there were worse ways to go around here. I dressed in one of Theresa's prettier black wool dresses. The style was only slightly outmoded, with a narrower skirt and longer sleeves than were currently in vogue. The dark color would, I hoped, successfully, hide the fact that I was both taller and slimmer than my mother. The discrepancies in height and girth were not very great, and the neckline of the dress was thankfully demure. The soft black wool gave my porcelain skin a delicate tint that pleased me very much. I couldn't see how the demon count could be so very angry with such a sweet-looking girl, her large blue eyes brimming easily with unshed tears. A black lace-trimmed handkerchief completed my toilette, and I was ready and waiting when Maddelena, looking more witch-like than ever, arrived back at my door to escort me into the royal presence.

It was my first good look at the palazzo—my unusual state of somnolence last night had, of course, left me unconscious of the decaying glory around me. I had been pleased, no, overwhelmed would be more apt, by the elegant splendor of my room and its appurtenances, but I could see from the cold and drafty hallways that the wealth had not been spread very far around Edentide. Cobwebs were strung from the distant corners of the ornate ceilings, dust accumulated on every available surface, and the brass (or were they gold?) sconces in the walls were sadly tarnished, with the candles throwing off only a fitful light. As I followed the squat, hunched-over figure of the housekeeper I was grateful that my too-short skirts enabled me to keep my hem from trailing in the dust, and my overactive imagination picked up the sound of large rodents scuffling behind me in the darkness. I peered back over my shoulder with a great deal of uneasiness. I did not care for rats.

"This is the third floor, signorina," Maddelena announced. "Your rooms are the only occupied ones on this level. I hope this will not bother you?" She grinned, and I knew she hoped nothing of the sort.

"Why should it?" I asked coolly, straightening my spine. "I like solitude."

The old witch shrugged. "Let us hope solitude is the worst you will experience." She continued down the hallway to a sweeping staircase, and impudently I stuck my tongue out at her sturdy little back. "The servants' quarters are on the second floor. The English servants, that is. The Italian servants have their rooms in the cellars."

"The cellars?" I shuddered. If the upper floors of Eden-tide were cold, slimy and rodent-ridden I hated to think of the condition of the cellars. "I would think you would rather be higher up . . . above the waterline, I mean."

"We are not given much choice. The *Inglesi* were brought here by the count's mother. They have ruled the palazzo ever since and will continue to do so." She spat, which I doubted did the filthy marble staircase much harm. She peered back up at me, her small black eyes shining in the dim light. "His rooms are on the second floor also . . . at the front of the palazzo."

"How interesting," I said mildly, hoping to convince the woman I had no desire to know of the count's sleeping arrangements. She cackled, however, and I felt a momentary temptation to push her down the stairs. I controlled my murderous tendencies.

The second floor was cleaner than the third, and more brightly lit. As we passed the landing I tried to peer down the long hallway, but the shadows made it impossible. For a moment I thought I could make out a pair of eyes glowing in the black corridor, and I stopped suddenly. But a moment later they were gone, and I told myself I must have imagined them. If I didn't take myself in hand before too long I would become hopelessly nerve-ridden in this macabre palace.

The first floor was far more reassuring. While not exactly clean and bright, it at least showed some small amount of housekeeping care. The brasses were polished, the furniture had seen an application of beeswax and lemon oil in the not-too-distant past, and the rugs were aglow with fresh colors, not the frayed and raveled remnants that had carpeted the cold, damp hallways upstairs. Even the dark and damp-stained portraits on the walls seemed to have more optimistic expressions on their ancient faces, but perhaps I was imagining that too.

I had fallen behind Maddelena, and now I rushed to catch up with her as she flung open a door into a warm and well-lighted room, announcing my name with great dignity.

"Signorina Morrow." I hesitated for barely a moment. That unfortunate English children's rhyme had popped into my head. *Come into my parlor, said the spider to the fly . . .*

Nonsense, I told myself firmly, striding into the room, only to have my hard-won courage vanish once more as the demon count repeated the very rhyme I had banished from my mind.

"Come into my parlor . . ."

Chapter Five

HE WAS LOUNGING negligently in a gold brocade chair, and as I entered the room he rose with lazy grace, just slowly enough to express his boredom with the custom and with me. He was dressed in black as he had been the night before, and his pale, handsome face was not in the slightest bit reassuring to me after I had had a full night's sleep. He looked down at me and smiled, a cool, calculating smile, and motioned me to a chair opposite him.

"Well, Charlotte Theresa Sabina," he murmured, "I trust you had a decent sleep. I have never had anyone find my company quite so strenuous as you, my dear. People usually manage to stifle their yawns when I bore them. Your candor in falling asleep was quite refreshing."

I could feel an embarrassed flush mounting to my face at his mocking words. "I . . . I apologize, Count del Zaglia," I said stiffly, formally. "It had been a very long trip, and then the wine on top of it . . ."

"Oh, don't apologize," he protested, raising a slim, elegant hand, and the bloodstone gleamed dully. "I was charmed, my dear. And you must call me Luc. Despite the vast difference in our ages I find so much formality wearying." He rose with a sudden, graceful move and paced restlessly across the room. "Some wine, my dear?" He paid no attention to my small protest, pouring me a goblet of the dark red stuff and carrying it back to me. I had no recourse but to accept it, and as I did my fingers touched that elegant hand. Ignoring the amused expression on his face, I pulled my hand away quickly, as if stung, spilling a few drops of the wine on my dress. His flesh had been as cold as the grave, and yet its touch seemed to burn me. With trembling fingers I brought the wine to my lips and took a deep swallow. It wasn't as bitter as last night's wine, and I took another gulp.

"Is Luc short for Luciano?" I questioned with an effort at casual conversation.

He smiled then, and I was not warmed. "No, my dear. It's Lucifero. The fallen angel. Apt, is it not?"

At that point I gave in. This was a different type of man, one I couldn't cajole with fluttering eyelashes and innocent smiles. Nor with tear-filled eyes . . . at best it would merely amuse him.

"Have I cowed you completely, my dear Charlotte?" he inquired solicitously, once more seeming to have read my mind. "I do hope not. I have been looking forward to battling you. Your dear mother was one of the most self-willed females I have ever encountered, and you have the look of her, no matter how hard you try to disguise it. That obstinate little chin, and the stubborn expression about your delightful lips. I do hope you won't capitulate too easily."

I lifted my head at that and looked him squarely in those magnificent eyes. "I won't," I promised him in a cold, angry voice.

The look of amusement deepened, and he reached out and took one of my unwilling hands in his fiery-icy grip. For a moment I tried to pull away, then let it rest there as he brought it to his lips. At the last moment he turned it over and pressed his mouth against my palm. The kiss he placed there seemed to scorch me to my very soul. It was both a threat and a promise, a declaration of war and a peace offering, and desperately I wondered how long it would take me to amass enough money to escape from the demon count. For escape I must, before it was too late.

A moment later he released me, turning from me as if I were no longer of any interest to him—as indeed, I suppose I was not. The May night had fallen, and a myriad of candles threw a fitful light into the dim and shadowy corners of the room. Now that Luc's overpowering attentions were elsewhere I had a chance to take in my surroundings. I was not reassured. The Palazzo Edentide was in dire need of money, and I wondered if my poor virgin body was going to be sacrificed upon its altar.

"We are expecting a guest for dinner, my dear Charlotte," his soft, slightly menacing voice broke through my reveries. "An old friend of mine . . . and yours, apparently. You shouldn't find you have much in common with him, I'm afraid. But perhaps with you here to lend countenance to my sybaritic bachelor existence we may expect to entertain a more suitable acquaintance."

"Suitable?" I questioned.

He shrugged his elegant, silk-clad shoulders. "At this point virtuous ladies of Venice would cross the street rather than be forced to acknowledge me. Or they would if it didn't necessitate falling into the canals. My reputation, dear Charlotte, is sadly wretched." He smiled that brilliant smile. "But now that you are here to reform me perhaps the matchmaking mamas will let me at their little virginal ninnies. The name of del Zaglia is old and respected, the title only slightly less ancient. Who knows whether certain social-climbing matriarchs might be persuaded to accept its less than worthy incumbent."

"I wouldn't know," I responded. "Are you desirous of finding a . . . a virginal ninny?" I tried to toss this off casually but a telltale blush mounted to my fair cheeks.

Luc noted it with an ironic twist to his mobile mouth. "My friends tell me it is time to marry again. I have been a widower for too long. Besides, all this splendor," he indicated the water-stained damask wall-covering and the cracked marble mantelpiece, "needs refurbishing. My own pockets are sadly to let. A fatal addiction to gaming, I'm sorry to confess."

He couldn't have looked less sorrowful. A sudden gnawing attacked my stomach, reminding me that I hadn't eaten in well over twenty-four hours. I cast a furtive glance around the room, hoping I might find a small tray of bread and cheese, or even a dish of stale comfits. There was nothing edible in evidence. Nobly I attempted to turn my thoughts away from such mundane matters, back to my sinister guardian.

"Perhaps you should control your fatal addiction," I suggested repressively.

"I could scarcely do that, my dear ward. One has one's standards to keep up, you know. You aren't, by any chance, possessed of a comfortable fortune?"

This time I flushed a darker shade, and the demon count stopped his restless pacing, arrested by my acute embarrassment. It would have done me no good to prevaricate—he was bound to find out sooner or later. Indeed, I was amazed he didn't know already.

I cleared my throat. "As a matter of fact, yes."

He flung himself back into the ancient damask chair, the spindly frame creaking in protest against his strong body. His curious golden eyes were fixed on my face once more, and I wished I could look elsewhere, anywhere but at that hypnotizing gaze. "Oh, really?" he drawled. "You interest me greatly, little one. How much of a fortune?"

"I beg your pardon?"

"I said, how much?" he repeated impatiently.

I repeated the quite staggering sum Cousin Horace had mentioned in a flat voice.

His eyes narrowed. "All yours?"

"All mine," I admitted unwillingly.

He leaned back, eyeing me speculatively for a moment. Then with one of those lightning-like moves I had already come to expect of him, he rose and filled my wineglass, pouring a generous amount of the ruby liquid for himself at the same time. "How very convenient my inconvenient ward has suddenly become! Tell me, Charlotte Theresa Sabina, who is in charge of your financial affairs? No doubt your very tedious Cousin Horace?"

This came as a surprise to me. I hadn't thought he knew anything of my British relatives. No wonder their disapproval had been so stern. *They could have given me more definitive warnings*, I thought gloomily, knowing full well I had only myself to blame for my current predicament. "I believe, my esteemed guardian, that you have been placed in control of my financial as well as physical and moral well-being."

He threw back his head and laughed. "But how delightful! And there's no need to marry you. Your dear father was a better friend than I realized."

I stared at him, amazed at his audacity. Before I could confront him with all the things I wished to throw in his sardonic face the door opened, and the elegant butler of last night ushered in my handsome French acquaintance, Jean-Baptiste Perrier.

He stopped short at the sight of me, however, staring in unfeigned amazement, and I watched him with equal interest.

He was dressed even more elegantly than the previous evening, and for the first time I realized how very attractive he was. His clothes were, of course, impeccable, his dark blond hair dressed with sobriety and verve, his feet and hands small and well formed. And his face, despite the amazed expression, was quite pleasingly handsome. Not as bristlingly masculine as my longed-for Holger, nor as dramatically beautiful as my amused guardian, he nevertheless was very, very attractive. His bearing was military, and for a rash moment I considered throwing myself on his mercy and at his small feet, and begging him for asylum, for protection from the saturnine monster beside me. Before I could speak, however, he recovered himself and greeted Luc in French-accented Italian.

"Your newest, Luc? I didn't know you cared for the virginal type. She's quite attractive, I must say . . . Let me know when you tire of her. I'd be more than willing to take her off your hands."

I nearly drew myself up to my full, enraged height before I realized I wasn't supposed to understand a word of this. Quickly I put a blank expression on my face, but a swift glance from Del Zaglia made me wonder whether I had been quick enough.

"My ward," Luc spoke in slow, deliberate English, "Miss Charlotte Theresa Sabina Morrow. Her father was an old and dear friend of mine. I believe you two have met, though not formally introduced. This is Jean-Baptiste Perrier. Vice-consul for the French embassy here in Venice. Not a very popular young man, are you, Perrier? But then, I find politics so fatiguing." He was as mocking with his guest as he had been with me, I was relieved to note.

Perrier, after a startled moment, bowed low over my hand with perfect manners, as if he had never even suspected I was a lady of uncertain morals. "*Enchanté, mademoiselle.* I am delighted to see you again. The sun will shine a little brighter for your presence in this wretched, waterlogged town."

I smiled up at him, relaxing for the first time since I had entered the room, warming to the obvious attractions of the young man. Here was something I understood, something I was used to. Luc del Zaglia's ironical toying with me not only frightened me, it went against all the normal laws of behavior in men.

"I must thank you for your good offices last evening," I said, leaning back in my spindly chair. "You found my guardian just in time. I was being plagued by an alarming fellow countryman of yours when Luc appeared like a *deus ex machina.*" I was aware of Luc's inscrutable smile, and I wondered whether my unthinking use of Latin had set off any suspicions. Or perhaps he was merely entertained at hearing himself referred to as godlike, however remote the connection.

I had misjudged the reason. Jean-Baptiste looked properly abashed. "I wish I could take credit, dear lady. Alas, I never did find Luc last evening. When I returned to the room where I left you it was deserted. I hope you suffered no great disturbance?"

"No great disturbance at all," I replied blandly, all too aware of the taut attention behind Luc's casual demeanor.

"Is this your first visit to Venice, Mademoiselle Morrow?" He changed the subject smoothly. I confessed it was, and he continued, a knowing eye cocked in Luc's direction. "Then perhaps your ogre of a guardian will allow me to show you the dubious glories of the Queen of the Adriatic. Most account St. Mark's piazza to be quite a sight, with the campanile towering above the handsome domes. I would consider it a great honor."

"Right to the kill," Luc murmured in French, and M. Perrier flushed. "It is up to Charlotte," he continued in the English I supposedly understood solely. "I'm sure I can trust you with my sweet, innocent ward."

"But of course, Luc, I wouldn't dream . . ."

"Because if you betrayed my trust," he continued smoothly, as if Perrier had not spoken, "I will be forced to kill you. And the Austrian government does so frown on dueling."

There was an uneasy silence for a moment, and I looked from one handsome, tension-filled face to the other, amazed at the suddenly rigid atmosphere.

As quickly as it had come upon them it disappeared, and a moment later they were drinking and laughing as if it were a normal house in any part of England, with pleasant, acceptable young men paying flattering attention to an eligible and not unattractive young lady. Except that one of those men had a peculiarly frightening streak, and the not unattractive young lady was plainly terrified of him, leaving only Jean-Baptiste with any chance of being what he seemed. And even of him I was not completely sure.

Chapter Six

DINNER WAS SERVED early, which was a fortunate thing for all concerned. By my third glass of the dry red wine my guardian favored, I was feeling dizzy and just the tiniest bit silly. Another glass would have undone me completely.

Fortunately for my addled state of mind Jean-Baptiste managed to take me in to dinner. I rested a confident hand on his strong. young arm, idiotically relieved that I wouldn't have to touch Luc's body until I was more myself. I seemed to react strangely to his flesh, and with my wine-induced inanity who knows what might have happened?

The food was well cooked, bland, and obviously British, a suspicion that was borne out by the nature of Jean-Baptiste's compliments. The first half of the meal I devoted to silent gorging. It wasn't until the savory arrived that I was able to lean back in the wretchedly uncomfortable chair and listen to the gentlemen's conversation with more than half an ear.

"It's become an outrage," the Frenchman was saying. "I would have thought the Austrians would have shown a little more sense. If the French were in power we would have found the felon and dispatched him before he'd committed a second crime. And now this latest atrocity . . . I wonder the Imperial Army dares show its face around here."

"What latest atrocity?" I questioned, temporarily replete.

Luc raised an eyebrow at me, pushing his untouched plate away from him in distaste. "You are still with us, *ma petite?* I thought we had lost you with the pasta." Before I had a chance to respond he continued smoothly, "Jean-Baptiste was just informing me of the latest murder. Hardly dinnertime conversation but then, the French are savages."

His guest laughed lightly, a dark look in his brown eyes belying his good humor. "You never eat anything anyway, my friend."

"And I doubt an entire massacre could daunt my ward," he responded. "Tell her the latest. She had best be warned."

Jean-Baptiste cleared his throat. "There exists, mademoiselle, in this benighted city, a fiend, a ghoul, so horrible I hardly dare venture to tell you of it."

"You fully intend to tell her, Perrier. Get on with it," Luc said cynically, his tawny, brooding eyes never leaving my face.

The Frenchman ignored him. "A fiend, mademoiselle, who preys on the living. One who takes the cover of night and attacks those foolhardy enough to venture out alone and untended. Poor helpless females without sturdy males to protect them."

"A thief?" I questioned prosaically.

"If only that were all," Jean-Baptiste sighed. "But their money is always left with the . . . the bodies. No, this . . . this thing is nothing but a foul and merciless killer, who preys on young women for no apparent reason. Three bodies have been found in the canals, mademoiselle. Three young women with not a drop of blood left in their corpses!"

My knife clattered to the plate as I stared at him in horror. "How could that be?"

A small smile played about Luc's lips as his eyes watched me. "The peasants say it is a vampire," he offered pleasantly. "A creature that takes the form of a bat and sucks the blood of its victim. We, of course, know better."

"Do we?" Jean-Baptiste countered. "Such things have been known to exist. Who can say that a vampire has not risen from its endless sleep and taken to stalking its victims along the waterways of Venice?"

"I can, my dear Perrier." Luc toyed with a knife, his slim, elegant fingers looking very dangerous. "The victims throats were cut, were they not?"

"Yes, that's true. But there still should be some blood left in the bodies." He held to his theory stubbornly.

"Vampires, my friend, exist only in the imaginations of frustrated spinsters and adolescent females." He cast a mocking glance in my fascinated direction. "It is my theory, Perrier," and there seemed to be a hidden meaning underlying his casual words, "that the murders are committed in a certain way to place guilt on an innocent party."

"For what possible motive?" His companion was equally cool.

Luc shrugged. "Who knows, my friend? Anyway, I would have thought you at least had more sense than to believe these ghost stories."

"I do not believe them," Perrier said with great dignity. "But I do not discount them without careful consideration. And I would advise you not to do so either, del Zaglia!"

There was a sudden, dangerous silence, a silence more frightening than Perrier's ghastly tales. Once more a palpable tension arose between the two seemingly friendly men. In desperation I broke in. "How perfectly awful!" I murmured in an idiotic voice. "And when was the latest victim found?"

That mocking smile that I was coming to expect played on Luc's face. "Last night, my dear. Probably just as I was bringing you back here the ghoul was about his business. Just think, if you had only managed to stay awake you might have seen him at work."

"Did you see him?" I inquired sweetly.

"Not this time. No doubt I will get another chance." He reached one long arm and poured himself another glass of wine, the only sustenance he took during that meal. "You may retire now, Charlotte, and leave us to our port and cigars as they do in your barbarous country. Jean-Baptiste and I will be going out gambling when we're finished so you needn't stand upon ceremony. Bid her good night, Perrier."

Thus prodded, the Frenchman jumped to his feet and bowed low over my hand, his golden mustache tickling me. "Would tomorrow be too soon to give you your first tour of Venice, mademoiselle? You may be assured you can trust me to protect you from our ghoul."

"Since the vampire only strikes at night I think she need have no fear on that account," Luc said gently. "And tomorrow *would* be too soon. She needs a complete new wardrobe before I allow her to be seen in public. She is hardly dressed as befits a ward of del Zaglia—she shows too much ankle and too little chest for a Venetian. Perhaps by Friday, if Signora Conticelli can be made to hurry."

I stared at him mutinously, not sure which enraged me more, his casual discussion of my anatomy or his curtailing of my freedom. "But I wish to go out sooner," I protested. "I'll feel like a prisoner!"

"That is indeed too bad," he murmured solicitously, unmoved. "But it cannot be helped. I think Friday would be the day, Perrier. You may fetch dear Charlotte in the early afternoon and even take her to Florian's for coffee if the mood strikes you. Good night, Charlotte." He rose with graceful indolence.

"But . . . but . . . ," I objected.

"Good night, Charlotte," he repeated more firmly.

Throwing my damask napkin down on the table with as haughty a gesture as I could manage, I stalked from the room. My lordly gesture, however, was completely ruined by the infuriating little laugh that followed me out the door.

HAVING JUST SLEPT a total of almost twenty hours, I looked forward to a restless night, but I overestimated my own recuperative powers. That last glass of wine had been strangely bitter, but despite my stomach's protests no sooner had I reached the oppressively elegant confines of my third-floor room than I was overcome with a sudden sleepiness. No sooner did my head hit the plump feather pillow than I was in a sound sleep that lasted well into the next morning, and was troubled only mildly by nightmares, the details of which were blessedly forgotten when I awoke.

As I lay there in the darkened room I listened to the footsteps by my bed, footsteps so soft and hesitant that I knew they couldn't belong to the delightful Maddelena. Cautiously I opened my eyes to behold one of the loveliest creatures I had ever seen.

Even dressed in the coarse, plain clothes of a servant, the girl moved with a natural grace and elegance that would have put a *principessa* to shame. Her midnight-black hair curled down her slender back, her liquid black eyes stared at me soulfully, her olive skin was smooth and creamy. Even her mouth was beautifully formed, with full red lips that were now curved in a surprisingly unpleasant expression, almost a sneer.

"The signorina would like her breakfast now?" she inquired in Italian, and the image was shattered. Instead of the lovely soft, slurred accents of the Venetian, her harsh voice clearly bespoke the poorer southern sections of Italy, even if she looked like a princess. I stared at her with my blankest expression.

"I don't speak Italian," I said in my clear, light tones, and the smirk broadened disconcertingly, making her angelically beautiful face almost ugly.

"Of course the stupid pig of an English girl can't speak Italian," she continued in that language, smiling sweetly. "It is only to be expected." One beautifully formed hand indicated the well-laden tray beside my bed. "And would the stupid pink and white cow of an English girl like her tray?"

I stared at her with gentle incomprehension, my mind working feverishly. Gesturing for her to place the tray on my lap, I gave her my sweetest smile. "Thank you," I murmured. "Er . . . *grazie.*" My pronunciation was deliberately atrocious, and she smiled once more, bowing that gorgeous head.

I couldn't help but sigh. I would have given ten years of my life to have looked like her. My pink and white prettiness I found dreadfully insipid, and as for my yellow curls . . .

So, apparently, did the servant. "I will be back to dress your ugly body in your ugly dresses," she cooed. "But you will soon find, stupid girl, that he will not look at you. Not when I am around." Curtseying politely, she slipped out of my room, leaving me with much to think about as I drank the hot, strong coffee and nibbled at the sweet biscuits.

THE DRESSMAKER, Signora Conticelli, was a round little bird of a woman, all darting eyes and quick, nimble hands that resembled nothing so much as claws. Even her fine feathers would have done justice to a parrot, as would her cawing voice with its incessant gossip. Maddelena presided over the fittings, keeping up a running conversation with the little dressmaker about the scandals and foibles of Venice's best families and the detested Austrian occupiers. The French were equally disdained, and the English—my humble self included—were looked upon with curious contempt. Surprisingly enough, Maddelena did not use my supposed ignorance of the language to insult me any more than she already had in English. I wondered if she guessed I was more learned than I appeared to be. If so, she was equally circumspect.

"Count del Zaglia would like the dresses by the end of the week," Maddelena informed the woman when she had finished her measurements and I was allowed to dress once more.

"The end of the week? Impossible!"

"Not impossible," the housekeeper corrected her. "By the end of the week, the count has said, and he shall have them."

Signora Conticelli bit her beaky lip and glared at me, as if I were to blame for the outrageous demands of my guardian. "And what exactly am I to make for the *Inglesa*? You have yet to inform me of that, eh?"

It was time I interfered. "Excuse me," I said brightly, "but do you speak English?"

The signora stared at me with mute dislike. "A bit, signorina, a small bit."

"But how shall I tell you what I'd like?"

Maddelena laughed, a harsh, guttural sound. "What an innocent," she said in Italian, then lapsed into her broken English. "It is not up to you what clothes will be made," she informed me, not without some pleasure at depressing my pretensions. "The count has already made a list of the proper clothing. There is no need for you to be consulted."

"But . . . but . . . ," I protested. "I wish to choose my own clothes!"

Maddelena shrugged. "That is a shame, signorina. When you have been at the Palazzo del Zaglia a bit longer you will learn that your wishes are of no importance whatsoever. It is what the count wishes that matters." She turned her broad little back to me and started out the door.

Signora Conticelli, packing away her tape measure, looked at me and shrugged, as if to say, "That's the way of the world." As indeed, no doubt it was in this backward country, I thought angrily. As the door closed behind her I resisted the temptation to send the china vase full of fresh-cut flowers hurtling after her in a sudden spasm of frustrated rage.

Chapter Seven

LUC DEL ZAGLIA did not dine at home that night. I told myself I was relieved as I partook of a light supper in my room overlooking the malodorous canal. After my nerve-wracking day I was in no mood for another session with the demon count. And there was not a trace of disappointment in me, I assured myself, picking listlessly at my delicious meal. I was merely tired and overwrought.

I had decided to investigate the crumbling Palazzo Edentide after Signora Conticelli left. It was bad enough that I was a prisoner in the mansion; I refused to be a prisoner in my room. If I met the count I would have more than a few things to say to him, concerning the high-handed way he arranged my wardrobe, for one thing. I was also more than curious about the very beautiful and very hostile maidservant of this morning. What caused her to be so extraordinarily rude to me? Or, more to the point, what caused her to be so jealous of the count?

The upper hallways were deserted. I went through the rooms with hasty inquisitiveness, finding nothing to interest me in the damp-stained wall hangings, the dusty furniture, the cobwebby curtains. It was obvious that no one had spent much time on the third floor in many long years, and I wondered why it had fallen into such disrepair. Money, or lack of it, I assumed. How had the late contessa felt about her home crumbling down around her ears? I supposed, though, Venetians had to become used to such things in an entire city on the brink of falling into the sea.

I was a bit more circumspect on the second floor. I remembered Maddelena's information that the despised English servants inhabited these rooms. I had yet to see these remnants from Luc's mother's rule, except for the very superior butler, and if he was any example, I could cheerfully have avoided the others. I stood before a door, hesitating, when it opened and a tall, middle-aged woman with a long, pointed nose appeared.

I must have startled her as much as she had me. She let out a small gasp, jumping back a few steps. I recovered first, recognizing her for the upper servant that she was. I was about to apologize for startling her and introduce myself when some small hidden instinct made me wait for her to speak first.

I had a trifle too long to wait. Her slowness was just bordering on the reluctant, and the look in her milky blue eyes was disturbingly sly. Very interesting, I thought.

"You must be Miss Morrow," she said briskly after a long moment. I nodded, waiting. "I'm Mildred Fenwick."

I smiled with just the right degree of coolness. "Yes?"

She appeared flustered, and I relaxed a bit of my haughty demeanor. "I'm Mr. Thornton's assistant."

"Who, pray, is Mr. Thornton?"

"The butler, miss. And the majordomo of this godforsaken house. Begging your pardon, miss. You took me by surprise—I'm sorry if I seemed rude. I serve as a sort of combination bookkeeper, seamstress, housekeeper . . ."

"I thought Maddelena was the housekeeper?"

She sniffed, that long thin nose pinching. "That peasant? She would hardly know how to run a gentleman's estate. She is in charge of the Italian servants, I am in charge of the British ones. Not that there are many left. Standards have become so lax."

"How very interesting," I murmured, looking vague. "If you would be so kind, Miss . . ."

"Fenwick," she supplied hastily, suddenly eager to please. "Mildred Fenwick."

"Miss Fenwick. As I was saying, if you would be so kind, I would greatly appreciate hearing exactly who are the members of this household. I find it all quite bewildering."

She straightened her thin, overdressed body. I noted for the first time the unlikely red shade of her too-tight curls, the small blue bow attached incongruously to one of the side ringlets. Miss Fenwick was obviously not free from vanity.

"My dear lady, if you would honor me for tea, I would be delighted to acquaint you with the workings of Edentide," she practically gushed.

"That would be very kind of you, Miss Fenwick," I acquiesced. "I really am most curious about this strange place. This is the first time I've ever left England, you know."

She responded to this ingenuousness with what I suspected was a false warmth and put one of her clawlike hands on my arm. "You poor child! It's no wonder you're all at sixes and sevens. I wish I'd never left that sceptered isle for this wretched swamp, indeed I do!" As she moved closer I caught the overpowering scent of cheap perfume, and I barely stopped myself from recoiling. "You come with me, my dear, and I'll ring for tea. Thank God we have an Englishwoman in the kitchens. I don't think I'd survive here if it weren't for a decent cup of tea."

The small salon she led me to was scarcely cleaner than the abandoned rooms on the third floor. Mildred Fenwick must have caught my uncontrollable reaction, for she quickly dusted off the table with her delicate lace handkerchief, laughing in a highly affected manner. "The servants are disgraceful," she twittered. "If I've told them once, I've told them a thousand times, they must dust and sweep every room twice a week, even the deserted ones on the third floor. Oh, I beg your pardon, you're on the third floor, aren't you?"

I agreed that I was, seating myself gingerly on the frayed silk cushions of an unreliable-looking sofa.

"That was none of my doing," she announced hastily. "I try and try, but in the end, who does that man listen to but his childhood nursemaid? She should have been pensioned off years ago."

"I beg your pardon, Miss Fenwick, but you've lost me."

"Maddelena!" she spat the name. "Nothing more than a filthy, ignorant old peasant. She was the count's nursemaid when he was young, over his dear mother's objections, of course. But in that one area the old count was firm, and poor Contessa del Zaglia couldn't budge him."

"You knew his mother, then?" A healthy curiosity was perfectly acceptable in an English ninny, and I didn't bother to feign disinterest any more than my companion hesitated in divulging the intimate details of the del Zaglias. "Knew her! My beloved Constance! Why, it was she who brought me here, may God rest her soul. When she married the count and moved to Venice she swore that she would have nothing but English servants around her. It was enough, she used to say, that she was forced to live in such a barbarous place, but she refused to be surrounded by foreigners all the time. There used to be a full complement of servants in the old days, of course. When my dear Constance was still alive, and when that poor girl who married the count was here. Three gardeners, four housemaids, a cook, two kitchen maids, butler, valet, two footmen, various ladies' maids. Only the laundresses and gondoliers were Italian." She sighed at the unhappy state of things now. "At this poverty-stricken time we have only Mr. Thornton—a most estimable man." I could tell the aging spinster had her milky blue eyes on him. Hence the absurd bow and the too-youthful curls. "He came over as footman and stayed when everyone else left. And Mrs. Wattles is still here, thank the Lord. She's our cook, and heaven only knows she'd be turned out if it weren't that Count del Zaglia detests Italian cooking."

"And the Italian servants?"

"Them!" Mildred Fenwick signaled her contempt with another expressive sniff. "Maddelena, of course. Antonio, the gondolier, who also assists as the count's valet. Several daily maids. And Rosetta."

"Is that the very pretty girl who brought me my coffee this morning?" I questioned innocently.

My companion looked at me for a moment, then opened her mouth like a fish, leaning closer to me and drowning me in her heavy scent. Before she could speak, Rosetta herself appeared, her sandal-shod feet noiseless on the faded and raveled carpet, her carriage far more naturally graceful than I had ever managed with years of practice.

She set the heavily laden tea tray down in front of Miss Fenwick with a loud thump. Obviously there was no love lost between the two women. Their conversation, therefore, surprised me.

"You are having tea with the little English pig, eh?" Rosetta questioned in her guttural Italian. "What good will that do you?"

"How do you know she doesn't speak Italian?" Mildred questioned sharply, then smiled at me with great innocence. "She's probably not as stupid as she looks, you know."

"Bah, she is an idiot. She won't interfere with either your plans or mine, signorina." She sketched a curtsey and vanished. Both Mildred and I watched her beautifully formed back till it was out of sight, both sighing for what nature had deprived us of.

"You were saying, Miss Fenwick?" I prompted.

"Call me Mildred, my dear," she said absently as she poured me a cup of nice dark tea and then watered it down until it undoubtedly tasted like the canals. "That, of course, was Rosetta. She serves at meals, does a bit of haphazard dusting here and there. That's about all. She's here for very obvious reasons."

"And those are?" I questioned, nibbling at the thickly buttered toast.

She cast a suspicious look in my direction, and patted her too-perfect curls. "I hate to be blunt, my dear, but you'll find out soon enough. Rosetta spends a fair amount of her time in the count's bedroom. Because of that, there's no disciplining her, nor forcing her to do a speck of work more than she cares to. I realize it's disgraceful, but we're among foreigners, Miss Charlotte. They aren't like us."

Amen for that, I thought fervently, disliking this pretentious woman more and more the longer I sat with her.

"But enough of such tawdry stuff. I presume you were on a tour of the palazzo when we met. I would be delighted to show you the rest of the place when we've finished this delicious tea." Mildred's mouth was full as she spoke, and the crumbs tumbled down her brown sateen front.

This was the last thing I wanted. I much preferred poking and prying by myself, but I could think of no good excuse to get rid of her, so I gave in with good grace, mentally planning a second tour later. I was graced by many sins, including pride, gullibility, and suspicion. Worst of all was a positively common curiosity that had been the despair of Theresa and led me into worse scrapes than I cared to remember. At this point I had no one to answer to but myself, and for not the first time I decided to indulge myself as soon as I got the chance. In the meantime . . .

"That would be delightful, Miss Fenwick," I said sweetly. "Mildred, then," I amended as she raised one of her thin hands. For the first time I noticed the surprisingly beautiful sapphire ring, and I wondered how an emigré servant could own such a fine piece. Her alert eyes caught my expression.

Instead of offering an explanation, however, she quickly hid her hand in her lap, away from my prying eyes.

I was not one to take my proper cues, however. "What a lovely ring, Mildred! Is it a family heirloom or a token from some admirer?"

The look she cast me was one of strong dislike, quickly masked by an innocent simper. "A token of affection, Miss Charlotte. I seldom wear it . . . it's too large for my delicate hands." She made no effort to show me her trophy, however.

"But what a shame! You should have it adjusted. I am persuaded that was a particularly fine sapphire."

"Oh, heavens, no, my dear," she tittered, beads of nervous perspiration breaking out on her lined forehead beneath the frizz of orange bangs. "Merely a very pretty quartz. What would I be doing with sapphires?" She laughed again, nervously.

What indeed? I thought grimly. Something very strange was going on at the Palazzo Edentide, and it didn't all stem from the villainous count.

The rest of the tour would have been tiresome were it not for the oppressive yet beguiling ornateness of the palazzo. Centuries of Venetian artistic genius had gone into the making of this dainty, elegant mansion, and centuries of Venetian love of beauty, art, and music had tempered the almost Eastern opulence with a sly charm, rather like a child dressed in its mother's clothes, dignified yet playful. As I wandered through the remainder of the thirty rooms of what Mildred stigmatized as a "small dwelling," I found myself responding once more to the enchantment of the Queen of the Adriatic. Were it not for the depressing correctness of my companion, I could have danced down the dust-specked halls, waltzed in the huge abandoned ballroom with the bright Venetian sunlight as my partner and the glorious ceiling (painted by Titian himself, Mildred assured me) smiling down on me. As it was I did neither, merely nodded solemnly at Mildred Fenwick's continuing round of plaintive remarks.

We ended our tour in the bowels of the house, the dark and dank-smelling kitchen. The room was steamy and odorous, a combination of oil, boiled mutton, freshly baked bread, and human sweat. Not terribly appetizing, I thought critically, and then turned to greet the cook with surprise and unfeigned warmth.

Mrs. Wattles was so round, so rosy-cheeked, so good-natured and so very *English* that I could have thrown my arms around her in sudden delight. Here was something I recognized, a part of England that would never change no matter to what heathenish places it was transplanted. Women like Florence Wattles had been ruling wealthy British kitchens since the time of William the Conqueror and perhaps even before. The very permanence of her sturdy frame and cockney accent set my mind at rest for the first time since I arrived in the strange, enchanted city.

Apparently I had almost the same effect on Mrs. Wattles, for she dabbed at her bespectacled eyes with her spotless apron with great sentimentality. "Eh, and it's a bit of old England like I thought I'd never see again. You're a blessed sight for these old eyes, miss, that you are. Only a pure young English girl could look like you, with that guinea-gold hair and the kind of skin these Eye-talian lovelies would murder for. It'll be a rare pleasure to serve you, miss."

For not the first time I wondered how such insipid looks as mine could command such admiration, but I dutifully smiled and blushed and thanked the dear lady.

"And good English food you'll be having, just like you're used to," she reassured me, shaking her head up and down vigorously so that her chins shook. "Master Luc won't stand for no Eye-talian food. Hates the smell of garlic, he does. Why, I once used just a touch in a pot roast; thought I might spice it up a bit, and do you know what happened?"

I confessed I didn't, and the voluble creature continued, "He walked right out of the house. Rose up from the dinner table, threw down his napkin, and stormed out without a word. And him having twenty guests to dinner at the time, mostly Austrians and Frenchies and the like." She sniffed. "Not that they deserved better treatment. Pack of foreigners. But it's a funny thing, miss. I was sure Maddelena told me to use garlic that day. I must have been mistaken." She sighed gustily, and I caught the faint trace of gin on her breath.

"Yes, you must have been," Mildred cut in coldly, and I could see there was little love lost between the two English ladies. We beat a hasty retreat as Mrs. Wattles invited me to stop in anytime and we could have a comfortable chat, but I was caught up in the sinister implications of the strange little episode that had preyed on the cook's mind. The count had a desperate hatred of garlic, had he? Now why did that ring such an ominous bell in my usually excellent memory?

"You'll have to excuse Mrs. Wattles," Mildred murmured conspiratorially, trying to slip one of her hands through my arm with ingratiating friendliness. With a fair amount of subtlety I evaded her pawing. "She's getting on in years and is prone to fancies. Besides, she drinks."

"Fancies?" I echoed.

"About the garlic. She's been listening to the Italian servants and refined too much on it. I do hope you won't be so gullible."

I stopped still in the middle of the hallway, the dark and gloomy ancestors of the del Zaglia family staring down at the two English ladies with amused disdain. "What would I have to be gullible about, Miss Fenwick?"

"Mildred," she corrected coyly.

I waved that aside impatiently. "What would I have to be gullible about?"

"Why, the supposed curse of the del Zaglias. It's all nonsense, of course. Do you think I'd work here if I believed a word of it?" Nevertheless, the older woman peered over her shoulder with a sudden nervous start.

"I have no idea what you'd do, Mildred. I scarcely know you. What is the curse of the Del Zaglias?" Some deep-seated cowardly part of me didn't really want to know, and for a moment I considered turning my back on her and running all the way up the flights of stairs to my bedroom before she could frighten me further than my own imagination had done.

She lowered her voice ominously. "It is said that the del Zaglias are . . . are . . . *vampiros.*"

"*Vampiros?*" I questioned. My excellent Italian had not encompassed that word, but there could be little question of its English translation.

"Vampires," she whispered. "The living dead."

"That's absurd," I lowered my voice also, the tiny hairs on the back of my neck standing on end.

"Of course it is," she proclaimed stoutly, her slightly protruding eyes darting nervously around in her head. "But still, there are disconcerting coincidences. No one ever sees the count when the sun is up. He never seems to eat anything, never attends church. And he hates garlic. You will also notice there are no mirrors in the house, except for your room."

I pulled myself together. "That's awfully little to condemn a man on," I said sternly. "You should be ashamed of yourself, spreading such rumors."

"You would have heard them sooner or later," she sniffed indignantly. "Better you heard it from someone who was on the count's side, and not one of his far-too-numerous enemies." She moved closer to me, and her scent was overpowering. "But I swear to you, miss, half of Venice believes it of him. They are all terrified. And sometimes when I see him, looking so much like a . . . a prince of darkness, I can't help but wonder . . ."

This was too much, even for me. Grimly I fought the thrill of horror that ran along my backbone. "You are a foolish, gossiping woman, Mildred," I said sharply. "You should be defending your employer, not spreading lies. I have a good mind to mention this to the count." I would do no such thing, but I was horrified by her reaction.

Mildred Fenwick screamed, a shrill, terrified shriek, and clutched at my resisting hand, babbling in her terror, "Oh, please, miss, don't. You wouldn't be so cruel, miss, you wouldn't! He'd kill me as soon as look at me, I know he would. Please, miss. And I'll return the ring, I promise."

It took surprising strength to pry loose her clinging hands. "Calm yourself, Mildred. I promise I won't mention it. But I trust you won't be so foolish to mention this ever again. It's both absurd and wicked."

"Oh, yes, miss. Thank you, miss. May God bless you, miss, for your kindness!" The poor woman must be a little mad, I thought.

I turned away and left her, making my way directly back toward the dubious haven of my own room, unable to rid my mind of the sight of Mildred Fenwick staring after me, a haggard expression on her pinched face, a look of fear and . . . was it pity . . . ? in her faded blue eyes. Just as I couldn't wipe from my mind the horrid image of Lucifero, so like the fallen angel, bending over some poor young thing and draining her of her life's blood. It wasn't my fault if in that image he seemed more like a lover than a murderer.

I remembered Jean-Baptiste Perrier's ghoul of Venice, and I couldn't help but recall the cold, amused expression on the count's face as he listened to the atrocities. In an upsurge of unreasoning fear, I picked up my skirts and ran the rest of the way to the third floor, locking the heavy door firmly behind me.

Chapter Eight

I SLEPT FITFULLY that night, which came as no surprise. I ate the large, garlic-less meal sent up to me by Mrs. Wattles more out of duty than pleasure, ignored the bitter red wine after a tentative sip, and roamed the confines of my room, pacing back and forth while I tried to reason with that base, superstitious, cowardly part of myself that usually remained under control. There was no denying that a good part of me was completely and totally terrified, believing in Mildred Fenwick's demon of the night and all the horrors accompanying it. Now I understood the looks, the terror, the horror on so many previously friendly faces when I spoke my guardian's name.

But that's absurd, I informed myself with a stern good sense that would have pleased my practical mother. The poor man couldn't help being desperately romantic-looking, rather like that previous intermittent Venetian, Lord Byron. It was his dark and brooding beauty that gave rise to these foul rumors, coupled with his cool, cynical manner, but any number of coincidences do not a fiend from hell make. Pleased with my rationalization I returned to a dream-tossed sleep. To my horror and displeasure, my dreams were of Count Lucifero Alessandro del Zaglia, but they did not present him in the guise of a murderer. Instead he kept intruding into my somnolence in the most *romantic* fashion, those cynical topaz eyes meeting mine with promises better left unspoken while his elegant white hands stroked me in ways no man had ever dared. The bloodstone ring gleamed against my pale skin. When I awoke I was hot all over, despite the chill damp of the room, and my hands trembled. Moonlight was streaming in my balcony, calling to me. I tried to ignore it, shutting my eyes against its silver beams, but the excess of sleep I had enjoyed in the past few days had finally taken its toll, and the night was far from still. Male voices seemed to echo through the ancient walls of Edentide, and I wondered whether our neighbors were having a party.

Finally I gave up trying to sleep. The May night was pleasantly cool on my thinly clad body, and without further hesitation I pulled Theresa's loosest dress over my thin night rail and padded barefoot down the dark, deserted hallways of Luc's palazzo.

I was as quiet as the grave. The folds of my dress made barely a whisper, and my bare feet on the chilly marble floors were cold but silent. It seemed to me that there were eyes everywhere as I crept down the empty stairs. *Nonsense*, I told myself briskly, and continued toward my goal.

It was not, as one might suspect, the kitchen. During my morning tour Mildred had indicated a small overgrown garden off the side canal. "No one uses it nowadays," she had sniffed, obviously suggesting I follow suit. Of course, I had no intention of doing so.

The door out into the night air opened with surprising ease, considering how noisy and rusted the more frequently used door hinges were in the decaying mansion. I stepped out into the still night air and gave myself up to the wonder of it.

Moonlight was everywhere, casting shadows on the tangled bushes, lending a flattering glow to the ancient marble statues that peopled the garden. As I moved through the moon shadows I fancied myself some mythical goddess, Diana the huntress, perhaps, with my bare feet and my loose clothing and outrageous lack of undergarments. I threw back my head, feeling my long hair curve down my back, and raised my arms slowly and luxuriously to the benign and mysterious moon . . .

"I didn't know you were a moon worshiper, little one," a dry voice broke through my reveries, and I dropped my arms and whirled around, stunned and embarrassed at being caught in such a compromising situation.

Luc was sitting on one of the benches that a few short moments ago was vacant, and the faint wisps of smoke from the slender cigar he was smoking added to the uncanny suspicion that he had materialized out of thin air.

"I . . . I didn't know anyone was out here," I stammered, edging nervously back toward the house.

His hand shot out and caught me in a hard grip that was belied by the unaccustomed sweetness of his smile. "Stay a bit, Charlotte. Humor your poor aging guardian on a spring night."

I eyed him with patent distrust, trying not to notice the sudden tumultuous pounding of my heart. A second later he released me, and I was about to run, then halted, uncertain of what I wanted.

Apparently Luc knew far better than I did. "That's a good girl," he said approvingly as, mesmerized, I sat down at the opposite end of the marble bench, out of reach but not irremediably so. "It warms me to see you being biddable for once."

That broke the moonlit spell. "It won't last long," I said coolly, and he laughed.

"Nor do I expect it to, my Charlotte. Bah, what a name! Tonight you look more like a Carlotta—it suits such a wild creature far better than the tame 'Charlotte.' I can't imagine what possessed Theresa to give you such a name."

My interest was fairly caught. "Did you know Theresa?"

A small smile hovered about his lips. "Only too well, little one. She was my late wife's second cousin, but they might as well have been twins. As alike as two peas in a pod."

"How ghastly," I said with heartfelt sympathy, and then realized the enormity of my faux pas. "I beg your pardon," I muttered incoherently, blushing. "I don't know what got into me. I . . ."

"It is only the truth. It was indeed ghastly, though I fared better than your poor father. His problem, you see, was that he really loved Theresa." He took a puff of his cigar, and his face in the moonlight was like marble, despite the lightness in his voice. "Whereas I cared not one whit for Sybil."

I stared at him, wide-eyed in wonder. "But then, why did you marry her?"

"My poor innocent Carlotta, do you still believe people marry for love? I married Sybil Brunwood because my mother desired me to. And my mother's wishes were never to be taken lightly. Besides, I had nothing better to do at the time, and it seemed an adequate match. Not brilliant, but then, my reputation at the time was already a bit . . . compromised."

"And was your mother pleased?" I tucked my feet up under me and clasped my arms around my knees, oddly enough feeling more comfortable with my formidable guardian.

"Ah, yes, my mother. She was perhaps the only one who was satisfied with the marriage. She was one of those indefatigable women who see things only as they wish to see them, and ruthlessly bend people and things to their will. It is because of her this palazzo is called Edentide. I am sure she wept prettily to my poor besotted father and begged him to make the place more like her beloved England, even to changing the name that had lived for centuries." Disgust was patent in his voice. "A few more tears and all the old retainers were replaced with cold British servants. It is no wonder that I have ever had a disgust of feminine wiles." I vowed to myself then and there never to weep in front of him. "My dear mother had her way for far too long, but Venice is slowly reclaiming her own." He looked out over the motley roofline with a dreamy gaze.

"And were you and Sybil happy? I questioned, ignoring the outrageous impropriety of asking such a question.

His answer was a short, sharp laugh as he stubbed out the slender cigarillo. "Need you ask, little one? Sybil was as cold, self-willed, and mean-spirited as your late mother. Apart from occasional efforts to provide myself with a son and heir I had very little to do with her."

Again I blushed, and I was grateful the shadowed garden hid it. "Perhaps she wasn't all that bad," I offered hesitantly. "She must have been very unhappy to have killed herself."

He shot me a look of surprise out of his golden eyes. "Sybil didn't kill herself," he said. "If you've already heard that rumor no doubt you have heard its alternative, that I murdered her."

A chill ran down my spine at the flatness of his words, but before I could speak he continued, as if compelled by the moonlight or the strange hour to confess.

"Sybil had been quite circumspect, but by accident I discovered that her childlessness was not caused by a failure in nature. When it came to avoiding what she wished to avoid Sybil was very clever, and she wished to avoid childbirth. When I discovered the lengths she had gone to I quietly arranged to divorce her."

He leaned back and stared into the starless sky, a distant expression on his fallen-angel countenance. "She did not care for that. Nor did my mother, but by that time I was past paying any heed to her wishes. I went to our villa in Treviso and told her my plans.

"Unfortunately a great many servants were in hearing, but none in sight. At least half a dozen heard her shrieking imprecations at me from the top of the stairs, at least half a dozen heard me reply as loudly and as angrily. And they all heard her screams as she plunged to her death on the marble floor below. But none of them," and his smile was both sad and chilling, "none of them could say whether it was my hand that pushed her, or her own evil temper that had overset her."

"And which was it?" My voice was little more than a croak.

He turned and seemed to see me for the first time. A smile lit his face, one that was both rueful and charming. "What a one I am, to be pouring out my inmost secrets to your delicate ears! You make me indiscreet, *mia Carlotta.*" And he reached over and ruffled my hair in a casual, friendly gesture.

It was the first time I could remember being caressed in such a careless, affectionate manner, and it was at that moment a small part of my starved heart fell disastrously head over heels in love with Luc del Zaglia.

"Go to bed, little one," he said softly, a laugh in his voice. "You will catch cold like that."

I tried to pull myself out of the adolescent stupor I had fallen into. I could only hope he hadn't read my reaction. "I couldn't sleep," I replied childishly, rising reluctantly to my feet and moving in the direction of the well-oiled door.

The look on his face was far from reassuring. "Next time, little one, you should drink your wine. You will find that you sleep far more soundly."

I was to ponder those words as I made my way back to the cool confines of my room. It wasn't until I was almost asleep that I realized he had never answered the naive question I had placed before him. Had Sybil's screaming tantrum sent her hurtling off the balcony to her death? Or had it been Luc's slim, elegant hands with the bloodstone shining dully and prophetically?

Chapter Nine

THE FIRST OF my clothes arrived the next morning from Signora Conticelli, turning my troubled thoughts down more pleasant channels. The softest, most delicate lace-trimmed undergarments I had ever seen quickly replaced my sturdy and scratchy cotton lingerie. The stockings were whisper-thin silk, practically transparent; soft new morocco leather slippers replaced my stouter English shoes. And the outer garments!

Apparently Luc was a stickler for the conventions of mourning. Everything was unrelieved black with a touch here and there of purest white: black dresses, black capes and manteaux and gloves and shawls and absurd little hats. I stared at the stuff around me in dismay. I had hoped, being so far from any member of my mother's family, that I might throw off my mourning with unseemly haste, and had greeted Luc's decree of a new wardrobe with secret relief. Apparently I had rejoiced too soon. I glanced at my disappointed face in one of the numerous mirrors that decorated my walls and sighed. There were mitigating circumstances, however. As I held up one new dress against my body I couldn't fail to notice how black complemented my round English figure. What looks I had were certainly enhanced by mourning. My cheeks were flushed, my blue eyes sparkling and seeming even larger than ever, so that they dominated my pale face with its small nose and overgenerous mouth. Even my hair seemed more golden, and I wondered cynically whether it was the flattering attributes of my black clothing or something about the Palazzo del Zaglia (or Edentide as Mildred insisted on calling it) that brightened my eyes. Had it something to do with the strange and beguiling tête à tête in the moonlit garden last night? I quickly shut such dangerous thoughts from my head.

I smiled up at the three pairs of dissimilar eyes staring down at me. Signora Conticelli watched me like a hawk, Mildred's milky blue eyes were damp with sentimental emotion, and Maddelena's beady black ones stared at me with unpleasant cynicism. "The count's orders are that your absurd English clothes are to be burned. You will be pleased to change immediately and give your clothes to Rosetta."

"But I wish to keep my old clothes," I protested, turning to a fluttery Mildred for support. "They belonged to my mother; they have sentimental value."

"Oh, I do think the count would understand your feelings in the matter, my dear Charlotte," the spinster said hastily.

"You will have to discuss it with the count," the old witch pronounced sourly. "In the meantime Rosetta will take them."

Rosetta was pleased indeed to take them. She watched me change with hooded, haughty eyes, pretending ignorance when I repeatedly asked her to leave the room while I undressed. She irritated me so with her superior smirk that I was tempted to give her a return insult in her own language, a temptation I controlled. My knowledge of Italian (and French and German, among others) was my one advantage in this threatening household, an advantage I meant to hold on to for as long as possible.

Actually, despite my jealousy of Rosetta's dramatic beauty, I preferred my body to hers. Her lush curves were edging over to fat, while my body was slim and lithe, with curves in the right places, and not too noticeable muscle in other useful areas. By Venetian standards (and by Luc's, no doubt) I was too thin, but I liked myself that way. And Mrs. Wattles's bland English cooking wasn't likely to add any extra pounds, thank heavens.

As I dressed I came across one major omission. "Where is the corset?" I questioned the indolent maid.

"*Scusi?*" she murmured as she lounged against the door.

"My corset?" I picked up my old one and waved it in her expressionless face. "There must be a new corset if everything else is to be replaced."

"No," she replied, displaying a small grasp of English.

"Then I'll have to wear this one," I sighed, pulling the instrument of torture around me with a sigh. Suddenly Rosetta was on her feet and babbling in nervous Italian, tugging at my hands, trying to pull the whalebone garment away from me.

"No, no," she cried. "He said you were not to wear one. I was to see that it is burned . . . you may not have it! Give it up, English cow!"

"Rosetta!" Maddelena appeared at the door, a disapproving expression on her habitually sour face. "What is the problem?"

"The corset, signora. She won't give it up."

The tug-of-war over my undergarments suddenly struck me as both absurd and undignified, and I let go. To my immense satisfaction Rosetta fell backwards, hard on her rather ample hindquarters, still clutching my poor corset like a trophy.

The housekeeper turned to me with a strange expression in her beady black eyes, what in a more pleasant woman I might have called amusement. The look was gone as swiftly as it appeared. "The count has given orders that you will not wear that . . . that thing, signorina."

I was outraged. "What right had he to dictate my underclothing?" I demanded angrily.

"The same right he had to choose it. Which he did, personally, signorina." She watched my blush with cold pleasure. "You are too thin anyway.

And the count considers corsets unhealthy. You may discuss it with him if you like, and perhaps he will relent. At the moment, however, you will let Rosetta take it with your other clothes. Such an uproar in a gentleman's home is unseemly."

I bowed my head, properly chastened. As if I would bring up the subject of my underclothing with Lucifero del Zaglia on the infrequent occasions that we met! Despite my outrage at his high-handed and embarrassingly intimate overseeing of my wardrobe, in this case I couldn't help being grateful. It would be a blessed relief to be free of that wretched thing.

I had more surprises in store for me in terms of my new wardrobe. Pulling the filmy black dress over my head, I couldn't help but revel in the luxuriousness of the fabric. Theresa had never been one to stint herself, but not even she had had dresses made of such thin, elegant Italian silk. As I presented my back to Rosetta for fastening I caught a glimpse of myself in the full-length mirror opposite me and let out an undignified gasp.

"This . . . this is indecent!" I protested to Maddelena. "I can't possibly wear anything so . . . so immodest!" I had never seen such an expanse of creamy white shoulders and breast in my entire life, not even in the demimondaines I had watched with furtive interest when I attended the opera in London. "Surely this is not at all the thing for a young lady?" There was a plaintive note in my voice. Despite my outrage I would have been blind not to notice how very flattering the lines of the dress were. Indeed, my shoulders and breast were part of my more pleasing physical attributes, and the immodest neckline did show them off beautifully—a small secret part of me wanted to see my guardian's reaction.

"All the young ladies of Venice wear dresses like this," Maddelena said positively, and I could not doubt her. "Not black, of course, unless they're in mourning, but décolleté like that. A higher neckline would be deemed prudish and old-fashioned."

I smoothed the skimpy material over my shoulders, wanting to be convinced. "I don't suppose I have any choice in this matter, either," I said. The dress was so very dashing. The loud slamming of my door aroused me from my conceited reverie, and I looked to Maddelena in surprise.

"Rosetta does not care for your dress, signorina," she remarked cynically. "She thinks the count will like it far too much."

I held my breath for a moment. "And what do you think, Maddelena?"

Those small black eyes, so like little raisins in her suet pudding face, met mine with cynical amusement. "I think, signorina, that you are already far too concerned with Signor Luc than you should be." And with that she turned and left the room, albeit more quietly than the infuriated Rosetta had.

IT WASN'T UNTIL evening that I finally saw Luc del Zaglia again. In the warm, sun-drenched Venetian light of day my moonlight madness seemed absurd indeed, and the horrid tales of ghouls, vampires, and the undead seemed all so much foolish chatter, unpleasant fantasies of ignorant peasants and nerve-ridden English spinsters. Daylight had added a healthy dose of practicality to my romantic musings. After all, this was the modern year of 1840 . . . such horrors belonged to the middle ages, not in such enlightened times as these.

The sun was just setting when I entered the west parlor on the main floor of the Palazzo Edentide. In the cold, damp place it was hard to choose a favored room, but of the myriad of parlors, small and large, this seemed the most comfortable. Its damp-stained wall hangings were of a soft rose hue, the frayed furniture comfortable, the tables surprisingly free from dust. The room received the full force of the afternoon sun on two sides, flooding the room with a water-dappled light reflecting from the canals that gave the eerie but not unpleasant sensation of being underwater. It also gave a spectacular view of the sun setting over the domed roofs of Venice, and as I had always had a weakness for both sunsets and sunrises I settled myself down in a well-stuffed rose-brocade chair and proceeded to watch nature's spectacle in all its awe-inspiring glory.

In silent wonder I watched the last dying rays touch the city with fairy light. In two short days, housebound days at that, I was being beguiled by this absurd, waterlogged place, and I could feel a treacherous little clutching at my heart as the sun dipped below the horizon.

A deep sigh escaped me, almost as if I watched my life slip below the surface with it.

"Why so sad, Carlotta?" Luc's voice came quietly across the room, making me jump out of my chair in fright.

"You scared me to death!" I said reproachfully after I had managed to catch my breath. My heart was still fluttering strangely beneath the low-cut bodice of the new dress as I turned and faced my guardian, keenly aware of those hooded amber eyes taking in every detail of my appearance with a disturbing mixture of amusement and interest.

He looked no different than before, despite the horrid rumors surrounding him and my brief stirrings of infatuation that had taken me by surprise last night. Indeed, as I took in his lean, elegant, black-clad length, the pale face with the black hair curling around it, with the odd mixture of the sensual and the spiritual playing over his arresting countenance, I could see how people could believe such absurdities as Mildred whispered. In the early dusk I half believed them myself.

"Not quite to death," he corrected gently, moving into the room with a sort of graceful glide. "You must strengthen your nerves if you are to survive in this damp place. Otherwise you will be seeing ghosts in every corner." He moved to the window and looked out over the still canals, then turned back to me. "Who knows, you could turn into a completely nerve-ridden mental incompetent and I would be forced to have you committed to an asylum. Leaving me with your healthy fortune." And he smiled, that beguiling smile that made his lightly spoken words all the more chilling.

He laughed then, with none of the mockery that had marred it previously. "I wish you could see your face, my dear ward. It is so expressive!" He left the window and moved closer to me, so close that I could feel my breath constricting in my chest, almost as if my stays were too tight, and I was not blissfully, sensuously free of the armor. He looked down at me from his great height, and there was an expression of tenderness in those hypnotizing eyes. "You must learn, *mia Carlotta,* not to believe everything I tell you."

I stared up at him in mute silence, unable to say a word. He had hit the nail squarely on the head. I believed every word he said, and I had the unfortunate suspicion that I would continue to do so.

Hastily I cleared my throat, hoping to break the spell he cast over me with such little effort. "I will try not to," I said gamely. "But I am very gullible."

He laughed again, and released me from his hypnotizing gaze. "I know, little one. I know." He moved away, and I let out a silent breath of relief. "It amazes me that one with your intelligence could be so."

The stillness then was awkward, to say the least. I watched him with sudden suspicion. "Intelligence?" I echoed in my lightest voice. "No one has ever accused me of that before." I batted my eyelashes in what I hoped was a dim-wittedly entrancing manner.

Luc was unimpressed. "Liar," he said softly. "But it is of no importance. For the time being you may keep your secrets, and I will keep mine." He took my arm in the lightest, most polite of gestures, and it was all I could do to keep from pulling away from his scorching touch, it unnerved me so. That sardonic little smile pulled at the corners of his mouth once more. "If you have no objections, my dear, a visitor awaits you in the east parlor. A very correct young Austrian soldier, I believe."

"Holger?" I demanded, delight sweeping over me. Here was rescue from my more wicked side.

"I have no idea." The boredom in his voice was belied by the quickening of interest beneath his drooping lids. "We shall soon find out."

An uncomfortable thought struck me. "You'll let me see him alone, of course?"

"Of course *not,*" he corrected gently. "Since I have decided to dispense with a duenna there is nothing for it but that I must serve in her place. Young ladies of good breeding do not hold conversations with young gentlemen unchaperoned."

"But I do with you!" I protested, and then wished I had kept my very large mouth shut for once. The smile on his face, instead of chilling me, warmed me in a most uncomfortable manner, so that I was blushing when I entered the room where Holger was striding around impatiently. Fortunately Holger, like most men, assumed my blushes were caused by shyness at meeting him once more, and he puffed up like a pouter pigeon as he bowed low over my hand, all the while unable to keep himself from stealing worried little glances at the tall, saturnine presence of my silent guardian.

I had wanted to throw myself onto Holger's manly bosom, so relieved was I at his return, but Luc had successfully put a damper on my high spirits, and I greeted my noble swain with a speaking look from my large blue eyes and a firm pressure from my hands. Holger didn't seem to notice.

"I am delighted to meet you, Count," he greeted Luc with great serious-ness, pumping his hand energetically for all the world as if he hadn't called the man a spawn of the Devil a few short days ago. "Your friendship for the Austrian Empire has been an excellent example for your not-so-amiable countrymen. I wish there were more like you."

I couldn't help letting out a little choked gasp at this, and quickly tried to turn it into a cough. One Luc del Zaglia was all the terrified town of Venice could stand.

Luc hadn't missed my reaction. Indeed, nothing seemed to escape those seemingly somnolent eyes. He smiled at Holger with great charm. "I thank you for your kind words, Captain. I am always happy to be of assistance to the glorious Austrian Empire and their representatives in our little city." The sarcasm was so obvious I wondered how Holger could miss it. But Holger, I was fast learning, was one to see only what he wanted to see, so he nodded in an odiously pompous manner and took my suddenly resisting arm in his. "If you will excuse us, Count. Charlotte and I have much to discuss."

He started to lead me into an adjoining room, but Luc moved smoothly in front of us, detaching me from the Austrian with so light a touch I scarcely would have noticed if I hadn't been so overly aware of everything about my guardian.

"*Miss* Morrow," the emphasis was light but unmistakable, "would love to talk alone with you, but unfortunately it cannot be." He shrugged, and the gesture was almost a parody of an Italian stage character's. "Society has cer-tain rules, and we, alas, must follow them."

Holger looked affronted, taken in by Luc's absurd playacting. "I've never heard that Luc del Zaglia was one to abide by the rules of society," he said sharply.

The demon count smiled slightly. "Ah, but that is for myself, Captain. When it comes to my innocent young ward, the rules are quite different. I am sure I can trust you to obey them." With that he led me to one of the more uncomfortable sofas in the room and with gentle force seated me beside him. I could feel the heat emanating from his body, and it so disturbed me I barely heard a word of the long, tedious conversation I held with Holger. Since I had found out previously that the Austrian did not seem to be overloaded with intelligence it required only half my brain to keep up with him; the other half was busy trying to figure out how to move farther from Luc, how to appear unflustered when his nearness was making my pulses race, my heart beat far too quickly and the breath constrict in my lungs. Never before had I had such a reaction to a man, and the thought of such strange and unaccustomed weakness on my part bothered me almost as much as the symptoms themselves. Try as I would to forget, my mind kept returning to last night in the moonlit garden, and his careless, affectionate caress that had upset me so.

I cast a surreptitious glance at his profile, the hooded eyes, delicate nose and high cheekbones, the expression arranged in an attitude of courteous attention to Holger's boring monologue. Could it be possible that he really was a creature of darkness, and the absurd and undignified things I was feeling were the results of a . . . a spell?

The idea seemed laughable, but I didn't want to laugh, Love was a comfortable emotion, what I could learn to feel for Holger, for Jean-Baptiste, perhaps. Warmth, affection, a yearning to take care of the silly creature. I could never love anyone that left me so bewildered. This quickening of my pulses and heat in my stomach could have nothing to do with those warm feelings that Theresa had reluctantly admitted existed between men and women. It must be the climate, I told myself. I was unused to the long, slow, warm days and the damp, chilly nights. I was also unused to such strange and overpowering creatures as my guardian. As soon as I got to know him better he would lose his appeal, his awe-inspiring qualities. He would be just another man, no wiser, no handsomer, no more enticing than any other. Once I understood exactly what he was, everything would be fine. I only wondered if that blessed day would ever come.

Holger said only two things during his hour-long visit that were able to distract me from my worried thoughts of Luc. The first was his mention of the murders.

"Another one gone a few nights ago, I hear," Holger said, with an uncomfortably sharp glance at my impassive guardian. "We're having the devil of a time catching up with this insane monster, but never fear, we will!"

"You think the man's insane, then?" I questioned abruptly.

Holger frowned at my daring to question his judgment. "Obviously," he replied shortly. "Only a madman would drain innocent young girls of their blood. All this talk of a vampire is so much nonsense. Simply some poor fool gone over the brink. We'll catch him soon enough."

"Let us hope so, Captain," Luc said gently, a smile hovering around his lips.

"In the meantime, Charlotte must not venture out unless she is accompanied by me," Holger announced with the air of an occupying army. As indeed, he was, I thought uncomfortably. "I will pick her up tomorrow in the afternoon and take her on a small bit of sightseeing."

"I beg your pardon," Luc corrected with great charm, "but Miss Morrow will tour Venice with her guardian and anyone else I choose to deputize. As for tomorrow, I'm afraid a rival has been before you, Captain. She is already bespoken."

He flushed an unbecoming red. "You allow her out with just anybody? Have her cancel the appointment!"

"I do not think Monsieur Perrier would appreciate that," Luc murmured. "Perhaps the next day, if she is not too tired."

"She is going with Jean-Baptiste Perrier?" At Luc's nod Holger let out an angry snort. "That little idiot! He cares more about his clothes than his country! I would think you would find her more of a man, Count." Obviously he thought himself the perfect candidate. Luc was not impressed.

"My dear Captain," he protested, "how was I to know of your existence when this previous appointment was made? My so-dutiful ward had failed to mention your obviously lengthy acquaintance, and she neglected to tell me entirely that you planned to call on us. So naughty!" He chucked me under the chin with one long finger, and I glared back into his impassive eyes. He was not pleased with me for omitting to mention Holger, and I tried not to let that unnerve me.

"I had always heard that you were a friend to Austria, Count." Holger was still sulking. Luc had obviously had enough of my admittedly boorish suitor, and he rose with languid grace, holding out one slim hand in obvious dismissal.

"I am a friend to Austria," he said gently, "and to France. Indeed, I am a friend to all, unlike some of my hot-blooded compatriots down at the Caffe Mondelo. Revolutions are so tiring."

"You would not find them so if you were trying to control them," Holger snapped, shaking the count's hand with obvious distaste, then bowing low over mine and pressing an unfortunately damp one on my hand. "The day after tomorrow, Charlotte," he announced, more a threat than an invitation. "No excuses."

I smiled sweetly. "I would be delighted, dear Captain. Till Saturday then."

A curious silence reigned over the room when the captain had departed, shown out by the very correct Thornton. I had the feeling Lucifero Alessandro del Zaglia was not pleased with me. It was to my great surprise that I watched him look from the ancient bloodstone ring he was contemplating and smile at me with his full charm.

"And where did you meet your stalwart young suitor?" he questioned idly, but I knew the question was far from casual. "I had no idea you were so well acquainted with members of the occupying army."

"Do you disapprove of the Austrians?" I countered sweetly.

"I disapprove of no one and nothing," he returned lazily. "I do not make judgments. You didn't answer my question."

"I met Holger on the coach. I'm sorry if I didn't think to mention him, but I doubted I'd ever see him again." I hated to apologize, but in this instance I felt his well-concealed annoyance might be justified.

"You underestimate your charms, my dear. Why shouldn't he follow up on your no doubt delightful relationship?"

I hesitated, but only for a moment. I was being baited, a thing I disliked intensely, and Luc was a master at it. "Because the moment I mentioned my guardian's name all my fellow travelers turned pale and crossed themselves in horror. My sturdy swain was visibly shaken at the thought of you. However, he seems to have recovered in short order."

He seemed completely unmoved by my words. A gentle smile played about his thin, well-shaped lips. "How very interesting, to be sure. And where did Von Wolfram join the coach?"

"Just north of the border. Why do you ask?"

"Mere curiosity, little one. How extremely coincidental that Holger von Wolfram should pick your coach of the many that pass through on their way to Venice. I would advise you, my dear, to be wary of the good captain. He is not entirely the fool he appears." He rose and sketched a negligent bow in my direction. "And now, my dear Charlotte, I am desolated to inform you that I must leave you once more this evening. I'm sure Mrs. Wattles will provide you with an excellent repast."

"But . . . where are you going?" I had the temerity to ask, momentarily bewildered. I had certainly displeased him greatly—"Charlotte" was so cold and unfriendly compared to the warmth of "*mia Carlotta.*"

He smiled that charming smile once more. "Why, to visit my mistress," he replied sweetly. "And to gamble away your fortune. *Buona notte,* little one." A moment later he was gone, leaving me with a curiously bereft feeling I told myself was relief.

Chapter Ten

MY TOUR OF Venice the next day was the first relatively normal time I spent since I first arrived. Jean-Baptiste Perrier, nattily attired in a coat of bottle-green linen, fawn-colored trousers, and gleaming boots, was all attention and subtle flattery, treating me with the combination of deference and charm that I had come to expect from the men I had met. Only Luc seemed immune to my attractions. This was no doubt a much needed blow to my disgusting vanity, but the thought made me frown.

"But why do you look so fierce, *ma petite*?" Jean-Baptiste murmured solicitously as we skimmed the dark green waters of the Grand Canal in an exceedingly elegant black gondola, past the pink and gold fairy palaces that leaned this way and that in the spring sunshine. I admired them with impartial approval, but secretly I saw nothing to touch the decadent, eroded, brave beauty of Edentide. "You aren't a victim of . . . of seasickness, are you?" The idea creased his handsome brow, no doubt from the worry that I might disgrace myself and soil his too-elegant clothes.

"No, I'm a born sailor," I replied, smiling at him with my best smile. Hoping to obtain some information from him, I threw caution to the winds. "As a matter of fact, I was thinking about my guardian."

My companion had been leaning closer than I would have deemed proper, but at this he pulled back, an unreadable expression on his handsome face. "Indeed?" His voice was not encouraging.

There was nothing like coming to the point, I decided. "How long have you known him, Monsieur Perrier? What is he really like?" I hesitated, then rushed on. "To tell you the truth, the man terrifies me."

He permitted himself a smile at that, showing a set of small, perfect teeth. "I'm sure that is just what dear Luc has in mind. He loves to frighten people. It's only a game with him, Mademoiselle Morrow. You mustn't take him seriously. Underneath his rather frightening exterior Luc del Zaglia is just another aristo, with too much money and too much time and too little to occupy himself. So he spends his nights frightening ignorant peasants and silly little girls." He shrugged, letting out an indulgent little laugh that grated annoyingly on my nerves. Presumably I was one of those silly little girls.

"As for what he really is like," he continued smoothly, "who knows? Without a doubt he is far too intelligent for his own good. I have never seen him do a kind deed or say a good word about anyone. His sexual and financial appetites are reportedly rapacious, his sense of honor perhaps strong enough when he cares to exert it. The games he plays are silly, Mademoiselle Morrow, but underneath it all I think Luc del Zaglia might be a very dangerous man. I would advise you to be careful."

"It isn't really up to me, is it?" I replied, somewhat nettled. "He is my guardian, completely in control of me and my fortune. He could do anything he pleased."

"You need have no fear for your fortune, Mademoiselle Charlotte," he soothed, his brown eyes nonetheless perking up at the mention of money. "Luc has no need of it. He's unbelievably rich. Perhaps the richest man in Venice."

"But he gambles all the time! He said he has lost his fortune," I protested.

"Luc does indeed gamble all the time. And he always wins. That is part of the cause of his satanic reputation. Half the people he plays with believe he can't lose because he's made a pact with the Devil. Personally, I disagree."

"Do you play with him?"

"Of course. And I lose. But one day I won't." There was a note of steel beneath his light tone, a note that made me suddenly very uncomfortable, rather like looking into a still pool of water and seeing a dead toad floating on the clear blue surface. I was to remember that thought long afterward, when it was almost too late.

Sensing my unease, Jean-Baptiste smiled at me with a charm that couldn't begin to come close to the hypnotizing enchantment of the demon count's smile. "As for your fears, *cher mademoiselle,* you must banish them. Luc is my friend, but I have no intention of letting him damage such an enchanting little flower such as you."

I didn't know how to reply to this, so I contented myself with a small, tentative smile. It was the proper gesture, for Jean-Baptiste secured my willing hand in his strong, well-manicured one and held it tightly for the rest of the trip. And try as I would to derive some small bit of comfort from the touch of his warm flesh, my heart remained stubbornly disturbed.

I WAS ON MY way up to my bedroom when a door on the second floor opened and Rosetta stepped out. I stopped to stare at her in amazement, my stupidly innocent mind uncomprehending why she should be so disarrayed. Her long black hair was loose and tangled around her sensuous face, her eyes were dreamy, her cheeks flushed. Her white peasant blouse was still undone, showing an indecent amount of her full, milky breasts, and she was barefoot. Her eyes met mine, and her full red lips curved in an insolent smirk.

"What . . . what were you doing in there?" I stammered, caught off guard. The smirk broadened.

"Those are the count's rooms," she replied.

A hot flush mounted my pale skin, and I cursed myself for being such an idiot. "Oh," was about all I managed before taking to my heels and practically running the rest of the way up to the third floor and the sanctity of my bedroom. I was consumed with an overwhelming, burning rage that I told myself was disgust for my guardian's libertine propensities. The fact that it was Rosetta's eyes I wanted to scratch out and not Luc's made no difference to my rationalizations. But I couldn't control my imagination, couldn't keep myself from seeing those slender, white hands reach out and fondle Rosetta's olive skin. I slammed the door behind me as loudly as I dared and sank into an overstuffed slipper chair, staring disconsolately out the window.

If I would only face the truth, I would have to admit that Luc del Zaglia fascinated me for the very things that would have revolted most properly bred young ladies. His flagrant sex life should have horrified me. Instead I was filled with a burning rage that I couldn't avoid recognizing. And for a brief, cowardly moment I wished I was back in England, not so terribly beyond my depth in the mysterious and ancient city of Venice.

DINNER WAS SERVED in my room again. Rosetta, now properly attired and shod, served it, her magnificent brown eyes chastely lowered and her nasty Italian tongue miraculously silent.

For my part I ignored her as best I could, sampling the plain baked chicken and polenta without much appetite. I remembered Luc's words about the wine and sniffed it tentatively. It smelled bitter, and I put it away from me, feeling restless and irritable. "I presume the count has gone out?" I finally broke down and questioned my unwilling maidservant.

She nodded, obviously not eager to give me any more information than she had to. All right, my girl, I thought, pushing the tray away and rising. If Luc was safely out of the palazzo till near daybreak I would be damned if I would stay cooped up in my elegant prison. Reaching into my already well-stocked wardrobe I pulled out a warm wool shawl. In another moment I was out of the room and down the stairs, leaving a suddenly terrified and incoherent Rosetta babbling after me.

The formidable Thornton was lurking about the hallways as I reached the front door. I should have known he would be on duty only when I wished the cursed fellow elsewhere. He stared down his long, thin nose at me with rampant disapproval.

"Where, may I ask, miss, are you going? It is not at all proper for a young lady to venture out unchaperoned after dark."

I smiled sweetly at him, but there was no softening in his pale, granite-like face, and I wondered how he could arouse such tender feelings in Mildred Fenwick's skinny breast. "I am going for a short walk, Mr. Thornton.

I will be back directly." I started forward again, but his smooth voice brought me up short.

"May I suggest, miss, that you take Miss Fenwick along with you? Or at the very least Rosetta?"

If he thought Rosetta would be protection along the narrow alleyways that passed for streets in Venice he was sadly optimistic. She would more likely stab me in the back and dump me into the canals. For some odd reason she considered me a rival. I told myself she was being ridiculous, but secretly I only wished I were.

"No, thank you," I replied politely, waiting for him to open the door for me. "I will be fine by myself."

The man was obviously torn. His dislike of me was warring with his sense of propriety, not unmixed with what was probably a very healthy fear of his employer. "The count won't like it," he warned, verifying my suspicions.

Since he couldn't make up his mind I pulled open the massive front door myself, surprised at the silence and ease with which it opened. "Blast the count," I observed sweetly, and swept out into the murky Venetian twilight.

The freedom was delightful, a physical aura that made me feel like skipping down the cobbled alleyways in my new slippers. The streets were deserted, and a light mist was falling, accompanied by a deep fog that made it impossible to see more than a few feet ahead of me. But I was too determined to wrest my bit of freedom from a tyrannical fate, and I firmly made my way toward what I hoped was the small square, or *campo*, that I had seen from one of the drawing room windows. A short stroll around it and then back to the palazzo. No harm would have been done, and I would feel like a different person. I needed to feel that I could . . .

"*Bon soir*, mademoiselle," a husky voice spoke in my ear, and a burly arm went around my throat before I could cry out. "It is such a pleasure to see you, mademoiselle, after these many days. I have been waiting, watching the Palazzo del Zaglia. I knew you would venture out alone sooner or later, and I was right. And now, if you'll be so good as to come with me."

I had no choice. I was being dragged through the fog-shrouded streets, a hand clapped over my mouth so that I could not scream, that arm still around my throat, choking me. I drummed my heels against the cobblestones, kicking at my enemy, but he seemed possessed of a superhuman strength. *This is hopeless*, I thought. *The ghoul of Venice has gotten me, and in the dense fog no one could see us, no one could help.*

"How unfortunate that del Zaglia did not see fit to place a better guard upon you," the man chuckled in my ear. "If he weren't so high-and-mighty, he would know that I am not a man to be crossed lightly. I saw you first, and I intend to have you. It was promised. Once we're back in my room it'll be too late, eh? And then what good will it do for him to rant and rave?"

I stiffened with recognition. I had heard that voice before, had felt those cruel, punishing hands on me. It was the lecherous Frenchman from the embassy. Georges, Luc had called him. I was about to breathe a sigh of relief when a particularly vicious yank slammed me against a stucco wall, dazing me. When my head cleared we were in a dark, foul-smelling stairway, with Georges dragging me up the steps regardless of my struggles. As I banged against the risers I gathered my breath to scream loudly.

"Go ahead and scream," he offered jovially, having divined my intention. "Anyone who can hear you will pay no attention. I have had other women here in my rooms. Other women have screamed." He laughed, a low, incredibly evil laugh, as he reached the landing and kicked open the door. Flinging my frightened body into the pitch-black room, he turned from me and locked the door. I lay there in a trembling huddle, wondering what in the world I could do.

"Del Zaglia will kill you," I said bravely, struggling to rise from my ignominious position on the floor with an attempt at dignity. "He is not a man to be trifled with."

"He will not dare make a scene," Georges scoffed, lighting one of the lamps and illuminating a filthy, cluttered room that stank of sour wine, garbage, and unwashed clothing. He was very drunk, but that didn't mitigate the danger. He was obviously the sort that too much wine makes a little mad, and there was no reasoning with a madman.

He swayed back and forth, staring at me out of feverish, swollen eyes. "Del Zaglia would not lower his aristocratic self to brawling over a woman of ill repute."

"I am not a woman of ill repute," I said hotly. "I am his ward."

"Is that what he calls you?" Georges snorted. "It makes no difference to me. Take off your clothes."

"Go to hell," I snarled, rising to my feet and edging back to the door. "Do you think del Zaglia's pride would allow him to let you take his possession? He'll rip you into pieces."

"I doubt it," Georges spat meditatively. "But you just might be worth it." And then he lunged.

Chapter Eleven

IF GEORGES HAD been expecting a frail little English flower he was doomed to disappointment. A proper maiden would have stood there and screamed, calling on the Lord and other sundry intangibles to deliver her. Being more practical, I made a last minute dart out of the way, so that his heavy body hit my shoulder, knocking me against the wall instead of onto the tumbled bed. A moment later he was on me, mouth slobbering at my shoulder as he ripped away my dress. I lay there passively for a moment, just long enough to lull his suspicions, then brought my knee up sharply into his groin.

His scream brought me a great deal of satisfaction, as did his rolling over in pain, clutching himself and groaning. "I'll kill you," he panted, struggling to rise.

"I think not," I answered pleasantly, bashing him on the head with the first thing at hand, which happened to be a full bottle of wine. The bottle broke, splashing my tormentor with the red stuff that mixed with the frightening amount of blood as he collapsed in a stupor on the littered floor of his room. I stood over him, panting, ready to do battle with the broken shards if need be. But the fight had gone from Georges.

I prodded him tentatively with a foot, wondering if I had killed him. The thought didn't move me particularly, but I felt some relief when he moaned. Dropping the rest of the bottle on him, I quickly found my shawl, wrapped it around the remains of my dress, and ran from the room out into the miasma of Venice.

The mist had risen, making the streets once more visible. Much good it did me. In that headlong flight I had had no chance to see where Georges was dragging me, and having never been out of the palazzo except by gondola, I knew this area of Venice not at all. I remembered that it hadn't taken long for Georges to reach his filthy little room. Indeed, I probably hadn't been gone from Edentide for more than an hour. Huddling deeper into my shawl, I struck out in what I hoped was the direction of the palazzo, keeping a weather eye out for a resurrection of Georges.

It was well over an hour later that I finally found the narrow little campo that stood a few short steps away from the del Zaglia mansion. From the street side Edentide bore no resemblance to the palazzo I knew, and I passed it twice in the twilight before I recognized it. In my desperate search I had had to fend off the helpful suggestions of half a dozen men; three Austrian soldiers, two Venetians and a French merchant. Even now I could feel masculine eyes appraising me from a distance, and, lifting my sodden skirts, I ran the rest of the way down the alley, nearly slipping on the damp, slime-covered steps as I collapsed against what I hoped to God was the right door, sobbing with fright and exhaustion as I pounded helplessly against the unwelcoming portal.

A moment later I was inside, the warmth and light momentarily blinding me. I looked up to thank the unyielding Thornton, and instead met the compelling golden stare of my demon count, who towered above me.

"Out for a stroll, my dear Charlotte?" he murmured icily, those extraordinary eyes narrowed in fury at my disobedience.

I stared up at him, feeling the color drain from my face. All my superstitions came to the fore again. "I . . . I . . . ," I stammered helplessly, and then compounded matters by dropping to the marble floor in a dead faint.

I couldn't have lost consciousness for long. The next thing I knew I was being carried through the dark, damp halls of the palazzo in a strong pair of arms. I could feel the slow *thump, thump* of his heartbeat beneath my head, and I remembered feeling a small, silly surge of relief. Surely a real vampire couldn't have anything as mundane as a beating heart.

He kicked open the door to the west parlor. A blazing fire welcomed me, and I thought it time to bestir myself. I squirmed, but the iron bands around me only tightened. Moving across the room with effortless grace, he deposited me on the comfortable settee.

I considered continuing my providential faint, but my curiosity got the better of me. I opened my eyes and stared up at the imposing figure of my guardian.

The expression in his golden eyes was unreadable, but the set of his mobile mouth was not. Lucifero Alessandro del Zaglia was in an absolute fury, and I shrank back among the cushions.

"Thank goodness you've found her!" Mildred Fenwick fluttered from the doorway, wringing her thin hands that were now free of jewelry. "I was afraid something terrible had happened."

Luc didn't bother to raise his eyes from me. "I rather think something terrible did happen. Bring some warm water and bandages." A slender, pale hand reached out and gently pulled the shawl away from me, exposing my ripped gown, the bruises and bite marks on my shoulder.

"Oh, my goodness!" wailed Mildred, starting into the room.

"At once!" he ordered, not bothering to look away from me. Without another sound she vanished, leaving him to touch my aching cheek gently, bringing his hand away stained with blood. He stared at it meditatively, and I wondered whether it whetted his appetite.

As if he could read my absurd thoughts, his eyes met mine, and he smiled, that gentle little smile that so unnerved me. "I was about to scold you quite severely for leaving the house unescorted, but I do think you have learned your lesson, *poveretta.*" He reached out once more and smoothed the tangle of blond curls away from my face. "Haven't you?"

I was caught like a rat in a trap. "Yes," I whispered, aching for him to continue touching me, continue soothing away the terror and upset of the last few hours. A moment later Mildred was back, followed closely by Maddelena.

"What has happened?" the latter demanded in Italian, eyeing me with surprising concern.

"I have yet to find out, Maddelena," he answered. In English he said, "I will take care of my ward alone, thank you, ladies. If you could see that a bath is brought to her room and a fire laid, I'm sure she'd be very grateful. Wouldn't you, my dear?" Still caught by his inexorable will, I nodded, watching them leave me in his clutches with a wave of desperation. I didn't know if I could bear to have those slim, sensual hands ministering to me. Luc del Zaglia knew far too much about arousing women. I fancied he knew very well that his touch on my face was exciting rather than soothing me, and was doing it deliberately.

He dipped a cloth in the warm water, touching it to my face with a gentle hand. "And now, *mia Carlotta*, you will tell me who did this to you, and what exactly happened."

I hesitated, sensing beneath his tender care a deep, killing fury that I was terrified of arousing. But I knew he would have the truth from me sooner or later, and it would go easier with me if I told him what he wanted to know. "The man from the French embassy," I said after a long moment. "Georges. I don't even know his last name."

"Martin." He gave it the French pronunciation. "Not that it matters. He won't have it for long." And I knew from that soft voice that I had signed his death warrant. "Continue."

In as few words as possible I told him of Georges's abduction in the campo, the long haul to his rooms, the fight therein. A small laugh escaped him as I recounted the efficacy of my knee, all the while he was carefully washing away traces of blood from my face and neck, his hands seeming to caress my skin, the bloodstone ring shining in the candlelight, hypnotizing me.

"And then I hit him over the head with the wine bottle and escaped." I finished, my breath suddenly constricted as he pulled the torn gown away from my shoulder, exposing even more of my breasts than the indecent gown had. Luc, however, seemed unmoved, and I supposed he had seen a great many women in far less clothing than I was wearing.

"How very resourceful of you, little one," he murmured. "Did you kill him?"

"I don't think so," I confessed. "There seemed to be a great deal of blood. I rolled him over to see if he was dead, but he groaned a bit. So I left him there."

"How unfortunate. It would have saved me a bit of trouble. I shall have to kill him myself, then." This was said so casually that I barely took in the meaning.

I sat up quickly, holding my tattered dress against me. "Must you?" I questioned. "A severe beating would do just as well, wouldn't it?"

"Such a violent child. No, a severe beating would not be at all the thing. It would only enrage the man further, so that he would be obliged to try to kill either you and/or me at the first chance. Besides, I shall enjoy killing him. Your tender heart does you credit, *mia Carlotta*, but I'm afraid I can't allow myself to be swayed."

"He doesn't need to die!" I insisted, chilled. "He . . . he didn't rape me . . . he only tried. Surely you could show a little mercy?"

"Do you think he would have shown you any mercy?" he countered, throwing the cloth back into the water with a splash. "Are you certain you knocked him unconscious before and not after the fact? English girls are notoriously innocent; perhaps you didn't realize what he was doing, eh?"

A deep flush flooded my face. "I am not quite a fool. I would know if I had been . . . had been . . ." the words failed me, and Luc's lip curled in silent amusement. He was so damnably close to me that I couldn't think straight, couldn't talk straight.

"Perhaps," he said, running his hand along my neck, the skin burning mine, "I should find out. Just to set our minds at rest." His head bent down toward mine, and I shut my eyes, waiting for the feel of his mouth on mine.

It never came. A moment later I felt him move away in a sudden rush. I opened my eyes to see him standing by the balcony overlooking the Grand Canal, his back to me, while Mildred Fenwick, unaware of the devastating scene she had interrupted, fluttered around me with wringing hands and chirping noises.

"A bath is all ready for you, my poor child. And then into bed you go! I'm sure this has all been too alarming. But that's what comes of living in a city full of heathenish foreigners." She colored, casting an apologetic glance at Luc's rigid back. "Begging your pardon, Count."

He ignored her, turning back to me with a bland expression on his pale, handsome face. "I'm going out. I trust you have learned the folly of disobeying my orders, Charlotte. You are lucky you didn't suffer any more serious consequences. See that she gets straight into bed, Miss Fenwick. And make sure she drinks her wine," he added sharply, striding from the room before I could get out a single word of the many things that I wanted to say to him. I stared at my innocent helper with frustration, but she was far too busy clucking over me to notice.

In an hour I was bathed, dressed in a warm flannel nightgown, and tucked safely into my large, comfortable bed. Refusing the soporific wine, I lay awake for long, restless hours, turning among the suddenly constricting sheets, fighting against the smothering pillows, listening for the sound of

Luc's return. He would have to return by sunrise, I thought sleepily, determined to stay awake that long. When I heard him come in I would tiptoe downstairs and confront him. Beg him once more to spare Georges's life. And perhaps have him finish what he started in the west salon of this crumbling palazzo.

Chapter Twelve

IT WAS WELL past noon when I awoke the next day. The sun was directly overhead, reflecting off the canal and shining with translucent green light into my bedroom. I lay unmoving in the bed, waking very slowly, aware of my stiff, aching body, that same dry taste in my mouth, and a profound sense of unease. And then I remembered last night.

A tray rested beside my bed, a cup of cooling chocolate beside the now empty glass of wine tempting me to arise. Slowly I sat up, sipping at the rich sweet stuff as I tried to remember when I had succumbed and swallowed the bitter-tasting wine. It was all a hopeless blank to me, and I turned my cloudy brain instead to the problem of how to save Georges.

Without a doubt I hated the creature with his cruelty and brutish, animal lusts, but I certainly did not want to see him dead on my account. Beaten, humiliated, yes, but not dead, and certainly not at Luc's hands.

And then the memory of Luc's hands made me grow hot all over, and I could only be grateful that the madness of last night seemed to vanish in the golden light of the sun. Would I have really gone down and confronted him last night upon his return? It would have been tantamount to throwing myself into his arms. I shook my head with disgust at my own weakness. If I was not more careful I would end up being seduced and abandoned by an unprincipled and no doubt degenerate rake. I would do far better to concentrate on the heavy but intermittent attention of Holger, or the flattering regard of Jean-Baptiste. Luc del Zaglia, as the Frenchman had pointed out, was a very dangerous man. Surely I had too strong a sense of self-preservation to want to be caught in that whirlpool he represented.

My reflection in the mirror was not reassuring. A large welt cut across my neck and shoulder, a mark that would surely be obvious in my low-cut dresses. Even worse was the scrape on my cheek, the bruises on my throat, and my cut lip. Georges had done his work well, and I shuddered to think what would have happened if I hadn't managed to stun him with that bottle.

The sight of my wounds should have aroused me to a vengeful fury, but I remained adamant in my determination to save the wretched Georges. As soon as I dressed I drafted a short note, warning Georges that Luc intended to kill him. Sooner or later I would find some way to have it delivered, and then my conscience would be at rest. Georges had been terrified when Luc interrupted him at the embassy. Apparently Luc del Zaglia was enough to put the fear of God into anyone, not just a gullible little fool like me. A warning should manage to frighten Georges out of the city, with luck, out of the country. And if he happened to meet with a shipwreck or carriage accident on the way, I could greet the news with unimpaired good cheer, as long as I knew neither Luc nor I was responsible.

For a short time luck was with me. No one was in sight when I made my cautious way downstairs, a heavy shawl pulled around the low-cut shoulders of my gown, my slippers silent on the dusty marble stairs. I was able to find Antonio with no sharp-eyed witnesses around to watch as I slipped both the note and my small remainder of money into his greedy paw. With mixed feelings I watched him disappear down the corridor. I had no great hopes that the warning would reach Georges in time, but I had done my best.

"Signorina Morrow is feeling better?" A soft, sly voice broke through my reverie, and I turned to meet Maddelena's seamed face with unruffled calm. I couldn't tell whether or not she had seen me talking with Antonio, but I could only trust that she hadn't. I would have to continue on that assumption.

"A bit," I replied faintly. "I'm quite hungry."

"A good sign. If you would go into the smaller dining room Rosetta will bring you something shortly." She turned her squat body away and started down the hallway, in the same direction Antonio had taken.

"Where are you going?" I asked nervously.

She turned back, smiling a bland smile that disclosed brown and broken teeth. "Why, to see what you gave Antonio, of course."

I watched her go with a sense of fatality. I couldn't have the horrid man's blood on my hands, more particularly I didn't want Luc's beautiful pale hands further stained (if stained they were already). Antonio would hand over the message (though not the money) without further ado. There was nothing I could do but warn the man myself.

A few short minutes later I was making my furtive way through the cobbled alleyways of Venice. I had no idea how to get to Georges's hovel by gondola, and indeed, thought it safer to slip through the streets, swathed as I was in an enveloping black cape stolen from Mildred, hunched over like a woman three times my age. I caught no more than a couple of curious glances as I scuttled through the streets, clasping an exceedingly sharp and lethal-looking letter opener I had stolen from the Chinese desk in the west salon. I could defend myself from another attack, or so I told myself. I didn't really have a choice. So preoccupied was I in my thoughts and fears that I nearly ran full tilt into an Austrian officer in the street outside Georges's flat.

"Watch where you're going, you old hag!" I heard my beloved Holger snarl, shoving me against the wall with rude force. I was tempted to throw off my enveloping cape, but thought better of it. I watched in disbelief as what appeared to be an entire battalion of Austrian soldiers milled around in the streets outside, the sun shining on their spotless white and gold uniforms.

Even before I could make out the murmured comments of the soldiers I knew I had been too late.

One poor fellow, who couldn't have been more than seventeen, was leaning over and vomiting into the street. His friends were looking pale and unwell, and, deciding to risk unmasking, I hunched closer to my Austrian admirer.

"It must have been a large dog or wolf," a greenish-pallored lieutenant was saying, mopping his brow despite the cool spring breeze. "I've never seen anything like it. Just torn to shreds, he was."

"Nonsense," Holger maintained stoutly. "There are no wolves in Venice, and no large dogs on this island. It could only have been done by a man."

"What sort of man could inflict such carnage?" the other demanded. "Back in Austria we once found a young boy half eaten by wolves during a bad winter. That pales in comparison with this."

"Then what do you suggest?" Holger asked coldly. "Perhaps the ghoul of Venice is taking other forms now. First a vampire, now a werewolf, eh?"

"I . . . I never said a word about werewolves," the man stammered, crossing himself ardently. "There . . . there are no such things."

"Nor are there such things as vampires, my friend. Some fiendishly clever human being is murdering people in and around Venice and making it look like the work of supernatural beings."

I watched Holger with dawning surprise and suspicion. Gone was the dim-witted, pompous young suitor. The pomposity remained, but a shrewd intellect that had so far escaped my attention was making itself apparent. I felt a sudden chill, and, stumbling a bit, turned back toward the doubtful haven of Edentide. I had seen enough for one day. I had been too late for Georges, and were it not for my fears for the demon count, I would not have been sorry. As it was, I was now more frightened than I had ever been.

I made it back to the palazzo with only a few minutes to spare. No sooner had I taken off the enveloping cape and smoothed my tumbled hair than an imperious knock sounded at the front door. Quickly I ducked into the west parlor to straighten my shawl about me, keeping a sharp ear out for our visitor. But the walls of Edentide were thick and the noise from the canal even louder than usual, so I had to content myself to wait until the somber Thornton appeared at the door, accompanied by not one but two of my suitors.

Jean-Baptiste rushed to my side, barely leaving me enough time to appreciate the sumptuous effect of his pearl-grey costume. "*Ma pauvre petite,*" he murmured, taking one slim hand in his and planting a respectful kiss upon it. "Luc has told me of last night's outrage. That man shall pay for it, I swear to you! If Luc has not yet seen to it you may count on me to defend your honor."

Holger was only a few paces behind him, a sternly disapproving mask over his ruddy features. "That will be unnecessary, Perrier. For either you or the count."

Jean-Baptiste stood back and met Holger's icy blue eyes with a smirk. "Ah, my good Captain, have you already seen to the villain?" He bowed low. "My compliments on your speed. We both heard of it at the same time, and yet you took care of it with such dispatch." He sighed. "I am all admiration."

"I didn't do it!" Holger countered impatiently. "Someone else finished off Georges Martin before either of us could even plan a suitable punishment for his impertinence."

"Either?" I questioned, watching the two of them.

"Any of the three of us," Holger amended graciously, but I was no longer fooled by him. "I'm sorry to say that Georges Martin has been brutally murdered."

"That is a regrettable circumstance," Jean-Baptiste responded with false sorrow. "I was hoping I would have the pleasure of killing him myself. Or at least watching Luc do the honors."

Holger eyed the Frenchman in obvious disgust. "If you are so eager for the sight of blood, Perrier, you may view the carnage in Martin's apartment. I'm sure it will no longer bother the poor fellow."

"Gentlemen!" I held up a restraining hand, feeling quite dizzy. My imagination had always been overdeveloped. At the sight of my pale face they broke off their bickering, vying with each other to lead me to the frayed sofa.

"What monsters we are, *liebchen*, to talk of such a brutal thing in front of you," Holger murmured, his icy blue eyes not in the least sorry.

"What brutal thing?" Jean-Baptiste demanded irritably. "You have yet to tell us how the wretched Georges met his end."

Holger paused significantly, no doubt to savor the full effect of his disclosures. Fortunately I had a good idea of what his gory news would be, and I was prepared.

"Georges Martin was ripped to pieces by some very large and savage animal," he said solemnly, his cold, rather small eyes never leaving Perrier's unmoved countenance. "Either that, or by a madman."

There was a silence, one I felt called upon to break. "Oh, dear," I murmured inadequately, leaning back against the cushions and fanning myself uselessly with one limp hand. "How ghastly."

"Ghastly indeed, fräulein," Holger said heavily, the concern in his accented voice unmatched by the speculation in those eyes I no longer trusted.

"It does seem, Von Wolfram, that the Imperial Army is doing a wretched job of policing the canals and alleyways of Venice. This latest sounds like a variation of the work of our resident vampire."

"Don't be absurd," I snapped, much to their surprise. "There are no such things as vampires."

Perrier raised one of his immaculate eyebrows. "Really, my dear? I think you should ask your superstitious Italian and English servants if they agree with that." He took my limp hand in his small, neat one and brought it up to his lips with a gesture that a week before would have thrilled me. "You and I know it's nonsense, of course. As does the good captain."

"Indeed," Holger broke in, taking my other hand in an effort not to have Jean-Baptiste outdo him, "there is no ghoul of Venice, no werewolf or vampire. Merely a very clever, very dangerous man. As soon as I find out what is behind these seemingly random murders it will be only a short step to finding the villain. He must be an exceedingly brilliant, dangerous criminal, with a fiendish mind . . ."

"You wouldn't by any chance be discussing me, would you?" Luc's smooth voice startled the three of us, and we turned in unison to the door, where my elegant guardian lounged in Stygian splendor. Damn him, I thought, feeling the color rise in my face at the memory of our last meeting, of his gentle hands on my poor battered body.

"Luc!" Perrier let my hand drop lightly, not before bestowing a reassuring squeeze that reassured me not one bit. "You're up early today. The sun has barely set."

This was supposed to be a jest, but I couldn't help the little shiver of apprehension that ran down my backbone at the sinister implications of his lightly spoken words. Luc merely cast a cynical glance at his friend before entering the room, moving across the stained marble floor with a panther-like grace that made my stomach contract in the most alarming fashion. Taking my hands in his cool grip, he pulled me to my feet, his eyes sweeping over me in a manner that should have been solicitous, but in reality had the power to leave me more disturbed than I already was.

"I trust, my dear ward, that you have recovered from your upsetting experience of the previous evening?" The voice was soft and soothing, and for a moment I thought he referred to our almost-embrace in this very room. Then I realized he meant my near rape, and my color heightened even more.

"I am quite well, thank you," I murmured, dropping my eyes from an amused glance that suggested he knew all too well what I had been thinking of. "Were it not for this latest horror . . ."

I expected him to show surprise, demand information, but to my dread he seemed to know all about it. "The unfortunate demise of Monsieur Martin?" he questioned lightly, dropping my hands and moving over to the bell pull. "A most unpleasant fate, to be sure, but one he richly deserved. He hadn't long to live, anyway. I had intended to dispose of him this evening, but the ghoul of Venice seems to have forestalled me."

Out of the corner of my eye I saw Holger pull himself stiffly upright. "Are you sure it wasn't yourself that took care of Georges?" he demanded with a touch of belligerence that almost bordered on rudeness. "I wonder how you found out so quickly. I gather you only just arose?"

Luc met Holger's angry gaze with bland self-assurance. "My dear Captain, at least three of my servants informed me, complete with unnecessarily gruesome details about Martin's sad end. You should know by now that nothing stays secret in Venice for very long." As if on cue Thornton appeared at the doorway.

"You rang, sir?"

"Yes, Thornton. We would like wine for my unexpected but of course most welcome guests. And you may also inform the good captain of the cheerful news with which you greeted me this evening."

"About the Frenchman's murder, Count?" Thornton asked politely, and Holger's ruddy face flushed a darker, unbecoming shade.

"Exactly," Luc said smoothly. "Thank you, Thornton, that should be sufficient. I think a good claret would be in order."

As the butler withdrew a small moment of silence reigned in the room, broken only by the lap of the water against the *riva*, with the sounds of the gondoliers as they called their directions echoing through the twilight room. Both Perrier and Holger seemed abstracted, while Luc watched them with a cool smile curving his beautiful mouth.

It wasn't until Thornton returned with the crystal decanter of ruby wine that my suitors bestirred themselves. As if suddenly coming to his senses, Perrier returned to my side, his manner as smooth and flattering as before. With a great deal of expertise and delicacy he began to flirt with me, so gracefully that I couldn't help responding, all the time remembering the cold, speculative expression in his brown eyes as he watched my guardian, and knowing with a growing sense of irritation that he had no more real romantic interest in me than had Holger, who was now making jealous moves to push Jean-Baptiste away. They were both playing a devious game, one that included me as bait, and I thought I knew quite well who their quarry was: my indolent, sinister guardian, who watched all this attention with an indulgent eye.

My self-esteem had been dealt a mortal blow. No doubt I deserved being taken down a peg or two, and I thought with a twinge that I had asked for it, after accepting their slavish devotion with such an unquestioning complacency. As my two false swains wrangled over the right to take me to a band concert early the next week my rueful eyes met my guardian's from across the room. For the moment I hadn't bothered to shield my expression from him, and he read my newfound knowledge as easily as he might read a book.

He smiled then, a very gentle, mocking little smile, as if to say all men are fools, and lifted the wineglass to me in a silent toast. And I smiled back, in silent agreement, that all women were fools, too—and thereby took another dangerous step down the road of infatuation with my romantic and devious guardian.

A few moments later Luc arose with one of those abrupt, liquid gestures that startled me so. "I think, my dear Charlotte, that you should have a quiet supper and an early bedtime. Perrier and I have plans to go out this evening, and we shall of course include the good captain, leaving you to a quiet night alone. Unless you plan to disregard my warnings and go for another solitary stroll?"

I flushed under his mocking regard, my moment of charity gone, leaving me with unaccountable irritation and disappointment. Rising with great dignity, I wrapped my enveloping shawl around me to ward off the damp chill that seemed to creep through the windows from the canals below. "An early evening is an excellent idea," I said composedly, ignoring his acid comments. Bidding them all a graceful good night, I stopped before each one and gave them all my small, white hand.

Holger saluted smartly, his heels clicking together as he planted a loud, wet kiss on my hand. Jean-Baptiste was more delicate, murmuring a French endearment I pretended not to understand as his warm, dry mouth followed Holger's. And then I stopped in front of Luc, holding out my suddenly trembling hand.

He smiled down at me, not a trace of mockery this time, and took my shaking hand in his strong, fine-boned grasp. Once more he brought it to his lips, kissing my palm in a gesture that was so intimate I felt half faint.

"Good night, *mia Carlotta*," he murmured, leaning over and brushing a stray lock out of my eyes. "And lock your door," he added in a low voice that only I could hear.

I stared at him for a moment, and then he released me. Without another glance I ran out of the room, across the hall and up those long flights of marble stairs. When I finally reached my room I did just as he suggested, locking the inlaid door against the terrors of the night.

It wasn't until later, as I picked at the simple but nourishing meal Mrs. Wattles had thoughtfully sent up to me, that I wondered what exactly Lucifero Alessandro del Zaglia inspired in his gullible little ward, whether it was superstitious terror, or, to my suddenly observant mind an even more frightening possibility: was it an absurdly ill-placed attraction that was skirting the dangerous and illogical borders of love?

The moonlit canals of this romantic city met my troubled gaze and gave me the answer I least wanted to hear.

Chapter Thirteen

WHEN I AWOKE the next day, late in the afternoon, my head was like cotton wool, and my tongue like chicken feathers. I lay back among the linen sheets and soft goose-down pillows and closed my eyes against the late afternoon sunlight, too tired and muddle-headed to move.

"Are you awake yet, my dear?" Mildred Fenwick's bright voice disturbed the gentle daze in which I was floating, and reluctantly I turned my now throbbing head.

"Yes, Mildred," I sighed.

She bustled busily into the room, her pale orange dress matching her orange frizz of hair, both festooned with dark purple ribbons. "Thank goodness, dearie. You've slept like one dead. I've been in here every hour on the hour, looking for some sign of life, but you've been safe in the arms of Morpheus."

A quick dread pulled me fully awake. "Has something happened? Is Luc . . ." I let the sentence trail, misliking the cunning look in her milky blue eyes.

"No, my dear. Nothing new has happened. Not that I'm aware of, apart from the fact that Count del Zaglia left last night for parts unknown. I wondered whether your unusual somnolence had any connection with the count's sudden departure."

A hazy memory began to materialize in my mind, rather like coming closer and closer to a scarcely seen vision in a deep fog. Ribbons of mist began to dissolve away, and I stared into my memory in mute fascination, until Mildred's noisy snorting sound brought me back to the present.

"I beg your pardon, Mildred," I apologized absently. "I was just remembering the most extraordinary dream I had last night. I had no idea Luc had plans to leave us, but I'm sure in his absence we'll all fare very well, don't you think?" I looked pointedly at her ringless hand, and the spinster flushed.

"I'm sure you're right," she agreed after a long moment. "In any case, both your young men have called today, asking after you. I told them you were slightly indisposed but would be delighted to receive them tomorrow."

"That was very kind of you," I said with charming insincerity. I had no desire to see either of my so-ardent suitors. "In the meantime, I desperately need some tea . . ."

It took more than a few subtle suggestions to rid myself of the inquisitive creature. It was a good ten minutes before she left me alone to lie back in my bed and reconstruct the strange and compelling dream of last night.

I had dutifully drunk most of the sour, foul-tasting stuff Luc deemed suitable wine for a young lady, and, as usual, it was not long before I had fallen into a deep sleep. But this was not the long, death-like trance I had heretofore enjoyed since my stay in Venice. From the very first I was troubled by noises, voices whispering and shouting, footsteps scuffling on the dusty marble floors, doors opening and closing.

As if from a distance I watched my sleeping body rise from my bed and move to the door, soft linen night gown trailing in the dust, bare feet numb to the chill. I watched myself move as if in a trance through the darkened hallways of Edentide, moving nearer and nearer to the voices, the footsteps, the doors . . .

"Who's that?" a voice called out in broad Venetian dialect, but the sleep-dazed creature that was and wasn't me paid it no heed. A moment later a rough-looking peasant appeared from out of the darkness, grabbing me in a bruising grip, twisting my arms behind my back. I suffered all this with blissful unconcern.

Another voice broke through the stillness. "If you value your life, friend, you will release the girl immediately." Luc spoke in the same rough dialect, and his garb was as sturdy and simple as the peasant's.

"She's been spying," the man replied, loosening his grip slightly. "We can't afford to have witnesses tonight."

"I would think you would know by now that *I* decide what risks we can afford to take," Luc said with silky menace. Detaching the man's grip, he continued smoothly, "This is the young lady of the house. She is English and very stupid. Besides that, any fool could see she is sleepwalking. She is still asleep—she'll remember nothing of you or me tomorrow morning."

With one strong hand on my arm he began leading me away, back down the long dark hall I had traversed so blindly. My mind seemed wholly suspended from my body, so that while my brain worried about his proximity, my body was safe, and my body could revel in his nearness without the torment of an over-anxious mind.

There was an unusually grim expression in the count's dark, handsome face, and the golden eyes were bitter. I wasn't worried, however. I followed him happily enough, mindlessly, blankly assuming he would take me upstairs to his bed. In my dream it seemed like an excellent idea.

"I will take her from here," Maddelena appeared at the top of the stairs, and my anger and disappointment was so great I almost woke.

He stopped and looked down at my blank, guileless face, and his mocking reproach tore at me. "You gave her too much of the drug tonight," he said in a flat, dead voice. "I found her wandering down in the cellars. Giorgio was ready to cut her throat first and ask questions later."

"A thousand pardons, Signor Luc. But with such a stubborn one as this it is very difficult. Some nights she doesn't touch the wine, some nights a sip, some nights she drains the whole of it. There is no way to be certain; she is so willful."

"The drugging will stop, Maddelena," he ordered abruptly, still staring down at me out of those strange, beautiful eyes. Without any warning he pulled me gently into his arms, so that my head rested quite comfortably on his shoulder. I could feel the hardness of his chest in the rough peasant cloth pressed against my breasts through the thin cotton of my gown, and our hearts beat in counterpoint.

"What have we become," he murmured against my hair, "that we would drug a poor, innocent child like this? How could we have become such strangers to decency?"

Maddelena made some inarticulate cry of dissension but Luc ignored her. A hand came under my chin, forcing my head up to meet him. "Poor, lovely, lost child," he murmured in sweet, gentle Italian. "Whatever shall I do with you?"

Needless to say, I found all this very agreeable. With Luc's strong arms around me I felt safe and content for perhaps the first time in my life. The soft, soothing words made me want to purr like a contented kitten.

Abruptly he released me. "Take her away, Maddelena," he ordered hoarsely. "Before I forget myself." He vanished into the night like a creature of darkness, leaving me bereft.

AS I DRESSED that late afternoon, trying to blot from my mind the weakening and embarrassing memory of last night's dream, another strange thing happened. I heard a loud thump just outside my balcony, and without hesitation I flung open the shutters, determined to confront the eavesdropper.

Sitting at my feet was the largest cat I had ever seen in this city of large cats. Coal black as the prince of darkness himself, he stared up at me haughtily out of golden eyes that were a twin to Luc's amber orbs. Had I been a devout Catholic I would have crossed myself.

Instead I stumbled back into my room, controlling the nervous shriek that bubbled up within me.

"So that's where he's gotten to," Mildred's querulous voice floated in. "Nasty, dirty creature. I can't abide cats, but he is by far the worst!"

Reaching down, I lifted all twenty-some pounds of him and held him against me. "Where did he come from? I've never seen him before."

She sniffed disdainfully. "His name, I believe, is Patrick. I gather from Maddelena that he haunts the count's rooms exclusively. I, of course, would have no idea about that." Here she laughed coyly. "The rest of us never see him unless the count is gone. Here, let me take him." She reached out her thin hands, and Patrick showed the good taste to spit at her.

"Evil creature! If it were up to me I'd see him drowned. You'd best be careful, Miss Charlotte. He could carry rabies."

I hugged the huge creature closer to my breast, which seemed to please the immense feline. "I'll be careful, Mildred." I scratched behind his ears, and he looked up at me with dignified adoration. "I'll be very careful."

Chapter Fourteen

"MUST YOU WALK so quickly, Mildred?" I demanded irritably, struggling to keep up with her long-legged stride as her beanpole figure made its way hurriedly through the teeming crowds. "We are in no particular hurry, are we?"

She turned back with a guilty expression on her plain face beneath the fruit and feather trimmed bonnet. "No, of course not. I beg your pardon, Charlotte. Since you expressed an interest in Florian's I naturally thought you would be eager to arrive."

I sighed. "I *am* eager to arrive. But a few minutes won't make much difference one way or the other, will it?"

"Perhaps," my companion murmured cryptically, speeding up once more, her claw-like hand in the pale, lime-colored gloves digging into the tender flesh of my arm. Giving in, I quickened my footsteps to match hers, undeniably grateful for my first trip out of the oppressively beautiful Palazzo del Zaglia in two long weeks—weeks that had left me fretful and solitary, with only the large black cat, Patrick, for company. I would have been ready to die of boredom, had it not been for the amusingly obvious attempts of my false suitors to gain information from me.

"I have absolutely no idea where Luc has disappeared to," I replied limpidly to the fulminating Holger. "He certainly never confides in me. You'd do much better to ask Jean-Baptiste where he's gone to."

But Jean-Baptiste had been equally curious, if a trifle more subtle. "Surely, *ma petite*, Luc would never have left a charming, defenseless creature such as yourself without a word? He cannot have simply disappeared with not a mention of his destination?"

"I'm afraid he has," I replied, smiling with an equally fraudulent charm at the Frenchman. "One day he was there, the next he was gone. Pouf. Like magic." I was not above having a part in increasing Luc's supernatural reputation. "Maddelena probably knows where and how, but whenever I ask her she pretends not to understand."

"Ah, then you too are curious?" Jean-Baptiste pounced.

I opened my china-blue eyes as wide as I could, fluttering my long eyelashes provocatively. "But of course, Monsieur Perrier. I am exceedingly curious, about that and other things. After all, what else have I with which to occupy my days?

He allowed himself a small snort of frustration, and I leaned back, satisfied. He left with indecent haste, and it would have taken a dimwitted lady indeed to have clung to the belief that he had any interest in my heart. My supposedly shallow brain with its untapped store of knowledge, perhaps, and he might not have refused my pink and white body, if it were offered. Curiously enough, such debasing knowledge caused me only a momentary pang.

I tripped over a cobblestone, bruising my ankle and cursing pungently in Arabic. Mildred forgot her haste long enough to fasten her fish-like stare at me.

"What was that?" she demanded, fascinated.

"Bad words, Mildred," I replied. "Very bad words indeed. You are too young to know the meaning."

She flushed then, absurdly pleased, and patted her orange frizz of ringlets. And then her demon of speed caught up with her once more. "We must hurry," she panted. "The count is expected home tonight . . . I doubt he'd approve of this little foray."

My heart gave an uncontrollable leap. "He is? When did you find that out?" If my voice was breathless it was only to be expected at the speed we were rushing through the narrow lanes and squares of Venice.

Mildred shrugged her thin shoulders. "It seems obvious enough, though no one has said a word. Suddenly, after two weeks of sloth and idleness the Italians are making halfhearted attempts at cleaning. Your wretched cat has taken to stalking through the place looking for all the world like his master, and Maddelena has been uncommonly close-mouthed since last night. None of us had heard a thing, of course, but just watching that old witch scurry around has convinced Mrs. Wattles to plan on a full dinner."

"With no garlic," some demon prompted me to add, remembering with a fondness the nice garlicky meals we had enjoyed in Luc's absence. Mildred was too preoccupied to have caught my implication, for she merely nodded.

"If my guardian is returning tonight," I questioned patiently, "why did you wait until today to invite me out? We could have gone any time during the last two weeks."

"But he only asked to meet you yesterday," she replied artlessly, her eyes scanning the crowds at the café in the Piazza San Marco as we came to an abrupt stop.

"He? Who?" I demanded, sounding like an owl. "Who asked to meet me? What's going on?"

An ugly flush stained her faded cheeks, and she ducked her head. "There he is now. Come along, dear." Her hand fastened once more on my silk-clad arm, and she half pulled, half dragged me through the tables. I made no more than a token resistance, my curiosity thoroughly aroused.

A moment later we were standing in front of an exceedingly attractive, exceedingly British young man, while Mildred was making stammered introductions, beaming proudly, like a mother hen presenting a prize baby chick. I met the calm blue eyes of the well-dressed gentleman opposite me and nodded coldly.

"Mark Ferland," Mildred's voice died away as she saw the chilly expression on my face. I turned her with an icy glare.

"So, it is not an innocent visit to Florian's you had in mind after all, Mildred," I said coolly, ignoring Mr. Ferland. "I wonder what my guardian will have to say when I tell him of this afternoon's work." I reflected with some compunction that I was becoming a wretched little tattletale, but as usual I made the superstitious Mildred look panicked.

"Oh, no!" she said faintly, obviously distressed. Her accomplice put one strong, tanned hand on my arm, forcing me to meet his troubled gaze.

"I hope you won't do that, Miss Morrow." He spoke for the first time in a slow, deep voice, and despite my irritation I warmed to him. "Not before you've given me a chance to explain. You've been deceived, you're angry about it, and I can't blame you. But if you'll just give me a few minutes of your time you may find it in your no doubt generous heart to forgive me for this deception."

I regarded him coolly for a moment, half tempted to turn on my heel and leave him with the fluttery Miss Fenwick. He smiled then, such a nice, handsome smile, as different from that of my saturnine guardian as the day was from the night, and I told myself there would be no harm in at least giving him a chance to explain.

"All right," I said in the same cool tone, not giving him any encouragement. "You have ten minutes."

Once more he flashed that dazzling smile as he hurried to pull out a chair for me. In another moment he had placed an order for two strong coffees with the waiter and seen to the disappearance of Mildred.

"Where has Miss Fenwick gone?" I demanded as he seated his long, sturdy frame opposite me.

"She had graciously consented to let us alone for this short time. She, like most spinsters, has a very romantic nature."

Some hard little part of me broke at this, and I spoke with far more frankness than I usually reserved for the male sex. "If you are about to tell me, Mister Ferland, that you have conceived a desperate passion for me, and that all you desire is my company and, as a side benefit, information about my guardian, I will tell you right now you are wasting your time! I have heard that story far too often, and I'm growing tired of it." I sounded quite snappish, but the fumbling flirtations of Holger and Perrier had tried me more than I had realized, and I was damned (mentally I savored the sound of that word) if I would add another to my list of spurious beaus.

The Englishman looked momentarily disconcerted, and then he charmed me by laughing—a light, infectious laugh that melted an inch or two of my suspicious nature. "Very well, Miss Morrow. I see I will have to be frank with you. I was told you were very beautiful, but no one happened to mention that you were also equipped with a brain. I wouldn't have attempted subterfuge if I'd known you could be reasoned with."

Naturally I was not displeased with this blatant flattery, but I kept my stony expression. He sighed, and wasted more time stirring the steaming little cup of coffee the waiter presented him. Finally he looked up, his unassuming blue eyes smiling into mine in a way that would have charmed harder hearts than my poor starved one.

"I need your help, Miss Morrow," he said flatly. "Or, to put it more correctly, *we* need your help. The situation here in Venice is volatile, to say the least. The Venetians are moving inexorably toward a revolt against the Austrians. We want to be ready and able to assist them if and when that time comes."

"Assist whom?" I demanded, all at sea. "And who are 'we'?"

"Assist the Venetians, of course!" He looked shocked that there could be any doubt. "And 'we,' my dear Miss Morrow, are merely a group of concerned Englishmen who have banded together to give our unofficial aid to the Italians if and when they need it. With the unspoken consent of our own government, of course."

I considered whether or not to believe him. "Very well," I said after a moment. "What is it you want from me?"

"It is suspected, Miss Morrow, that your guardian is not what he appears to be," he began, and then broke off in confusion at my laughter.

"I certainly hope he is not," I said after my inappropriate merriment subsided. "But I would be greatly interested in what you think Luc appears to be."

"An indolent Venetian nobleman, with nothing to do but game and wench and frighten peasants. Oh, we've heard rumors, Miss Morrow. Supernatural suggestions which we have, of course, discounted. But the more we have watched him, the more we are convinced that Count Lucifero del Zaglia is definitely playing a dangerous game. We need to know what his affiliations are, what he knows, and what he's planning. Is he in the pay of the Austrians, the French, or is he a Venetian patriot rallying to the cause of a free and united Italy?"

I sipped at the strong poison those in Venice called coffee and watched my companion over the rim of the delicate little cup. "He does not strike me as a man with an ounce of idealism in him," I replied cautiously. "So I doubt he has any interest in a free Venice. Beneath his courtesy I suspect he detests the Austrians and mocks the French." I set the cup down in the saucer with a little clink. "No, I think you are mistaken, Mr. Ferland. Count del Zaglia is nothing more than an idle aristocrat . . . it makes no difference to him who rules Venice, as long as it does not interfere with his self-indulgent pursuits." Harsh words from his dutiful ward, but I had been nursing a grievous hurt since his abrupt disappearance two weeks ago.

"Perhaps you are right, Miss Morrow. But I don't think so. Would you . . . would you be willing to assist us and indirectly the British government in the meantime and disprove our suspicions?" This was suggested in a bland voice, but I wasn't lulled.

"Are you asking me to spy on my guardian?" I demanded bluntly, outraged and secretly thrilled. Life had been very boring with Luc gone.

He frowned in sudden concern, his broad, sensitive brow wrinkling. "Perhaps I've been wrong to confide in you. I may have misunderstood the situation. I was informed that there was nothing between you and del Zaglia. Was I mistaken?"

Now I was indeed angry. "Are you suggesting, Mr. Ferland, that I . . . that I . . . ?"

"No, no, of course not. It is merely that your reluctance to aid your government in a small matter concerning a man you met barely three weeks ago seems quite strange to me. You must forgive me for jumping to what seemed an obvious conclusion."

"You think that because I'm reluctant to spy on my guardian I must be . . . must be compromised. To put it bluntly, are you suggesting that I am sleeping with him?" I demanded, and was pleased to see the handsome Mr. Ferland flush. "And of course, to prove my innocence I must now agree to all your ignoble suggestions, trespass on the count's hospitality and betray him to you . . ."

"I believe it is your money that is supporting the count, not vice versa," he interposed gently, taking the wind from my sails quite effectively. "Large sums have been withdrawn from your accounts by your guardian during the last few weeks, you know."

The sun was beginning to set, and I felt an unaccustomed chill pass over me. I met Mark Ferland's eyes with sudden uncertainty. Luc would return tonight, would return in the darkness, where he belonged, and I was worried.

He placed a strong hand on mine in a comforting gesture, as if he could read my thoughts and fears. "It's not a very nice thing we're asking of you, Miss Morrow. If there was any way we could get the same information without involving you we would do so without delay. We need you. England needs you."

There was no way I could resist that. I was hit with a sudden wave of homesickness that threatened to make me burst into tears in the middle of Florian's Café. I bent my head lower so that he couldn't see the unshed tears in my eyes, and let my hand remain in his strong, comforting one.

"What would you have me do?" I said after a long moment, my voice husky and momentarily cowed.

He permitted himself a sigh of relief, squeezing my hand reassuringly. "Not much. Just watch, and report back to me when you discover anything.

You're far more observant than you pretend to be, and these Italians usually consider women to be of small intellect, rather like household pets. It shouldn't be any trouble to find out who del Zaglia's visitors are, what his political ties are."

"I doubt that he has any," I interrupted numbly, purposely dismissing my troubled dreams.

"And, most importantly, keep an eye out for any important papers that happen to pass through his hands, particularly if he has a secretive air about him."

I laughed again. "Luc always has a secretive air about him. I doubt I'll be of much help, Mr. Ferland."

"I have complete faith in you," he said stoutly. "I may as well tell you: The Austrians have a very talented and productive spy, and it would greatly aid us if we were to discover that spy and unmask him."

"And if Luc is that spy? What happens then?" He said nothing, and my temper flared. "And you don't think I'd be in any danger? That no one would want to prevent me from finding out the truth? What kind of fool do you take me for?"

"No one would harm you. I swear, on my honor. I wouldn't let anyone touch you." This was stated with such passionate sincerity that I blushed and looked away. Despite his businesslike demands, Mark Ferland seemed a great deal more interested in me than my two other suitors, and my faltering self-esteem rose a trifle in the face of his flattering regard.

I began gathering my things together, and as if on cue, Mildred reappeared across the square and began threading her way back to my side, a sentimental expression on her face. Standing up, I reached out one gloved hand and placed it in Mark Ferland's, unable to stifle the small thrill his sturdy grasp sent through me. He really was an attractive man, the kind of man I would eventually marry. A man without secrets was a refreshing change. "Good day, Mr. Ferland," I said.

"But will you help us?" he asked urgently, clinging to my hand while Mildred looked on with tears in her cloudy blue eyes.

"You give me little choice, Mr. Ferland. I will do my best, but I make no promises."

"That is all I ask, Miss Morrow. I will look forward to seeing you again soon." Reluctantly he released me, and as I turned away I allowed myself a romantic sigh. I would do as he asked for a variety of reasons—reasons consisting of boredom, anger with my guardian, and an insatiable curiosity I usually kept well under control. I was just as eager as Mark Ferland to find out what secrets lay behind Lucifero Alessandro del Zaglia's inscrutable behavior. Not totally unimportant to my motives was the chance of seeing such a splendid specimen of the British male as Mark Ferland once more. And besides, there was that perfectly valid and troubling reason: what was Luc doing with my inheritance? I doubted that I'd be able to stop him from throwing it away at the gaming tables, but I'd at least like to know such a thing was really happening.

The ride home through the rapidly darkening twilight was spent fielding Mildred's questions. For reasons best known to herself she decided we'd return by gondola, and in the end I was glad she did, although usually I preferred to walk, savoring each tiny moment of freedom in this unfree society. We had scarcely disembarked from the gently rocking boat when the stiff, practical form of Thornton appeared at the door. One look at his gloomy face and his curt beckoning gesture and I knew Luc had returned.

Chapter Fifteen

"QUICKLY," MILDRED whispered. "You can sneak up the servants' stair if you're very quiet. I'll go in and meet him."

I remained stubbornly where I was, foolhardy to the last. "Why should I sneak?" I demanded. "There is nothing wrong with our going out to Florian's, is there?"

She cast me a look of exasperation mixed with dislike. "You do not think he will object to your meeting the handsome Mr. Ferland while he is away? The count is obtuse about certain things, but I don't think this will be one of them."

"Perhaps you are right," I conceded, pleased at the thought. "I don't think I would care to explain . . ."

"Explain what, my dear?" Luc's voice interrupted me, the very gentleness of his tone panicking me. He appeared on the green-stained marble steps, and for a moment I was totally and completely horrified at myself, wondering what in the world had induced me to agree to spy on this overwhelming creature. In the two weeks of his absence I had forgotten quite how disturbing an effect he had on my brain and my senses. His tall, almost sinister form stood framed in the doorway, an ironic smile on his wickedly handsome face as he held out one slim hand to me in a gesture of command rather than welcome, and the bloodstone ring gleamed dully.

As I felt myself slipping back into that abyss of terror and superstition that threatened to engulf me, I thought back to Mark Ferland, and from somewhere deep inside me I was able to call forth hidden reserves. I straightened my spine, threw back my head, and met Luc's clear amber eyes with a fine show of bravery. "Explain why we were so late in returning to Edentide and not here to welcome you properly. Though of course, we had no idea when you were to return, any more than we were prepared for your departure." Some waspish part of me made me mention this. "Miss Fenwick was kind enough to accompany me to Florian's this lovely afternoon. I hope you haven't been here too long."

I sounded like Theresa at a garden party, the cool English lady making polite conversation, even to a demon. Luc smiled, moving forward and taking my unwilling hand in his strong, cool grip.

"Little one, I have angered you," he murmured gently, mockery in his light eyes. "I would never have deserted you without a word if I knew you minded so much."

"I minded not one bit!" I said quickly, pulling my hand away from him. "I merely have been bombarded by your friends day and night, asking over and over again where you are and when you will return."

"Which friends?" He said it softly, but I wasn't fooled into ignoring the seriousness beneath his light tone.

"Holger and Jean-Baptiste. They seemed most eager to get in touch with you."

"You undervalue yourself. I have no doubt it was merely an excuse for them to call on you while your ogre of a chaperone was away. You seem to have wreaked havoc on hearts all over Venice."

"Perhaps," I said slowly. It wouldn't do for him to realize just how observant I was. "But I place no reliance on either of them."

"You are wise not to do so," he observed, leading me into the warmth and light of the palazzo. "Never fear, *mia Carlotta*," and his voice caressed my name, "in due time I will find you a suitable husband. You are still little more than a child."

Needless to say I found this generous offer totally infuriating. "No, thank you, signor. I am entirely capable of finding my own husband."

"I'm sure you are, my dear," he said gently. "But I think I prefer to choose." He smiled down at me from his great height, and once more I was reminded of the rumors that flew around Venice. He had never looked more satanic, with those light, piercing eyes, that cynical mouth, and the black wings of hair above his high, pale forehead. Satanic, dangerous, and very, very handsome. I tried to summon up the image of Mark Ferland, and failed.

DINNER THAT NIGHT was slow and stilted. Luc was preoccupied, staring, eating nothing as usual, drinking surprisingly large quantities of the dry red wine he favored. To my surprise no wine was offered me, just as none had appeared on my dinner tray during the time he was gone. I toyed with my food, wondering whether to try to initiate a new topic. Any remark I made he would either ignore or reply in absent tones. There was evidently a great deal on his mind, and I would have given much to find out what it was.

Finally he rose from the table, leaving me with my mouth half full of a rich, creamy rice pudding. "I'm afraid I must abandon you once more, little one. Various duties call . . ." he let it trail as I stared up at him, stricken. "But don't look so desolate! I promise to remain home tomorrow and you may tell me all that you did while I was gone. I am pleased to see you care so much for my company."

At this cynical remark I flushed, swallowed the last of my dessert and rose also. "It is entirely up to you," I murmured.

"That is right, my dear. It *is* entirely up to me," he interposed gently. "Now go to bed like a good little girl."

Needless to say, at the advanced age of almost twenty, one doesn't like to be called a little girl. "But where are you going?" I asked in an innocent a voice.

He hesitated, then shrugged. "To see my mistress," he replied, watching my expression with some amusement. "And to gamble more of your fortune away. I trust that meets with your approval."

A surprising flash of anger swept over me, anger for his mocking of me, anger for my own vulnerability. In that flash of fury a dangerous idea came to me, and once there in my fertile brain refused to be dislodged. "As we have discussed previously," I said primly, "it is entirely up to you. Good night." I turned on my heel and stalked out of the room, outrage plain in my upright bearing. The soft laugh that followed me only stiffened my resolve.

When I got to my room I didn't bother to change from the elegant black silk evening dress I had worn to dinner. I knew I wouldn't have time. It was only fortunate that decadent Venice still had frequent masques, and ladies of quality could appear in public in domino and *maschera* to protect their reputations. I barely had time to change my shoes to my sturdier walking slippers and grab my reticule, thankfully full of *soldi,* not to mention the kitchen knife I had thoughtfully retained, before I sped silently down the seldom-used back stairs and out into the alleyway. Creeping into an arched doorway I had noticed earlier, I waited for my guardian to appear.

I hadn't long to wait. The fog was lighter than usual, and in a few minutes I made out his tall, graceful figure through the thin ribbons of mist that swirled around the streets. He was alone tonight—Jean-Baptiste apparently had no idea his friend and constant companion had returned. It would make it a little harder, with no chattering friend to distract him from the sound of light footsteps dogging him, but there was nothing I could do about it. I could only be thankful he hadn't taken a gondola, but was preparing to walk. Surely luck would be on my side tonight.

I waited for him to turn the first corner, and then slipped out after him. He would be easy enough to spot in a crowd. Most Venetians were far shorter than he was, besides lacking his almost theatrical presence. By the time I rounded the corner, however, he was much farther away than I would have expected. I had failed to take into account his long legs and the surprising energy he could exert on rare occasions. I sped up, desperate to keep him in sight as he turned still another corner, heading down an alleyway that led nowhere. I ran after him, turning at the same street and speeding down the narrow, deserted little lane until I ended, full tilt, against a man's broad chest.

I barely controlled my muffled shriek of terror as I felt my wrists caught in an iron grip, and as I looked up to meet the cool golden eyes of Luc del Zaglia through my half-mask. A wave of terror swept over me. It did me no good to struggle; his strength seemed supernatural, and after a moment I stood still, panting and staring up at him like a frightened rabbit. My one reflection was that at least he could have no idea who I was.

"It seems, signorina, that you were desirous of some company tonight, eh?" he spoke in a slow, deep voice. "Surely you are either very brave or very stupid, to have set your sights on me, when there are countless other gentlemen abroad tonight who would be glad of your company." He gave me a little shake. "One of your friends should have warned you about me, signorina. I have no need of paid companionship. If you were to offer yourself for free . . ." He let it trail, a trace of a smile on his distant face. And then without further warning the hands on my wrists pulled me closer, and his mouth descended on mine, ruthlessly, more to punish than to pleasure.

For the first kiss in my lifetime it was a shattering experience. For a moment I struggled, but I was no match for his incredible strength, for the shocking intimacy of his lips on mine. His mouth was hard, and to my utter shock I felt his tongue, playing with the seam of my tightly closed lips. I was so astonished I jerked away, belatedly realizing I wanted more. I fell back against the stucco wall of the house behind me and stayed there, awash with conflicting emotions, foremost among them disappointment. Disappointment that he had released me. He laughed then, and I reached out to slap his face. His strong white hand caught my wrist and twisted it until I cried out.

"You don't learn, do you?" he said softly, loosening his grip on me and running his thumb with sudden tenderness on the bruised part. And then I realized what had eluded me during the past few minutes. He had spoken in English the entire time.

I looked up into his handsome face with sudden suspicion, suspicion that was justified when he smiled an innocent smile that ill-accorded with his saturnine countenance. "The question is," he continued, "what shall I do with you now, *mia Carlotta*? Shall I send you home to languish in your room? Or, better yet, shall I assuage the no doubt mighty curiosity that sent you out alone in the night and take you to the den of iniquity I haunt nightly?"

"I . . . I would like to go home, please," I said in a small voice. His fingers continued to massage my bruised wrist in a hypnotic way.

"No doubt you would," he replied. "But your wishes have not much place in my scheme of things." He reached out and took off the mask, looking down into my eyes with a curiously tender expression. "I think it would be useful if you learned your lesson tonight. Besides, Silvana has been most curious about you. I cannot abide curious women." He tossed the mask into the street and forcibly placed my hand on his silk-clad arm. "Perhaps after tonight you will both keep your curiosity under tighter rein."

He set off again, back out the alleyway and down the street with me struggling to keep up with him. "Who is Silvana?" I questioned after a moment, my breath still coming quickly from the speed with which we were traversing the narrow streets of Venice and the proximity of the demon count.

"Still more questions? Silvana is my mistress. One of them," he amended, and drew me up the steps of an elegant, brightly lit palazzo only slightly smaller than Edentide.

Chapter Sixteen

THE SUDDEN juxtaposition of heat and light, noise and laughter replacing the dark, lonely, fog-shrouded streets of Venice made me sway as we entered the gaming palace, and it was only Luc's strong arm supporting me that kept me from falling. Ca' Bellini was one of those glorious pink and gold palazzos that lined the Grand Canal, but in this case the interior was more in keeping with the sumptuous, fairy-like exterior. Lights blazed in every corner, the walls were hung in deep rose silk, and the furniture, adorned as it was by the flower of the demimondaines, looked both elegant and comfortable.

I shook my head slightly, to clear away the mists, still too benumbed to prevent my guardian from removing my domino, exposing me in my deep black evening gown with the practically nonexistent bodice, with none of the shawls I usually wore to preserve my modesty. I couldn't ignore the fascinated looks of those present. Blond hair was not that unusual in northern Italy, especially in towns occupied by Austrians, but my hair was an unusual tawny gold that tended to draw far more than its share of attention. Coupled with my indecent garb and my dramatic escort, I felt I was the subject of almost every conversation, and the sensation was proving extremely unpleasant.

I pulled at Luc's arm. "Please," I whispered once more, beseechingly. "Let me return home. I'm sorry I followed you. Please."

He took no more notice of me than if I had been a gnat, and I gave up protesting. He was determined to shame and embarrass me, forcing me to associate with people I would never have met in England. I could see by the gowns and painted faces of the women present that in comparison I must look like a nun, and determinedly I kept my eyes straight ahead of me, ignoring the shrieks of laughter from the darkened corners of the far rooms, the indecent caresses that were going on around me.

With a careful solicitude that would have done credit to a knight of old, Luc drew me into the main gaming room, carefully pulling out a chair for me and providing me with champagne. I sipped slowly, taking in my surroundings and Luc's companions with wide-eyed wonder. No doubt they viewed me with the same surprise.

There was no way I could make sense out of the solemn and incredibly complicated game that held most present enthralled. Luc was the one exception—the look on his face signaled only intense boredom as he played hand after hand, and the huge pile of money grew beside him.

Jean-Baptiste was right: He never lost. If he was using my money for gaming I would be very rich indeed if he were to share even a small portion of his winnings. As I thought of Perrier I found myself longing disconsolately for his presence. At least he was too much of a gentleman to let me languish here in boredom and embarrassment.

I drained my champagne, and at an almost imperceptible signal from Luc my glass was promptly refilled. I continued to drink, enjoying the dry bubbly stuff far more than the sour red wine Thornton always served me.

"We have missed you, Count," a voice spoke from behind in soft, slurred Italian. "Something of great importance has come up." Luc gestured him to silence with a brief move.

"Later, Giorgio," he murmured gently in the same language. "When we are alone." He turned back to his gaming, for once less observant than usual. Had he paid more attention to his idiot of a ward, he would have seen her stiffen with shocked recognition. The indolent, well-dressed nobleman who had just spoken was none other than the threatening peasant of my so-called dream.

After that the hours dragged. Sipping on the champagne Luc provided for me, I watched him gamble and win huge sums of money with apparent unconcern, all the time my mind working feverishly. How could I have been so stupid, so obtuse, for so long? Now if only I had some inkling of what was behind Luc's plotting and scheming, his secret meetings. I stared at my guardian with anger, and then found those golden eyes fixed on my mutinous face. He cast a brief, meditative glance at Giorgio and then back to me, just long enough to know part of what I had guessed.

"Why so angry, *carissima*?" he murmured, mocking me. Those eyes knew very well the cause of my outrage.

"You . . . you . . ." words failed me. Angrily I drained my champagne, and immediately my glass was refilled.

" 'You' . . . what?" he prompted with a benign interest. I averted my gaze, but the sudden numbing pressure of Luc's hand on my wrist brought back all my attention. "I would suggest, *mia Carlotta*, that you quickly forget anything your busy little mind might think it has discovered. Vapid ignorance is much more appealing in innocent young girls."

"But I don't wish to appeal to you," I lied convincingly, biting my lip to keep from crying out with pain.

"You are wise beyond your years," he murmured, letting go of me suddenly. "In the meantime I think a quiet corner would suit you much better. As I have business to discuss," and his expression dared me to ask what, "I would be happier if you were safely out of the way."

The alcove to which he led me was free of the lovely, loose-mannered women that abounded in this elegant house. Once I was comfortably ensconced on a Recamier sofa with champagne at my right Luc took his leave, pausing long enough to place a gentle, lingering kiss on the red, throbbing mark on my wrist where his cruel fingers had so lately rested.

"Do not be too curious, *mia Carlotta*," he murmured. "For your sake as well as my own."

Needless to say, I paid no heed to his warning, but little good did it do me. It was impossible to keep track of all the people who desired a few words with Luc. He carried on at least twenty conversations, in French, German, English, and Italian. I strained to hear every word from my distant alcove, but the conversations could have been completely innocent, or completely damning. I leaned back on my silken sofa and sipped more champagne.

It was past two o'clock when Luc finally pushed back his chair and rose from the tables. The pile of money in front of him was astounding, even more so the fact that he left it as if it bored him, leaving his fellow gamesters to pounce on it with an avidity that chilled me. Taking my arm once more with great courtesy, he led me through the brightly lit halls, still as heavily populated as they had been hours earlier, into a small and quieter salon. Sitting in the middle of the room, surrounded by perhaps a score of attentive and admiring men of varying ages, was the most beautiful woman I had ever seen.

Her hair was a rich auburn, her pale white skin creamy and smooth and unblemished by any trace of freckling. Her nose was noble, her mouth sensuous, her dark green eyes sparkling with an allure she was providing all for Luc del Zaglia. Her white shoulders rose out of a pale pink gown that was not, however, quite the fortunate shade she undoubtedly thought it was. Her somewhat petulant face lit up at the sight of Luc, and she lifted one plump arm in greeting.

Dragging his reluctant and slightly drunken ward behind him, Luc moved across the room to her side with his customary grace. His kiss upon the heavily beringed hand was all anyone could hope for, and it was only wishful thinking on my part that made me imagine a mocking overemphasis. The lady laughed; a light, high laugh that no doubt charmed her admirers. Being a woman, I immediately noticed she was older than I had first thought. There was a calculating look in those dark green eyes and an expression of dislike as she glanced over my sober figure trailing behind Luc.

"Silvana, my jewel," Luc said with a charming smile, "may I present to you my ward, Carlotta Theresa Sabina Morrow?" There was always just the slightest emphasis on my third name, that curse from a classically minded godmother. I curtseyed properly and murmured a polite, if somewhat slurred, good evening.

Milady Silvana responded stonily, turning to Luc in a flood of Italian as patrician as her elegant bearing. "What a charming little girl she is, Luc! You did not tell me she was such a beauty. Life must prove a great deal more entertaining at Edentide since her arrival. Perhaps that is why you haven't been to see me in so long."

"My dove, you should know as well as I that I had business in Genoa these last weeks," he said in a gently chiding undertone. "I returned only this evening, and the first thing I did was fly to your side."

"With a stop at the gaming tables on the way?" Her pretty lip curled. "Does this one know anything?" She gestured to me with a graceful arm. "Does she understand Italian?"

"Supposedly not," he replied imperturbably. "Giorgio said you might have information for me?"

"She does not look as if she were burdened with much intellect," the divine Silvana said cattily, switching to a poorly accented and ungrammatical German. "But one can never be certain. I have a most interesting paper for you, my dear Count. I was hoping to be able to deliver it to you in private." She swept a look of acute dislike over my innocent face. "Apparently that is not to be."

"I beg your forgiveness, my goddess," Luc replied in his flawless command of the same tongue, and I wondered that the silly wench should be taken in by his outrageous flattery. "Shall I kiss your lovely hand once more and you can give it to me?"

She sniffed haughtily. "Giorgio will place it in your cloak before you leave. I believe he may have already done so. I had given up on you ever finding the time to spare for poor Silvana. I may remind you," she added, switching to an even more atrocious French that clearly revealed her well-hidden plebeian descent, "that I am not to be toyed with. My lovers have always been completely devoted to me until *I* dismissed them, and I am not about to be betrayed for a wretched little pink and white schoolgirl. Not by anyone, Luc del Zaglia, not even by you!" Two blotches of angry color stained her pale white cheeks as she cast an angry glance in my direction.

"My angel," protested Luc, obviously much amused, "are you jealous of my little ward?"

"She is ugly and stupid and no doubt an Austrian whore in the bargain," she purred, "but I do not trust you, my friend. Remember," she finished, still in her terrible French, "that I have had the richest and most powerful men of Europe at my feet."

"And no doubt you trampled all over them just as you demolish their languages," I snapped in my perfect French, unable to control my temper a moment longer.

Silvana's rage would have been magnificent enough, had it not been augmented by Luc's burst of laughter. The divine Silvana responded with some pungent and extremely idiomatic references in Italian to my parentage and sexual habits. I immediately replied in kind, shocking even myself. Silvana then added a few choice remarks about Luc, which fascinated rather than repulsed me, and I finished with a long and beautifully phrased denunciation of her predilection for Austrians, Arabs, and horses.

This was too much, even for Luc. Still laughing, he dragged me out of the room, barely in time to avoid Silvana's lunge at me. The room was abuzz with horrified conversation as half a dozen men endeavored to placate Silvana's outraged sensibilities, and, as I realized the last extremely obscene exchange had been in Italian, I felt a flood of mortification sweep over me. I had no time for apologies or self-recriminations, for we were out of the house in a few short moments, with a still-amused Luc pausing only long enough to feel for the crackle of paper in the pocket of his elegant black cape before he hurried me into the early morning streets of Venice.

During the short and silent walk home I several times considered apologizing, and several times thought better of it. Each time I remembered exactly what I said to his mistress, and the extremely indecent things she had replied, my resolution failed. We had reached the steps of Edentide before I could bring myself to speak.

I put out a hand to stop him. In the dark of early morning I couldn't read his expression, which was perhaps easier for me. "I am sorry if I insulted your mistress," I began stiffly.

"If?" There was a muffled laugh from the tall, cloaked figure. "Do you think there is any possibility that she wasn't insulted?" he inquired sweetly. "I am sure your suggestions left little room for misunderstanding."

I could feel myself flush, and damned the man and the champagne I had drunk in excess that night. "Your mistress," I observed charitably, "is a fish-wife."

"True," he allowed. "But she has her uses." I thought back to the mysterious paper that now resided in his pocket, and wondered whether I would have any chance of retrieving it if I fell in a deliberate swoon into his strong arms. I remembered the feel of his mouth on mine, and like a coward I decided I would rather jump in the canal than enjoy the mixed torment of being in Lucifer's arms once more. Sweeping ahead of him, I mounted the stairs and marched past the amazed form of Thornton into the dark and damp corridors of the Palazzo Edentide.

Chapter Seventeen

WHEN I AWOKE the next day it was a little past noon. The bright spring sunlight was fighting its way through my louvered shutters, giving my green damask paneled room its customary underwater atmosphere. The lithe form of Rosetta moved among the furniture with surprising stealth. I cracked open one eye, fascinated, while she pawed through my chest of drawers, through the delicate lace-trimmed underwear Luc had supposedly chosen for me, as she rummaged among my dresses hanging so neatly. There were almost twenty of them at this point, half of which I had yet to wear, and I wondered whether I should make a peace gesture and offer her one of them. We were close enough in size so that it wouldn't require much alteration. With this Christian thought in mind I rose up among my linen covers.

She let out a shriek, jumping nearly a foot in the air, and then turned on me with a malevolent expression on her beautiful face, a face that almost, but not quite, equaled her rival, the divine Silvana. "Stupid English cow," she spat in Italian. "You frightened me. Why don't you go back to England where you belong? You will only bring disaster upon him."

I hesitated only a moment. My secret was out in the open after my indiscretions last night, so I answered her in the same language. "Stupid Italian cow," I replied sweetly, "I intend to stay right here. What were you doing, going through my closets?"

Her mouth dropped open. It took her barely a moment to recover her composure, though, and she immediately took the offensive once more. "So, you speak Italian! It's not to be wondered at, such a dishonest one you are. And what he will think when I tell him you have understood every word he has said over the past few weeks, I shudder to think!"

I climbed out of bed and moved to open the shutters, wanting fresh air and sunlight to cleanse the room of her dislike. "You needn't trouble yourself, Rosetta. He already knows. And now, if you would be so good as to bring me my coffee . . ."

I had pushed her a little too far with my grande dame manner. Beneath my irritation I felt sorry for her, caught as she was in the trap of poverty and a hopeless infatuation with the demon count. I could sympathize with the latter problem only too well, and remembered my earlier resolve to befriend her.

I took a step in her direction. "Rosetta, I'm sorry if I've been rude. There is no need for us to fight all the time. I promise you, Luc has no interest in me whatsoever. Not a bit."

My propitiatory gesture was in vain, however, for the look she gave me out of her magnificently flashing black eyes would have shriveled a stronger soul than mine. "You are sorry for me!" she hissed. "How dare you! It is I who am sorry for you, stupid English girl. For I will win, and you will lose, and then I will laugh." She demonstrated, a deep guttural sound that was frightening in its malice. "In the meantime, I will be glad to bring you some coffee. And I hope you will be fool enough to drink it!"

With that she slammed out of my room, leaving me trembling slightly with the aftermath of her venom. From now on, it was obvious, I would have to take my meals directly from the hands of Mrs. Wattles. Rosetta apparently had some Borgia blood in her veins, and I didn't choose to be her victim.

MY NIGHT OF debauchery didn't have much effect on my spirits or my appetite. A slight, nagging headache disappeared after I gorged myself on some of Mrs. Wattles's freshly baked scones, accompanied by two full-size cups of Venetian coffee. With more energy than I usually commanded I found myself alone and bored in the west salon, with a full four hours before Luc would awake stretching ahead of me.

Not that his rising would make any difference to me, I quickly assured myself. The sooner I was away from his pernicious influence the happier I would be. To that end I decided my immediate duty was to recover that mysterious slip of paper before Luc had a chance to dispose of it. I could hardly search his rooms while he lay sleeping—the very thought terrified me. But a truly clever man wouldn't be likely to leave his secrets out in the most obvious place. I would make a casual search of some of the other rooms before sneaking into Luc's while he was at his inevitable gaming, though whether the divine Silvana would welcome him tonight was another question.

The ballroom at Edentide in the early afternoon was an eerie place. Dust motes sparkled in the air, cobwebs dazzled from every corner, and the dirt on the floor showed every footprint with minute detail. But something had drawn me back to this long-deserted room that had once held many gay parties, happy, laughing, elegant men and women, long before the Austrians came to power. Edentide was almost three hundred years old, built just as the great republic's glory had begun to wane. It was sad to think how the mighty had fallen.

It was more than mere chance that had brought me to this ancient haunt. While on my tours with Jean-Baptiste we had held a lively discussion of architecture, of all things, and he had disclosed the enchanting quirk several Venetian noblemen had incorporated into their palazzos. Small retiring rooms, hardly larger than closets, where the families could relax away from the constant pomp and glory that was life in *La Serenissima*. If such a room existed in Edentide, what would be a better place for Luc to keep his evil secrets? And what would be a more logical area of the palazzo than just off the seldom-used ballroom? So Jean-Baptiste had suggested, and I was more than eager to try out his idea. It wasn't until I reached the far wall that I had any success, however. I tapped a few times, and came up with a satisfyingly hollow sound, after a good solid hour of discouragement. Heartened, I edged my way further along, feeling along the ornate plaster molding with delicate fingers, until suddenly the wall in front of me gave way and I tumbled headfirst down a short flight of stairs.

I was momentarily stunned, not even hearing the ominous slamming of the door behind me. I lay there on the hard stone floor, struggling to get my bearings. As my senses gradually returned I found myself shaking with excitement. It was a little room, exactly as Jean-Baptiste had foretold. I pulled myself to a sitting position, ignoring the aches and pains of my bruised body, while I looked around me. From my ignominious spot on the floor I could see a tall, enclosed bed, and an absolutely horrid suspicion swept over me. Suppose I had by accident fallen into Luc's bedroom? And suppose, instead of being asleep, he was at rest in his coffin, waiting only the setting of the sun to rise and resume his evil deeds?

"Don't be absurd!" I spoke out loud in a small, brave voice. "There are no such things as vampires." With this bold thought firmly in my conscious mind I rose, discovering with relief that the bier-like structure was indeed a simple bed, and at the moment it was unoccupied.

My quick surge of relief was replaced by a sudden, more terrifying, more real fear. The steep stone steps I had so gracefully tumbled down led up to a blank stone wall. No molding, no discernible doorway, no handles—nothing visible to afford me exit the way I had entered.

A half hour's desperate scrabbling made me accept the fact that I was trapped in this charming little boudoir. The only possible means of escape was a small, narrow window through which my English hips would never have fit. On top of that, it allowed for a two-story drop into the murky waters of the Grand Canal, a contingency that thrilled me not one bit. Screams, calls, and shouts for help availed me nothing. The Grand Canal was fully as noisy as any street in London, despite the relative quietude of the main mode of transportation, and my desperate calls faded in the hubbub. Perhaps later at night someone would hear me, but for the time being I had no option but to lie down on the charming little cupboard bed and await my rescue. Since the furnishings of the room consisted only of the bed, the first comfortable chair I had discovered in all of Edentide, and an entirely empty chest of drawers, there was little to distract me from contemplation of my troubles. I curled up on the fine silk coverlet, shed a few tears of self-pity, and drifted off into a comfortable siesta.

WHEN I AWOKE it was dark. The din from outside seemed to have quieted somewhat, and I half rose from the bed, wondering whether I should try my luck at shouting for help once more, when the noise that must have first woken me came again. A moment later a crack appeared in the far wall, opposite the small flight of steps, and a thin shaft of light fell into the room, over my huddled figure.

"Who is it?" I whispered, petrified. "Who is there?"

A low laugh that chilled me to the bone emanated from that anonymous sliver of light, and I could feel a scream of terror rising in my throat like bile. Before fear took complete control of me the door opened the rest of the way, illuminating my guardian in all his satanic splendor.

"Have you enjoyed your incarceration, Charlotte?" he inquired pleasantly, moving into the room and thankfully leaving the previously undiscovered door ajar behind him. The lamp in his hand cast fitful shadows over the thick stone walls, adding to the eeriness of the room and the man looming over me.

"You knew I was here, all the time?" I demanded in a hushed voice, stupidly not moving from the unconsciously provocative position on the tumbled bed.

His small, mocking smile showed he was not unappreciative of the picture I made. "I heard you calling for help, little one. This closet," one slim white hand gestured at the little room, "abuts my rooms. I also heard you tumble in here an hour ago. And Rosetta slammed the door behind you in quite a lively fashion."

"Rosetta?" I must still have been sleep-fuddled. "Are you sure?"

"Very sure. Two sets of women's shoeprints lead across the ballroom to the secret doorway; only one pair, that of flat sandals, leads back. A simple question brought about the correct answer." His light eyes were cold and distant, and I could find it in my heart to pity the poor Rosetta.

"But why didn't you let me out earlier? What time is it?" I cried, bewildered, as I struggled to rise from the soft bed.

"It is early evening," he replied with amusement, his eyes alight with a curious expression in their depths. "And I was not about to rouse myself to extricate you from a dilemma you thoroughly deserved." He moved across the floor, setting the lamp down on the little dresser and looming over me. "Tell me, Charlotte, why are you spying on me?" There was a quiet seriousness to his tone that almost made me want to confess. But I knew better than that.

"Spying?" I laughed incredulously, amazed that I could sound so innocent. "Why in the world would I want to spy on you?"

He reached out and took me by the shoulders, pulling me up with a steely strength that in no way reassured me. "Why, indeed? I wonder who you have been meeting during the time I was gone? And whom have you agreed to help?"

I stared up at him mutely, mesmerized by the quiet menace of him. If I spoke I knew I would betray everything. My only hope was for silence.

The fingers tightened on my shoulders, causing me to wince in pain. The stony face above me was unmoved. "There are ways, Charlotte Theresa Sabina, of making you tell me everything I want to know." One slim hand came up under my willful chin, forcing me to meet his distant gaze. "Ways pleasant and not so pleasant."

I vaguely wondered if I looked as terrified as I felt. His small, gentle smile seemed the epitome of evil, and I wondered whether it would help me to scream. I doubted that it would.

"First we will try the unpleasant way," he murmured, and slapped me hard across the face.

I was so astounded by the suddenness of his attack that I fell back on the bed, my eyes filling with tears of pain and fury. A moment later he grabbed my arm and dragged me to my feet once more.

I flinched, expecting another sharp blow, my mouth stubbornly shut against a cry for mercy. He was going to kill me, I knew that full well, and pleading would not help.

He gave me a little shake, so that my eyes flew open to meet rueful ones. *"Poveretta,"* he murmured, touching my bruised cheek with sudden tenderness. "And now we will try the pleasant way." Carefully he drew my shivering form into his arms, causing me to give way completely. He sat down on the bed, and I lay against him, drenching him with shuddering tears that I was unable to control. I cried for the pain, for my guilt in deceiving him, for my desperate longing for him that was becoming more and more unbearable.

When the tears finally subsided I felt him shift my weak and trembling body around in his arms. He moved my head to face him, leaned down, and kissed me.

There was never any question of my not responding. I was drowning, drowning in the feel of his mouth on mine, his clever hands caressing my body, drowning in the overwhelming emotions that washed over me and broke like waves. All my longings, all my love, all my horrified fascination broke free from my iron control and turned me into a helpless, pulsing creature, a slave to Luc del Zaglia's whims. This time when his tongue teased my lips I opened them, letting him kiss me with such completeness that I was ready to flop back on the bed and drag him with me. When his mouth finally lifted and began to travel down my neck I heard a helpless little moan that I distantly recognized as my own.

Suddenly a great noise broke through my dazed trance, a pounding and shouting that seemed to echo through the tiny room. With deliberate care Luc put me from him, a disturbing smile on his face as he slowly rose and went to investigate the commotion. Fortunately he left the hidden door open, and in a few short moments I had pulled myself together enough to rise from the bed, pulling my tumbled clothes about me in embarrassment, and ran through the door before Luc could imprison me once more. At that moment, however, he appeared to have forgotten me entirely. I caught a glimpse of his back as he left his bedroom, his head deep in conversation with someone who looked suspiciously like Giorgio, his voice pitched far too low for me to make out a word. It was with mixed feelings that I watched him leave. Remembering the last few moments in the little room beside this one, I could have preferred his less pleasant ways of making me talk. I would have recovered from a beating far sooner than I expected to recover from the demon count's shattering embrace.

Pulling myself out of my reverie, I looked about me with sudden interest. I was in that holy of holies, the one room I had yet to see among the forty odd rooms in the Palazzo Edentide. Luc's bedroom was dark and ornate, the bed a mammoth affair even larger than mine and draped in jade-green hangings. Candles burned low in the sconces and the ornate crystal chandelier, lending a warm, romantic glow to the room, minimizing its size and making it surprisingly cozy. And there, ensconced in majestic glory, was my fair-weather feline friend, the black, satanic Patrick.

"Greetings, old friend." I scratched behind his ears, and he purred condescendingly. "I am glad to see you exist on your own, and not as a form your wicked master takes." Patrick made a small, deprecating sound. "Now if only you could speak, noble one, all my problems would undoubtedly be solved."

I glanced around the room, my wicked eyes lingering on the counterpane, and some small, sinful part of me wondered how Luc would respond if he returned from so necessary an errand and found me waiting in his bed.

"Damn the man!" I said out loud, having finally shocked myself. Even Patrick looked affronted. I was begging to believe Luc really was possessed of the Devil. How else could such a cool, secretive creature have made me forget my upbringing, forget every tenet of decent behavior and bring me to such a hopeless, indecent pass, longing for his illicit caresses? With a sudden upsurge of fury at myself, I strode over to the armoire and systematically began to search through his pockets, through the neatly folded clothes in the drawers, through the papers in his desk, all the while followed by Patrick's calm, unwinking eyes. And there was nothing, absolutely nothing of interest. Bills, memos of credit, and a very great deal of money tossed around loosely, like trash. But no list of Austrian spies, no plans for rebellion. Nothing to incriminate or exonerate him.

In fact, I noticed nothing sinister at all about the room until half an hour later, as I bolted my own door and dragged a heavy chest of drawers across it, and I remembered the complete and astounding lack of mirrors in the demon count's bedroom. I didn't believe in foolish superstitions, but for the first time in many years I prayed before I went to bed.

Chapter Eighteen

"I DON'T KNOW whether I would feel safe that far away from land," I protested. "I don't swim, you know, and even the gondolas make me nervous." This was a lie; I had swum almost as soon as I could walk, having lived on the shores of a gentle river in Devon, but the last thing I wanted to do was commit myself to a picnic with Jean-Baptiste Perrier of the roaming hands and the calculating eyes. I was afraid he could see right through me, in another few minutes he would know what had almost happened last night between Luc and his ward and would somehow turn it to his advantage.

"Come, come, *ma petite*," he scoffed jovially, drawing his tan kid gloves through his perfectly manicured hands and smiling down at me. The strong Venetian sunlight was a blessing and a benediction after the fog-shrouded evenings that were playing havoc with my sensibility, and I wanted nothing more than to remain in this little garden for the rest of the afternoon while I decided how I would face Luc, and what my attitude would be after the near-compromising situation last night. I doubted if I could hold out against him if he tried again, the key word being if. I couldn't figure out whether he put his hands on me to punish me or because he wanted to. I almost reconsidered Jean-Baptiste's flattering invitation. I would have gone with him gladly, if only I could trust him, but in his own neat, polite way he frightened me as much as Luc did, and in far more subtle ways.

"Ah, you have already promised yourself to the Austrian gentleman, eh?" he said suddenly. I opened my mouth to protest and shut it just as quickly as Thornton led Holger's mountainous form out into the tangled garden.

"Fräulein." He bowed low over my hand and clicked his heels. "You shouldn't be out in such bright sunshine. You will ruin your lovely complexion." He nodded to his rival and took the seat beside me on the marble bench. Patrick, comfortably resting in my lap, cast him a look of acute dislike. "I assume you were just leaving, Perrier," he added coldly, dusting off his neat coat.

Jean-Baptiste smiled, exhibiting his beautiful pearl-like teeth. "By no means, my dear Captain. I was in the midst of trying to persuade Miss Morrow to accompany me on a picnic, to Torcellano. She claims she is afraid of the water, never having learned to swim."

"You cannot swim, fräulein? It is not surprising for ones of your country; nevertheless, I think you should rectify that if you intend to remain in this wretched city. There are too many canals you could easily tumble into if you are not careful."

Did I imagine the hint of menace beneath Holger's heavily accented English? Suddenly the bright Venetian sunlight no longer seemed so bright, and I felt a shiver steal over me.

Looking up at my two suitors, I gave them both an impartial, brilliant smile. "Your concern warms me," I murmured, not warmed one bit. "And Jean-Baptiste, I would love to accompany you, and I do trust you implicitly, but with Luc so recently returned from Genoa I don't think . . ."

"Genoa, was it?" Holger pounced, and Jean-Baptiste appeared equally gratified. I cursed my idiot tongue, wondering whether I had truly set the cat among the pigeons this time.

Patrick, as usual, appeared to have read my thoughts. After taking time to snarl at my two suitors, he rose and stalked majestically off, presumably in search of some misguided pigeons from the piazza.

"Or was it Padua?" I murmured, half to myself. "No, I am sure it was Verona, that was it. I get these northern towns so confused. Whatever, with my guardian so recently returned I don't like to make any appointments without his express permission. You understand?"

"Mademoiselle, I understand only too well," Jean-Baptiste said sweetly, those too-clever eyes watching with a speculative gleam. "I will merely have to look elsewhere for feminine companionship." His eyes focused on something over my shoulder, and I turned to see the sultry gaze of Rosetta. She bestowed a stunning smile on Jean-Baptiste, and I wondered uneasily how long she had been hovering behind me.

"Tell me, Rosetta," Perrier said smoothly, "do you think your so-harsh mistress will allow you the afternoon off to accompany me on a small picnic? Miss Morrow is too afraid of the water to come, so I shall have to leave her in the captain's capable hands."

Rosetta swayed closer, her ample hips wiggling provocatively. "I would be honored, signor," she breathed, casting a scornful glance in my direction. "I am sure Maddelena will give me permission."

My second faithful suitor cleared his throat. "I'm sorry I can't oblige and spend the afternoon, fräulein, but duty calls. I merely stopped by for a moment to see that all goes well with you."

"All goes well," I replied, hiding my cynicism. I wanted neither of them to bear me company that day. After the entirely distressing events of the last few days I was more and more determined to unmask Luc del Zaglia for what he was. What that would be still escaped me, but I had resolved to find out as soon as possible. Before it was too late.

My best time for snooping was during the afternoon rest period that was honored by both the Italian and the English servants. Not a soul would be up and about during those long hot hours of midday, and I knew exactly what I intended to do. I would continue my search of the palazzo, the search that had been terminated so abruptly when, with Rosetta's assistance, I had tumbled into Luc's closet.

It had occurred to me sometime during the early hours before dawn that the logical place to hide secrets might not be one's bedroom, but in one of the myriad of unused rooms, rooms that the servants did not bother even to dust. Consequently, at one thirty, after a heavy noontime meal and a restless half hour on my bed, I crept down the third floor hallway in my stocking feet, every nerve attuned to an untoward sound, though with Rosetta safely off an a picnic I felt I could count on being unmolested during my investigations.

It wasn't until the fifth room that I had any success. After fighting through dust, rat nests, and horrifyingly large spider webs I at last came upon something of more than ordinary interest in the bottom drawer of a damp-stained desk in one of the smaller, more decrepit bedrooms. A beautifully inlaid box, locked against prying fingers, met my eyes. The ornate clasp looked flimsy enough, and I carried the box out on the small balcony to get a better look at it. One of my hairpins should do the trick nicely, I thought, reaching behind me. A familiar scent teased me, and I felt a swirl of skirts, and then everything went black.

I WAS ONLY unconscious for a few moments. I was vaguely aware of being lifted by someone with seemingly unlimited strength. I made a brief attempt to struggle, still befuddled by the blow on the back of my head, when to my horror I felt myself being tipped out into the cool Venetian air. Soft breezes swept by me as I hurtled downward, and a moment later I was immersed in the cold, dark waters of the canal.

I seemed to sink down and down. Instinctively I had held my breath when I first hit the water, and by the time my feet touched the slimy bottom my lungs were near to bursting. I gave myself a push, and felt my foot stick for one horrifying moment. And then I was spiraling upwards.

A moment later my head was clear, and I sucked in deep gulps of air with tearful gratitude. Carefully I treaded water, recognizing with despair that my waterlogged skirts would drag me back down before long, opened my mouth and screamed at the top of my lungs.

That forced me back under water, and this time I swallowed quarts of the filthy stuff. I came up again, gasping and choking, and screamed again. Unfortunately the room I had exited so precipitously overlooked a small side canal, one free from traffic and witnesses. The noise of the Grand Canal must have drowned out my calls for help, and as I screamed again I felt myself slipping back into the water for what I knew would be the last time. Even the best swimmer would be helpless against the weight of four petticoats and a heavy skirt. My lack of shoes was the only thing that had preserved me this long.

The water closed over my head once more, and I felt myself sink into the blackness.

WHEN MY SENSES returned I was lying face down on the cobbled alleyway, vomiting canal water, while my back was being pushed and pummeled by a pair of pitiless hands. I tried to call out for mercy but nothing more than a croak issued forth. My rescuer must have heard, however, for I heard an exclamation of relief as I was turned over on my back. The sight that met my dazed eyes was the worried blue gaze of Mark Ferland.

"Are you all right?" he demanded, his hands passing over my body to ascertain my wounds in an entirely pleasant manner. "I was nearly too late."

I smiled wanly, and reached a limp hand to touch his dripping face. "I'll be fine," I croaked, fighting down the urge to rid myself of more lagoon water. "How did you happen . . . ?"

"I've been watching the palazzo," he admitted, looking a trifle abashed. "Ever since you agreed to help us I've been worried about you. Luc del Zaglia can be extremely dangerous. Apparently my worries were justified."

"You think Luc did this?" I questioned in a hoarse whisper. My throat ached from the water and the subsequent retching. "He couldn't have!"

"Then who else?" he demanded logically.

I just shook my head before such a natural question. "I have no idea. Three people heard me say this morning that I couldn't swim. It must have been one of them." I shook my head to try to clear away the confusion. "Holger or Jean-Baptiste or Rosetta." I tried to recall a fleeting impression I had had, just before I had been hit. One of sense or smell. But it escaped me.

"Captain von Wolfram is on duty in the piazza at this moment," Mark corrected me. "I saw him scarcely an hour ago. And Perrier and the Italian girl went off some hours earlier, heading in the direction of Torcellano. There is no one else it could be."

I still refused to accept it. "Luc knows I am spying," I admitted reluctantly. "He is very suspicious of me. But there are easier ways of ensuring my silence than throwing me in the canal." I struggled to sit up, and his strong, gentle hands went behind my wet back. "We shouldn't rule out the servants. There is something underhanded about them."

"Tell me."

I quickly related the tale of Mildred and the magnificent sapphire ring, the odd conversations and strange looks I had observed. Mark shook his head as he helped me to my feet.

"It's possible," he admitted, "but I doubt it. Mildred is harmless and silly—I can't see her tossing you out a window." He looked down at me, deep concern in his warm eyes, and I should have felt warm and flattered. He was the perfect man for me. Instead I felt nothing warmer than gratitude.

"It's amazing you survived that long in the canal, not knowing how to swim," he continued, unaware of my wayward thoughts.

"Oh, I know how to swim," I reassured him. "I merely used it as an excuse not to accompany Jean-Baptiste on his picnic. I don't trust him."

"And I don't trust del Zaglia, for all your determined championing of him. Let's just hope that next time he won't be more fortunate when he decides to dispense with his rich ward."

I began to shiver then, more from reaction than from the warm spring air. I looked back up at the palazzo, the sinister marble walls with the green lichen seeming to ooze from the stone, and I wondered if I could see a face peering down at me from the third floor. I squinted, and made out the elegant form of my feline friend, Patrick. A moment later the apparition vanished, and I decided not to mention anything to my companion. But somehow I could not feel easy.

"I'd better go in and change before the servants wake up," I said reluctantly, struggling to my bare feet. "There is no way I can thank you." On impulse I reached up on tiptoes and bestowed a grateful kiss on his smooth-shaven cheek.

Absurdly, he blushed, and I wanted to love him even more. Even time wouldn't change a thing.

"I wish you didn't have to go back," he said.

"You were the one who asked me to help," I pointed out.

"I know. I've regretted it ever since. Just remember, I'll be watching. Either I or a friend. And if anything goes wrong you can send a message to the little tailor's shop in the Campo San Paolo. Ask for Giacomo."

"I'll remember," I promised, lifting up my wet, heavy skirts and running off around the corner on bare feet. Both doorways, I knew, would be guarded by a sleeping Cerberus—Antonio on one, Thornton on the other. My best way in was the ground floor balcony that led off the dining room. I had eyed it carefully on previous occasions and it appeared low enough for a lady of sufficient athletic prowess to scramble up to and down from. In my wet condition it took considerably more effort than I had imagined, but within five minutes I had half crawled, half jumped onto the outside lip of the ledge, indelicately hoisted myself over the wrought-iron railing, and sped upstairs, hoping the puddle marks would dry in the hot sunlight. I could place no reliance on the marks obliterating themselves in the cool, damp hallways, but with luck no one in this household would notice. If they did, I could always come up with a suitable lie.

As I rubbed my naked, shivering body down with a thick towel and tried to assemble something passable out of my canal-drenched hair, my mind kept wandering to my demonic guardian. I couldn't help wondering whether he had braved the terrors of the daylight to cast me out of the third-floor window so that I would surely drown, leaving only Patrick as a mute witness to the regrettable accident. Or whether he had sent a henchman. Or whether, as I hoped and prayed, it was someone entirely different, with no ties to Luc del Zaglia except an unceasing enmity. And I wished with all my heart that Jean-Baptiste hadn't been on a picnic with my self-proclaimed enemy, Rosetta, and that Holger had not been so noticeably on duty. I would have gladly believed murder of any of those three, rather than of Luc.

Pulling on a warm wool wrapper, I gave in to my exhaustion and the still energetic revolutions of my stomach and lay down on my bed. A large thud sounded, and Patrick, a concerned expression on his elegant face, stalked across the floor, leapt on my bed, and proceeded to curl himself up at my stomach, purring noisily. With a brief caress for my self-appointed protector, I leaned back and slept.

Chapter Nineteen

AFTER MY HARROWING experiences of the afternoon, I was in no mood to put up with Luc's sardonic innuendoes. For once I hoped he would spend the evening out, so I would not have to endure his disturbing company. As luck would have it, for the first time in weeks he showed no disposition to rush away from the dinner table. He merely sat there, toying with a bone-handled fruit knife, as his topaz-colored eyes watched me in silent absorption.

It quite put me off my feed. Even Jean-Baptiste's unusually jovial company failed to lighten the atmosphere, and our stilted conversation petered out after the cheese course.

"Did you know, Perrier," Luc's voice suddenly broke the uneasy stillness, "that my poor ward narrowly escaped death this afternoon?"

I looked up, startled, and my eyes flew to Luc's unreadable face. Out of the corner of my eye I could see the Frenchman's look of suitable concern, and yet a suspicious and totally unjustified thought entered my mind. Perhaps the news of this afternoon's near drowning was not totally unexpected.

"What's all this?" he demanded after a pause that was just a shade too long. "You never mentioned such a thing, my dear. Mademoiselle Morrow?"

"No, she didn't, did she?" Luc said softly, and a chill ran down my spine. "Perhaps she didn't want to alarm me. Nevertheless, she fell into the canal, and it was only the fortunate and highly coincidental appearance of a fellow countryman of hers that saved her life."

"No!" Jean-Baptiste protested, suitably amazed.

"Yes, my dear fellow," the demon count corrected. "The noble hero dragged my fair ward to the side of the quay and rescued her from certain drowning. I am still at a loss, dear Charlotte, as to how you happened to be in the canal in the first place, and how this young man happened to be so fortuitously close at hand. It is still too early in the season to attempt swimming in our lovely waters."

I knew I was pale from the strain, and I glared at my mocking guardian with suitable rage that failed to quell him one bit. "I was pushed out of a window," I replied stiffly, and was enraged to see him stifle a little spurt of laughter. "Probably by you," I snapped, tossing down my napkin angrily. "As for the Englishman, it is sheer luck that he appeared. For all you could care I could have drowned. Were you by any chance watching all this, hoping I'd sink into the canal and leave you in control of my fortune?" It was a shocking thing to say, but I had had enough of my so-called guardian toying with me, like a feral cat with a mouse. I was sick of being mouse-like.

"Mademoiselle Morrow!" Jean-Baptiste remonstrated, clearly shocked.

"No, don't stop her, my friend, I find it fascinating to hear of all the terrors an adolescent mind can concoct. No doubt she was doing her usual job of rummaging through some deserted chest of drawers or desk in one of the unoccupied rooms, tripped on a frayed rug, and over the balcony she went. Tell me, *carissima*," he continued, and his voice was silky, "have you ever read *Northanger Abbey* by one of your so-talented countrywomen?"

"Certainly," I replied stiffly, at a loss. "I have read all of Miss Austen's works. What has that to do with the matter?"

He smiled enigmatically. "You should take the time to reread it, little one. It might keep you out of trouble, instead of wasting your time snooping around. You were probably leaning across the balcony, trying to peer into our neighbor's bedroom. I would put nothing past you."

"Luc, I must object to your unkindness," Jean-Baptiste protested. "The poor girl must have suffered a dreadful shock; there is no cause to berate her like this!"

"Am I berating her?" Luc demanded innocently of the world in general. "I put up with her prevarications and curiosity with the patience of a saint. Even her outrageous suspicions I accept with equanimity. Tell me, *mia Carlotta*, did you know this English fellow?"

"I have no idea who he is," I muttered ungraciously, feeling curiously and irrationally in the wrong.

Luc smiled, his brilliant, blinding smile. "You see, my dear Perrier, another lie. The man is Mark Ferland, he is in some way attached to the British consul, and my ward and the redoubtable Miss Fenwick had tea with him at Florian's not two days ago." He shrugged his black-clad shoulders expressively, a demonic gleam in his light eyes. "I will have to talk with Mister Ferland himself. Perhaps he will be more willing to come up with the truth." He rose then, in the warm glow of the candlelight towering over me. "Let us go in search of the gentleman, Perrier. Secrecy wearies me."

Jean-Baptiste rose hastily, sneaking a worried glance in my direction. His warm eyes met my pleading ones, and he gave me a slight nod, just enough to reassure me. Perrier would not allow my guardian to commit what might be another in a long line of brutal murders. The episode of Georges Martin would not be repeated.

I simulated a yawn. "Do as you wish. Your suspicions are quite as outlandish as you deem mine to be. Nevertheless, if it will set your mind at ease, I hope you find Mr. . . . Mr. Ferland, did you call him . . . ? and that he will be able to satisfy your questions." I yawned again, and rose. "Good evening, gentlemen." I was inordinately pleased with my indolent act as I glided by my two companions. Before I was out of reach, however, Luc's hand shot out and grabbed my wrist in a hard grip.

I stifled my instinctive shiver, determined not to react to the pressure on my wrist, the feel of his skin against mine. I looked into his eyes and found no enjoyment of his cruelty, no delight in hurting me, just an expression of mocking sadness that somehow tore at me more than anything else might have. I bit my lip to stop its trembling, and he loosened his punishing hold on my wrist. Without another word I turned and ran from the room.

IT WAS VERY sudden. One moment I was deeply asleep, the next wide-eyed and motionless in terror. I lay unmoving beneath my heavy covers, not even daring to turn my head. Moonlight streamed through my shuttered balcony door, casting patterns on the marble floor with its elegant, slightly moth-eaten rugs. The silence was so deep I could feel it pressing on me from all sides, and yet I knew, somewhere deep inside of me, that evil was in the room—an ancient, terrible evil so vast I couldn't even begin to comprehend it, an evil with its roots in eternity.

Summoning all my courage I moved my head a mere fraction of an inch, then a bit more, then completely around. My lovely, elegant room, which at times seemed more a prison than a haven, was deserted. Not a living creature was in sight, not even Patrick, and yet I knew I was not alone. Something so terrible it defied description watched me, waited for me. Slowly I turned my head back to the moonlit reflection on my floor, and watched with horror as a figure just beyond the slatted balcony door blotted out those lines of light.

My nerve broke, and I rose out of bed, shrieking like a banshee. A moment later I had flung open the door and ran down the hall, dressed skimpily enough in a thin cotton nightdress, barefoot, with my hair tangling down my back like a wild woman. Just behind me, so close I could imagine its foul breath on my neck, was the indescribable horror I was trying so desperately to escape.

I practically tumbled down the long flight of marble stairs, catching myself just in time, twisting my ankle in the process. The few second's delay brought the sounds of pursuit even closer to my panicky ears, and, sobbing with hysterical fright, I ran on, down to the first flight, trying vainly to peer over my shoulder into the dark from whence I came, afraid I would see what frightened me so. In my blind panic I ran straight into a very large, solid body in the middle of the first floor hall.

My reactions have never made sense to me. When I looked up and met the unreadable topaz eyes of my guardian, I should have shrunk away in horror. Instead, with all the illogic I alone seem to possess, I threw myself, cowering, into his arms, whimpering and sobbing like a child in unreasoning relief.

Strangely enough, he asked no questions. His face was grim as he enfolded me into his strong arms, and through my tears I noticed that he was in his shirtsleeves, the white linen shirt unbuttoned to the waist, exposing a tanned, smooth chest, the significance of which escaped me until many days later, when it was almost too late. His heart was pounding beneath my head, slow, even beats at variance with my fluttering pulse.

"There . . . there was something in my room," I managed to stammer after a long while. "Something cold and evil and . . . and horrible."

"What?" he asked flatly, perhaps hoping to calm me by his prosaic question, his hands gentle but firm on my trembling body.

"I don't know," I cried, shaking all over from cold and fright, and, I must admit, excitement caused by Luc's proximity. "I didn't see anything more than a shadow on the floor, but I felt its presence. It was real, and horrid!" I was still crying, unable to stop it, and he reached out a slim hand and brushed away the tears.

"Very well, little one, I will go and check on this 'thing' that frightens you out of a good sleep. And you will see it is nothing more than bad dreams." But he made no move to release me, and I clung to him in desperation, more terrified than I had ever been in my short, eventful life at the thought of being alone in this damp and decaying palazzo, alone and victim to that ageless evil.

"Please!" I pleaded through my tears. "Don't leave me. I . . . I . . ." As I realized what I was asking I fell silent, biting my hand to try to still the sobs that were racking my body so inexorably. I could feel him looking down at me. Without another word he scooped me up into his strong arms and started down the hall.

His bedroom was very dark. Only the moonlight provided illumination, shining on the large bed, still neatly made. Kicking the door shut with his foot, he moved across the floor on silent feet, making light of his burden. Patrick's golden eyes glowed from the foot of the bed as he watched us with sleepy curiosity.

With the grace that comes from long practice Luc stretched out on the bed, still holding my shivering body in his arms with a tenderness I wouldn't have thought him capable of. Slowly, gradually, my sobs lessened and then ceased altogether, and I nestled closer, my head against the hollow of his shoulder.

A few moments later all that was left of my hysteria were a few lingering, shuddering sobs, and then, lying so safely and comfortably in the demon count's arms, I slept.

Chapter Twenty

IT WAS IN THOSE dark, still moments immediately preceding dawn that I awoke. In my first few moments of half-consciousness I was aware only of the most profound serenity I had ever known in my life. Totally at peace for perhaps the first time, I snuggled closer to the object that seemed to emanate such warmth and protection.

And then suddenly I was completely awake, still not daring to move a muscle, as I became chillingly aware of exactly where I was: lying in the demon count's arms, for all the world as if that was where I belonged.

Through the darkened shutters I could make out the first traces of daylight, a daylight that was surely never allowed to penetrate into the secure reaches of Luc's bedroom. Slowly, carefully, I moved out of the protecting circle of his arms, almost crying out with the physical pain of separation from him. Sitting up on the still-made bed, I looked down at my guardian's smooth, untroubled face.

He slept as one dead, did Lucifero del Zaglia, an unpleasant notion on my part that I couldn't rid myself of. At some point during the night he had drawn a rich velvet throw over us, and with an inaudible sigh I slipped from beneath it, my bare feet cringing as they touched the chill marble floor. Pulling my disordered nightdress around my chilled body, I was conscious of two overwhelming emotions. First was a desire to crawl back into that bed beside him, and second, outraged and illogical fury that the demon count, self-proclaimed lecher and despoiler of virgins, had allowed his ward to sleep the night through unmolested in his arms. Was I so unattractive? I demanded of myself. Did he agree with Rosetta's estimation, that I was a stupid, ugly English cow? Surely I had practically offered myself to him last night, and he hadn't even bothered to take me! I could hardly acquit him of noble motives. I doubted he knew the meaning of morality.

Suddenly my eyes fell upon a beautifully inlaid rosewood desk beside the bed. On it was a book, with a sheaf of papers hastily stuffed inside it. I hadn't the nerve to read them—Luc could awake at any time and disprove the rumors of the supernatural that surrounded him. But I doubted he would.

Hastily I took up the papers and tucked them down the front of my thin night gown. I turned back to look at my guardian.

Staring down at the chiseled perfection of his alabaster profile, I wanted to scream and weep and hit him. I had to content myself with slamming the heavy, inlaid door very loudly behind me.

IN THE EARLY hours of the dawn the halls of Edentide lost their terrifying qualities. Indeed, before last night I had never been frightened, and in the rational light of day I decided it must have all been a nightmare, an unexpected reaction to my near drowning of the previous day. So silent was I on my cold, bare feet that I crept up on the redoubtable Thornton, still in rather grimy shirtsleeves, as he perused some small, fascinating object in one of his meaty paws.

"Good morning, Thornton," I greeted him serenely, and was diabolically pleased to see him jump with unaccustomed nervousness, dropping the small object he had been fondling onto the floor where it rolled and came to an abrupt rest against my toes. Thornton dived for it, but I was too quick for him. I retrieved the object, suffering only from a bruised forehead as Thornton careened against me. He drew himself stiffly upright, his clear, colorless eyes taking in my scanty clothing, bare feet, and generally tumbled appearance with an interest mixed with an unlikely nervousness.

"If you please, miss," he said in a wheedling tone of voice, holding out his thick hand. "That's my property you've got there."

What I "had there" was a small, exquisitely-shaped sapphire heart, obviously designed to be worn as a pendant. It seemed curiously familiar, and as I cast my mind back, for once my hazy memory did not fail me. A dark, damp-stained portrait in one of the unused third-floor bedrooms portrayed a typical Venetian beauty, with her heavy blond curls, large drooping eyes, and imperious nose. On her somewhat thick neck rested this very pendant, and on one plump hand was the sapphire ring Mildred Fenwick had paraded about with earlier.

I smiled sweetly. "I think not, Thornton. What would you be doing with a sapphire pendant?"

Being unoriginal, he came up with the same excuse Mildred had offered. The beads of nervous sweat stood out on his high-domed forehead. "Sapphire, miss? Surely not! That there is a piece of quartz. Belonged to my dear mother, God rest her soul. The only thing she could leave to her Bert, and I've treasured it always. It's not worth much, miss, just sentimental, y'know." His perfect butler's accent was slipping in the agitation, and he rubbed his bony hands together nervously.

"Really?" I said innocently. "And what were you planning to do with this worthless little souvenir?"

He licked his thin lips, his pink tongue darting over them like a snake's. "We all fall upon hard times, miss. The master isn't one to remember to pay regular, and I've had a few unexpected expenses. I was planning on selling it, much as it breaks my heart to do so." He held out his hand again, and I could see it trembling slightly. "Give it o'er, miss, please."

"How glad I am to hear you say that, Mister Thornton," I chirruped with bright enthusiasm that secretly made my head ache. "Unfortunate that you have fallen on hard times, but fortunate for me. I have taken an instant fancy to this worthless piece of quartz, and I shall have the count reimburse you for it. I'm sure once he sees it he'll decide on a suitable recompense for you, my dear Thornton."

And then, with the jewel still clutched tightly in my hand, I swept up the stairs, for all the world like a duchess in full court dress, rather than a barefoot, thinly clad English girl a little too foolhardy for her own good. I left Thornton babbling strangled protests and excuses in my wake.

My room was just as I left it the night before. The bedclothes were tumbled on the floor, the shuttered balcony door still tightly closed against intruders and the bright Italian sunlight. Suddenly I was very, very tired.

I retrieved the papers from their uncomfortable nest in my bodice and stared at them absently. They made little sense to me, and I wondered if it was my faulty Italian that made the hastily scribbled words appear like gibberish. Or was it perhaps a code?

I would let Mark sort it out. At that moment I cared not one bit about Lucifero del Zaglia. That son of Satan was more than capable of taking care of himself.

I tucked the papers under my pillow and turned to face my room. Pulling the dresser that contained my frivolous lace underclothing against the door to prevent unwarranted intruders, I pulled the bed back together and crawled wearily beneath the sheets. Whatever evil had entered my room in the dead of night, it would certainly never bother me during the blessedly safe hours of daylight. And with an idiotically free mind I fell back into a deep, dreamless sleep.

THE SUN WAS beginning to set when I finally awoke. My room was in an eerily murky half-darkness, and the remembered terrors of the night came rushing back. With trembling fingers I lit the lamp beside my bed, illuminating the untenanted corners of my vast room. The sapphire pendant winked at me from the bedside table, and I decided that the first order of business would be to hide it until I decided what I would do with the lovely thing. I was loath to present it to Luc, and yet let Thornton get his ham-handed fists on it I would not do.

I climbed out of bed and was suddenly assailed by a weak, dizzy feeling. My mind quite naturally jumped to the conclusion that I was drugged again, when I belatedly realized I hadn't eaten in almost twenty-four hours. For a solid trencherwoman like myself that was something of a record.

Sapphire still clenched in my fist, I hurried to the large armoire, determined to dress in the first thing at hand and then sneak down the back stairs to raid Mrs. Wattles's better than well-stocked kitchen. I swung the door open and stood there, numb with horror.

A moment later, the still, bloodless body of the once-lovely Rosetta tumbled at my feet, her pansy-brown eyes staring sightlessly in that white, cold face. I stumbled backwards, but by some hideous misfortune the dead girl had landed on my trailing hem, so that inadvertently I dragged the body part way across the room before it lessened its death grip. I stumbled back against the bed, gathered sufficient energy and began to scream, loudly and shrilly, over and over and over again.

I ACCEPTED THE proffered glass of wine gratefully, draining it with indecent haste after one long suspicious look in Luc's direction. My eyes strayed around the small, formal little salon Holger von Wolfram had chosen for his base of operations. The candlelight successfully hid the fraying carpets, the soiled slipcovers, the chipped and peeling paint. The look my one-time suitor cast upon me was cold and unsympathetic, and I wondered that I had ever been taken in by his spuriously dull-witted demeanor.

"Perhaps, fräulein, you will be good enough to repeat for me the happenings of last night," he ordered stiffly, glancing down at some mysterious papers beneath his heavy fist. "I would like to be clear in all matters before I make my arrest."

"You know who did it?" I asked breathlessly, leaning forward, my eyes carefully avoiding the unreadably dark expression on Luc's face. He was leaning against one damask-covered wall, having ironically declined Holger's offer of a seat in his own house. I had yet to exchange a word with him since the previous midnight, and my poor mind was beset with conflicting emotions as far as my demonic guardian was concerned. Outraged pride, anger, embarrassment, and most of all, a sneaking, overwhelming fear for his safety made my hands tremble so that I had to clench them tightly in my lap.

Holger cast a meaningful glance at my unconcerned guardian. "I have a very good idea," he said pompously, and I felt the fear clutch at my heart a little more tightly.

"I awoke in the middle of the night," I began, leaning back in the uncomfortable chair in an attempt to appear at ease. "I felt there was something in my room, something . . . something evil." Even now, remembering my unreasoning terror of the night before, my mouth went dry. "I could see someone's silhouette out on the balcony, outside my shutters."

"And?" he demanded impatiently.

I was aware of his determination, his furious regard, as I was aware of Luc's golden eyes watching me from across the small room. "I . . . I jumped out of bed and ran downstairs," I stammered.

"Did you call for help?"

"No, at least, I don't think so. I was too frightened even to think." I looked up into Holger's grim face with my most appealing expression, and for a moment the stern lines softened into what might have been sympathy but bore more of a resemblance to lust. "I thought I was being chased, though now I realize that is not so."

"Why do you realize that, fräulein?" he pounced.

"Because I ran into the count, and there was no one following me. No one at all."

Holger turned to Luc. "Is that true?" Skepticism was heavy in his accented voice.

Luc shrugged. "True enough. My ward was most probably terrified by some nightmare. She had suffered an unfortunate dip in the canal yesterday, and it must have upset her more than she realized."

"That still does not account for the serving girl," Holger snarled. "Have you some easy excuse for that?"

A brief, chill smile flitted across his saturnine face. "But of course, my dear Captain. This house is easily accessible if someone truly wanted entry. No doubt the ghoul of Venice decided my house would be a perfect place to dispose of his most recent victim. Maniacs quite often have bizarre senses of humor, I've been told. He must have crept in one of the ground-floor entrances, followed Rosetta upstairs, and murdered her, stuffing her body in the nearest available closet. Which sadly belonged to my impressionable ward."

"Very convenient. And when do you think all this happened?"

I could feel the trap closing in, and I wanted to call out, to warn Luc to be careful. But for once, wisely, I kept my mouth shut.

"I would imagine sometime in the early evening," he replied. "While we were at dinner, no doubt. Before Charlotte went up to bed."

"And that's where you are wrong!" Holger shouted, causing me to jump nervously. "I place you under arrest, Count Lucifero del Zaglia, for the murder of Rosetta di Serbelloni, among others."

"My dear Von Wolfram," Luc protested wearily, "Whatever for?"

"Because the surgeons say without a doubt she died somewhere between the hours of midnight and dawn—the hours when you are free to roam this damp, wretched city, committing foul and loathsome crimes. No one else in this house would be free to wander around during those dark hours without arousing comment. You have been watched, del Zaglia, and we know for a fact that you never left this house last night. No, you stayed here to claim your newest victim. I only wonder that Fräulein Morrow has survived in your hellish clutches for so long!"

All this was very stirring, but Luc rose to his full height, almost half a foot taller than Von Wolfram, a tired expression on his face. "Are you sure you're not Italian, Captain? Such a love of melodrama, to be sure. I did not murder

Rosetta between the hours of midnight and dawn."

"So you say," the Austrian sneered. "But where is your proof?"

For the first time since I had left Luc's bed my eyes met his, and the rueful expression in their golden depths threw a new fear into me. I knew he would not say a word, would be convicted of a murder I alone knew he couldn't have committed, rather than speak out and sully my reputation. I almost burst into tears at his nobility, determined to speak out myself and save him. I needn't have bothered.

"My proof sits in front of you, my good Captain. Miss Morrow was with me from a little before midnight until dawn this morning."

All of Holger's regard for me could not have been specious, for he blanched visibly at Luc's idly spoken words. "No!" he protested.

"Yes," Luc mocked him. "Is it not true, little one?"

I threw him a glance of intense dislike. "As Count del Zaglia has so chivalrously stated, I spent the night with him," I said in a cold, slipped voice.

"In his bedroom?" Holger gasped.

"In his bed."

Suddenly the Austrian crashed his fist down on the delicate papier-mâché table in front of him. "I will not have it," he screamed in German. "It is lies, all lies!"

"It is the truth," I replied wearily in that same tongue.

"Do you realize, young woman, that this will very likely be reported in the newspapers?" he demanded after a long moment. "The international press has been most concerned with the ghoul of Venice. Any news about his latest atrocities are sent by correspondents all over the world. The London papers have been especially interested, and will be likely to reprint your guardian's alibi. How would your friends and relatives react to that, eh? Your name besmirched before all the world?"

"I'm sure they will think it no more than I deserve," I replied wearily. "And now, if that is all . . ." I rose, keeping my eyes away from that area of the room that Luc dominated.

"I have not dismissed you," Holger snapped.

Suddenly I was very angry, at Holger and Luc in particular and men in general. They sickened me, and if I spent another minute in their company I would lose control completely.

"Well, I have dismissed you!" I shouted suddenly, slapping at his restraining hand.

"I must warn you, *gnädiges Fräulein*, that this man will not escape me for much longer. That he had wickedly seduced you is to be expected, that you would lie for him is also obvious. But his free days are numbered, and where will you be once your protector is gone?"

I pulled against his hand in vain. "Don't you realize," I said wearily, "that you are mistaken? He didn't murder Rosetta. I wouldn't lie for a murderer."

He sneered. "I care not whether he murdered a hundred maidservants. If you have no idea what his crimes are far be it from me to enlighten you. Perhaps he will tell you next time you are in bed together."

Unthinkingly I reached out and slapped his bovine face. It was like hitting a boulder. He didn't even blink. "And when we have your beloved Luc, and have dealt with him as we deal with all traitors, then you will have to turn to me, my dear fräulein. And after I have suitably disciplined you I'm sure we will get on quite well." He turned and smiled evilly at the demon count. "She will be quite amenable after a while. Tell me, my dear Count . . ." The next words were so incredibly obscene I could scarce understand him. Luc was not so afflicted.

A moment later I was free from Holger's steely grasp, and the Austrian was lying on the floor, holding his stomach and groaning in pain.

"Go to your room, Carlotta, and lock yourself in," Luc ordered, his negligent grace vanished.

"You don't have to tell me that," I snapped. "But I'd rather use another room."

A brief smile lit his dark face. "You are frightened of ghosts, little one? You may of course stay in my room."

My reply was slightly less obscene than Von Wolfram's question, but Luc only laughed. "Maddelena will show you to a room that is at least halfway clean."

Holger was beginning to drag himself to his knees, groaning and clutching himself as if in mortal pain. I turned to go, and then my wretched weakness forced me to turn back. "You will be all right?" I questioned reluctantly. "He won't imprison you for striking him?"

An expression I couldn't read flitted across his dark, handsome face. "Do not worry about me, little one. I don't deserve it. Besides, the Devil looks after his own."

There was nothing left for me to do but leave the two men alone with their mortal enmity.

Chapter Twenty-one

FOR ONE WHO had suffered through such an incredibly varied and eventful thirty-six hours I slept surprisingly well. Maddelena, with an ill-concealed contempt, showed me to a smaller, less grand back bedroom on the second floor. The clothes still in the closet left little doubt that this had been Rosetta's room, and that fact, coupled with the room's unfortunate view of the side canal that had provided me with my recent bath did little to reassure me. The cold gleam in the housekeeper's black-currant eyes added to my unease. I had ventured to say something suitably sympathetic about Rosetta, but the old witch had forestalled me with a shrug of her heavy shoulders.

"That one!" she spat, which couldn't hurt the dust-caked floor. "She was born to die thus. If it hadn't been the *vampiro* it would have been one of her many lovers."

"The . . . the *vampiro*?" I echoed nervously.

Maddelena's laugh was not pleasant. "That's what they are saying, signorina. Best to lock your door tonight."

That was my second warning, one that I did not need. "I have every intention of doing so," I replied with dignity, "though I don't see how a locked door would keep a vampire out if he truly wanted to enter."

"True enough," she nodded seriously. "You must rub the door and windows with garlic. They can even sneak in through the keyhole. They have been known, signorina," she leaned closer, "to take the shape of bats in order to gain access to their victims. I should beware of night-flying creatures if I were you."

Her heavy breath left me no doubt that she'd be safe from the garlic-hating fiends of the night. "I could tell you many things," she added in a deep growl. "Many ways to protect yourself. A cross made of rose thorns, wolfbane, a mirror. But I think you are wise beyond your years. If the *vampiro* truly wants you, nothing will stop him." She moved away, leaving me quaking in cowardly terror.

"Who are you talking about?" I demanded in a frightened croak. Quickly I cleared my throat. "Are you talking about Luc?"

An amazed expression crossed her evil, suet-like face. "The count?" she echoed, astounded. "But no, signorina. I speak of the ghoul, the *vampiro*, not of my noble master." And without another word she left.

IT WAS WELL into the next day when I awoke, and for a moment I lay in the strange bed, wondering where I was. I'd been sleeping far too much without the help of the soporific wine, but Maddelena could always put something in the food. A noisy purring reminded me that I was not alone, Patrick having deserted his master for one more in need of consolation. I was blessed with forgetfulness for only a few moments, and then it came back to me.

Mentally I reviewed my position. I was a golden English virgin of almost twenty years, possessed of a large fortune and an evil guardian who was most likely a murderer, vampire, an embezzler, and a spy. I was also quite stupidly ignoring all the suitable handsome young men because I was obsessed by the man. Or should I say creature?

I had further complicated my life by severing my ties with England and placing myself in this monster's hands, then turning around and promising to spy on him for the sake of my country and a young man's lovely blue eyes and broad shoulders, a young man I should fall in love with and knew I never would. Two people I had known were dead, brutally murdered. Hidden in my room was perhaps incriminating evidence, evidence that could free me from the legal hold Lucifero Alessandro del Zaglia had over me. I wasn't sure anything could destroy my fascination. Hastily I put aside any doubts, any feelings of guilt I might have. After all, I could trust Mark to do the right thing, couldn't I?

Before my better self could rise up in protest, I jumped from the bed. By instinct rather than thought I dressed quickly in the cleaner of Rosetta's two dresses and surveyed myself in the mirror, only the second I had seen in this mirrorless house. The clothes were big on me, to be sure, and nothing could disguise the disgusting "Englishness" of my appearance, but unless anyone looked closely I could pass. The Austrians had occupied Venice for years before I was born; there was no reason why I couldn't be the offspring of those fair-haired invaders and a local woman. After perusing the empty hall-way I started out the door. I could only hope no one had bothered to rummage through my bedclothes. If the incriminating papers were gone so was my last hope.

The third floor was deserted. Since I had been moved it was now completely untenanted, and the brief glimpse I had had of the new girl brought in to take Rosetta's place assured me that she would rather face the fires of hell than venture onto the haunted third floor. I knew I could trust the vague and fluttery Mildred and her cohorts to feel the same way.

My room was just as I had left it, with the fortunate exception of Rosetta's body. I couldn't keep my nervous eyes from darting to the spot where she had fallen, searching for bloodstains. But of course there would be none. Holger had only verified what I had known instinctively. When the poor dead beauty had been placed in my closet she had been practically drained of her rich red blood.

Quickly I averted my eyes. For one horrid moment as I scrambled around my bed I thought the papers were gone. A moment later I was dizzy with relief. During my nightly tosses and turns I had merely dislodged them. They were now down around the foot of the bed, happily disguised by the rumpled bed linens. Of the sapphire pendant there was no sign, and I could only surmise that Thornton or Mildred had taken advantage of the confusion and repossessed it.

I did not even pause for a cup of the rich, strong coffee Mrs. Wattles made so well. I was out of the house before anyone could stop me, marching briskly down the narrow streets. The sun was beating down on my head, gilding the oriental domes of the city, turning the dark green canal waters a silvery color. And suddenly it felt very good to be alive, very good indeed. Not dead and bloodless and in some pine coffin like poor, unhappy Rosetta. My feet were light over the cobblestones, and I met the smiling faces of the Venetians I passed with equal cheer only slightly dampened by my guilt. I had no right to feel happy with the horrible things that had been happening around me. But it was a lovely afternoon, and no matter how ominous my situation might be, there was still unbidden the memory of sleeping in Luc's strong arms.

In my present costume I didn't dare stop at Florian's for a desperately needed breakfast. Looking as I did, I doubted they would serve me. Indeed, it was a little too close to the Quadri, the café frequented by the hated Austrians, for comfort. Holger von Wolfram was the last person I cared to run into on my current mission.

Instead I had a delicious breakfast of coffee, sweet rolls and rich, creamy butter at the small café in the same campo as Giacomo's tailor shop. Once I had eaten, my spirits soared even higher, and I contemplated never returning to the dark and decaying palazzo on the Grand Canal. But then, if I did so I would never see Luc again.

"Why do you ask for the *Inglesi?*" the small, dark little tailor demanded, perhaps fooled by my excellent Italian into thinking just what I wanted people to think.

"Why should I know him?" he added, shrugging hunched shoulders. "I have done work for many *Inglesi*, many Austrians also. I cannot remember everyone."

"But he told me," I insisted anxiously, my earlier good mood vanishing at this sudden setback. "He said I could get in touch with him here. His name is Ferland, Mark Ferland."

There was no softening in the black, unreadable eyes of the tailor. After a moment he shrugged again. "Perhaps I can help you, signorina, perhaps I can't. I would suggest you return home, and if I run across this Mr. Ferland I will have him get in touch with you."

"But I can't!" The thought of trying to hide the papers that now seemed to burn against my skin terrified me. I knew that if I didn't place them in Mark's strong, capable hands soon I would weaken, my resolve would crumble, and Luc would once more win.

"Then you will have to wait," he said resignedly. "Perhaps he will show up today, perhaps not. If you refuse to return home you may stay in the back room. If he is going to come he will be here by three."

"Three!" I could feel fresh tears starting. "That is hours away!"

"Two hours, signorina," he grumbled. "I do not want you here anymore than you wish to be here. It could cause me great trouble with the *Tedeschi*, and I have no wish to get in trouble with those Austrian *bastardos*. Already I have been indiscreet. Either retire to the back room or leave my shop."

I had no choice. As I slipped behind the heavy curtain into the dark, airless little cubicle Giacomo had optimistically referred to as a room, all my fears and doubts came crowding back. I sank down into a corner of the stuffy closet and leaned back against the wall. At least, I thought with the last glimmering of humor I would muster for the next two hours, I would be safe from *vampiros* in this atmosphere.

During the next two hours I alternated between hope and despair, anger and a cheerful courage, determination and a treacherous weakening whenever I envisioned the sinuously graceful form of the demon count. Surely I was doing the right thing, giving my cares and worries over to Mark Ferland. There could be no doubt, could there? And if Luc was not doing anything wrong, it could do no harm. If he was as evil as people imagined, then he deserved whatever punishment fate meted out. Fate, or me, I wondered guiltily.

The bell in the small campo outside the tailor's shop tolled three o'clock, slowly, sonorously, and I climbed stiffly to my feet. I should have been furious, saddened, exhausted. But, truth to tell, those hours had passed swiftly, and now I was free from having to make any more choices. I had tried to tell Mark, truly I had. That he hadn't shown up was no fault of mine. I could in all good conscience return to the palazzo, destroy those papers, and meet Luc's golden, all-seeing eyes with bland innocence. He would come to no harm through me, much as he doubtless deserved to. A great weight lifted off me.

"Charlotte?" A soft, British voice whispered, and the weight descended full force. Mark had arrived after all.

THE WALK BACK through the narrow, twisting alleyways was filled with mental torment. Even having my limp hand held in Mark's strong, capable one did little to allay my fears and doubts and, most of all, my guilt.

"This is magnificent, Charlotte!" he had crowed, sweeping me into his arms in surprising exuberance when he'd perused the papers. "I couldn't have asked for anything better. The code should be simple enough to decipher—just a few days, more or less."

"What . . . what will it say?" I asked faintly, staring at my treachery with a jaundiced eye.

Mark shrugged those broad, sturdy shoulders. "Who knows? That del Zaglia is a traitor, perhaps. But a traitor to whom, that is the question? In the meantime, your work is done. You have only to wait until I send word for you. We can leave Venice before the week is out."

"Leave?" I echoed vaguely. "We?"

A crestfallen look came over his face. "You'll come with me? I know it's been far too short a time, but I thought, considering the circumstances . . ."

"You thought what?"

"That you might be willing to come stay with us for a while. I've told my mother all about you. I know she'll love you at first sight. I realize we barely know each other and these things take time, but I was hoping you might reciprocate my feelings . . ."

I could feel an unaccustomed blush rising in my cheeks. "I am not . . . indifferent to you, Mr. Ferland. I would be charmed to meet your mother," I said with stilted formality. "It's just . . . so sudden."

A light blazed in his warm blue eyes. "I wouldn't have dared to bring it up so soon, Miss Morrow, but I doubt that Venice is a very safe place for either of us much longer. There's just so little time."

"So little time?"

"Von Wolfram grows more and more suspicious of the interfering English, as he calls us. He's a lot more powerful than he appears to be, and not a good enemy to have."

"I've become aware of that," I said drily.

"There is a ship leaving within the next two days. I've reserved a single cabin for you," Here, ridiculously, he blushed. "I've spoken to the captain, and he assures me there will be room to stow a single man."

"I think, Mr. Ferland, that you should stop calling me Miss Morrow if we are to travel together," I said, and found myself swept into a crushing embrace that should have been eminently satisfying. If it lacked the breathless, drowning quality of Luc's intermittent caresses, neither did it contain any fear, of my suitor or of the deep black depths of the unknown. It was no one's fault but mine if I emerged just a trifle disappointed.

Fortunately, Mark was too caught up in making plans for our future to notice my abstraction. Being a serious and sober Englishman, he never openly proposed, but I was well aware that he had every intention of marrying me, once, of course, his mother approved.

He didn't want me to return to Edentide, but I wasn't ready to burn my bridges. I would only do so if a monster on the other side, and my heart remained stubbornly hopeful.

Against his better judgment he left me beneath the balcony. The tall, brooding windows of the old palazzo looked lifeless in the late afternoon sun, and yet a strange prickling on the back of my neck told me someone was watching.

"You should go now," I whispered, ducking into the shadows under the marble ledge. "If anyone should see you . . ."

"If anyone should see me they'll think twice about interfering with you," he said with reckless confidence. "You're not alone any more, Charlotte."

The disloyal thought came to me—how much pleasanter, more sensuous was the name Carlotta than plain, stuffy Charlotte. I summoned up my best smile, deciding not to tell him that, in fact, I was alone, and would be until I was safely aboard that ship. The ship that loomed more like a punishment than a haven. In answer to my shaky smile Mark pulled me into his arms, kissing me with a healthy ardor that left me dangerously unmoved.

"Only a few more days, my dear, and we'll be safe," he said in a damnably loud voice. I tried to look misty-eyed, but my nervousness was quickly overpowering me. I pushed him away as gently but firmly as I could, returning his quick, impassioned kisses and wondering if I had made a very grave mistake.

But no, I thought, watching him hurry down the street until he was out of sight. The mistake I was making was in having any doubts at all about the suitability of the match. He loved me; he was kind, handsome, and noble. I could love him. Couldn't I? I simply had to!

I leaned wearily against the cool marble wall and watched the sun sink below the roofline of the ancient city. A real man, I told myself angrily, would not have let me return to this den of demons no matter what I demanded. A real man would have taken me back to his room and hidden me there, and damn propriety and people and everything.

But no, Mark Ferland would never so dishonor me, I thought bitterly, scrambling up over the iron railing and landing lightly on my thin-soled sandals. He must be a perfect gentleman, he must respect me enough to put my life in danger. If I made it safely back to my room I would lock my door and stay in there until Mark came to get me, I thought mutinously.

"Did you have a pleasant walk, Carlotta?" Luc's soft, menacing voice came from directly behind me. I whirled around, wondering whether I should leap off the balcony and risk a few broken bones rather than meet those hypnotizing golden eyes and the graceful, delicate, murderous hands of my guardian, adorned so prophetically with the gleaming bloodstone ring.

I put my hands back on the railing, about to leap. "Don't be any more of a fool than you've already been," he said sharply. "Your stalwart young lover isn't around to catch you. It's a great deal safer climbing up than jumping down."

I hesitated for a moment longer, but in the rapidly growing darkness the cobblestones below looked far away indeed. Squaring my shoulders, I turned and walked into the room. After all, what could he possibly do to me?

By the time I got close enough to see his face I nearly broke and ran. Beneath the cool, icy composure was an expression of such dark anger that I quaked at the sight of it. I felt smaller and weaker than I ever had, but some last vestige of bravery forced me to come directly up to him, my tousled blond hair reaching only to his shoulder.

He was dressed all in black, as usual, with the obligatory trace of white in the linen shirt that was open to the waist. He must have just risen, I thought stupidly, and found I was lost.

I looked up into those brooding eyes in his pale, sensual face, and a feeling of inevitability came over me, so that I stood there, motionless, mesmerized, trapped by his inexorable will. After a time that could have lasted seconds or hours, he spoke.

"Where are the papers, Carlotta?"

I didn't bother to deny it. "I gave them to Mark."

No expression crossed his face. "I should have known. I underestimated you, little one. A fatal mistake, it seems." His hand reached out and gently stroked my neck above the low-cut peasant blouse. His skin on mine seemed to burn with an icy fire. "You look quite fetching in Rosetta's clothing. Have you some unconscious wish to be with her throughout eternity?"

I knew then that I had very little time left on this earth. This pretty, decaying little room would be my last sight on earth—that, and the beautiful face of my murderer, who was looking down at me with such a closed, angry expression. He was all everyone suspected, a vampire, the ghoul of Venice, and I would be his final victim before Mark deciphered those damning papers and had him arrested. But by then it would be too late for me.

"No," I said, and my voice came out in a croak. I couldn't move; I was frozen in place with his hand on my neck, his golden eyes capturing my helpless ones.

"It is only what you deserve, little one," he murmured, and his mouth moved down and brushed my lips, very lightly. He kissed my eyes, my cheeks, my chin, soft hurried little kisses that made me feel dizzy and dreaming. *This must be death*, I thought, not minding one bit.

"Look at me, Carlotta," he commanded, and, startled out of my reverie, I looked up. It seemed to me I had never seen a face so evil or so sad, so beautiful or so death-like. Without further warning his head moved down and I felt his teeth on my neck, sharp and painful, felt the blood come just before the blackness closed in.

Chapter Twenty-two

THERE WAS SOMETHING very wet and icy cold on my neck, interfering with my embarrassingly erotic dreams. I batted away at the hands that were pressing the compress on me, and felt them imprisoned in a strong grasp. Stubbornly I clung to my state of sleep. I was dead, I had no intention of giving up this pleasant dream any sooner than I wished to.

My tormentor thought differently. My hands were loosened, and I snuggled back amid the soft covers, prepared to drift off once more, when I was spattered with myriad drops of cold water. My eyes flew open in rage.

"Hell and damnation!" I began, and then faded out. I was in Luc's bedroom . . . the warm candlelight was strong enough to tell me that much. Sitting on the bed beside me and holding a cold compress to my neck was my murderer, an amused, rueful expression on his face. He reached into a golden basin and splashed me with more water for good measure. I was too astounded to say a word, just continued to stare at him in shock.

"Little one, do not look at me like that," he pleaded, a note of laughter in his voice. "I couldn't resist; you looked so gullible. I had no idea you would faint."

His words made no sense. "Am I dead?" I asked with great practicality.

He pulled the compress away, and I could see faint traces of blood on the wet cloth. Dipping it into the basin and wringing it out before reapplying it to my neck, he kept his eyes averted. I squirmed as the icy material touched my skin, and reached out to capture his hand. That was one of many mistakes.

"Am I dead?" I repeated, holding onto his hand like a lifeline.

He smiled that bewitching smile. "No, *mia Carlotta*, of course not. I let my wicked temper and my even worse sense of humor get the better of me. You were staring up at me, convinced I was all sorts of fiends, and I decided to prove you were right. I only meant to scare you." He looked truly repentant, an unusual expression for Luc del Zaglia. Repentance and something else played over his expressive countenance.

Without another word I let go of his hand, sitting up abruptly, determined to leave the bedroom. I was unceremoniously pushed back against the pillows. Luc's contrition hadn't lasted long.

"Where do you think you're going?" he asked, and a shiver ran down my backbone.

I struggled against his hand, fury and embarrassment fighting for control.

"To my room, of course. You've had your amusement at my expense. I want to leave."

"My dear child," he said sweetly, tossing the compress in a corner and bending over me, "I have not yet had my amusement with you. You are going to stay in this room until I send you away, and you will not leave a moment sooner."

As I looked up into his hooded, topaz eyes there was no mistaking his meaning. But I was still unable to grasp it. "You . . . you don't want me," I stammered stupidly. "I spent the entire night with you already and you didn't touch me."

A mocking grin twisted his lips for a moment. "I was, for once, a gentleman. You were cold and frightened, *mia Carlotta*, and I didn't want to take advantage of you."

"And now?" I demanded, a small knot of dread inside me warring with another, unspeakable reaction to his nearness. "I'm still cold and frightened."

He shrugged. "I can wait no longer for you, little one. You have precipitated things with your meddling and spying. I must leave at dawn, but not before I've taken from you what's rightfully mine."

Panic burst forth in me. "You're wrong. I'm . . . I'm no longer a virgin. Mark seduced me weeks ago!" I added triumphantly, hoping he'd believe me.

He shook his head, amused. "I'm not interested in your virginity, my love. I had expected as much. What I am going to take from you," he said, leaning down and brushing his lips across my forehead, "and what you're going to give to me," his lips gently touched the wound on my neck, "is your love." And his mouth took possession of mine.

I felt as if I were drowning, drowning, with his mouth on mine. If his first kiss had been astonishing, this one was life altering. When I gasped his tongue pushed into my mouth, touching mine, stroking mine, and I shivered with shock and delight. I was drowning and never wishing to surface again, I wanted to lose myself in this dark desire, fear and passion warring for control. A part of me had wanted this since I first saw him. I had longed for him, been terrified of him, hated him. And damn me for a fool, I loved him.

Without knowing how it happened my arms were around his neck, pulling him down to me as I answered his mouth, inexpertly, but with all the passion that thrummed through my body. His hands were cool and gentle on my flesh, slowly and sensuously depriving me of Rosetta's baggy clothes before I even knew it, before I could summon some vestige of protest at his expert handling of me. I lay naked on his bed, the candlelight casting a golden glow over my body that was matched by the glow in his eyes as he slid down beside me. He leaned down and traced the smooth surface of my skin with his mouth, his hands running along the sleek lines of my hips, his breath coming more rapidly now, matching my own desperate excitement. My heart was pounding wildly, my head was spinning, and I knew I must be mad, to let him take me like this, but I didn't care. I moved underneath his probing hands, sighing with surprised delight only slightly clouded with the thought of all the women and all the years that had taught him how to pleasure one so.

"Little one," he whispered in my ear, his tongue sending little shivers of delight through me. Obediently I followed where he led, mindless, thoughtless, a slave to the wild passion he was arousing in me. I slid my hands beneath the loose white shirt, pushing it from his strong shoulders, and his skin was warm, golden and I moved my hands down over his chest, his stomach, the sleek muscles that covered him, reveling in the feel of him.

One of his hands moved lower, between my legs, touching me in a place I seldom touched myself. Vainly I protested, but he was inexorable, and in truth I didn't want to deny him, to deny myself. I was wet down there, which should have embarrassed me, but I stopped thinking when the first shiver of astonishing pleasure shook me, followed by a second, and then a third that was so powerful I was sobbing against his chest, clutching at him in my need.

"Please," I whispered, not knowing what I was begging, not caring, only wanting him so that I thought I should die, wanting some mysterious more that I knew awaited me beneath his strong hands, his strong body. He smiled down at me, no longer demoniacal, his topaz eyes warm with love and tenderness as he kissed me gently, his mouth fastening on mine and deepening as he moved over me, pushing my legs apart so that he lay between them.

We were skin to skin, and I hadn't noticed when he'd removed the rest of his clothes, and I tensed in sudden panic. I could feel that hard rod of flesh, that piece I didn't even have a name for, between us, and I knew there was no changing my mind. I didn't want to.

"This will hurt, my angel," he whispered in my ear, "just this one time. I would spare you if I could, but I can't keep away from you any longer. Forgive me." He raised his hips, and I felt him against me, against that private, secret part of me, and he was pushing inside me. He was right, it hurt, and I bit my lips as unbidden tears filled my eyes, but he didn't stop. I didn't ask him to, just clung to his shoulders as tightly as I could until I felt a tearing inside me, and I cried out in pain as he sunk deep inside me, our bodies tight together.

He kissed the tears that had rolled down my cheeks, kissed my mouth with their salt still on his lips. "That's the worst of it. Soon it will be much, much better." As he felt me relax beneath him he began to move, slowly at first, and I decided he was lying, it still hurt. And then the pain began to recede, as other feelings took over, frantic ones, and I clawed at his back, trying to pull him closer still, as he slid his hands under my hips and brought me up to meet his thrusts.

It was instinctive, preternatural, this rhythm that I somehow knew, and each time he pushed inside I arched up to meet him, looking for something, I wasn't sure what. One hand slide between our sweating bodies to cover my breast, his fingers plucking at the nipple, and the sensation was like a fiery line down to our joining. I was panting in need, when he leaned down and put his lips on my nipple, sucking it into his mouth, his teeth brushing against the flesh, and I cried out as my body seemed to ripple around his invading flesh.

He slid his hand down, between our bodies, but I was past noticing details, so lost in the deep, dreamy world he'd wrapped me in, my skin sensitized, my entire body on the very edge of explosion. I felt a vague fear—what would happen when I let go? Would I lose myself entirely? Would there be anything less?

He was moving faster now, thrusting into me, and I was meeting him, tiny sparks covering every inch of my flesh. He touched me then, hard, and I felt my entire body convulse and shatter as wave after wave of reaction swept over me. He went rigid in my arms, pulsing inside of me, before he collapsed on top of me, gasping for breath as I was, our hearts beating closely together, and I was crying like a silly child, unable to help myself.

He rolled on his side, bringing me with him, holding me close against his chest where I hid my face, content to hide from him, from myself, from the world. But Luc was not one to let me take the easy way out. When my helpless little sobs had ceased, a gentle hand came under my chin, drawing me up to face him with tear-stained cheeks.

"Such a liar," he said gently, wiping away a tear with one long-fingered hand. "I knew Ferland had never had you. You were too besotted with me to pay any attention to him. You are such a terrible child, I can't imagine why I love you."

My heart seemed to stop, then start all over again, beating against my ribcage as if it would break through. "What?" I whispered, not believing my ears.

He smiled, that same mocking, loving smile that so destroyed me, but he wouldn't repeat the words, so that I doubted I'd heard right. Instead he drew me back into the shelter of his arms, holding me like a child, until we both slept.

Chapter Twenty-three

I LOST ALL SENSE of time, lost in a hazy dream of sensuality. A few hours later he awoke me with a tray of hot, steaming soup and crusty bread.

"You probably haven't eaten in days," he smiled at me with that new, loving smile so devoid of mockery.

I watched him out of silent eyes, unmoving, both shy and wary at this new side of the formidable Luc del Zaglia. "Come," he said, placing the tray beside me on the rumpled bed. He was dressed in a pair of sleek, close-fitting black breeches, a snowy shirt hanging loose and unbuttoned around his tanned torso. His black hair was rumpled, and his feet were bare. It was this last that suddenly loosed the hold on my tongue that fright and timidity had placed there. I smiled up at him, a blush suffusing my skin as my eyes met his wicked golden ones.

"I can think of a great many things I would rather do than eat," he murmured, one elegant hand tracing my neck with a light touch that sent shivers of delight through my responsive body. "But Maddelena is already fiercely disapproving, and it was all I could do to beg this from her."

I struggled to gather my wits about me, sitting up with the linen sheet clasped demurely around my body. "Maddelena?" I questioned, horrified but reaching for the soup with surprising hunger. "She knows? What about Mrs. Wattles? And the other servants?"

He shrugged, watching me eat with quiet amusement. "They have all decamped, all but Maddelena. And Antonio, of course. Apparently the word has traveled very quickly around Venice. My arrest is imminent. The Austrians now have proof that I've been working diligently for their overthrow for the last ten years."

I had the grace to blush in guilt and shame. "Arrest?" I echoed, the spoon halfway to my mouth. "Should you still be here?"

He smiled, and I blushed again. "No, little one, I should not. Which is Maddelena's contention. But I know Von Wolfram and his cohorts better than they know themselves. First light will be soon enough." He reached out and took a piece of bread from the tray, nibbling at it absently. "It is just as well the noble Thornton left with his female accomplices. I would rather not have to avoid their prying eyes when I leave this morning."

"They were stealing from you," I ventured.

"I know that quite well. It suited me to have it so. It kept them occupied, and it cost me little enough. However, I did not go so far as to let them leave with the contents of my mother's jewelry box. Maddelena very cleverly substituted a bag full of costume jewelry for the real thing. I imagine Thornton will be quite chagrined when he tries to arrange passage out of Venice with the proceeds from those trumpery pieces. And I was able to discover, *poveretta*, that it was Mildred who threw you in the canal. Apparently you had stumbled upon their secret cache during one of your many searches, and she panicked."

"Poor Mildred," I sighed, leaning back. "Life cannot have been very pleasant for her. I can't say I'm not glad they're gone, though."

He took another piece of bread and sopped it in the dregs of the soup. He met my quizzical expression curiously. "What is wrong?"

I found that I, too, could shrug. "It's just that I've never seen you eat before."

He laughed. "Maddelena would bring me meals during the day. I used to watch you, staring at me out of those great blue eyes of yours as I drank my way through meals. You were so delightfully transparent." He reached out and moved the tray from the bed. I could feel my heart pounding beneath the sheets as I watched him, the shadows cast by the candlelight playing over his tall, lean form.

"Shouldn't you escape now?" I asked again. "Holger hates you—he isn't going to let you go easily."

He blew out one of the candles, turned to me and smiled. "Yes, Carlotta Theresa Sabina," he murmured tenderly. "I *should* leave. But I have no intention of doing so a moment before I am ready to. It is only just after midnight. I have a great deal I want to do before dawn." And he leaned down and pulled the sheet away from me with deliciously slow deliberation.

It was the sunlight that awoke me next. It was streaming in the shuttered balcony door, casting slats of light across my lover's face. I savored the word. As I lay beside him, trying not to waken him, I was conscious of many things. The first was my body, which ached in every muscle, every nerve ending, and yet had never felt so alive. I shut my eyes and reveled in the sense of completeness, of physical well-being that was at direct odds with the sudden onrush of overwhelming terror. It was way past dawn, and Luc was still here.

I opened my eyes and met his solemn golden ones, glowing in the early morning sunlight as he watched me. A slow smile curved his lips.

"You should be gone," I whispered. "It's late."

"True enough," he replied, stretching like a well-rested cat. I alone knew how little rest he had had. "You have worn me out, little one." With one lithe move he was out of bed, staring out the crack in the shutters with an unreadable expression on his face. He turned back to me, and gone was the tender yet fierce demon lover of the night before. "You will do several things for me, Carlotta," he said abruptly, pulling on his clothes.

I nodded obediently, trying to shut my mind to the overwhelming fact that he was leaving.

"You will meet with your handsome young Englishman today, as you have arranged." He ignored my gesture of repudiation. "You will leave Venice with him on the ship he has arranged, and you will marry him as you have planned."

All trace of languor had gone, and all trace of love, I told myself, staring at him in sullen rage. "I can take care of my own life, thank you," I said icily, casting about me for some remnant of last night's clothing. I came up with the shirt Luc had worn, and I drew it around me with a chilly dignity.

He watched me gravely. "I am still your guardian, little one. Ferland is safe, secure, and he obviously loves you. You would be well advised to do as I say."

"And how will you enforce your will?" I snapped back, determined to let my anger keep the tears away. "I most certainly will marry Mark, if he'll have me after you . . . you dishonored me!" The phrase sounded ridiculous in my ears, so far removed was it from the night I had just spent. Luc apparently thought so too, for a small laugh escaped him, which inflamed me even more. I jumped out of the bed, pulling the silky folds of his shirt around me to preserve what shred of modesty I had left. "Damn you to hell," I spat at him. "I hope Holger catches you and hangs you."

"He may very well do that," he replied calmly, and the awful truth of that remark struck me dumb. I stared at him in shocked silence, the tears slipping down my face.

And suddenly I was in Luc's arms, sobbing with fright and anguish, my words incoherent. And through my tears I thought I heard the sound of soldiers outside Edentide. But it was still too early, it must be my tortured imagination.

He scooped me up, holding my frail, shivering body against him as he carried me across the room. A moment later we were in that little closet I had been imprisoned in just a few short days ago. It seemed like centuries. He put me down on the bed with great gentleness. He stood up, looking at me with a tender, loving expression that made me weep even more. He put one hand out to brush the tangled hair away from my forehead, and I grabbed it like a lifeline.

"Don't leave me," I begged brokenly, foolishly.

He took a deep breath, and suddenly he was beside me, on me, in me, taking me with a force and a loving brutality that sent me deeper into ecstasy tempered with despair. It was almost over before it had begun, and as I lay panting in his arms, trying to regain my tremulous control, his voice whispered in my ear.

"That is my seed within you, little one. Make sure Ferland brings up my bastard well." He pulled away from my clinging arms abruptly. "I would wish that you would make your home in Somerset," he added softly. "I have always had a fondness for that country, and it would please me to think of you living among those rolling green hills."

I heard him move to the door, and I shut my eyes, unable to bear watching him leave me. "Maddelena will let you out, *mia Carlotta*," he said, shutting the door behind him with a tiny click. I jumped up, running to the door and beating on it. It was no use, I was locked in.

I thought I heard him whisper from behind that heavy barrier. "Do not forget me, little one." And then the door to his room slammed shut, and I knew he was gone.

Suddenly other noises intruded in my ringing ears, noises more ominous than anything I had heard so far. I rushed to the narrow window, straining to see into the narrow street below. And all I could see was the white and gold uniforms of the Imperial Austrian Army. As I watched them mill around through dazed, dry eyes, I was suddenly aware of something clutched tightly in my fist. I opened my cramped fingers and saw Luc's bloodstone ring.

HOURS, LONG, LONG hours later the door to my prison opened slowly. My eyes met the tear-ravaged countenance of Maddelena. "They have taken him," she said slowly, painfully. "He never had a chance. They have taken him to the New Prisons and they will execute him as a spy."

And something cold and hard formed within my breast, a pain so deep and terrible that not even tears could assuage it. I met Maddelena's accusing expression dry-eyed.

"Then we must get him out," I said defiantly. "Somehow, some way, we must get him out."

THAT, OF COURSE, was impossible for two women. I pleaded with Holger that afternoon, but to no avail. He merely smirked at me with open contempt and lasciviousness, the cruel expression in his ice-blue eyes promising worse to come. Jean-Baptiste answered none of my desperate missives, and all attempts to visit Luc proved useless. I returned to the palazzo at dusk, exhausted and in despair. It was not with any great joy that I greeted the news that Mark was awaiting me in the small salon.

I moved slowly down the hall, aching in every part of my body and soul. If I thought it would have done any good I would have fled upstairs and avoided him completely. But there was always the chance that Mark could undo the terrible wrong he had done. I opened the door and stood there, cold and still.

"Charlotte!" He rushed across the room and folded me into his sturdy embrace. "I came as soon as I heard. They have taken del Zaglia?"

I nodded, not trusting myself to speak. Sensing my deep unhappiness,

Mark drew away and looked down at me, his strong hands resting lightly on my arms. "And you blame me, my darling. You have every right to. If it weren't for my stupidity everything would have keen all right. Someone must have been watching me for weeks, and I thought I'd been so careful. I had just finished decoding the papers when someone hit me on the back of the head. When I awoke the papers were gone." Gingerly he rubbed the back of his head, wincing slightly to illustrate his point. "And it was all for nothing. He was on our side—one of us. Word reached me from Lord Bateman this morning. Luc del Zaglia is a well-concealed patriot, not a traitor to Venice and his own people. He'd been working with our people for years, but of course they never bothered to tell me that." He sounded plainly disgruntled. "If only I'd known!"

"He's going to die," I said numbly, moving away from him to stand by the window. The dark green waters moved sluggishly beneath me, and numbly I wondered what it would be like to slip back into those chill, dark depths. "We have to do something!"

"Charlotte, my dearest, I know. But what can we do? I have tried to talk with Von Wolfram, even had the English ambassador intervene. But it is useless. They mean to make an example of del Zaglia, and nothing anybody does or says will make any difference. I doubt even the king could interfere!"

"Then he will die," I said dully. I could feel my aching body folded into Mark's comforting embrace, and I resisted only for a moment. I was so very tired.

"There is nothing we can do, my dear. Do not grieve so. It seems very likely that he was the ghoul of Venice. If he doesn't deserve to die for his political activities, he certainly does for his fiendish murders."

I turned on him in a blind rage. "Don't ever let me hear you say such a thing again!" I shrieked. "Luc is no more a murderer than you are."

A perplexed look crossed his face as he soothed me. "Of course not, dearest. You should know, of course. I have arranged for proper food and bedding to be provided for him until . . . that is . . ."

"Until they murder him."

"Until his sentence is carried out. Remember, he hasn't even been tried yet."

"A mere technicality."

"He did send a message, though." Eagerly I turned to him, hoping against hope for some word of love from the demon count. A moment later my hopes were dashed. "He wants you to leave Venice immediately. With me or without me, he said. It's all the same to him. But leave Venice you must." There was no suspicion in his handsome, trusting face, only deep concern.

"I can't. Not until I know . . ."

"There is no doubt, Charlotte. I have arranged passage for us on the *Devon Queen.* The captain will marry us as soon as we leave port and reach the open seas. You must promise me you'll come."

"I can't marry you," I said lifelessly. "I spent last night with Luc." I waited for the anger, the repudiation to cross Mark's face, but he merely nodded sadly.

"I cannot say I'm surprised. I've always known you've had complicated feelings for the man. It doesn't matter a bit, darling. I love you, and once you are free of his spell you will come to realize that you love me, too. Maddelena has already packed your trunk. I'm taking it with me tonight, and tomorrow morning at ten o'clock we set sail. I'll come and fetch you."

"I won't go with you," I cried. "I can't leave."

"You'll go with me," he replied gently. "If for no one's sake but his." Once more he swept me into his arms, not kissing me, just holding me close against the warm strength of him, so that my resolve began to weaken. I was so tired, I wanted more than anything to give myself and my trouble up to his strong, comforting arms. I watched him leave in the early evening sunset, mixed feelings warring in my breast. So caught up was I that I failed to notice Maddelena's silent entry into the room.

"You will go with him," she stated flatly. "There is nothing you can do for the master. It is better that you go."

I didn't bother to turn around and face her. "I am staying."

"Do not be a fool!" she flared. "If he has any chance at all of escaping do you think he wants to worry about whether or not you're safe?"

"He wouldn't worry."

"And if he cannot escape," she continued inexorably, "do you think he wants you there, watching, as he comes to a terrible, shameful end? If you think that, you are an even bigger fool than I thought you."

It took me a while, but I knew when I was defeated. I finally turned around and met her angry eyes. "And what will you do?"

"I have family in Genoa. I will go there, once I know there is nothing more that I can do for him. We must still have hope, signorina," she added in a kinder tone of voice.

"Yes, we must still hope." I moved listlessly across the room, my black silk skirts trailing in the dust. I could be more grateful that Luc had chosen black for me. Mourning seemed to be a constant state for me. I would mourn him for the rest of my life. "Mr. Ferland will come to fetch me tomorrow morning. Could you awaken me by seven?"

Relief crossed her suet-pudding face. "But of course, signorina. I will call you."

Chapter Twenty-four

I SLEPT FITFULLY that night. Despite Maddelena's protests I returned to Luc's rooms, determined to spend my last few hours in this decaying palazzo in Luc's bed, the scent of our lovemaking around me. But the much-needed sleep eluded me—it was well after midnight that I finally drifted off, after being tempted to ask Maddelena if she still retained any of the drug she had used so cheerfully on me when I first arrived in Venice. When sleep came at last it was deep, only to be cut short by what I thought was the sound of rats scrabbling over in the area of the desk.

The lump at my feet, obviously Patrick, was unmoving, so slowly, carefully I opened my sleep-glued eyelids. A small glow of candlelight split the gloom, and I lay there, still and silent, as an obviously male shadow moved through the room. He was bent over Luc's desk, rummaging through the papers with a surprising disregard of the room's occupant. And then I realized my intruder probably had no idea I was there.

I contemplated screaming for help, but the only other person in the house was Maddelena, and she was three flights down in the bowels of the house, fast asleep in her basement quarters. She would never hear me.

Antonio, Luc's valet, might still be on the premises. I had seen him skulking around, surreptitiously keeping out of my way. Perhaps it was he searching through Luc's papers. I kept my tired muscles rigid, too terrified to move. For suddenly that dark, dank, hideous sense of evil was upon me, and I knew without a doubt that the ghoul of Venice, Rosetta's murderer, was in the room with me.

The horror I felt was so complete that it must have communicated itself to the sleeping feline, for Patrick rose suddenly, his back arched, and hissed at the creature by the desk. The intruder whirled around to face my cowering form.

"What are you doing here?" My voice quavered as I attempted to question him with some degree of normal outrage. He was not fooled.

"Why, *cherie*," he protested with silky charm, "I would never have thought to find you here in Luc's bed. At least, not with Luc so tragically detained elsewhere. I thought I would have to search through this wretched pile of stones for you."

"You wanted to see me?" I sat up slowly, very slowly, so as not to arouse his suspicions. "Could not it have waited until tomorrow?"

"Ah, but it is you who wanted to see me," he replied smoothly. "Three desperate notes I received from your fair hand. I merely wanted to tell you that I am sadly unable to help poor Luc." He smiled then, displaying his small, pearl-like teeth, and something inside me snapped.

"You betrayed him," I whispered.

"But of course," Jean-Baptiste returned calmly. "It was necessary."

"Why?"

"Because Luc has proof that I am an Austrian spy. No one else in this damp, benighted city knows that, not even the noble Captain von Wolfram. If such news leaked out, my life would be worth nothing."

"Your life is worth nothing already," I said with deep contempt.

He smiled again, that charming, terrifying smile. "A matter of opinion, *ma cher*. The French government still employs the guillotine, and I have no desire to follow my grandparents. But a man must make his fortune in this world, and one man's treason is another's patriotism."

A small silence reigned. "All right," I said. "So you are a spy, and Luc knows it. Now that you have taken care of him why are you here?"

"Various reasons." He waved one slim, small hand airily. "Proof still exists somewhere in this house of my so-called perfidy. And, of course, I had to finish with you." The smile on his face was ferocious, and I was suddenly frightened. "You see, my dear, I have had to do all this without an appreciative audience, and I have this overwhelming need to confess to someone. You have been my choice."

"Lucky me."

"Lucky you, indeed. You will go to your death knowing the full scope of my genius. You alone will be able to appreciate my cunning."

"I will go to my death?" I echoed.

"But of course. Who do you think is the ghoul of Venice? Not Luc, with his theatrical flair and his midnight prowls, although he was the one who inspired me."

"You?" From the moment I had recognized that familiar sense of horror I had known, but I wanted to hear the words from him. "But why?"

He leaned back against the wall, negligently, brushing an imaginary speck of dust from his immaculate coat. "Well, I must confess that the first murder was none of my doing. Some lovers' quarrel, no doubt. But because of Luc's supernatural affectations, suspicion pointed his way, although it was, of course, impossible to prove anything. That gave me my inspiration. I took care of the other young ladies, carefully leading all the evidence directly to Luc's door. But that damned Von Wolfram ignored it!" An expression of outrage came into his sulky voice. "Georges, of course, was the perfect victim. I thought after that there would be no doubt."

"You murdered Georges?"

Again that horrible smile. "Indeed. I also enticed him into abducting you.

I have been very busy the last few months, doing everything I could to destroy del Zaglia before he destroyed me." He stood upright and began moving across the room towards me. "Rosetta was simple enough, and if I had only been able to finish with you that night everything would have been so nicely resolved. I was very angry with you, *ma cher.*"

"I . . . I am sorry I was so unobliging," I stammered, moving my feet around to the side of the bed. It was very dark in the room. The first traces of dawn were coming through the slatted shutters and the single candle let out only a fitful glow.

He shrugged. "Do not be frightened, *cherie.* Just think, you will be joining Luc. I won't hurt you very much." As if by magic a huge, glistening knife appeared in his hand as he continued to edge toward me. Suddenly he pounced.

But he had failed to account for Patrick. With a savage yowl, the cat sprang, leaping onto Perrier's shoulders with claws fully extended.

That moment was all I needed. I slipped past him, the knife grazing my shoulder, and ran, barefoot and screaming, out into the deserted hallway.

THE SLUGGISH FIRST light of dawn was fighting its way through the grimy windows of Edentide as I stumbled down the long, curving marble staircase, my pursuer close behind me. My mind was an unthinking mass of terror, and I headed blindly toward the cellars, toward Maddelena, the only one I thought could help me in this deserted mansion. I heard the monster trip, fall heavily, and his curses gladdened my heart as I ran ever faster.

I had forgotten, in my terror, that I had no idea exactly where Maddelena's apartments were. I found myself in the long, dark, water-drenched basements with a myriad of doors around me, trapped in the middle of the long stone walkway that led the length of the house to a small doorway onto the canal. On either side of the path was green, slimy ooze, ahead of me the canal, and behind me the ghoul of Venice. The beady eyes of rats that had so far escaped Patrick's vigilance winked in the fetid darkness, and, shuddering, I stumbled to a halt. I had no place to turn. I started to run back, but my path was blocked.

"You shouldn't run, *ma cher.*" His voice came from the darkness, eerie and cheerful. "I will always catch you. You merely make it more painful for yourself. I was disposed to be merciful, but now you have made me very angry. Very angry indeed. I am afraid I will have to make you pay for it."

The knife glistened in his hands as he moved toward me on his absurdly small, neat feet, clad in highly glossed boots. I was mesmerized by the evil in his face, the glimmer of the knife, the faint glow from behind him that was growing steadily brighter.

He had almost reached me. "There is someone behind you," I said calmly. A dark shape had materialized behind him, and I felt a faint hope.

"Don't be absurd," he scoffed. "It won't help . . . you cannot fool me." The knife glistened. "I will tell you something that might aid your departure. Your lover has escaped. Late last night, I believe. By this time he will be out of the city, out of the country. There is no help for you."

"He escaped?" I echoed, joy ringing in my voice.

"He will be free to mourn you," Jean-Baptiste mocked, his arm raised to slash me. Coward that I was, I shut my eyes and prepared for death.

It all happened at once. A voice I had thought never to hear again cried out, "Get down, Carlotta!"

Two screams broke the damp stillness, a death scream from Jean-Baptiste as a battle-ax cleaved his skull and a cry of horror from me as I hid my eyes from the bloody sight. A moment later I was enfolded in Luc's arms, my face hidden against his shoulders as he held my shaking, sobbing body.

It was a long while before he spoke, and when he did his voice was harsh. "I am sorry, little one. I should have warned you about Jean-Baptiste, but there wasn't time. I could only pray I would get back here before it was too late."

"You shouldn't be here," I managed to blurt out against the muffling folds of his cape. "You should have escaped while you had the chance."

He moved my head up to face him, keeping my face firmly averted from the bloody sight to our left. "And then you'd be dead, *mia Carlotta*. I had no choice." He leaned down and kissed me lightly on the lips. "I'm sorry his death had to be so gory, but it was the nearest weapon I could find when I saw him heading down into the cellars."

I allowed myself a moment to enjoy the taste of his mouth on mine before reality took control once more. "You must leave immediately," I said, breaking away. "Before Holger comes here."

He shrugged. "It is too late. I'm afraid they followed me. Giorgio is waiting in the side canal, but I doubt we'll make it. I worry about you, *poveretta*. You are leaving with Ferland?"

My eyes met his, and I could read nothing but a cool concern in them. I had no choice but to nod.

"Good. Go upstairs and stay with Maddelena until it is over. Either I will escape or I won't. There is nothing more you can do." He pulled me back into his arms, kissing me hungrily. And then he turned me around, swatted me on the bottom, and said, "Go."

I ran back along the passageway, determined not to look back. I had no intention of hiding with Maddelena, even if I could have found her room. I was going to distract Holger until Luc got away.

I barely had time to make it to the drawing room before a furious, red-faced Holger appeared, accompanied by what seemed to my terrified eyes to be at least fifty soldiers.

"Your lover, fräulein, has escaped!" he thundered.

I smiled politely, trying to act as if I normally entertained the Imperial Army at six in the morning dressed in my thin nightgown, with bare feet and a knife scratch on my shoulder. "Really?" I murmured innocently. "How inefficient of you, Captain."

"We have followed him to this house, fräulein!" he announced, his face mottled with rage.

"Really?" I said again. "Well, I haven't seen him. Do you intend to search the house?"

"We do indeed!"

"Well, then, I suggest you start in the cellars," I suggested affably, knowing the masculine mind well enough to be sure he would do the opposite, giving Luc a few more precious minutes.

Immediately Holger ordered his soldiers to begin searching the attics, meanwhile casting a triumphant look in my direction, and I relaxed a bit. I started for the door, only to be brought up short by Holger's ham-handed fist. "You will stay here with me, fräulein. I will not have you warning him."

"I have no intention of warning anyone, Holger," I said with some asperity. "I merely wanted to find some more suitable clothing."

He allowed a small leer to escape his stern face. "I find your apparel eminently suitable, fräulein. And when we have recaptured your lover and executed him I will undertake to show you just how suitable such raiment is."

"How dare you!" I said frostily.

"Oh, I dare a great deal. You are an enemy of the Austrian empire. It is my duty to teach such enemies a lesson. You will not leave Venice, fräulein, until I give you permission to do so."

"And if I complain to the British consul?"

"We will be most apologetic. But adamant. You are needed for questioning." He smirked.

His plans worried me not one bit—it was mere bluster to frighten me. The more minutes passed the calmer I felt. Surely he had long enough to escape by now. He must be safe.

A sudden shouting dashed my hopes. Holger thrust me aside and rushed to the window. "There he is!" he muttered grimly, drawing his pistol. I ran to his side, fighting for the weapon, shrieking at him. But to no avail. Throwing me against the marble doorway, he carefully aimed the pistol at the swiftly moving gondola. Wisps of fog moved in and out, obscuring his vision. He swore, and I watched, stunned, praying for the mist to thicken. At that moment they moved into a clear spot, and Holger fired.

Luc's tall, strong body recoiled, and without warning slipped from the gondola and sank beneath the murky surface of the canal.

A screaming and wailing came from the doorway, and Maddelena rushed into the room, her apron thrown over her face as she howled in grief. Numbly

I stared out into the mist-shrouded canal, watched hopelessly as Giorgio circled round and round, searching for some trace of his compatriot. Minutes passed, minutes that seemed like hours, and finally he gave up and began rowing slowly away through the fog. Holger once more raised his pistol, but I knocked it away.

"Murderer! Haven't you killed enough for one morning?" I spat at him.

His cold blue eyes never leaving my face, he reholstered his gun. "My men will call for you this afternoon, fräulein. Be ready." And he strode out of the room issuing orders in a stentorian bellow that I would barely hear above Maddelena's weeping and wailing. I waited until they had left the palazzo, thankfully having never reached the cellars and their grisly occupant, and then I moved slowly to her side, feeling like an old, old woman.

"You will come to England with me, Maddelena. There is nothing for you here." Grief-stricken, she nodded, raising her head to look at me out of tear-streaming eyes.

"He loved you, signorina," she said slowly. "Yes, I will come with you."

Chapter Twenty-five

SEPTEMBER WAS A beautiful month in Somerset. The leaves were turning a lovely golden brown, the earth was warm, and the sun shone surprisingly often. During the long, miserable months of June, July, and August it had rained and rained. The gloom of the weather had matched Maddelena's and my mood, but as the September sun appeared more and more frequently our spirits lifted in spite of ourselves.

As I strolled carefully along the well-trod path behind my little cottage, with the ever-faithful Patrick stalking placidly behind me, I thought back over the last four and a half months and hoped devoutly that I would never have to suffer through such a time again. But then, how could I? The one man I would ever love had died; I couldn't imagine caring that much for anyone again, unless it was the child growing steadily within me. And I had vowed to myself to protect that little one with every breath I had in me. Nothing would ever come to harm him, and I had Maddelena's devoted assistance in that resolve. Mark's also, should I ever accept it. So far I hadn't.

I seldom met people during my long, solitary walks through the northern corner of Lord Bateman's lands. My little cottage was part of his property, rented to me in honor of my valiant efforts in the cause of Italian freedom and unity. Lord Batemen, an attractive old reprobate of some fifty-odd years, had always been a revolutionary, ever ready to support insurgents in any country but his own. During the last fifteen years he had concentrated his energies and considerable financial resources in the cause of Italy. It was he who had sent Mark to Italy and indirectly assisted in some of Luc's expeditions, and when I had first made inquiries about housing in Somerset, his lordship had quickly offered me his cottage at a nominal fee. Not that the fee had mattered. I had discovered, upon arriving back in England, that not only was my substantial fortune untouched by Luc's hands, but his own surprisingly healthy inheritance was mine also. For the first month I had done nothing but mourn with no company but Maddelena and the ever-serene Patrick. Neither had cared for the trip to England, crammed as they were in my stuffy stateroom, Maddelena suffering dreadfully from seasickness and Patrick from a hatred of confinement. Indeed, with two such miserable roommates I could scarcely wait for the journey to end.

The peace and fresh air of the country did wonders for the two of them long before I began to rouse myself from the stupor of pain and guilt Luc's death had thrust me into. But as I found what I had wanted so much coming true, I began to accept life once more. My first move was to have Luc's fortune put in trust for our child. Once that was taken care of I had retired to Lord Bateman's dower house, there to while away my confinement in as much contentment as I could command under the circumstances.

In the first few months I accepted the flattering invitations issuing from Bateman's Folly. Highly colored accounts of my heroism in trying to save Venice's most recent martyr, Luc del Zaglia, preceded each introduction, until I was ready to scream. The only sympathetic face there belonged to the great Italian patriot, Guiseppi Mazzini, who would look at me out of his sad, dark eyes and talk about flowers and children instead of the interminable babble of politics. I couldn't help being grateful to him, and it was his absence alone that I missed when my pregnancy began to show and I resolved to stay closer to home.

I seldom passed any of the villagers on this secluded path. If I happened to, they would nod and tip their hats to the poor, sad widow-lady, Mrs. Ferland, casting furtive glances at her feline companion. I looked down at the bloodstone ring on my finger. All the jewels that Maddelena rescued from Mildred and her cohorts had somehow found their way into my baggage, but I hadn't had the heart to touch any of the glittering diamonds, emeralds, and sapphires. The bloodstone ring was enough.

Had it been up to me I would never have accepted Mark's name, even on such a superficial basis. I would have borne Luc's child proudly. But between Mark and Maddelena's protestations I had come to accept that I should not put that burden on a helpless child. Between the two of them a bogus marriage with Mark's nonexistent brother was concocted, and no breath of scandal was attached to me as I spent my quiet, secluded summer days, even when my supposed brother-in-law took every possible excuse to visit me and see how I was doing.

Each visit was accompanied by fervent proposals of marriage, and as the time passed my resolve began to weaken. I loved Mark; I would be safe and happy with him. But I didn't love him enough, and I couldn't bring myself to give him less than he deserved.

My trailing black skirts caught in the fallen branches, and I yanked them free nervously, leaving Patrick to chase after the blowing leaves, forgetting his stateliness for a moment. I was still able to wear my old clothes. Maddelena had let them out a trifle in the waist, and no one as yet could tell I was four and a half months pregnant unless they looked closely. And so far no one had had that chance. Until today.

I was avoiding my latest problem. A simple missive arrived this morning from Lord Bateman. A hero of the Venetian conflict had arrived that weekend, fresh from Italy, and wished to pay his respects to Luc del Zaglia's ward. No doubt I would like to hear the latest word from that bedeviled city. His lordship's friend would be pleased to call upon me at four o'clock that afternoon.

Lord Bateman was very high-handed, I thought angrily. But then, I had come to expect that from him. It was time I turned back, time I made sure that Maddelena and Bitsy, the cheerful young woman brought in to help, had managed a creditable tea for this Italian gentleman. No doubt they had degenerated into one of their countless battles, and it would be up to me to brew the tea and supervise the setting of the tray. I was getting tired more easily as my child grew, and I wished in vain they would learn to get along. But Bitsy maintained that Maddelena was a witch and Maddelena maintained that Bitsy was an addlepated gossip. Both were right, but beside the point.

My doctor had ordered long walks to keep me fit. I was in perfect health, he said, and would no doubt bring forth a large, lusty baby with no difficulty whatsoever. I only hoped and prayed he was right, in the meantime doing absolutely everything he suggested with a religious fervor. I remembered Luc's face in the garden, when he had spoken of his wife's deliberate childlessness, and determined not to fail him in this.

It was a little past four by the time I arrived back at the lovely weathered stone cottage that had held Bateman dowagers since time immemorial. Bitsy was waiting for me, her eyes as large as saucers in her bovine face.

"Oh, madam, there's been such an upset. The old witch has taken to her bed with the vapors, and the gentleman's waiting for you in the garden. I said as I didn't know where in the world you were and perhaps he might come back another day, but he said he'd wait. "

Alarm burst within me. "I'd better go up and see Maddelena. Serve the gentleman tea and send him on his way, Bitsy. Tell him I'm unwell, that I appreciate his calling but that I'll have to see him another day."

"I don't think he'll listen, ma'am. I don't know as I dare to tell him you won't see him."

I made an impatient gesture. "What are you frightened of, you silly goose? He's not some ogre, is he?"

Bitsy sighed gustily. "Oh, no, ma'am. Mrs. Ferland, that is. He's ever so handsome."

That should have warned me, but worry for Maddelena and annoyance overruled my thinking processes. "Very well, I'll see the man. You go up and check on Maddelena and make sure she's all right."

"Me?" Bitsy squeaked. "She'll put the evil eye on me."

"I'll put the evil eye on you if you don't do as I say," I snapped. "Where's the tea tray?"

Bitsy pointed, and I grabbed it and stormed out into the garden, determined to rout my intruder in a few short sentences.

Patrick had prowled ahead of me and was now most unaccountably busy rubbing ecstatically against the stranger's black-clad leg. His back was to me as

I walked through the door. He was staring out over the rolling green hills, and I felt a start of pain so sharp it was almost physical. His back, the way he held his head, was so like Luc. I wondered if I would ever get over imagining his face in a crowd.

"I beg your pardon," I said nervously, and he turned around. The tea tray crashed to the flagstone terrace as I stared at my beloved's face. And then everything swam before me, and I nearly joined the broken crockery.

A moment later I was thrust gently but firmly into a chair with my head between my knees, a difficult feat considering the beginnings of my stomach. Thankfully Luc was unaware of that aspect of the situation. I could feel his hand at the back of my neck, rubbing the nape with a touch that almost made me swoon anew. After a few deep breaths I sat upright, my eyes meeting the amber gaze I thought never to see again in this life.

"You're not dead," I said foolishly. But then, there's not much witty or entertaining one can say in such a situation.

He smiled. "No, I am not dead."

"But Holger shot you. You drowned," I insisted dazedly.

A smile cracked his tanned face. "Captain von Wolfram had no way of knowing that I had been swimming in those canals since I could walk. The bullet lodged in my shoulder, and I was able to swim to one of the many underwater entrances along the Grand Canal. It was only fortunate that the tide was coming in." He looked down at me, an enigmatic expression in his golden eyes, just enough reserve to prevent me from throwing myself into his arms as I so longed to do. "You should not have worried, Charlotte. Like our friend Patrick, I have nine lives."

"You must have given up quite a few already," I replied breathlessly. Charlotte, he called me. He was obviously displeased with me. My heart sank.

"Perhaps." He moved away from me then, his eyes never leaving my face. "I have had a great deal of difficulty tracing you, my little ward. After you and your husband arrived in England you seemed suddenly to disappear. It was sheer chance that I met Lord Bateman in London and he happened to mention the widowed Mrs. Ferland who once was my ward. And still is, for that matter. When do you become twenty-one?"

I hadn't even thought of that aspect. "Within a year."

"And what happened to Ferland? I understand from your idiot of a maid that his brother is courting you, and an announcement is expected momentarily." There was a gentle question in his voice as he stood over me. I had forgotten how very tall he was. He had lost weight during the intervening months, and the added gauntness made him appear even taller. But for once he seemed neither demonic or frightening.

"Charlotte?" he said impatiently. "I asked what happened to Ferland?"

I pulled myself together. "I'm sorry. I . . . it's just that I have never seen you in the sunlight before." I kept expecting his lean, handsome face to crumble, his liquid eyes to dissolve, and his mobile mouth to decay before my eyes. He remained, resolutely alive and in one piece. "Mark . . . caught a fever. He died three months ago." The lie came off my tongue unbidden, and I folded my arms in front of my gently swelling stomach. I had no idea why he had come to see me, but I was determined to find out before he knew of the child I carried—if, in the face of his remoteness, I decided to tell him at all.

"And you are about to marry his brother?" The question was sharp and cold, his face unreadable as always.

"I . . . I had thought to," I lied, not liking his abrupt questions. "Have you seen Maddelena? Oh, but you must have."

He allowed a small smile to curve his lips. "Yes, I saw her. Not a coherent word did I get from her, just prayers and rejoicing and weeping and wailing. Did she carry on like that when she thought I was dead?"

"Yes." The idea of his death seemed to amuse him, and rage flared within me. "I, of course, danced in the streets after watching you drown."

His smile broadened. "Still the sweet-tongued little girl you always were, eh? Are you wondering why I came to see you?"

"The thought crossed my mind. I assume you want your money back. Not to mention the bag of family jewels you had Maddelena conceal in my trunk. I will instruct my lawyers to arrange the transfer of funds," I said coldly, wishing he were dead after all, rather than have my short remembrance of love destroyed. "It will take a while . . . I put it in a trust fund. But you should have it before long."

"I thank you," he said gravely. "But actually that is not why I came to see you."

"No?" My voice came out cold and hard, admirably hiding the fact that I was near tears.

"No, little one," he murmured, taking my hand and pulling me reluctantly to my feet. "You are not going to marry Ferland's brother. I am still your guardian, and I refuse to give you permission." From my numbed hand he drew off my wedding ring. "And you are not going to wear this anymore, either." He glanced down at it and frowned suddenly. "This is the ring I left with you." he said abruptly. "Why are you wearing it? Couldn't Ferland provide his own?"

I tried to snatch it away, but I was always helpless against Luc's superior strength. "Leave me alone," I shouted suddenly, unable to bear any more. I tried to pull away, but now he held both my wrists in his steely grip. "Please," I whimpered, those damned tears spilling over once more. "Go away."

"You will make Maddelena very unhappy," he said in a calm voice.

"You make me very unhappy," I stormed back.

"But I told her I had come to marry you. It set off a spasm of rejoicing that finally carried her off to her bed. What will she say when I tell her you refused me?"

"Refused you?" Now I was furious. "You haven't asked me. You've never asked me a thing, you've always told me, and tormented me, and teased me. And now, for reasons unknown to me, you decide to marry me. God knows what you've been doing for the past four and a half months—you certainly were too busy to let us know you were alive." I wondered whether Maddelena had divulged the secret of my pregnancy, but I didn't dare ask in case she hadn't. Instead I ranted and railed at him, inwardly begging him to tell me what I wanted and needed to hear.

"Venice was a little difficult to escape from with a price on my head and a bullet in my shoulder," he said stiffly. "And what about you? I had no desire to intrude on your honeymoon," he said furiously, his angry voice filling the garden. "I was scarcely cold in my grave before you danced off to marry that English idiot!"

"I did not! And besides, you told me to!"

"I thought I would be unlikely to survive. I assumed you knew better than to obey me," he shouted back. "You never obeyed me before! Did you, or did you not, marry Ferland?"

"Damn you, no! And I won't marry you either. I can't imagine why you'd want me. It can't be for my money—you've plenty of your own." I had to bite my lower lip to keep it from trembling.

He pulled me into his arms then, holding my body close against him so that my struggles were useless. Gradually they ceased. "No, *mia Carlotta*, it is not for your money, or your charming tongue and friendly ways." He pulled my head up with sudden force and kissed me, long and deep until I was shaking and breathless. "And it is not even for that, delightful as it is." He kissed me again, more gently this time, and I could feel my bones melting within me. "It is because, Carlotta Theresa Sabina, I love you and you love me. And despite my dangerous life and advanced age, I intend to live a long time, and I want to spend that time with you. If I didn't marry you I don't doubt you would run off with the first pair of broad shoulders you saw."

I gasped in protest, and he kissed me again. I was so blissfully happy I didn't care that he was squashing his son and heir. "And I intend to have many, many children by you," he continued, "and they will all grow up to be revolutionaries, sharp-tongued shrews, or vampires, depending on their talents."

I smiled up at him, clearly besotted, and the look in his golden eyes was all that I could have asked for and more. I put his hand on my swelling abdomen. "And what will this one be?" I asked shakily. "I think he will have to be a demon count."

For the first and last time in our lives I had truly taken him by surprise. And then his laugh rang out through the hills over Somerset. "A demon count he will be," he agreed, and pulled me back into his arms.

The End

The Demon Count's Daughter

With love, for Uncle A.

Chapter One

IT TOOK ME most of the evening to pack. My supposedly vanished impulsiveness stood me in good stead as I went through my wardrobe with ruthless abandon, choosing the dullest, plainest clothing I owned. I debated for a full minute over the moderate hoop that was de rigueur for a fashionable young English girl in 1864, remembering at last my modern, collapsible model, which would just fit into my one large carpetbag. I doubted I could manage to carry more than that on horseback, and horseback seemed the only way I could escape to the coast without dear Uncle Mark alerting the country-side. I had every intention of writing him a polite note, explaining it was my patriotic duty to follow my other godfather's quixotic suggestion and make straight for Venice, the city of my father's birth. The trip would take me no more than a week, I estimated, and by the time I reached Venice, Bones would have convinced Uncle Mark there was nothing to worry about, at the same time dispatching his guardian angel to see that I came to no harm.

I stared across the room to the full-length mirror, the wavering candle-light giving my flamboyant looks a warm, melting sheen they usually lacked. It was fortunate that Bones had started the whole thing by suggesting I travel to strife-torn Italy. I would have an extremely difficult time trying to sneak there in disguise. There are very few women of my proportions wandering around Europe.

I could have wished my resemblance to my beloved parents a little less pronounced. From my father I inherited raven black hair that was thick and unruly and always managed to escape even the most severe pinnings. My eyes were golden like his, but undeniably warmer with what I have been told is a sweetness of expression to equal my mother's. I had her retroussé nose, rather than Father's Roman one, and her full, red lips. If I hadn't been cursed with such an extraordinary body, I would have been quite pretty.

But there fate and family resemblance had let me down. From my father I had been bequeathed a generosity of height that left me towering over every man I had ever met, with the exception of my father, my older brother, and a one or two foppish young men I had met last year in London.

From my mother I had inherited curves so voluptuous as to be down-right embarrassing. As the years passed and I began to ripen, I sought desper-ately to try to tone down my overly feminine attributes. But all the running, jumping, climbing, and horseback riding only served to develop me more fully, so that I had no choice but to become accustomed to the wide-eyed astonishment my first appearance elicited. Men's eyes usually glazed over when introduced. Looking up into my eyes, their second reaction was either a stiff invitation to dance or a quick tussle in the garden. It was no wonder I had barely lasted a month in my disaster of a season. It was my own secret sorrow that I had longed for some man of a different sort to carry me away from all that superficial glitter. But such a man didn't seem to exist. At least I hadn't met him in twenty-three years.

All in all I was hardly the type to blend into a background, and I could only hope I would be able to accomplish Bones's mission while appearing to be a simpering tourist. If not, well, I needed an adventure, and a trip to Venice and the long-deserted family palazzo would be adventure enough in itself, even if it failed to include midnight meetings and secret information.

I paused momentarily in my hasty packing and thought back to Lord Bateman's startling proposition this afternoon.

"I need you to go to Venice," Bones had announced with his usual startling abruptness, the china teacup trembling only faintly in his aged, cadaverous hands. "There's no one else who's so admirably suited for the job, or you know I wouldn't ask. Your parents aren't around to hold you back, and you're just wasting your time moping around. It's time you did something."

"I'm willing, Bones," I answered mildly enough, accustomed to my godfather's excitability and impulsiveness. "To what job am I admirably suited?"

He barely hesitated. "My dear Luciana, I shouldn't ask it of you. But I do ask it, because I know you and trust you. The political climate of Europe right now is like a tinderbox. Austria is just about ready to hand Venice over to France in exchange for various political amenities. My sources tell me that once that happens it's only a matter of time before Napoleon III cedes it back to Italy."

"But that's splendid!" I breathed, eyes aglow.

"Yes, and no. It is indeed splendid if all works out," he harrumphed. "Unfortunately, there have been a few obstacles thrown in the path of independence for La Serenissima. That's where I need your help.

"The powers that be in Venice do not fancy losing their somewhat tarnished jewel of a city. Therefore General Eisenhopf and Colonel von Wolfram have managed to obtain a certain very incriminating document. If that document were to be published, all our hopes would be dashed."

"What document?" I brushed the crumbs from my drab riding habit.

"A foolhardy document, fully authenticated, stating France's intention of attacking Austria once they have regained possession of Venice. Using that well-situated city and the Veneto as a base of operations. A stupid piece of business that Napoleon III rashly concocted a number of years ago, a plan he has no intention whatsoever of carrying out. But, needless to say, all Franz

Josef needs is a hint of such a thing and years of careful diplomacy will have been wasted. Europe is about to explode; we must move very, very carefully."

"But why haven't these two Austrians produced this paper?"

"They are too busy bargaining. Neither Eisenhopf nor Von Wolfram have decided which they'd prefer: money or power. The price they're asking is far too high, anyway."

"But what can I do, Bones?" I cried. "Of what possible use could I be?"

Bones leaned back in his chair, a crafty smile playing around his withered lips. "Eisenhopf has one major weakness, and that is for women, particularly tall young women with abundant physical charms. In other words, someone like you."

"And you want me to seduce this old general into giving me the paper?" I jumped ahead, a little surprised. Lord Bateman was an unconventional godfather, but this was a little extreme ever for him.

Bones looked shocked. "Good God, no! You would never even come near the man. You will merely sneak into his room in the guise of a lady of the night while he's safely out of the city. And while you are there you'll retrieve the paper, hand it over to our informant, and return to England, secure in the knowledge that you have saved Venice."

"It sounds simple," I said, trying to control the fire of excitement that was sweeping over me. "But how am I to manage all this? Gain admittance to his room, among other things?"

"All that will be taken care of. The general's valet is a very stubborn, pro-Austrian creature. Fortunately his brother-in-law is a different sort entirely. It was Tonetti himself who came up with the idea, approaching our best man with it. You'd be working with him, Luciana, though of course I'd have a guardian angel watching over you."

"And what makes you think we can trust this Tonetti?" I questioned warily.

"The best of all reasons. Money."

"But haven't you countless trained women who'd be better able to do the job?" I felt compelled to ask, though I knew deep inside that I would strangle anyone who tried to go in my place.

"No doubt. But none of them are del Zaglias." He leaned forward and clutched my hand with the intensity of a fanatic. "Venice has suffered under the Austrian yoke for so long the people are becoming dull and sullen. Even the *dimostrazione,* which has kept social intercourse and the upper classes out of Venice, has begun to lose momentum. You, my dear, would put new life into the movement." He sighed. "The beautiful daughter of one of Venice's bravest sons, returned to save that gallant, beleaguered city . . ." A grim smile lit his aged face. "What with your ancestry and the general's penchant for large and beautiful young ladies, we could scarcely do better."

A little flattery only added fuel to my eagerness, and there I was, five hours later, furtively packing my bags.

My beloved parents and six brothers were off in Scotland, leaving me in the care of various young and old retainers and the myopic supervision of my second godfather, the very correct, somewhat fumbling Mark Ferland. I hadn't needed Bones's warning not to tell Uncle Mark. I knew from long association that Bones's former agent looked back on all that derring-do with embarrassed dismay.

"Miss Luciana, what are you doing in there?" A querulous voice sounded at the door, and I thanked heaven I had had the foresight to lock it. Maggie had the sharpest eyes and the quickest tongue of anyone I had ever known, and ever since my mother had made her my personal maid and companion, nothing in my life remained private. I had no intention, however, of taking her to Edentide if I could help it. For one thing, her curiosity would be bound to interfere with my meetings with the mysterious and romantic-sounding Tonetti, and for another, she had a roving eye to equal the worst rakehell, and I had no doubt that the combination of her randiness and the Italian male would end in a brouhaha I could well do without. Besides, I was jealous.

"Not a thing, Maggie," I yawned convincingly. "I was tired from my ride over to Lord Bateman's and thought I'd get an early night's sleep." I bounced a few times on the bed for effect. "You may have the rest of the evening off," I added grandly.

"Oh, indeed?" Her voice was wry, and it was all I could do to remember that she was two years younger and a head shorter than me. "And why have you locked your door, tell me that?"

"Did I?" I murmured vaguely. "It must have been an accident. You know how these old doors are. Never you mind, Maggie. I'm too tired to get up and unlock it. I won't need anything more tonight. Why don't you go and visit Bitsy?"

"I have better things to do than spend my evenings with my mother," she replied pertly. "But I don't like the sound of you, Miss Luciana. You never tire so easily. Are you sure you're not coming down with something?"

I laughed with what I hoped was suitable heartiness. "I'm as strong as a horse, Maggie. It must have been too much sun."

"Very well, miss. I can't say as I wouldn't appreciate an evening off. That William has been at me something awful . . ." Her voice trailed away as she wandered down the hall, and I breathed a sigh of relief. Maggie was much too sharp by half, and even if I hid all the evidence of my intended flight, I doubted I could deceive her eagle eye.

I slept fitfully that night, tossing and turning and wrapping my long limbs in the linen sheets so that I felt as if I were in my winding sheet. First light found me wide awake and alert. I had never needed more than a very few hours of sleep. Dressing quietly, I slipped out my door and down the deserted hallways on silent feet, smugly aware that Maggie had failed to hear me from her adjoining closet. Of course there was no guarantee that she had actually slept in her own bed that night. Chances were she hadn't.

But my luck held all the way out to the stables. The only servant awake and moving around was a young groom of no more than thirteen, who sleepily saddled my younger brother's mare, accepted my notes for Maggie and Uncle Mark, and watched me ride off into the brilliant dawn with an incurious yawn on his young face.

I MADE EXCELLENT time that first day despite my concern not to overtire poor old Marigold, my ancient, but stately, mare. When night fell my first concern was to see to her well-being, and I conscientiously provided her with a good crop of grass to eat. As for me, I did equally well with the remains of a loaf of bread and a huge chunk of cheese stolen from the kitchens on my way out of the house and slept the darkness away quite comfortably under a hedge with my serviceable brown wool cape wrapped snugly around me to protect me from the chill of an August night in England.

By the next afternoon we were in Bournemouth, both of us rather the worse for wear, but our spirits intact. Marigold, after having been relegated to a boring life as a child's palfrey, was enjoying her sights of the wide world, though I didn't doubt she would retire gratefully back to pasture once her adventure was over. Indeed, she greeted her stall that evening with a whinny of tired pleasure, settling in with a sigh.

As luck would have it the Channel packet wouldn't leave till the next morning, and there was nothing I could do but take a room at the cleanest-looking waterfront inn I could find. And it was there they found me, tucking into a massive meal of pheasant, lobster, ale, and greens.

"Ahem." A loud throat-clearing broke through my food-clouded reverie, and I looked up with a sinking feeling to meet the stern blue eyes of my other godfather, Mark Ferland. Standing by his side, her pert face set in an abnormally grim expression of profound disapproval, was Maggie.

I swallowed, once, twice, determined to regain my aplomb. I smiled up sweetly as the pheasant made its way down my throat and signaled the waiter for more plates. "Uncle Mark! Maggie! What a lovely surprise! Are you planning to accompany me to Venice?"

My bright innocence stopped Uncle Mark for a moment, but Maggie was undeterred. "No, we aren't, Miss Luciana, and well you know it. We've come to take you back to Somerset, and no more of your tricks."

I surveyed my maid for a moment, my mind working feverishly while, with my usual amazement, I took in her far from prepossessing appearance.

Maggie Johnston was a cheerfully well-endowed girl of twenty-one with a pert little nose and a sharp tongue, copper curls twisted up on her small head, a rosy complexion flushed with annoyance. Her weakness for pretty clothes was apparent in the fanciness of her blue-sprigged traveling dress, and I knew half her irritation was for the dust on her elegant toilette. I smiled up at her beguilingly. Next to my mother and our ancient Maddelena, she was the woman I loved most in this world.

"Oh, for heaven's sake, sit down and stop glowering at me, Maggie," I exclaimed, pushing a chair out for her. "You, too, Uncle Mark. You're wrecking my appetite with your sour faces."

Maggie's glower abated only a trifle as she seated herself with ladylike grace. Uncle Mark, as usual, took his cue from the strongest personality present. His troubled eyes moved from Maggie back to me with vague concern.

"Now see here, Luciana," he began pompously, knowing full well how foolish he sounded. "As your godfather and the only man around who can stand in *loco parentis*, I must insist that you return with us immediately. When Bones told me you'd gone racing off I couldn't believe my ears. It's just not done, Luciana, my dear, and you know that as well as I do."

I leaned back and stared at them, a mutinous expression settling around my mouth. "There is little that angers me, Uncle Mark, but the one thing I detest is being told what is and isn't done," I said in firm voice. "It *is* done, because I have just done it. And if you intend to try to take me back home, you had best be prepared to use physical force. I won't leave without kicking and screaming and telling everyone you are white slavers bent on abducting me."

"Luciana!" Mark pleaded helplessly. "What would your father say?"

"He'd be very amused," I replied, not at all sure I was right. My father had a severe streak underneath his cynical lenience, a streak I had crossed, to my sorrow.

"We could always drug your wine, Miss Luciana," Maggie suggested pleasantly.

I grinned. "Are you sure you have no Italian blood, Maggie? I'm glad to be forewarned; I'll make sure I drink nothing that has passed your fair hands."

"For God's sake, Luciana, you can't be meaning to pursue this mad course!" Uncle Mark interrupted, running a harassed hand through his thinning brown hair. "Bones told me about your mission—it's not the child's play you seem to think. This man could be dangerous—there's no way you could be protected all the time. Isn't there some way we could dissuade you?"

There was, but neither of them was imaginative enough to threaten writing my father. The thought of his traveling to Venice to retrieve me would have put a swift end to Bones's wild scheme, but I counted on their knowing, if they had thought of such a possibility, that it would sign Luc del Zaglia's death warrant. The Imperial Army of Austria had a very long memory. "There is no way you could dissuade me," I said firmly. "You could always accompany me, of course."

I was fairly certain that Uncle Mark was Bones's hand-picked guardian angel, and I had little doubt he would succumb rather than let me go off on my own. Maggie was a question mark however.

My two pursuers shared a glance. Mark shrugged first. "It seems I have little choice, Luciana. As a gentleman and your godfather I could hardly watch you run off to that hotbed of espionage and insurrection without at least offering my protection."

I smiled my gratitude, breathing a sigh of relief. "And you, Maggie?"

She shrugged her plump shoulders in the stylish dress. "That William isn't half the man I'd hoped he'd be. Perhaps I might do better with a foreigner. Your father is a fine figure of a man, Miss Luciana. If any of them Eye-talians come close I'd be a happy woman."

"Take it from me, my girl," Uncle Mark said morosely, dwelling on ancient injuries, "there's no one like Luc del Zaglia." He refilled our wine glasses, then held up his glass in a toast. "To Venice, ladies! And let us pray I'm not making the worst mistake in a mistake-strewn life."

I lifted my glass, looking him squarely in the eye. "To Venice," I echoed. "To a free Venice and an end to Austrian tyranny!"

"To Venice," Maggie said dreamily, "and love."

I hesitated, but only for a moment. It was long past time to toss my bonnet over the windmill. I laughed aloud. "To Venice," I echoed, "and love."

Chapter Two

THE TRAIN BEGAN its way along the long Austrian-built causeway as we started on our last lap of the hurried, exhausting trip to the fabled city of Venice. I peered out through the soot-stained windows, eager for my first glimpse of the place that had meant more to me than the land of my birth, but in the late summer's twilight I could barely see the domed skyline in the distance.

"We're almost there." I turned to my companions. Maggie had her face pressed against the window while Uncle Mark nodded wearily and buried his nose once more in the paper. "Aren't you excited, Uncle Mark?" I demanded sternly. "We've finally reached our destination."

He put the paper down and sighed. "I must say I'm glad all our traveling is over. Though I'd be much happier if you saw reason and returned on the next train." He shook the paper into neat folds. "And no, I am not excited to be in Venice once more. My memories of the place are not my fondest."

"Why not? You met Mama there." I am a bit inquisitive, and at times lacking in tact.

"Because, Miss Busybody, I also met your dear father there, who proceeded to steal your mother away from me."

I had known all this for years, but never failed to be fascinated by it. "Pish, tush," I dismissed his complaints heartlessly. "Mama and Father were made for each other. You should have known that."

"Nevertheless," he announced with injured dignity, "I have never taken a bride."

I reached out and patted his hand, chagrined at my unsympathetic tone. "That is indeed a great shame, Uncle Mark, for all the women of the world." He cast a suspicious look at me out of his nearsighted eyes, but I spoke in all seriousness. "If it's any consolation to you, you've been my parents' best and dearest friend."

He sighed, a sound halfway between complacency and despair. "Yes, it's true," he said heavily. "It's probably just as well I never married. It wouldn't have been fair to give a lady only half a heart."

A small, strange noise came from Maggie, one I recognized as a snort, and I cast her a severe glance. I found my Uncle Mark's posturings as a heartbroken swain infinitely touching despite the fact he was, without a doubt, a born bachelor uncle.

"Best put your hat on, Miss Luciana," Maggie announced after an emotional pause. "And fix your hair. You do look a sight."

I rose and peered into the velvet-framed mirror the Austrian engineers had thoughtfully provided the first-class passengers on this most modern of railway cars. Black hair was straggling over my green-clad shoulders, my sooty lashes added to the circles around my large topaz eyes, and my narrow face was pale with fatigue. Incompetently, I stuffed my hair back into the loose coil I usually wore, pulled on my far-from-fashionable bonnet, and, as an afterthought, stuck my tongue out at both my reflection and my disapproving maid.

"I scarcely do you credit, Maggie," I noted, watching her as she stuffed filmy scarves, French novels, and half-eaten chocolates into one of the bandboxes she had brought along.

She cast a disparaging glance over my attire and sighed gustily. "I've long ago given up on making a fashion plate of you, Miss Luciana. I'm waiting till you fall in love. *Then* you might take some interest in your appearance."

"You may have to wait awhile," I warned her, striding nervously around our small, private compartment as the train began pulling to a stop.

"I've waited long enough already," she said sternly, primping in the mirror. "If you'd only . . ."

"Oh, please, Maggie, don't scold," I begged, practically dancing with excitement. "I want this moment to be perfect."

She sighed again, and Uncle Mark smiled benevolently. "Well, missy, I believe we've arrived. Would you like to be the first one out? To get your view of the city alone?"

I leaned down and gave him an exuberant kiss. "You know me so well, Uncle Mark. Bless you." With a shrieking of steam, grinding of gears, and clanking of metal, the great engine finally ended its seemingly endless journey. Within a few moments more our door was opened and the steps lowered. With my heart pounding beneath my stiff green traveling gown, I put my gloved hand on the sooty railing and stepped down onto Venetian soil for the first time in my life.

My first sight of Venice was as astounding as I had expected it to be, though the subject matter I focused on with my excellent eyesight was far from what I had anticipated. Watching me from halfway across the crowded, dimly lit station was the most extraordinary man I had ever seen.

He towered over the Italians around him, even topping most of the much taller Austrian soldiers that milled aimlessly about the station. His hair was dark gold and cut long in that style that looks natural rather than contrived. His nose was straight, his mouth beautifully formed, his expression unreadable at that distance. But I knew with a certainty he watched me as I watched him, as I looked into the most beautiful silver-blue eyes I had ever seen. Never had I seen a man more handsome, with the possible exception of my father. And then he turned slightly, and I saw the scar.

Cut into one side of his magnificent face, starting up in the hairline and ending just above his strong jaw, was a fine, white line, marring his perfect beauty, yet somehow enhancing it. That one terrible imperfection mocking his handsome face and turning it into something far beyond mere good looks. A gusty sigh escaped me.

"'oos that, Miss Luciana?" Maggie cooed in my ear, her eyes bright at the sight of an attractive male.

I stifled the jealousy that swept over me. "Isn't he the most handsome man you have ever seen?" I whispered.

She looked at me in amazement. "No," she said bluntly. "He's not half bad, but I would hardly say *the* most handsome. In the top fifty, perhaps . . ." she allowed cautiously, peering at him.

Shaking my head, I closed my eyes and sighed. "*The* most handsome, Maggie. Without question."

"What's all this?" Uncle Mark demanded, climbing from the railway carriage and unceremoniously pushing Maggie out of the way. "What's going on with you two?"

"Miss Luciana's fallen in love," Maggie announced, and I kicked her.

"Uncle Mark, who is that man?" I questioned urgently. "He must be British . . . no other race could look quite so arrogant."

"Which man, m'dear?" he murmured, casting myopic eyes out over the crowd.

"Why, over there . . ." I looked again, and to my disproportionate sorrow I found that he had disappeared. "He's gone," I said flatly.

Maggie looked up from nursing her wounded leg, and the look in her hazel eyes was sympathetic. "Don't you worry, miss. You'll see him again. If it's meant to be."

I shook my head nervously, as if to deny my reaction to myself and to her. "Why, whatever do you mean? I'm sure you're making a mountain out of a molehill. He was just a very handsome man, that's all. I would hardly be human not to notice."

"That's all well and good, miss. But you've never noticed before." She held up a thin, work-worn hand to hold off my protest. "Never you mind. I'll say no more on the matter. Not now, leastways."

"Seen an attractive fellow, eh, Luciana?" Uncle Mark boomed, still a few minutes in the past. "Well, chances are you'll meet him soon enough. Society, that is, English society, moves in very close circles in these foreign cities. Bound to come across the fellow sooner or later. Unless he's entirely ineligible, that is."

"For God's sake!" I swore, desperate. "The two of you are practically marrying me off, and I've never even spoken to the man. I wish you would just . . ."

"Yes, Fraulein?" A guttural German voice spoke from behind me, and I whirled around nervously.

My first sight of the hated Austrian army was fairly prepossessing. The young man in front of me could scarcely have been much older than I. We were of the same height, yet somehow his cold blue eyes seemed to look down on me with a sneer I found distinctly irritating.

"The Fraulein has yet to go through customs," he said stiffly. "If you will be so kind . . . He gestured to his left, and with dismay I saw a long line of my fellow passengers, their luggage pawed through, their faces set in angry expressions of rage and exhaustion. "We have been having a bit of trouble with a small band of insurgents," the man continued blandly, "making it necessary to search all visitors' luggage for contraband. I am sure the Fraulein will be more than happy to assist the Austrian army in their duty."

"Now see here, Captain!" Uncle Mark blustered, and I quickly shushed him. There was obviously no help for it. I gave him a polite nod accompanied by the merest trace of a smile. "Of course, Captain." I headed off in the direction of the disgruntled line, and once more his hand came down on my silk-clad arm. I halted, looking pointedly at the offending member until he removed it.

"We have a special place for you, Fraulein del Zaglia," he said heavily, and at the mention of my name my backbone stiffened in alarm. "Your companions may join the others, but we are determined to give you a better-than-average welcome. It is not often one of the ancient Venetian families chooses to return to their water-drenched city. The Imperial Army is very interested in your reason for doing so and most concerned as to whether we can expect the joy of your father's presence before too long, eh?" He smiled, revealing so many white, shining teeth I was quite revolted.

"My father has no intention of returning to Venice," I replied stiffly. "Not until the invaders have left."

My captor glowered, his heavy hand descending once more. Against my will I felt myself being forced toward a dark and sinister-looking doorway, and I bit back the temptation to scream for help. Screaming would do no good . . . the Austrians were in charge here. They would be far more likely to assist the brute by my side. And all poor Uncle Mark and Maggie could do was stare at us helplessly.

"Telfmann!" A voice broke through my red haze of anger, and the hand released me immediately.

"Sir!" He saluted smartly, and I followed his gaze.

The officer who had accosted us was somewhere near middle age. He could have been anywhere from forty to sixty, with closely cropped blond-gray hair, cold, cold blue eyes, and a hard expression on his handsome, slightly bovine face.

"You will leave Fraulein del Zaglia to me," he said softly, menacingly in

German. Thanks to my educated mother, I could understand every word. "I gave you orders that she was to be brought to me with the minimum of fuss, and I see you struggling all over the station with her. You have been inept, Telfmann."

"But sir," he protested, "how was I to know she was a bad-tempered giantess?"

I snorted indelicately, and the cold blue eyes met mine for a brief moment. I was not reassured.

"The Fraulein, like her mother, obviously understands German. You may leave us, Telfmann. I will deal with you later."

The younger man left quickly, protesting angrily in a muttered undertone, as I turned to face his replacement.

Having let my guard slip momentarily, I was anxious to regain lost ground. I put out one hand and gave him my most enchanting smile, reserved for Austrian pigs. "If you knew my mother then you must be Holger von Wolfram!" I cried ingenuously. "Mother has told me all about you." And Bones, too, I added silently, recognizing him as my enemy.

There was no change in his hard expression. "No doubt," he replied caustically. "And your father also, *hein*?" He cast a questioning glance back at the curious figures of Maggie and Uncle Mark, and even from a distance I could see Maggie's instinctive preen. Holger von Wolfram was far from unattractive, and Maggie, English as she was, lacked my instinctive hatred for the Austrians.

"That is my maid and companion, Maggie Johnston," I offered brightly. "She's accompanying me on my small version of the grand tour. I decided when I reached France that I simply couldn't return home without visiting the family seat in Venice." I gestured toward Uncle Mark's stooped figure. "And you remember my godfather, Mark Ferland?"

"I am acquainted with Mr. Ferland," he said dryly. "And that is your reason for being here, Fraulein? To visit your heritage?"

I let out a light trill of laughter. "But of course! Why else should I venture alone to such an insalubrious place? No doubt my parents would disapprove heartily, but I failed to notify them of my intentions." I smoothed my bottle-green skirt, peeking up at the soldier with what I hoped was demure charm. "I'm sure I'll receive a great scold when I return."

"Your parents do not know you are here?" he demanded, an expression of disgust crossing his stolid face. "Bah, you are just like your mother! No doubt"—and here he smiled evilly—"your father, when he hears what you have done, will come and fetch you home again?"

And how you'd like that, I thought. "Oh, no. I expect to be back long before he even finds out I've gone. And they'll trust Mr. Ferland to take good care of me should I be delayed."

"You expect your business to be concluded so quickly, then?"

"Business?" I echoed innocently, enjoying this verbal fencing. My mother, in her tales of Venice, had failed to mention how very acute the good colonel could be. "What do you mean?"

He smiled. "Why, your pilgrimage to your ancestral home, of course. What else could I possibly mean?" He cleared his throat loudly, and I jumped. "Though I must warn you, Fraulein, that Venice is a dangerous place for people here on less innocent . . . business." There was a slight emphasis on the last word, and I barely controlled a shiver of dismay.

"I have no intention of doing anything more dangerous than sightseeing," I replied brightly, hiding my uneasiness like a practiced spy. "Really, Colonel, you sound like something out of Byron . . . full of dark deeds. Do you think someone will stab me and drop me in the canal?"

He bowed over my hand with mock gallantry. "It could be arranged, Fraulein. If necessary. *Auf Wiedersehen.*"

It took me only a moment to recover from the threat. "Goodbye, Colonel. Perhaps we will see you again before we go."

"Have no doubt of it, Fraulein."

"Are you all right, Luciana?" Uncle Mark demanded as I finally reached his side. "Who was that fellow?"

"Do you remember Holger von Wolfram, uncle?" I questioned, and was not at all reassured to see the ruddy color drain from his face.

"Couldn't likely forget him. He nearly murdered your father, Luciana. He's a dangerous man, through and through. I advise you to keep clear of him." He paused, a puzzled look on his distinguished face. "Can't understand why he's still in Venice. He always hated the place. When I knew him twenty-five years ago he seemed a man destined to rise to the heights of his profession. Could have gone anywhere. Very strange."

"Well, I thought he seemed very attractive," Maggie announced obstinately. "In a fierce, angry sort of way. He seemed quite taken with you, Miss Luciana. If you're not interested I might try my hand there. It might be a treat to have an older man for a change."

"If you dare," I said angrily, "even think about consorting with the enemy, Maggie Johnston, I will personally see that you are strangled and dropped in the Grand Canal. That was how the Council of Three used to get rid of their enemies, you know." I tugged uselessly at the ill-fitting jacket. I was still shaken from my unexpectedly sudden encounter, and surreptitiously I cast my eyes around the crowded train station. If Tonetti was there, I could not tell. I would simply have to wait for him to make himself known to me.

Maggie was about to answer pertly when she recognized the abstracted expression in my usually mild eyes. "I'm only funning, Miss Luciana. You wouldn't think I'd actually lower myself to waste my time on an Austrian, would you? I doubt I'll have time to get through the Venetians." She chuckled, and reluctantly I smiled.

"Let's go home. Let's change our clothes, have some tea, and get to bed."

"I'd love to, Miss Luciana," she replied. "But where would 'home' be?"

"Why, Edentide, of course," I replied.

Chapter Three

AT ALL EVENTS, we didn't arrive at Edentide until early the next afternoon. "Dash it, no one's been in the place in years, with the exception of a few old retainers at infrequent intervals," Uncle Mark protested as we glided down the moonlit Grand Canal. I watched the silvery water float by us almost in a trance, forgetting for a moment why I was here in the enchantment of the August night. Uncle Mark pulled at his sparse and graying mustache, determined to hold my attention. "The place should be infested with rats. Best wait until we can send a few people in there to clean it up."

"But I can't afford to wait," I said stubbornly, pulling myself out of my moon-clouded dreams with an effort. "The sooner I take up residence, the sooner this Tonetti can contact me and I can set about Bones's business. Maggie and I are perfectly capable of doing a hard day's work. We can scrub and clean enough rooms to live in in no time at all."

"I must say I don't like the sound of this Tonetti fellow. Anyone who'd help land a lady in a compromising position can be no gentleman."

"Oh, I have no doubt he's not a gentleman," I said cheerfully. "I'm hoping he's a rake and bears a striking resemblance to the man I saw in the train station tonight."

"Von Wolfram?"

"No!" I shrieked.

"Telfmann?" Maggie questioned, but I could tell from the sly expression in her eyes she knew perfectly well who I meant.

"No," I repeated in a milder tone of voice. "But it doesn't matter what he looks like, as long as we're able to do what I came here for. And you're not to interfere, either of you," I added warningly, placing no reliance on their agreement.

"How can you expect me not to interfere?" he demanded irritably. "You're putting your head in a noose, and it's my unfortunate duty to protect you."

"You can protect me," I allowed him graciously, "but you can't interfere, or I'll have you carted back to England by one of Bones's henchmen."

"You couldn't!" he harrumphed.

"Oh, yes, she could," Maggie informed him grimly, recognizing the determined expression on my face. "Best leave her to handle it as she thinks best. In the meantime we have more important problems to deal with."

"And what problems are those?" I demanded.

She sniffed at my disavowal of the obvious. "Why, to find out who that devastating fellow was, to meet him again, and to do something about your wretched wardrobe. *I* wouldn't be caught dead in things you wear."

Normally I ignored Maggie's constant complaints, but for some reason tonight they struck a responsive chord. Perhaps it was the mood of the magic city, the wide expanse of the Grand Canal stretching out around us. Perhaps I had just reached the age to be interested in men. Or perhaps it was that man.

"May I suggest," Uncle Mark interrupted dryly, having recovered his equilibrium, "that we continue this discussion later? And that in the meantime we have this villainous-looking gondolier head for the nearest hotel catering to *English* travelers and plan what we shall do next. I know"—he held up a restraining hand at my bubbling protest—"you want to go directly to Edentide. No doubt we shall pass it on the way. If you do insist on cleaning the old wreck yourself, I will do all I can to assist you. But after a week of traveling I think we all deserve a good night's sleep on clean linen in a rat-free bedroom. Do you not agree?"

"You promise to let us go to Edentide tomorrow?" I demanded suspiciously.

"I most solemnly swear," he pledged, holding up his right hand in a theatrical gesture.

"In that case, an *English* hotel," I mimicked him, "would be most welcome."

NO SOONER HAD I reached my small, clean, English bedroom than I fell into a long, exhausted sleep, which was only slightly troubled by dreams. Dreams of the mysterious and romantic Venetian spy, Tonetti, who bore a startling resemblance to the scarred Englishman.

It wasn't until midmorning that I awoke, sunlight streaming in my hotel windows. Still in a stupor of sleep, I stumbled to answer the incessant knocking at my door and in a daze received an armful of flowers from a smirking chambermaid.

By the time I tipped her and locked the door behind her inquisitive figure, I was wide awake. It took me only a moment to find the note amid the fragrant mimosa blossoms, only another few seconds to scan the scrawled and ill-spelled message.

"Sweet Goddess," it began, "I saw you last night and gave to you my heart. Only say I might dare to hope. A brief glimpse of you is all I crave. I will be at the Merceria this morning by the perfume stalls. One small glance is all I ask, my precious pigeon. I live only for that moment. Your devoted slave, Enrico Addonizio Valentino Tonetti."

The scent wafting from the paper assured me that my admirer had already spent far too much time by the perfume stalls. I hesitated for only a moment. I ordered a brief meal and gobbled it in two minutes flat. Then I wasted another half hour pawing through my meager wardrobe, looking in vain for something the slightest bit flattering. Everything was either a muddy brown or a dull, bottle green, four years out of date, and more suited to a governess than a del Zaglia. I had always been bored with clothes and the tediousness of being fitted and pinned and poked, and the result was a very depressing wardrobe. It was a little past ten when I hammered on Maggie's door, bursting into her room with an excited good morning.

She eyed me from beneath the covers, a sour expression on her face. "What time is it?" she muttered suspiciously.

"Incredibly late, my girl. Past ten!" I threw open the shutters and stared out at the canal below me, my nostrils taking in the strong reek of sea water and garbage as it floated by.

"Miss Luciana," Maggie began in a dangerous tone of voice, tossing back the light covers, "we didn't arrive in Venice until past nine last night. We didn't reach our rooms at this bleedin' hotel until after midnight, and we've been traveling hell-bent for the past week, during which I've not had a decent night's sleep the entire time. And you have the bloody nerve to come bouncing in here when I've just begun to catch up on me beauty rest . . ."

"Botheration!" I dismissed her complaints cheerfully. "Just look out at this beautiful city and tell me that you want to sleep some more!"

With great dignity and bedclothes trailing, she stalked to the window, stuck her curl-papered head out, withdrew it, and stalked back to the bed. "Yes!" she said succinctly, sitting down with a plop.

"With all those so very handsome Venetian men wandering around down there? And me with shopping to do, and no one to come with me and help me deal with them all?" I questioned mournfully.

In a twinkling the bedclothes were on the floor, followed by Maggie's nightgown, curl papers, and chin strap. Another couple of minutes had her turned out in great style in a cherry-red striped gown, which made me appear the gangling servant, towering as I did behind her in my sober green dress.

"And what shopping have we to do?" she demanded, pulling her reticule over one heavy-boned wrist. Despite my length my bones were delicately shaped, preserving me from looking too much a freak, and every now and then I thanked providence for that small mercy.

"Cleaning supplies, food, etc. The Merceria should be the place for all that. And I thought . . ." I let it trail off in sudden embarrassment.

"Yes?" she demanded, casting a knowing eye at my blushes.

"I thought we . . . we might visit a dressmaker. I've heard a great deal about the Venetian dressmakers," I excused it lamely.

"Absolutely not!" she said stoutly, striding out into the hallway. "We will buy some lengths of cloth, and I will make some dresses for you. These

Eye-talians cannot be trusted when it comes to the dressing of an English lady."

"But I'm half Italian," I argued. "And besides, I thought you fancied the Venetian men."

"I do, indeed. But what's good enough for me doesn't come close to being good enough for you, Miss Luciana. We might buy you some Venetian lace," she allowed generously. "But you'll leave it to me to make it up."

MAGGIE, WHEN SHE got the bit between her teeth, was not to be moved, and indeed, in this case, I was just as happy to let her have her way. Having an eye for clothes and limited means, she'd learned to take a natural talent for the needle and turn it into an art, making some of my mother's most elegant dresses, and I had only to exercise the mildest of restraints as we pored over the bolts and bolts of rich fabric.

"I absolutely won't wear pink," I said firmly, dismissing a pastel silk an eager merchant in the Merceria thrust forward for my maid's exacting eye. The scent stalls were not far away, and I scanned them eagerly, hoping to recognize my partner in crime. I turned back to Maggie after a moment, none the wiser. "I need something more subdued." I shifted the huge bundle of soaps and rags that we'd bought earlier, trying to make my point.

"All your life you've worn subdued clothing, Miss Luciana, and where has it got you? It's time for something more daring. That's it!" She pounced on a length of deep rose, holding it aloft with a cry of triumph.

"That's still pink," I said mutinously, won over despite myself by the glowing shade of the silk. I couldn't control the eerie sensation that we were being watched, and once more I shifted our purchases, casting a searching eye over the assembled shoppers. There was no sign of any devoted admirer, no sign of anyone the least bit suspicious-looking. The bustling, crowded shopping area of Venice, with its rich smell of spices, ancient fish, and fresh flowers, was even blessedly void of the bright white-and-gold uniforms of the Austrian invaders. I shook myself nervously. Tonetti hadn't promised he'd contact me—he'd said he only wanted a glimpse. Well, I had the nasty feeling he was getting an eyeful.

"Perfect," Maggie breathed over the silk, ignoring my objections, which were halfhearted anyway. "With a deep flounce in the skirt, a small crinoline . . ." she sighed dreamily, "and lace around the necklace. You'll look a dream, Miss Luciana."

"I do hope so," I said cynically, dropping soap on my foot. "Not that it matters."

"Of course it matters," she said stoutly. "And don't think I don't know what prompted this sudden interest in clothes. I'll tell you what: Each time you see your mysterious gentleman, I'll make you a new dress. That way you could get yourself a husband and a new wardrobe at the same time, the one helping the other, so to speak."

The rest of the soap followed onto the cobblestones, accompanied by packets of tea, sugar, ginger biscuits, and nectarines. "You'd best pick out some more material, Maggie," I said in a strangled voice. "He's over there." At the sight of the Englishman, Tonetti fled my mind completely.

She whirled around, nearly dropping the lovely rose silk into the mud along with our food. "Where?" she demanded.

"Stop staring," I hissed. "I don't want him to see us." He was quite a way up the alley, his back to us, the dark blond hair glinting in the sunlight that played cruelly on his scarred cheek. Maggie followed the direction of my gaze, sighing soulfully.

"I do think that scar is ever so romantic," she breathed. Turning briskly back to the eager vender, she pointed toward a bolt of deep blue cotton with tiny white flowers. "We'll take that, too." I turned around to protest, but she merely met my objections with a bland smile. "A bargain is a bargain, Miss Luciana."

My once-bulging reticule was sadly depleted at the end of our bartering. Out of the corner of my eye I had watched the tall Englishman, covertly fascinated by his long, lean body. He seemed to have no particular business in the Merceria, merely wandering from stall to stall, paying no marked attention to anyone or thing. Not even, unfortunately, to me. For a moment I toyed with the idea that he was, in fact, Tonetti, and then reluctantly dismissed it. I had Bones's assurance that Tonetti was Venetian, and the man ahead of me was most definitely British. That, combined with his total lack of interest in me, forced me to abandon the romantic hope that he was my confederate. Turning to Maggie I suggested in an offhand whisper, "Why don't we just . . . sort of wander around and look at things?"

She grinned up at me. "I'm game if you are, Miss Luciana. Wouldn't want to let a live one get away." She trotted pertly off in his direction, leaving me to struggle behind, still clutching my myriad of parcels, desperate to stop my impulsive maid before she made a spectacle of the both of us. As we neared the Englishman she suddenly disappeared down a side lane beside a fish stall.

Rushing after her, I took no notice of the proximity of our innocent quarry. Suddenly a foot was stuck in my hurried path, a hand gave me a rough shove, and I ended sprawled on the ground, my poor damaged parcels around me like presents around a Christmas tree.

Two strong, tanned hands reached down for me, and I was gently, inexorably pulled to my feet to enjoy the quite novel sensation of looking *up* into the warmest, bluest eyes I had ever seen. I smiled up at him in dazed delight, and those beautifully shaped lips curved into an answering smile, which made the scar on his right cheek stretch and the small, fine lines around his eyes crease. And then, as if it had never been there, the smile disappeared from his face like the sun going behind a cloud, replaced by a look of stiff suspicion.

"I trust you're all right?" His voice was coolly, beautifully British, deep and rich despite his sudden, inexplicable dislike of me.

"Quite," I replied hurriedly. "Thank you so . . ." Before I could finish my thanks I found my arms filled with my bundles.

"Think nothing of it," he said brusquely. "But I suggest, miss, that you watch where you're going next time." And with that he disappeared into the curious crowd of shoppers, much as he had the night before.

"Well, of all the rude . . ." I sputtered, staring after him with indignant fascination. I had never met anyone so impolite in my short, sheltered life. It was both novel and disturbing. Added to the already upsetting effect the man had on me, it took a few moments before I realized that Maggie had reappeared at my side.

"Are you all right, Miss Luciana?" she inquired anxiously. "I hope I didn't push you too hard."

I stared at her in amazement. "Damn you, Maggie," I cursed when I got my breath back. "What an idiotic idea! I've got bruises from head to toe, a scratch on my face, our food is probably ruined . . ."

"But you got to meet him, didn't you?" she demanded, as if that were all that mattered.

As indeed it was. "I did. And he was abominably rude. I've quite lost interest in the man, I assure you. Mind how you carry that silk, you'll drop it!" I muttered as we threaded our way back toward the hotel. Her answer was a disbelieving laugh.

So caught up was I with indignant fascination that I failed to pay much heed to the handsome, aging gondolier who stared at us with intense interest out of moist, spaniel eyes. With a brief glance I dismissed him as one more hapless male bemused by Maggie's twitching little bottom or her companion's statuesque and overgenerous proportions. The scarred Englishman had banished all thought of my mission from my featherbrained little head.

Chapter Four

MY ARRIVAL AT Edentide, the ancestral home of the del Zaglias for generations untold, was hardly befitting the return of the native. Uncle Mark was up and fuming when we arrived back at the hotel and accompanied us down the wide, green expanse of the Grand Canal in a high dudgeon, scarcely replying to my commonplace pleasantries.

"You would think," he uttered in awful tones at one point, "that one of you would have more brains than a peahen. In a strange city, on a mysterious and dangerous mission, and the two of you run off like giggling schoolgirls and return loaded with dress material and tea! Absurd!"

"But, Uncle Mark," I protested sweetly, "we needed the tea. And the cleaning supplies. We could hardly set up housekeeping in a filthy dungeon without tea, could we?"

"You already know my opinion of your intended residence," he growled. "And what do you intend to do with the pink silk . . . scrub floors with it?"

"Rose silk," I corrected absently. "Maggie's going to make me a dress."

"Harrumph. So I gathered. Not that you don't sorely need one. Never saw such a shabbily dressed girl in my life. Nevertheless, your first morning in Venice is hardly the time or the place to embark on a new wardrobe."

"I disagree," Maggie piped up with her usual pertness.

"*You* would," he said morosely. "I should have known Luciana would wander off like a curious child, but I thought you would be able to exercise a little more control over her."

Maggie laughed. "Small chance of that happening, Mr. Ferland. Now or ever."

We were so busy wrangling I hadn't noticed our large and ancient gondola had pulled along a deserted, moss-coated marble quay. Looking up with a start, I had my first conscious view of Edentide in all its gloomy, ancient, marble glory.

There wasn't much color to her at this point. The last twenty years must have dealt harshly with her, for I could scarcely imagine my fastidious father inhabiting a place anywhere near this state of decrepitude. Gargoyles with chipped and broken noses adorned the corners of the top floor, the wrought-iron balustrades were rusted from the salty sea air, the shutters were closed and angry-looking.

I must have appeared somewhat daunted, for Uncle Mark let out a sour laugh of triumph. "You see what I mean? This never was a very welcoming place, even when your father made some effort to keep it up. I doubt it's even safe to walk in there anymore. I presume you've thought better of your rash plan?"

"I most certainly have not!" I climbed out of the gondola with surprising ease and scrambled onto the slippery quay. "I know perfectly well that father has sent regular sums of money to keep Edentide from sinking into the lagoon. Just enough to preserve it until the Austrians leave. I have no doubt we'll find it sturdy enough."

"And you think these villains would actually put the money to its assigned use?" he scoffed.

I met his gaze calmly. "Do you think they would dare not?" This, of course, was unanswerable, and Uncle Mark scrambled out of the gondola with far less grace than I had managed. Maggie fared worst of all, requiring the strong arms of the handsome gondolier to practically carry her onto the fondamento.

I kept an expression of curious interest all during our long and disheartening tour of Edentide. Uncle Mark and I were both right. It *was* filthy and mildewed and rather horrid. It was also blissfully free of rats, thanks to the presence of three rather fat ginger cats with clean habits, and the floors and walls were as solid as when the first piles had been driven into the soft mud of the lagoon.

I had immediately been attracted to the small salon on the west side of the house. The walls were covered in stained golden silk, the sconces were tarnished, the furniture frayed. But once I flung open the shutters, a great deal of sunlight and fresh sea air poured in, and I was able to view the carnage around me with a bit more equanimity.

Then began the orgy of cleaning. We decided not to bother with any floor but the main one, and Maggie and I spent the next five hours scrubbing, dusting, sweeping, beating rugs, washing windows, beating feather ticks, while poor Uncle Mark was instructed to cart various articles of furniture up and down the dirty marble stairs. By the approach of five o'clock we had gotten the west salon in charming order, with a clean floor, shining sconces, scrubbed upholstery only slightly more frayed than when we had entered the house, and polished tables and desks. I sank onto a particularly inviting chaise longue, feeling incredibly tired and incredibly dirty but very pleased with myself. Maggie plopped into a chair beside me, a streak of soot across her flushed and glowing face.

Uncle Mark, ever the perfect English gentleman, lounged by the balcony, not a hair out of place, not a wrinkle in his beautifully tailored jacket.

"You seem fairly settled," he allowed handsomely. "I suppose you'll do well enough for a few nights until you tire of this roughing it. I still wish you'd reconsider and return to the hotel with me tonight."

"After all our work?" I demanded in weak outrage, too weary to protest more loudly. "Never. We have our own neat and clean bedrooms . . ."

"With beds that I single-handedly wrestled down those damned stairs," he interrupted in a petulant voice.

"Which you nobly wrestled down the stairs," I inserted dutifully. "Even the kitchen is clean. Maggie and I will do splendidly, thank you."

"Absolutely, sir," Maggie joined in with a small show of energy. "And you can trust me to look after Miss Luciana. Lord knows I've had enough practice."

"But you weren't enough to stop her from running off with the traveling circus when she was fifteen, were you? Gone for a week before they found her, what?"

"Unfair, Uncle Mark!" I cried. "I was only gone overnight. I'd always wanted to be a tightrope walker."

"And what did your father say to that, eh? One of the blessed del Zaglias joining a circus. Bet he rung a rare peal over you that time."

"As a matter of fact he told me that if I still wanted to be a tightrope walker when I was eighteen he would see that I had lessons. I didn't, of course. And I must say, I think I've found my *metier*. Being a spy is a great deal of fun." My lips curved in a reminiscent smile.

"Damn it, girl, when you smile like that you look the spitting image of your mother." He shook his head. "I wish I could be easy about the two of you. At least two people that I knew personally died violent deaths in this house not twenty-five years ago."

If I was daunted I did my best not to show it. "I have no intention of following suit. You may come and check on us tomorrow morning. If you come early enough we may even feed you breakfast." I rose, and reluctantly he headed for the door, muttering dire predictions all the way out.

"And now, dear Maggie," I sighed as I wandered back in, "all I need to make me blissfully happy is a cup of strong tea, some dinner, and a bath."

"Tea, I can get you. Even dinner I can provide if you'll settle for some fried sprats and cornmeal mush . . ."

"Polenta," I corrected gently, not at all displeased by this typical Venetian menu.

"But a bath is one thing I cannot and will not do. If you think, Miss Luciana, that I am going to heat and carry buckets and buckets of water . . ."

"No, no, no," I soothed her. "Just wishful thinking. I feel so dirty; there's nothing I'd like more than . . ." I broke off as a delightfully wicked idea came to my ever-active imagination.

"I don't like that look in your eye, Miss Luciana. It bodes ill for someone."

"Pish and tush," I replied. "I am going to get clean, and in the easiest way possible. I'm going swimming."

"Where?" she demanded, and then a look of dawning horror appeared on her face. "Oh, no, miss. You can't mean it! Not in this dirty canal water."

"I certainly do. Father used to swim here all the time. I saw some boys swimming when we arrived. The canal on the side of the house is deserted . . . no houses or windows face on it but ours. And it will be a very short swim."

"I've never known you to take a short swim. I think you must be part eel yourself. And you're far more likely to come out dirtier than when you went in."

"Ah, but Maggie, you don't understand the secret of the Venetian garbage system. The ebb tide carries all the trash and sewage out into the open sea every day, and the return is fresh, clean sea water. Can't you smell . . . the tide has just come in." I took an appreciative sniff of the clean, watery smell, and Maggie took a disdainful sniff of disapproval.

"You're mad, Miss Luciana. But there's no telling you. Go on ahead—I can't stop you. But you'll have to sleep in your canal slime . . . I've told you already I won't get you a bath."

It took all my powers of persuasion to convince Maggie to accompany me down the long, dark, dank passageway that led under the house to the side entrance. Various rustlings in the dark left me with the gloomy conviction that the cats had not been quite as efficient as I had hoped, and the green moss growing along the sturdy and uncracked marble foundations added to the eerie atmosphere of the place. If I hadn't made such an issue of swimming in the first place, I would have suggested we turn back.

"Gawd, this is an awful place, ain't it?" Maggie whispered as we neared the end of the pathway. "I wouldn't like to be locked down here on a stormy night."

"Don't!" I shuddered. "We mustn't be superstitious. It's just another part of the house—a little bit damper, but nothing else."

"Isn't this where your father killed the—?"

"Please, Maggie!" I shrieked, and my voice echoed down the cavernous crypt. "I'd rather not think about it." Thankfully, I swung open the old and rusty door after a nervous moment fiddling with the bolts. "That was all a long time ago. It really shouldn't bother us in the least."

"Well, it bothers me. And what bothers me more, Miss Luciana, is what you're intending to wear for this twilight swim you're planning." She cast a suspicious glance over my rumpled skirt and blouse. "I hope you have more sense than to consider going in the altogether. That's bad enough in Somerset, but here with those Eye-talian brigands . . ." She shivered in delicious anticipation, obviously longing to run into an Eye-talian brigand in the altogether.

"But Maggie, I'd drown if I wore all this," I pointed out with great practicality.

"You've got a chemise on, haven't you? And pantalets? Indecent, of course, but better than nothing." I was quickly peeling off the grime-stained outer layers, and I nodded in compliance. The chemise was made of fine lawn and Venetian lace and came to just above my knees; the pantalets were short and frilly and absurdly dainty.

When wet, I knew they would be just as bad as the infamous "altogether," but I didn't bother informing Maggie of that fact. I sat down on the moss-coated quayside and dangled my bare feet into the splendidly cool salt water.

"I don't really fancy waiting alone in this great dark hole while you paddle around," Maggie warned. "In and out—that's all the swimming you'll do today, my girl."

"Yes, Maggie," I replied meekly, taking the pins out of my heavy hair and letting it hang like a thick, black curtain down my back. We were far enough away from the lights and noises of the Grand Canal so that I felt completely private. Especially now, at what appeared to be the dinner hour for so many of my fellow Venetians. Bracing myself against the dock, I slid slowly and quietly into the cool, green depths, letting out a long sigh of delight before taking off in strong, rapid strokes toward the end of the house.

"That's enough, Miss Luciana," Maggie called out uneasily. "Come back now."

"I can't!" I protested. "I've barely cooled off. Give me a few minutes more, Maggie."

"I don't like it here. Come now, or I'll leave you. I swear I will."

"Go ahead!" I called gaily, forgetting the eerie passageway and its ancient ghosts. "I'll be in directly."

"Miss Luciana, come now!" There was thunder in Maggie's voice, a thunder I chose to ignore.

"Go ahead and start supper, Maggie," I replied, floating on my back and wiggling my toes. "Or else you can come in and fetch me," I added wickedly, knowing how Maggie detested water in any form other than a tepid bath.

"Damn you, then!" she cried, and vanished from the dockside. I did a shallow dive and began a leisurely examination of the underside of Venice. When I surfaced for air the side of the old house looked different. It took me a full minute to realize that the water door was firmly closed, with no outside handle. It took only a small push from the water to ascertain that it was indeed locked.

Chapter Five

FOR A LONG moment panic set in, and I sank beneath the salty waters of the lagoon like an idiot. I surfaced quickly, coughing and sputtering and choking, my eyes stinging from the bite of the salt. Placing two hands on the moss-covered marble quay, I tried to pull my tired body upward, but the seaweed growing in slimy profusion gave me no purchase, and I slipped back beneath the now treacherous waters, my hands scrabbling desperately at the dock. Again I surfaced and tried to crawl out; again I felt my hands slip, my nails tearing helplessly. I tried to call for help, but the exhaustion of the past week and day had caught up with me with evil speed, and all that came forth before I slipped beneath the canal was a hoarse croak.

While my body was weakening my mind was working feverishly. I wasted valuable time cursing myself for being a careless idiot, for trying to swim in an unfamiliar place when I had already pushed myself too far and too fast. And as I made my way wearily to the blessed surface, I weakly realized it might be the last time.

Blinded by the sea water and desperation, I reached out one last time for the marble fondamento, gulping in the sweet night air. Once more I felt myself begin to slip, and I resigned myself to an early, albeit fitting, watery grave when suddenly I felt my weak wrists gripped tightly by two iron hands.

It was then I began to struggle in earnest until a deep, sure British voice that I recognized instantly cut through my panic. "Calm down," he ordered sternly. "I've got a hold of you. You'll be out in a moment. Just take deep, slow breaths."

Numbly I complied, and in a few seconds I felt myself being pulled out of the water with a sudden jerk of quite impressive strength and dumped on the slime-covered quay.

I sat there in a wet and sorry heap, my breath coming in long shudders, my body trembling from the aftermath of fear and the suddenly chill night air. My rescuer knelt beside me, and as I turned to thank him I came face to face with the angriest blue eyes I had ever seen.

"Do you realize," he began in an icy voice, stripping off his jacket to reveal a set of powerfully built shoulders, "what an idiotic, dangerous thing that was for you to do? A child would have more sense than to go swimming unattended in a strange place." While his voice was rough with anger, his hands were gentle as they lifted me and drew the warm linen jacket around my shivering body. "You should have some sort of keeper, someone to make sure you get into no more trouble. Venice is a dangerous place for fools and innocents."

"Which am I?" I questioned weakly, not really minding his harangue as long as he kept those gentle, reassuring hands on me. Both my parents had hot tempers, and I had come to associate being yelled at with people who loved me. I felt positively cherished as the nameless, scarred Englishman lit it into me.

"Both," he snapped, smoothing my wet, tangled hair away from my face. "You should turn around and go straight back to England," he said in a calmer tone. "This is no place for you."

"How do you know I've come from England?" I questioned with spy-like surprise, remembering my duties belatedly.

He hesitated for only a moment. "You know as well as I do that I saw you arrive last night. And your voice is as unmistakably British as your face is Venetian."

I smiled at that, obscurely pleased. "Well, I can't go back to England right now, even if I wanted to. I have business here."

"You are far too young to have business that couldn't be better conducted by the men in your family," he said in an oppressive voice.

"I am just as capable as the men in my family," I snapped, struggling out of my very comfortable position, which was half in his arms.

A look of amusement passed over his face. "God help your family, then." He helped me to my less-than-steady feet, catching his jacket deftly as it slid off my shoulders. "Are you quite all right?" A note of concern had slipped beneath his cold reserve, and it . warmed me despite the chill damp of my skin.

"I'm fine," I replied, holding out my hand politely. "And once more I must thank you, Mr. . . . ?" I let it trail meaningfully.

The mocking smile was very much in evidence now as he took my hand to his lips and kissed it with the lightest of touches. "I would suggest, Miss del Zaglia, that you keep my jacket for now. Your costume, though extremely attractive, is a bit too revealing for polite society, even in Venice."

I looked down at the sheer, clinging lawn that covered my ripe curves, and a warm blush mounted to my cheeks and spread all over the large expanse of visible skin. Snatching back his jacket, I pulled it around me in sudden and unusual modesty, barely managing to stammer out my thanks.

It suddenly seemed very still and quiet, alone with him on the slime-covered fondamento outside the austere and gloomy environs of the Palazzo Edentide on a cool August night. The sounds of the Grand Canal seemed soft and far away, and I had the odd, by no means unpleasant, feeling that we were alone in this world, my nameless scarred Englishman and I. And I knew with an ancient and sure instinct that he had the same eerie feeling. A gentle hand came under my chin, drawing me up to face those deep, troubled eyes as his other hand once more smoothed my wet locks from my face. The smell of the sea was strong on my skin and his hand, and the soft night breeze played through his dark gold hair, ruffling it just slightly.

"Take care, Luciana," he said in a soft voice, and my stomach seemed to contract within me at the sound of my name on his lips. "The world is full of cruel, evil people, people who want to hurt innocent young girls like you. Take care," he repeated gently, his hand an unconscious caress on my cheek.

"I can look after myself," I replied in a hushed but firm tone.

He looked down at my damp, scanty clothing, barely covered by the warm folds of his jacket.

"Really?" he said skeptically. "I do hope so, Luciana. I do hope so."

A sudden scraping at the door brought us both out of our reverie, and in a moment he was gone, swiftly and silently, so that were it not for the warm, soft folds of his coat around me, I would have thought I had dreamed his presence.

"Are you all right, Miss Luciana?" Maggie demanded, peering through the gathering dusk. "I thought I heard someone walking around upstairs, calling me. It must have been my imagination, for no one was there. When I came back down the door here was shut and locked." She couldn't quite keep the worry out of her voice.

I moved into sight, careful to keep a matter-of-fact note in my somewhat shaky voice. "I'm fine, Maggie. I had a little trouble climbing back out onto the fondamento, but a gentleman helped me."

"What gentleman?" she demanded suspiciously, squinting down the canal.

A seraphic smile creased my lips as I preceded her into the dark, damp cellars of the palazzo. The cellars that had seen death already in this century. "You owe me another dress," I said sweetly.

With a great deal more bravado than wisdom Maggie and I both came to the comforting conclusion that the nonexistent wind had shut the heavy, rusted sea door, with the force of it closing the sticky latch once more. That selfsame wind was also responsible for the voices and footsteps that had called Maggie away from my side—an illusion, nothing more. In the meantime, however, we locked and bolted the sturdy door down into the cellars, and every few minutes one of us would cast a nervous glance in the general direction of the wide marble stairs, expecting heaven knows what sort of ghost to make its sepulchral way down the recently dusted steps.

Between the two of us we managed a creditable job of the sprats and polenta. By the time we had finished eating a disgustingly huge amount, drunk several quarts of strong tea, and washed the dishes, bed seemed like a most pleasant place to be. It took all of Maggie's powers of persuasion to talk me into staying up another hour and helping her cut out the first of my dresses, and by nine o'clock I flatly refused to do anything more on it.

"I'm exhausted," I complained bitterly, struggling to my feet and staring down at the scraps of rose-colored silk that would somehow, inexplicably, become an exceedingly flattering dress.

"I never thought to hear you say that, Miss Luciana," Maggie replied pertly from her kneeling position, her mouth full of pins. "Go on to bed, then; I'll be along shortly." She let out a short, sharp laugh. "And don't think I don't know why you're so eager to go to bed for once."

"Whatever do you mean?"

"You want to dream of your handsome pirate. Well, it can do no harm," she observed magnanimously. "And once we have you looking more like a lady . . . well, who knows what will happen? I think, Miss Luciana, that you should just forget why you came here and concentrate on that gentleman. Spying's no ladylike occupation. You should be married and have one or two little ones running around by your age."

The thought of marriage with the aloof Englishman was curiously enticing, and reluctantly I put a tight rein on my imagination. "I can't forget why I'm here, Maggie. No matter how much I'm tempted, no matter how much I wish I could, I can't." Unconsciously I stiffened my backbone. "Good night, Maggie." The only reply was a derisive snort.

My small bedroom had obviously been a dining salon at one point. Most of the furniture had been too rickety to be of much use, and Uncle Mark had obligingly dragged it off to the section of the cellars I had designated for storage. Instead of wobbling, frayed furniture, the room now boasted a small, ornately carved wooden bed with plain white cotton hangings to protect me from the noxious sea airs, a plain table and chair, an armoire, which had required Maggie's and my help in wresting it from one of the second-floor bedrooms, and a small, very old, and exquisitely beautiful Oriental rug. Maggie had closed the shutters to the small balcony, effectively cutting off any fresh air on this close, still night. The balcony overlooked the side canal that had almost caused my death that evening; but looking down at it from the safe height of my room, it seemed calm and gentle and once more welcoming on such a sticky night. Firmly I put that thought from my mind, blew out my lamp, and undressed slowly and thoughtfully in the dark. I was asleep in a few short minutes.

I FELT THE BED sag beneath his weight as he sat down by my sleeping body. Those hands that had rescued me from a watery grave were warm and gentle on my face, waking me just enough so that I turned and offered my mouth to his insistent touch. I could feel the weight of his lips on mine, and I let out a little sigh of pure pleasure as I squirmed like a kitten.

His mouth left mine and traveled in short, delicate kisses, over my cheeks, my eyes, my brow, my soft, silky hair, as his hands gently pulled away the thin cotton sheet that lay over my nude body. He pulled it only as far as my hips, and then his mouth moved down my neck, leaving a trail of fire in its wake as he drew me up into his arms.

I lay there for a moment, enjoying the feel of his arms around me, his mouth on my neck. And then the feel of those strong, beautiful hands on my naked skin awoke a response in me I barely knew existed. His wrists lay against my breasts, and I reached my arms around his neck and drew him closer, closer, until we were kissing once more, his mouth hot and demanding, his warm, clever hands on my breasts causing me an almost unbearable mixture of pain and pleasure.

I let my mouth trace the thin, angry line of his scar, and then his head moved down, down, until his lips found my full breasts, bared beneath his touch, and his hungry mouth fastened on my taut and straining nipples, kneading, sucking, and biting them, until I moaned aloud with delight. I laced my fingers through his thick, long hair and held him closer, ever closer to me, writhing on the bed as he pulled the sheet away from the rest of me, his lips . . .

The yowl of a Venetian alley cat brought me suddenly, swiftly, horribly awake, and I lay alone in my narrow bed, the sheet at my feet, covered with a thin glow of sweat, trembling with the chill of the night air. A dream. It had all been a licentious, voluptuous, embarrassing, delectable dream. I wanted to cry out in rage and frustration.

A shudder passed over my body, swiftly followed by another and then another. Stumbling from my bed I crossed the mosaic floor on bare feet and found the armoire in the fitful moonlight. I took the Englishman's coat from its hook and wrapped it around my naked, shivering body. Climbing back into my soft bed, I heaved a sigh that was an odd mixture of contentment, relief, and disappointment. And in another moment I was sound asleep, this time for the remainder of the warm and sultry Venetian night, whose warmth could turn suddenly, bitingly chill.

Chapter Six

I SLEPT LATER than usual the next morning. By the time I struggled out of bed, forced a comb through my salt-tangled hair and arranged it in a simple manner, threw on a wrapper, and washed my face, it was close to ten o'clock. I found Maggie sitting in the salon, sewing industriously on the rose-colored silk, a cup of tea at her left elbow, her neat little feet perched on a petit point stool only slightly frayed from age and damp.

"You look quite demure this morning," I observed, pouring myself a blessedly strong cup of tea. "How long have you been up?" I wandered over to stare out at the noise and bustle of the Grand Canal.

"Any number of hours now, Miss Luciana. I've been to the square to buy milk from those cunning little milkmaids. I've had breakfast, and made a great deal of progress on this dress." She held it up for my inspection, and indeed, it had begun to take shape in an amazingly short amount of time. "And you've received an invitation."

I turned back quickly, almost spilling my tea. "Already?" I exclaimed, remembering my seemingly futile trip to the Merceria yesterday and Tonetti's secretive note. "From Tonetti?"

"I sincerely doubt it," she replied wryly. "It's from the embassy. Lady Bute, the consul's wife, to be exact. For tea this afternoon. I was so bold as to tell the messenger you'd be pleased to attend. I think we can thank your Uncle Mark for that particular attention. Lady Bute was one of his old flirts."

"How do you know that?"

She waved an airy hand. "Servants have ways of picking up on things," she replied, looking in no way like a servant in her elegant green muslin dress that was deliberately cut just a trifle too low for daytime wear. "You know what that invitation means, don't you?"

"I haven't the faintest idea, other than a possibly boring afternoon with a bunch of stuffy people," I said rudely. Formal teas had long been a bane of my existence, providing far more punishment than pleasure, and I wasn't looking forward to this afternoon's treat.

"It's Lady Bute's official monthly tea," Maggie explained with great patience. "All those people who are anybody will be invited. Including your mysterious friend who arrives so opportunely."

She made a neat little knot and cast a suspicious glance at my happy face. "You needn't be quite so jolly, Miss Luciana. He might not be there."

"No, you're right, Maggie." I waltzed around the room in the strong Venetian sunlight. "He'll be there, I know he will. I . . . I don't suppose there's any chance the dress . . . ?"

"Will be finished in time?" she continued for me. "Why do you think I'm sitting here on such a glorious day? I may have to sew you into it, but you'll have it to wear this afternoon. Your Uncle Mark will be calling for you at three."

I swooped down and gave her an exuberant hug, careful to watch my surprising strength or I could have cracked a few ribs. "Bless you, Maggie! What more could I ask?"

"That we get out of this devilish situation your impulsiveness hurled us into with our skins intact," she suggested morosely.

That afternoon I dressed with far greater care than I usually expended and consequently Uncle Mark was left cooling his heels in the salon for a good twenty minutes while Maggie sewed me into the rose-silk dress. She had done an admirable job of it—the soft folds hugged my uncorseted body and draped gracefully around my narrow hoops. The deep fold of Venetian lace around the shoulders set off the warm tones of my skin to perfection, and as I moved it rustled in a soft, feminine manner. We had worked a full hour on my thick, straight black hair. The damp sea air had given it more weight than usual, and as Maggie twined and plaited and pinned, small tendrils escaped the severe style and framed my face in a flattering fashion. I applied rose hips to my cheeks, charcoal to my already dark lashes, gardenia scent to my wrists, breasts, and the nape of my neck. When I was finished Maggie drew back and looked at me in astonishment.

"My Gawd, Miss Luciana," she breathed in amazement.

"What's wrong? Don't I look pretty?" I demanded, worried that I had been too partial to my reflection in the gold leaf mirror.

Maggie shook her curly head. "No, dearie, you aren't pretty. Not a bit." She laughed as my mouth drooped. "You are absolutely beautiful. I never knew you could be such a looker."

"You swine!" I shook her. "You frightened me for a moment." I pranced in front of my reflection, turning my full, graceful skirts this way and that. "Will he think so too?"

Maggie had no doubts as to the identity of *he*. "He'd be half-mad not to. You look just like that picture your pa has in his study. Of the lady."

"The Giorgione Madonna?" I supplied, amazed. "I really do? She's beautiful!"

"And so are you," Maggie said stoutly. "If you'd just keep those spirits under control. You have the same serene sort of looks. When you aren't being wicked, that is."

"I'll work on it, Maggie," I promised solemnly, turning to give myself one last smug grin in the tarnished surface of the mirror.

Uncle Mark's reaction was fully as flattering as Maggie's, though not quite so amazed. "I always knew you were a beauty," he said loyally, helping me into the gondola with surprisingly careful hands. "How could you help but be, with parents like yours?"

This was unanswerable, and the trip to the British Consulate was quick and silent. Uncle Mark seemed vague and abstracted; even more so than usual. Only once did he break the stillness.

"You still haven't heard from Tonetti, have you?"

I started guiltily, then met his worried blue eyes with a limpid expression. I had already determined not to confide in anyone if I could help it, smugly certain I could handle it far better without his meddling. Besides, I told myself virtuously, he would only worry needlessly. "I haven't heard anything yet," I replied with sweet innocence. "I expect to any day now."

"I don't understand it," he said worriedly, more to himself than to me. "I would have thought someone would have made contact by now. We've been here almost forty-eight hours—usually these people don't waste any time." He sighed, looking at the magic city as we glided by with blind eyes. "I can't rest easy until I've gotten you safely back in Somerset. This was a crazy idea to begin with. Bones must be senile!"

I listened to him in silence. "What's done is done," I said with great originality. "We should hear something soon. No doubt we'll be back in England before you know it."

"I only hope it's before your father knows it. I shudder to think of his reaction when he finds I've accompanied you here."

I patted his hand reassuringly. "His reaction would be far worse if he found that you had let me go alone."

"Yes, that's true," he muttered, brightening somewhat. My father had the ability to terrify most of his acquaintances when he chose to, and Mark Ferland was particularly vulnerable.

I stirred uneasily, and the gondola rocked slightly as it sliced through the dark green water. "Well, it should all be cleared up in a while," I said optimistically, wondering whether I ought to take Uncle Mark into my confidence. Despite his vague demeanor, he had some experience in the field. I sat there in a quandary, unable to make up my mind.

"I must say Venice agrees with you," my godfather continued thoughtfully after a moment. "Perhaps Bones knew what he was doing after all when he sent you. I only wish he'd had the foresight to send someone along to protect you." *But didn't he send you*, I thought suddenly? And if not, who and where was the watchdog Bones had promised me? I opened my mouth to question him when the gondola pulled up along the quay outside the British Consulate, and in the bustle of disembarking and greeting our various fellow guests, all of whom seemed to know Uncle Mark and my parents intimately, the subject was lost, not to return until late that night when I was alone and half-asleep.

We were halfway across the formal receiving room on the third floor of the old palazzo that had become the consulate, making our leisurely way to greet our hostess, Lady Bute, when I whispered uneasily to my godfather, "Everyone is staring at me. I must look a freak in this pink dress." Years of doubt and horrid self-consciousness about my unusual height came flooding back to me, and I felt like sinking through the polished marble floor.

Uncle Mark stopped short, turning amazed eyes on me. "My dear girl, they're not staring at you because you're tall—they're staring at you because you're beautiful. Remember, Luciana," he admonished sternly, "you're a del Zaglia."

Unconsciously I threw back my shoulders and smiled at the assembled multitude. The number of smiles I received in return amazed me.

"My God," I whispered, amazed, "I believe you're right, Uncle Mark."

Lady Bute was a very carefully preserved blonde somewhere on the shady side of fifty. She greeted her old beau, Uncle Mark, with a noisy and enthusiastic kiss on the lips and looked as if she were about to bestow the same salute on me upon our introduction. I quickly proffered my cheek, clanging into her chin with jarring force, and then drew back, aghast at my unusual clumsiness.

Lady Bute, far from being irritated, let out a high little trill of laughter, squeezed my hand with surprising strength, and waved my godfather away with one plump, bejeweled wrist. "You are Luc and Carlotta's daughter! How I've longed to meet you, my dear. No one ever told me you were such a beauty . . . every eye is upon you today. I feel quite put out."

No one had ever told me I was a beauty, either, I thought, and then realized that was untrue. My parents had always made me feel exquisitely lovely. It was only when I was away from their protective, sheltering love that I felt overgrown and lost the natural grace that was mine.

"Sit beside me, my child, and we shall enjoy a great gossip. There's nothing I don't know about who's in Venice, and I'm dying to hear the latest from your dear family. How many brothers do you have now? Was it three?"

"Six," I replied, smiling. "The youngest is Marco, who's barely a year and a half."

"Your mother never ceases to amaze me," she said sincerely. "The lucky creature."

We passed the next half hour in an extremely agreeable fashion. It seemed there were very few people present at the formal tea who hadn't a scandal hidden deep in their past, a scandal Lady Bute had managed to unearth long ago. So fascinated was I in all this that I failed to notice Uncle Mark's defection with a pretty, blue-haired widow, or the arrival of my mysterious gentleman, until a pause in Lady Bute's voluble conversation allowed me to cast a casual eye over the proceedings.

From my vantage point in the little alcove at the head of the room I could see him clearly, towering over the various international guests with easy grace. As far as I could tell he had yet to see me. Or if he had, he hadn't cared, I thought morosely.

"Who are you looking at with such a curious expression, my dear?" Lady Bute demanded, her long nose itching for more gossip. "Do I detect an expression of romantic longing on your lovely young face? You shouldn't be so transparent, my girl. Gentlemen should be kept guessing."

Blushing, I tried to deny any romantic interest. As my protests came out in stammered half-phrases, an old campaigner like Lady Bute was not fooled for a minute.

"I beg you, darling, tell me who he is! I can be discreet, I promise you." Unlikely chance, I thought cynically, closing my mouth tight against my usual longing to confide in anyone or anything. "I do so love romance," she twittered on. "Is it an attachment of long standing?"

I had to laugh. "It isn't an attachment at all, my lady. I was merely curious about one of your guests." *Should I keep my mouth shut or should I not?* I wondered feverishly beneath my calm expression. I doubted I would find such a gold mine of information again. And what harm would it do if she knew of my interest? I would be gone from Venice in a few short days, never to return until the Austrians had finally departed.

Lady Bute's sharp little eyes, like hard, shiny marbles, followed the direction of my limpid gaze, and widened in consternation. "Evan Fitzpatrick!" she exclaimed in an undertone, and I turned to her eagerly.

"Is that his name? I've seen him any number of times since I've arrived, but we've yet to be introduced. Would you . . . ?"

"Introduce you? Never," she said flatly, a deceptively merry expression in those eyes.

"But why not?"

"My duties as the wife of the consul, my dear, do not include introducing young ladies of proper upbringing to men who are scarcely gentlemen."

"Scarcely gentlemen?" I echoed, puzzled. "He seems perfectly genteel enough. I don't understand."

"You've talked with him?" she edged closer. "My goodness, what an intrigue! I didn't know Evan had ever bothered to exchange more than two words with a young lady of virtuous ways. This is absolutely fascinating. Tell me, where did you meet him?"

"At the Merceria," I replied. "And the train station. And outside Edentide." For the first time the coincidence seemed unpleasantly striking. "He's very rude," I added.

"Yes, that's Evan," the older woman said fondly. "Hated you on sight, didn't he?"

I remembered his gentle hands smoothing away my sea-damp hair, the look of concern in his angry, silver-blue eyes. I smiled reflectively. "Well, no, not really," I allowed.

"Then you've worked some sort of spell on him," she said flatly.

"Why? Why won't you introduce me to him, why is he not quite a gentleman, and why should he hate me on sight?" I demanded, unable to tear my eyes away from the back of his neck, the lovely way the overlong dark blond hair curled around his collar, the deceptive strength in those shoulders.

Lady Bute hesitated for only a moment. "Very well, my dear. I will tell you what I know of Evan Fitzpatrick, and then you will see just how totally ineligible he is. We shall take a short stroll on the north terrace, where we are unlikely to be interrupted. Come with me." She rose to her small height with classic dignity, and I followed suit, towering over her and feeling like a giantess. "My, you are a Juno, aren't you?" she said sweetly, drawing her arm through mine and leading me away from the multitude out onto the flowered terrace.

"To begin with," she said in a lowered voice once we were alone, "he is divorced." The tones she spoke in suggested an axe murderer at the very least, and I sighed with relief.

"Is that all?"

"Isn't that enough? But no, that is not all. England must have changed if the young people accept divorce so easily. In my day divorced people were not received."

"But you receive Evan Fitzpatrick?" I pointed out.

A sly smile creased her aging face. "Indeed, I do. But you'll find, my dear, that there are very few men as handsome as Evan Fitzpatrick that I don't receive. But I also do not introduce them to the innocent daughters of the nobility, be they Venetian or English."

"And what else is so horrid about him?" I demanded, feeling absurdly protective. "Did he abandon his poor, frail, helpless wife?"

"As a matter of fact Amelia was the most ghastly bitch. She had the morals of a Roman, and didn't bother to hide it. Daughter of a duke, but the most ill-bred creature I have ever met. She gave Evan that attractive scar, you know. I believe she did it with a letter opener."

"My God," I whispered in horror. "Is that when he divorced her?"

"Heavens, no! It wasn't until two or three years after that. They have a son. Sweet young boy, I believe; goes to school in England somewhere. It wasn't talked about openly, and the divorce trial was closed, but I have friends in high places. It turned out that the dear Amelia had a particularly nasty habit of having her five-year-old son watch while she disported with her current lover. Or lovers, as the case may have been. If the poor child was uncooperative she would fly into one of her maniacal rages. I gather she broke his arm in three places. *That* was when Evan divorced her."

I felt like throwing up. "I would have murdered her," I said quietly.

"Well, as a matter of fact, there was some question of that. A few years after the divorce she was found strangled in a Paris bordello which catered to odd tastes. No one was ever caught, but it was rumored that Evan might have finally gotten his revenge. He was wandering around Europe at the time. Still is, I suppose, though he's been in Venice for almost a year now."

"And for divorcing that . . . that monster of depravity he's ostracized from society?" I demanded, outraged.

Lady Bute shrugged, leaning against the marble balustrade and plucking a bright orange nasturtium from the flower box. "Such is the way of the world, my dear. There are certain rules, and if we relax them, civilization will topple."

"Civilization will not topple if people are sympathetic to a man who's obviously been through hell," I said crossly.

"Sympathetic?" she echoed, amused. "He wouldn't thank you for that, my dear. And I have a double reason for not introducing you. He detests women. Ever since Amelia he's decided we're all either sluts, teases, deviants, or useless, idle gossips." I could recognize who fell into that last category. "You wouldn't get a decent word out of him."

"I've already had several."

My companion sighed gustily. "Perhaps you're the one to convince him he's wrong about our fair sex. I must confess, if I were unmarried and ten years younger, I'd be tempted to give it a try myself. I do so love a rake."

"A rake! I thought you said he hated women?"

She smiled, a sly, secret smile. "But those, my dear, are the best kind."

Chapter Seven

THERE WAS NO changing Lady Bute's determination not to introduce me to my scarred Englishman. I couldn't help but wonder whether jealousy might be behind it.

"Well, then, I will simply have to introduce myself," I declared sweetly, heading back toward the gathering.

"You wouldn't dare!" Lady Bute scurried to catch up with me, dropping the torn petals on the marble terrace, her expression both aghast and amused. "My dear, remember, you're a del Zaglia!"

"That's exactly what I am remembering," I replied stoutly. "My parents would never approve of ignoring a man for such idiotic reasons."

A note of panic crept into my companion's voice as she placed a restraining, jeweled hand upon my arm. "I'm not saying you should ignore him. If you meet him you should nod pleasantly and walk on. But to actually seek out his company . . . She shuddered delicately, and I laughed.

"Never fear, Lady Bute," I reassured her, detaching her clinging hands with gentle strength, "the Lord protects fools and innocents. And I have it on the best authority that I'm both."

As I started off toward my quarry I thought I heard her mutter, "No doubt," but I was set upon my course by this time and ignored the carping remark.

Evan Fitzpatrick was standing in a corner, deep in conversation with a voluptuous blonde lady in an indecently low-cut dress for that hour of the day. As far as anyone could tell he was completely unaware of my presence, but I knew that was untrue. He was as fully aware of me as I was of him, and I found the thought oddly intoxicating.

As I neared his corner of the room some of my bravado had begun to fade. I could scarcely barge into the middle of his seemingly fascinating conversation, hold out one slender hand, and announce my name. Besides, in some obscure manner he already seemed to know who I was.

I cast a desperate glance around the room, hoping to find Uncle Mark. He could perform the introductions I so desperately wanted. But his graying head was nowhere in sight, nor was there anyone else with whom I was more than casually acquainted.

From out of nowhere a cup of tea was thrust at me, and unthinkingly I accepted it, not bothering to see who offered it. I took a large gulp out of the strong, peaty stuff, my eyes still upon my quarry.

Another swallow and absently I glanced down at the saucer in my hand, and the small twist of paper that was rapidly soaking up the slopped-over tea.

In the blink of an eye I had the damp missive safely tucked in my ever-present reticule, my heart beating faster than usual as I glanced around me with feigned interest. For a moment all thought of Evan Fitzpatrick fled my mind as I searched the crowds for a suspicious face. Everyone seemed intent on their own concerns, and I moved closer to Evan and his obviously Austrian harlot.

I edged near enough so that I could hear his voice, that cool, clipped, British voice, which for some reason had the power to move me more than any voice I had ever heard. His scarred side was toward me, and once more I wondered at his disfigurement's ability to render him even more attractive. At that moment his eyes met mine, then passed over me with complete and bone-chilling indifference.

I stood there helplessly, stunned by his cool disdain. For a moment I imagined how amused Lady Bute would be, having informed me that it was my duty to give Evan the cut direct, she would be delighted to know that *he* had taken that prerogative.

Momentarily gloomy, I searched around for a quick exit before I made a complete fool of myself. A very handsome, somewhat overscented Venetian manservant of uncertain age hovered nearby. As my eyes met his he immediately began bearing down on me, a large silver tray full of teacups and cookies balanced precariously. The crowds thinned out in front of him, and he continued forward, obviously with the blissful assumption that all would move out of his elegantly graceful way. My evil half took over, my delicate foot slipped out, and the servant, the tray, and all its contents crashed into Evan Fitzpatrick and his companion, covering the sensuous blonde with crumbs and tea, staining her low-cut lavender dress and dowsing her elaborate curls. Evan had moved in time, receiving the dregs of a cup or two, and my own rose silk escaped with only a drop on the hem.

The blonde shrieked in German words no lady should ever use, and I was doubly glad I had managed to inundate both a hated Austrian and an *inamorata* of the man I was thinking of as *my* Englishman. I turned suddenly, and my self-satisfied smirk met his cool, deep blue eyes. Immediately I changed my expression to one of deep concern, but it was too late. A look of reluctant-amusement crept into his eyes, and a slight smile curved his lips. Grinning back unashamedly, I turned and swept away from the melee, pleased to have survived, and even won, that last encounter.

Uncle Mark was waiting for me on the side terrace. "What's all that screeching in there?" he demanded. "Never heard such a racket in all my life. These parties are getting damnably underbred."

I thought of Evan, and barely controlled my impulse to rise to his defense. Mark had disappeared so early he probably hadn't even noticed his presence.

"Some Austrian lady," I replied calmly. "And I use the term 'lady' very loosely, indeed. A servant spilled a tray of tea and cookies all over her." I smiled.

Uncle Mark met that smile. "Assisted by a certain young English lady, no doubt?"

I nodded, descending the polished marble steps. "Do you know, uncle, I feel more and more Venetian the longer I stay here. And yet I also feel more and more British. It's very confusing."

"I dare say," he replied absently. "That's what comes of intermarriage. Now if your mother had seen fit to marry me . . ." He handed me into the gondola.

"Then you would have had a nice, placid, blond English daughter," I completed the sentence. "With no such problems to contend with."

"I would hope," he said sincerely, "that our daughter would have been just like you."

I was touched, but couldn't help laughing. "I doubt you would, dear uncle. I am very much my father's daughter. If your wife had given birth to me there would be little doubt as to what she'd been doing nine months before."

"Luciana!" Uncle Mark protested, deeply shocked. His outrage was enough to last the trip back to the slime-covered portal of Edentide, but it also fortunately rescued him from his increasingly sentimental moods. It was all I could do to be polite and leisurely with the latest missive burning a hole in my reticule and my patience. By some stroke of fortune he decided to leave me at the door, and it took only a small amount of subterfuge to escape Maggie's watchful eye long enough to untwist the sodden piece of paper and decipher the blurred message.

"My beloved! I long for a brief word, a glance, a touch! A midnight rendezvous would greatly benefit many people. Be so good as to wear a mask and domino. A gondolier will be waiting by the Rio di S. Felice at eleven-thirty. Be there, or I will throw myself into the canals. Your most devoted servant, Enrico Tonetti."

The note was poorly spelled as before, and I was more conscious than anything of a feeling of desperate uncertainty. I longed more than anything to crumple the thinly veiled instructions and grind them beneath my heelless morocco slippers.

Quickly I pulled myself together, casting a speaking glance at my misty-eyed reflection in the gilt mirror. "For shame, Luciana!" I scolded in a soft voice. "What would Bones think of you, ready to abandon the future of Venice for the sake of a pair of silver-blue eyes? What would your ancestors think, one of which was a cousin to a doge? What would your father think? And even worse, what would your mother think?"

Ah, but Carlotta Theresa Sabina Morrow del Zaglia would understand very well, I realized, thinking of my mother with belated fondness. But I knew with a sinking certainty that if I abandoned my quest, even if they all forgave me, I would never forgive myself.

Crumpling the note slowly, I was brutally aware of how alone and unprotected I was. I wished more than anything that Evan Fitzpatrick would appear as suddenly and mysteriously as he had already in the past two days, watching over me as I entered into the lion's den.

I dressed once more in one of my bottle-green dresses, hanging the rose silk in the cupboard with meticulous care. Maggie's questions seemed to have no end, and I answered them the best I could as I ate a nervous, scanty meal in the west salon and prepared for my first crack at espionage.

"Well, then, Miss Luciana," Maggie demanded as she finished the last of the fried eels that somehow failed to excite my appetite, "what do you think of him now? Don't you think you might do better with one of those nice young men from home that have been buzzing around you this past year or more? Johnny Phillips or the Viscount Herington?" She knew the answer before I even spoke it. A lifetime together banishes a lot of surprises.

"Maggie," I said in a quiet, determined voice. "I think you should be the first to know. Once I'm finished here in Venice I intend to marry Evan Fitzpatrick or die trying."

An unreadable expression passed over Maggie's pert face. "And what do you think your parents will say to that?" she questioned prosaically.

"I don't care. I think they'll trust my judgment, but if not . . .," I shrugged, signaling my unconcern. "The main person I have to convince is the bridegroom."

"Yes, well, that might take some doing. You won't get very far without his consent, and, if you don't mind my saying so, you haven't much experience with the ways of the opposite sex. You have to handle them very carefully to get them to do what you want—you have to convince them it was their idea in the first place."

I shook my head, smiling. "No, Maggie. I have no intention of tricking him. I will simply show him that he can't live without me."

"And how do you intend to do that? By knocking tea trays over his lady friends?"

I thought back to his amused smile, and my lips curved softly. "Perhaps. I'll simply have to take each day as it comes. Would you care to place a little wager on the outcome?" I questioned in dulcet tones.

She shook her head. "Never, Miss Luciana. I've seen you with that set expression on your face before, and never in twenty years have I known you to fail at what you set out to do when it came to something you really cared about. No, I have no doubt you'll get what you want. But I'll be mighty interested in how you set about doing it."

"I'll keep you informed," I promised, glancing at the ornate clock that was miraculously still in working order. Quarter past nine, and I still had to sneak up to the second floor and the cavernous closet where I remembered seeing an ancient mask and domino during our cleaning spree. I yawned hugely. "My, I'm exhausted. I can't imagine why I'm so tired all the time, Maggie. Aren't you tired, too?"

The look she cast me from her heavily fringed brown eyes was just slightly suspicious. "I've never known you to sleep so much in my entire life. Are you sure you're feeling all right, Miss Luciana?"

"Never been better," I said stoutly, simulating another yawn. "I'm just tired, that's all. Why don't we both go to bed early tonight and start the day at a more reasonable hour?"

"I think nine o'clock is a very reasonable hour to start the day," Maggie grumbled. "No one's up but milkmaids before then." She shook out the folds of the blue flowered dress. "Besides, I'd rather stay up and finish this. It does me no credit at all to see you wandering around Venice in those ugly old things." She cast a contemptuous eye over my tired old dress.

"Suit yourself," I said with an excellent show of unconcern, rising from the chaise longue and yawning once more. "I'll see you in the morning, then."

"Miss Luciana . . . ," Maggie peered up at me. "You're up to something."

"Up to something? Why, Maggie, how absurd!" I laughed convincingly.

"I've known you all my life, Miss Luciana," she said in a sober voice. "And I know when you're up to something. And knowing you, it's bound to be dangerous. I just want you to know, Miss Luciana, that I've loved every moment I've spent with you."

"Humbug!" I said bracingly. "You didn't care at all for the time I ran off with the circus, nor for the time I tried to go on the stage. And I shall continue to lead you a merry dance for as long as you care to follow. It will take more than a pack of Venetian and Austrian scoundrels to make an end of me." I gave her a brisk, bone-cracking hug. "Good night, my dear. And don't worry about me.

"How can I help it?" she asked of the room in general. "I wish to God your father was here."

"To protect me?" I questioned.

"No," she grumbled. "To beat some sense into your idiotic skull."

Chapter Eight

IT ALL PROVED far easier than I would have thought. The domino was right where I remembered it and was only slightly moth-eaten. My escape from Edentide was easily accomplished through the garden door, with no sound from the west salon to worry me about Maggie's surveillance. The gondolier looked vaguely familiar, and I wondered uneasily as I stepped into the gently rocking craft whether he had been dogging our footsteps during the entire last two days. As we pulled away from the quayside I saw a small, dark figure scuttle into the shadows, and suddenly I felt very small and very alone, surrounded by threatening creatures of the night. Surreptitiously I reached down and patted the huge kitchen knife I had secreted in one of my capacious pockets. Having willfully done away with what I assumed was Bones's protection, my hapless Uncle Mark, I would have to rely on myself alone. The thought was not overly reassuring.

We toured the back waterways at a leisurely pace, and I willed myself to relax. A strange sort of yowl suddenly welled up from the stern of the boat, and I felt my skin crawl in horror. The yowl was followed by another, and then another, and with near hysterical relief I recognized it. It was neither an infant being strangled nor one of those infamous Venetian alley cats. My gondolier had decided to serenade me.

There was no way I could silence the ghastly sounds of his reedy, nasal tenor with the unfortunate tendency to aim a little high for his pitch. Gritting my teeth into a semblance of a smile, I leaned back among the shabby cushions and trailed a languid hand in the warm salt water. Surely we would reach Tonetti soon, and he would put a stop to this God-awful caterwauling.

I still held a trace of hope that Tonetti and the urgency of the situation would send all trace of Evan Fitzpatrick from my fickle mind. I had already an image of Tonetti: tall, broad shouldered with raven dark hair, a cynical, dashing smile on his mobile mouth, strong yet gentle hands, and a charmingly deferential, flattering manner. In looks he would be startlingly like an Italianate version of Evan Fitzpatrick, in manner completely opposite. I sighed, and then winced, as my gondolier started on a new aria.

"Saaaaaaantaaaaa Looooooooocheeeeeyaaaaa," he howled, and my head began to pound. Just when I thought I could bear it no more, the gondola slowed, the voice mercifully stopped, and we pulled alongside a mooring pole outside an ancient pink palazzo, completely dark and deserted. As a matter of fact the entire waterway was devoid of people, and my skin began to prickle. It would be such an easy matter to dispose of an innocent, inquisitive young English lady. I watched the gondolier tie up to the mooring, once more trying to place the familiar shape of him.

When we were secure he turned and minced over to me, a difficult task in the rocking boat, and the fitful moonlight illuminated his face.

"You're the servant from the embassy!" I cried, in mingled relief and disappointment.

To my amazement he sank down on the cushions beside me, grabbed one hand in his soft, white ones, and pressed a very wet kiss upon it.

"Savior of Venice!" he declaimed thrillingly. "You see before you your humble slave, Enrico Tonetti! I am ready to lay down my life for you and the cause of a free Venice! I have only lived for this moment!"

Every word was vibrant with passion, and I stared at him with mingled amazement and distaste. "Mr. Tonetti . . . I . . . ."

"No!" He held up one slim white hand, heavy laden with rings. The scent of lilac was strong about him—no, almost overwhelming—and it clashed badly with the Macassar oil that slicked down his thinning brown hair over an obvious bald spot. His eyes were brown and spaniel-like and deliberately full of devotion, his mouth thick lipped and wet, his smile shy, ingratiating, and totally false. "You must call me Enrico, my sweet little pigeon. Or Tonetti, if you must. But none of this formal, English 'Mister' . . . ." Once more he kissed my hand. "We are in this together, eh? Two agents with a duty to perform. For you, dear lady, I am . . . ."

"Mr. Tonetti!" I snapped sternly, nettled. "I don't know why you are acting like this, but believe me there's no need. We are going to work together, not have an affair! If you would be so kind as to move back a bit . . . ?" Belatedly, he did so. "And if you could bring me up to date on the situation here in Venice. Have you any idea how I shall get into the general's rooms . . . ?"

Tonetti shrugged his thin shoulders sulkily. "I beg your pardon, dear lady. I cannot help it. It comes naturally to me. All my life I have adored the ladies. When I see a beautiful creature like yourself, all common sense is thrown to the winds. I promise I won't forget myself again." And to prove it, he pinched me.

I responded by socking him in the jaw, and tears of pain and hurt sprang into his expressive dark eyes. I judged him to be somewhat past forty, with the vain hope that he appeared fifteen years younger. "I trust you to behave yourself, Tonetti!" I said, sounding like a schoolmarm. "I gather this business is new to the both of us. If we can't rely on each other, I don't doubt we'll be in a rare pickle."

"Ah, but you are one of the aristocracy," he complained in a gentle sort of whine. "Nothing will happen to you other than they will deport you and slap your pretty little wrist. Tonetti will be garroted." He made a nasty strangling noise in his throat, and I shivered.

"Then why are you taking such risks?"

He struck a pose, with one hand in the Venetian night and the other in the area of his heart. "For the glorious cause of a free and united Italy!" he cried.

"For the money," I corrected cynically.

"That, too," he agreed, dropping his hand swiftly. "What with the *dimostrazione* keeping everyone out of Venice, it is hard for a man to make a living. And I have a wife and nine children to support."

"I am sure it is very difficult," I soothed. "What do you usually do? Are you a gondolier?"

He looked affronted. "Gondolier? Pah!" he spat into the canal. "Dear lady, do I look like a gondolier?" he demanded, and courtesy required me to assure him he did not. "When society is more normal, madonna, I am Venice's very finest gigolo."

It took me a moment to digest this casually offered information. "Doesn't your wife mind?" I choked out after a long moment.

"But why should she? She knows I am perfectly safe. It is all for looks, the *bella figura*, you know. What my sweet Maria doesn't like is when I don't bring home enough money, and then I must lower myself to more menial tasks, such as using my brother-in-law's gondola to bring in a few scudi." He sighed with the injustice of it all.

"But I thought your brother-in-law was General Eisenhopf's valet," I protested. "I thought that was how we were to gain admittance to his rooms . . ."

"My dear lady, I have seven sisters. All of whom have husbands. It is my brother-in-law Federico who has the gondola. My brother-in-law Livio is the valet. And I don't wish to involve him if I can help it. He will only want a share of the money."

I could not fault the man for his candor. "Have you made any plans?" I brought him back to more important matters. "How in the world are we to accomplish this?"

"Dear lady, of course I have made plans!" he appeared affronted. "It is all very simple. Sometime this week General Eisenhopf will be out of town on a very secret mission. Only his valet knows of this, apparently. He is planning to leave in the early afternoon and tell no one. You will simply dress in your most becoming dress"—a small sneer accompanied his glance down at my bottle-green costume showing through the domino—"and walk right into his room. Many women have done so; it will not be remarked upon. Your Italian is the pure Venetian kind; there will be no suspicions. While you are there you will search the room, and once you have found the paper you will leave, telling the guard outside you were tired of waiting for the old pig. I will be right outside the barracks, ready to receive you and your paper. And I will then take you back to the palazzo, you will board the next train for England, and Venice will be saved!" His voice rose to theatrical heights once more, and the lilac perfume wafted over me.

"And when is all this to happen?" I inquired sweetly.

"I will have to let you know." He lost some of his bravado. "I have not yet ascertained when it is that the general is leaving. Perhaps if you could meet me in the piazza tomorrow, I may have some word for you. But believe me, dear lady, there will be no danger to you whatsoever. It is I, Tonetti, who takes all the risks, and you who shall reap all the glory!" The nobility of this left him much moved.

"And you, Tonetti, will also have all the money," I remarked caustically. "That should comfort you on your long, gloryless nights."

"My nights, dear lady, are always filled with glory. You need only ask my wife." He drew himself up with full dignity.

"I am sure they are. I have not yet spoken of you to my Uncle Mark. I felt he would only complicate matters."

"Very wise, signorina. And what of that sweet little bambina who follows you everywhere?" He kissed his hands expressively.

"She is not to know anything either. The fewer people who know of this, the better. I doubt that either of them would be much good in a crisis."

"Then it is just the two of us, dear lady!" Once more he tried to embrace me, but a sharp elbow in his ribs dissuaded him.

"Just the two of us, Tonetti," I agreed, my heart sinking with a sudden, awful foreboding. "God help us."

Chapter Nine

"FOR GAWD'S SAKE, slow down, Miss Luciana!" Maggie panted behind me, scuttling gracelessly over the cobbled bridge that spanned the small canal. "Why are we in such a hurry?"

Abruptly I stopped, and Maggie crashed into me, my tall, strong body absorbing the blow with no trouble. Holding up the leather and gold cover of my book, I adorned my face with an idiotic simper for the edification of all around on the crowded thoroughfare, both Venetian and Austrian.

"Maggie, dear, I haven't done any sightseeing. And Mr. Ruskin's book is sooo fascinating," I cooed. "If only I could understand him a little better." Pouting prettily, I batted my eyes at a passing Tedesco who smirked in response, his thick Austrian lips curving in a leer. I dropped my voice so that no one else could hear. "Besides, I expect things to come to a head quite swiftly. If I'm to see anything at all of Venice before I leave, I'd better hurry."

If the prospect of our imminent departure didn't fill me with overwhelming pleasure, it was not to be wondered at. I had barely spoken two words to Evan Fitzpatrick, and how I would remedy that situation in the time allotted me was beyond imagining. My first duty was to Venice and Tonetti, but I knew in the question of Evan I would have to move fast. If I didn't secure his attention here in Venice, I might as well give up hope. In stately England the man wouldn't be allowed in the same county as me. I quickened my steps.

"If you fall, Miss Luciana, and soil your new dress," Maggie threatened, panting beside me, "I personally will push you in a canal. Right in front of a gondola."

I looked down with pleasure at the blue-and-white-flowered cotton dress swirling about my blue leather shoes. "Maggie, I'll guard it with my life," I swore, smugly aware of how pretty I looked in the new dress. Before I had time to congratulate myself too warmly, we were upon the piazza with the golden-domed, ornate splendor of St. Mark's and the Doges' Palace ahead of us.

"Will you look at that," Maggie breathed. "Is that where we're going?" She thrust one ripe hip forward to catch the attention of a handsome young gondolier.

I nodded. "It is indeed. We'll start with the basilica, then perhaps climb the Campanile, then the clock tower, and then the Doges' Palace. And after that we'll stop at Florian's Café for sugar and water." Tonetti, in parting,

195

hadn't said where or when he would meet us. All of Venice eventually ended up in the piazza, and I intended to partake of its myriad treats fully, leaving it up to the perfumed gigolo to find me.

"What a treat," Maggie said with less enthusiasm. "Why don't we start with the church, then the palace, and see how our energy holds out. I've been staying up late sewing for you, miss. I'm tired!" she yawned convincingly, winking unabashedly at the now-staring Venetian.

"Well, you can sit at Florian's and drink coffee while I continue exploring," I agreed with a show of reluctance. "But I'm sure you'd be missing a great pleasure."

"Pleasures like that I can afford to miss every now and then, Miss Luciana. Let's start with the church."

IN A WAY I could understand Maggie's boredom. St. Mark's was gloriously ornate, the mosaics glowing with color, the golden altar, bronze doors, marble columns, all contributing to an aura of somehow pagan splendor that wasn't much in keeping with my image of the holy mother church. This was the heart and soul of Venice, and yet somehow I wondered if it were the heart and soul of Luciana Carlotta del Zaglia. I had always assumed it was, but now suddenly I was having doubts.

"What does Mr. Ruskin say about this?" Maggie questioned in somewhat strident tones, pointing to a glorious mosaic of Salome in a stunning red medieval dress, dancing with lascivious abandon with John the Baptist's head borne aloft above her typically Venetian blond plaits.

"Not much," I replied, leafing through the tedious little book. "But she is magnificent, isn't she?" I stared up at her in profound admiration. "That's what I'd like to be like," I sighed longingly. "Bold and beautiful and seductive and powerful."

"I would say you've got a fair start," she remarked pertly. "I only hope you don't have men who scorn you decapitated."

I laughed. "A fitting punishment. I can't say as I blame the woman."

"Let's try the Doges' Palace," Maggie sighed after a moment, "and then we might go for some coffee. The café on the left as we came in seemed very pleasant."

"Maggie!" I murmured, shocked. "That was the Quadri. It's patronized by the Austrians and their sympathizers. Never the Venetians!"

"But Miss Luciana, you aren't Venetian either. You're three-quarters English, and there's no way you can change that."

I opened my mouth to protest, then shut it again. The simple truth was inescapable. "Well, even if I have a great deal of chilly English blood," I snapped, "it doesn't mean that I have to approve of the Tedeschi."

"Especially not with your parentage, Miss del Zaglia," a smooth Austrian voice broke through as we stepped into the dazzling sunlight, and it was all I could do to turn a bland, polite face to Holger von Wolfram.

"How nice to see you again, Colonel," I murmured calmly, batting my eyelashes in a manner that left the Austrian entirely unmoved. "My disapproval of the Imperial Army doesn't necessarily have to extend to individuals."

He bowed with perfect gallantry at my flirtatious remark. "I would hope not, Fraulein. Each of us has our duty to perform, no matter how unpleasant we may find it, but we must only hope that one can somehow remain friends."

A small chill ran down my spine. "And what unpleasant duties have you to perform, Colonel?"

He smiled, and the chill deepened. "But I was speaking of yourself, clear Fraulein. Have you seen the Ducal Palace? You must be sure not to miss it before you return to England. Which I trust will be soon. For your sake, as well as that of others."

I gave him a smile to match the dazzling brilliance of the Venetian sunlight. "I will see the Ducal Palace very soon, Colonel. In a matter of minutes, in fact. And I will be sure to pass on to my friends at home everything I see and hear while I'm in this glorious *Italian* city."

"You willfully misunderstand me," he growled. "Your parents did not warn you about me."

"Oh, yes, they did," I corrected him cheerfully. "But I choose not to be intimidated by an aging toy soldier." Nodding my head regally, I swept by him, with a nervous Maggie in my wake.

"Should you have been so rude, Miss Luciana?" she demanded, horrified, as we strode across the piazza toward the Ducal Palace with well-disguised haste. "He seems a powerful enemy to make."

"I didn't just make him my enemy," I turned and said coldly, still shaken from the encounter. "He's been my enemy since long before I was born. I no longer care who knows it." I started forward again. "Come along, Maggie."

A loud groan answered me, and I whirled back to find my maid clutching her ankle, an expression of agonizing pain on her suddenly pale face. "Maggie, what's wrong?" I demanded.

"A stone in my shoe, Miss Luciana. I think I'd best go back home. You go on ahead without me. I'll be fine." She took a few hobbling steps.

"I'll do no such thing. The Doges' Palace has been here for centuries, it will last a bit longer. I'll go get help." Briefly I thought of Tonetti, and abandoned the idea as hopeless.

"Don't be an idiot," my polite maid whispered sharply. "Go on ahead to the palace. A certain gentleman has been watching us from the portico, obviously awaiting us. It won't do you any good to have your chaperon trailing around after you." I looked up sharply, expecting to see Tonetti. Instead, Evan Fitzpatrick's tall form disappeared into the palace just ahead of us.

"But Maggie, your foot . . ." I protested weakly.

"There's nothing wrong with my damned foot," she hissed. "Go on ahead. I'll go back over the Rialto Bridge and get you a bolt of nice, soft muslin. In a warm, butter yellow, I think." And she hobbled off with amazing speed, leaving me staring after her with mingled amusement and fear and absolute amazement that wherever I happened to go in this city of water I would always run into Evan Fitzpatrick. It must be fate, or God's will, or something equally nebulous. And there was nothing I could do but stifle my conscience and give in to that fate. Tonetti and the future of Venice could wait another afternoon.

There was no sign of him when I entered the Ducal Palace. Throwing back my shoulders, I started forward.

I found him all alone in the square drawing room at the top of the great golden staircase, staring up with seemingly rapt attention at the ceiling painting, which my guidebook informed me was by Tintoretto, entitled "Doge G. Pruili with Justice, Peace, and St. Jerome." If I hadn't known better, I would have thought the Englishman had been following me, rather than the other way around. The room was deserted but for the two of us, and, after casting only a cursory glance at the florid masterpiece above my head, I cleared my throat alarmingly.

His extraordinary blue eyes swept over me in complete unconcern and then went back to their perusal of the ceiling. Undaunted, I took in all the glorious details of him—a far more impressive work of art as far as I was concerned.

He was so delightfully tall I could scarce believe it after a lifetime of being surrounded by short men. I knew from experience that he topped me by a good three inches, almost as tall as my father. Coupled with his broad, strong shoulders, which stretched the careless black coat he wore with such a dash, it was enough to make any young girl swoon. His legs were long and well-muscled, his ungloved hands both strong and sensitive-looking. The dark blond hair fell away from his face as he looked upward, his strong nose and chin in profile, the scar away from me. With great determination I dropped Mr. Ruskin on the floor with a loud thump, consigning Tonetti and his plots to a temporary perdition.

Once more he turned from his endless admiration of the tedious work of art, his eyes sweeping from my book on the marble floor, to my face, to the floor once more. A cynical smile curved his lips, and he moved with pantherish grace to retrieve the fallen Mr. Ruskin.

He would have turned away without a word if I hadn't quickly spoken. "It's a very boring book, you know."

He halted, reluctantly. "Is it?" he sounded very bored himself.

"Yes, it is," I pushed on. "I came upon one sentence that had two hundred and thirty-five words in it. Truly! I counted everyone."

Some of the mockery faded from the smile, leaving genuine amusement. "I have no doubt that you did. If you will excuse me, Miss . . ." He started to go, but once more I detained him.

"You knew my name two days ago."

The brief smile was chilly now. "Did I? Well, I have since forgotten it."

This time I did hold out my slender, gloved hand. "Then I shall have to remind you. My name is Luciana Carlotta del Zaglia."

He continued to stare down at me, making no attempt to take my hand, no attempt to introduce himself. I could feel my face flushing beneath his cool, aloof regard. "And your name is Evan Fitzpatrick," I pushed on.

"I can thank Lady Bute for that, I suppose," he said coolly. "My dear Miss del Zaglia, I would suggest you refrain from accosting strange men in your peregrinations around Venice. Despite Lady Bute's assertions, I am a gentleman, but the next man your wayward fancy lights upon might not be one. Good day to you." He turned that lovely, broad back on me and strode out the door, leaving me gasping with hurt, indignation, and rage.

Before I had time to master my conflicting emotions, one of the side doors opened and two surprisingly rough-looking Venetians entered. I peered at them closely, but neither was my absent gigolo. As I watched them move into the room, I thought absently how sweet it was that the lowest of Venetians would still be interested in their local treasures, the other part of me still envisioning Evan Fitzpatrick's head on a plate with me in a red dress like the mosaic Salome's, when suddenly I realized that the two brigands were not looking at the ceiling. They were looking straight at me and moving toward me with a great show of determination, something that looked ominously like a rope and a sack in their filthy hands. "That's the girl," the first one muttered. "It should be simple enough."

I darted to one side, but they were too fast for me. One meaty hand grabbed my wrist, while another cuffed me across the face with a force that stunned me, but only momentarily. A moment later I was down on the hard, marble floor kicking, biting, and scratching, my tormentors rather ineptly trying to control a giant madwoman as she fought tooth and nail.

One of the creatures kept trying to force a filthy rag into my mouth, and I barely had time to scream for help before I felt myself choking. A knife flashed, and I grew still, knowing my furious strength could do little good against that shining blade.

"That is very good," one of the men chuckled, his mouth showing stained and broken teeth. "The English lady will keep her mouth full of that, won't she? No more screams for this 'Evan,' eh?"

He yanked me to my feet and began binding me roughly with the thick hemp rope. The sack he held in one dirty hand was a capacious one, but not made for my noble proportions, and he tossed it in one corner with a curse.

"We'll have to take her out the back way, Gianni," he muttered. "The Tedeschi want her alive."

"I don't think you will." A dry, English voice broke through, and the three of us turned in amazement to see Evan Fitzpatrick standing very coolly in the doorway.

They hadn't had time to secure my bonds, and after a short struggle I slipped them off as my two abductors began circling round, edging toward Evan with murder on their swarthy, villainous faces. Yanking the rag out of my mouth, I spat a few times and then commenced screaming at the top of my rather powerful lungs.

Gianni turned back to me, rage and confusion on his bovine face. The knife flashed, and I felt the sleeve of my dress rip, followed by a trail of wet, warm blood down my arm. My first thought was of Maggie's rage at the destruction of her newest creation, and then I realized the danger in which both Evan and I stood.

"Goddamn it, Lucy, run!" Evan shouted, as the other villain jumped on him, and for a moment the two of them were a hideous, frightening tangle of thrashing limbs, the knife gleaming as they rolled around the floor. Gianni stared, unable to decide who to stab first, me or the Englishman, and I took advantage of his indecision to fling the heavy rope in his face.

It was like a red flag in front of an angry bull. I heard a hideous grunt behind me, but I had no chance to see who was the victor. I began backing away from the Italian, slowly, and he followed me just as slowly, an incredibly evil grin on his face. And then, horribly, I felt the solid marble wall behind me and knew I could escape no farther. I shut my eyes and prepared to meet my death.

Another hideous grunt followed, and I opened my eyes once more to watch Evan grappling with him, a cold, murderous expression on his face, which was even more frightening than the simple malice of my abductors. Loud noises and running feet came from the corridor. "*Avanti*, Gianni," the first man shouted as he struggled to his feet. With a sudden burst of strength the second man flung Evan aside, and I saw the knife flash. And then they were gone, leaving their two wounded victims.

I met Evan's eyes across the room. He was panting, disheveled, and blood oozed from a cut high up on his thigh. I could feel my hair slipping from its pins, and the wetness at my fingertips told me my own wound was bleeding in a cheerfully profuse manner.

Limping slightly, he moved across the floor and retrieved the shawl I had dropped during the melee. "Wrap this around you," he ordered tersely, holding it out to me.

Numbly I did as I was told, my eyes never leaving his pale, sweat-streaked face. We could hear voices from a great distance heading our way, and without another word he grabbed my good arm, his touch surprising me with its magnetic effect.

"Let's get the hell out of here," he muttered, dragging me forward out the door down the glorious, wide, golden stairway, our mingled blood leaving small patches on the floor.

"But shouldn't we report this?" I demanded breathlessly, feeling stupidly weak.

"To Holger von Wolfram?" He questioned cynically. "I think not. Who do you think sent them? Those two men are known to be Austrian hirelings. How bad is your arm?" His voice held a rough concern that made me bless my shallow wound.

"Only a scratch, I think. And your leg?"

He smiled down at me wryly, and I was in love. "It'll do. Can you manage to walk a ways?"

"I think so." Holding on to him like this, I was fully capable of walking miles. "Where are we going?"

"To my flat. Since you're so anxious to compromise yourself, that should please you no end." I was about to flare up at him when I saw a wince of pain flash momentarily in his beautiful eyes. And I knew he would never make it to his quarters alone. I summoned up my best smile, held on to him a little more tightly, and said nothing, smiling like the Giorgione Madonna Maggie had likened me to. And if there was a touch of Salome in me, how was anyone else to know?

Chapter Ten

I HAVE NEVER had so long or so nerve-racking a walk. Blindly I followed where Evan led, knowing by the inexorable strength of his muscles that he must be in great pain, but his face was smooth and expressionless. I draped my shawl around my arm, allowing it to trail down so that it hung and obscured his wound.

Across the wide, tourist-filled expanse of the Piazza San Marco, down narrow alleys, past churches and small canals and shops and palazzos, I walked until I thought I should faint with the tension and the heat. And suddenly La Fenice Theatre loomed up in front of us, and Evan's feet finally slowed their relentless pace until we came to a small, neat, pink building with window boxes brimming with nasturtiums of a riotously clashing orange and red.

"You'll have to keep your voice down," he warned me, his face still blank. The only inkling I had of the strain he was under was the unnatural paleness of his face, paleness that touched everywhere but the thin, red line of his scar. "My landlady is a very strict widow who doesn't approve of ladies in gentlemen's rooms."

I nodded, following him silently up the narrow, twisting stairs. It was as well he had warned me; it was all I could do not to cry out as his customary grace deserted him for a moment and he stumbled against the wall. Hastily he pulled himself upright, leaving a dark red splotch of blood on the whitewashed surface.

Vainly I tried to scrub at the mark with my now blood-soaked shawl, but it only served to smear it. "Leave it," he ordered briefly, and continued upward. There was nothing I could do but follow.

It was dark in the apartment, but blessedly cool after the burning heat of the midday sun. I stayed just inside the closed door, leaning against the wall and willing my cursed dizziness to pass. Such feminine weakness was not at all like me, and I could have wished for a better time for this sudden upsurge of delicacy. I took a few deep breaths, determined not to swoon, when I felt myself caught up in a pair of strong arms. The sensation was so pleasant I gave up all idea of fainting. And then the darkness closed in.

WHEN CONSCIOUSNESS returned I was lying stretched out on an exceedingly comfortable sofa. Evan was beside me, bending over my arm and cleaning the long, deep scratch with assiduous care.

"Damn!" I said loudly and clearly, and those silver-blue eyes met mine for a startled moment.

"Damn what?"

"I have never fainted in my entire life," I assured him ruefully. "I certainly picked a fine time to do so."

"Never fainted?" he mocked. "How can any properly brought up young girl of these times and fashions say such a thing?" His voice was rough, but his hands, as they carefully washed my wound, were incredibly gentle.

"I've never worn a corset," I explained reasonably. "Most women swoon because of tight lacing."

The look from those eyes was definitely perplexed, and too late I realized the impropriety of my words.

"Oh, damn," I said again. "I shouldn't have mentioned corsets, should I?"

"Certainly not. You also shouldn't say 'damn' so frequently," he said calmly, wrapping my arm in clean, soft linen. "What would your parents say if they heard you?"

I chortled. "They'd probably say, 'Damn it, don't swear so much.'" I eyed his handiwork with professional approval. "You do seem to take an inordinate amount of interest in my parents," I observed casually.

He leaned back on his heels, wincing slightly. "It fascinates me that they would let such an unprincipled hoyden as yourself loose upon Europe. I think a few years in a convent would do you a world of good." He rose, swaying imperceptibly, and a moment later I was on my feet.

"Sit down and let me see your wound," I ordered sternly, staring up into his scarred face with a determined expression.

"Certainly not," he snapped, manlike. "I'm entirely capable of taking care of it myself."

"Don't be absurd," I snapped back. "I have a great deal of experience in medical matters. I used to assist the village doctor in all manner of things. I've helped babies being born, amputations, typhus . . ."

"Then a mere knife wound should be too trivial for one of your vast experience. Unless you were planning on amputating."

"Evan," I said in a low, dangerous, not-to-be-thwarted tone of voice, "I must insist that you take off your pants and let me take care of your wound."

My voice trailed off before his burst of laughter. "You certainly are direct and to the point, aren't you?" he said after a moment. "Well, my dear child, if you have no modesty, I'm afraid I do." He limped over to a chair, lowering himself gingerly, and with the aid of strong fingers and a letter opener proceeded to rip away the remainder of his pants leg.

It was a great deal worse than I had expected, and as I knelt there on the floor, holding a wet compress to his thigh, I wondered that he had been able to walk so far with what had appeared to be only mild discomfort. "This must hurt you," I muttered under my breath as I tried to clean up the wound.

"Thank you, it does," he replied politely, watching me out of hooded eyes as I knelt between his long legs and worked on his wound. "You'll have to disinfect it," he said after a moment.

"I know that, much as I dislike the thought. Do you have any whiskey here?"

"Would an English gentleman's home be complete without a bottle of whiskey?" he mocked. "Over by the table." As I came back and knelt once more in front of him, some devil prompted him to tease me. "I do hope you're enjoying this, Lucy. Lady Bute will be dying to hear all the details of your encounter with the evil divorcée."

Calmly I poured whiskey all over the deep wound, wickedly pleased to see him stiffen in pain. "I have no intention of confiding this afternoon's adventures to Lady Bute. Perhaps I should tell you that you are not of such all-consuming interest to me as you seem to believe."

"Should you tell me that?" he said in an odd tone of voice.

I looked up and met his silver-blue eyes with a clear gaze. "Of course, I should. But it would be a lie." And with a splendid show of unconcern I went back to my task, wrapping the strips of linen around his lean, muscled thigh with only the slightest shaking of my hands, and I controlled my desperate urge to throw my arms around his waist and rest my head against his broad chest with more real effort. When it was done I looked up again, surprising an odd expression on his face, one that I couldn't read at all.

"I've done my best," I said briskly. "It's my professional opinion that you should stay off it for the next few days."

"Is it now? And who's going to wait upon me, bring me my dinner, pour me my whiskey?" he questioned softly. "Were you planning to volunteer?"

Shaking my head, I rose abruptly and walked halfway across the room. His proximity had been even more disturbing than I had let myself realize. "I could do with a cup of tea," I said after a long moment. "Would you care for some?"

He nodded, pulling himself to his feet. "You'll find everything you need in the kitchen. In the meantime I'll change my clothes. And no"—he held up a restraining hand as I impulsively moved forward—"you may not help me. I am still entirely capable of taking off my clothes without your assistance. When I've changed and the tea is ready, my dear Lucy, I will be ready for your explanation." His eyes were like blue smoke. "And I expect it to be believable."

I found myself singing as I bustled around his kitchen, happier than I remembered being in a long, long time, despite the throb in my arm and the worry in my mind. I couldn't betray my business here in Venice—Bones would kill me. The more people who knew of my mission, the less chance of success. But oh, I did so want to confide in him!

I made the tea strong and peaty, a noble restorative, and carried it into the drawing room just as Evan emerged from the far doorway, dressed in a pair of soft brown pants and shirt sleeves. As I stared at him in witless admiration, I thought once again how very attractive men were in their loose white shirts, the collars unbuttoned to show the beginnings of a tanned throat. He moved across the room with the barest trace of a limp and took the tray from my nerveless fingers. And unbidden, the thought flashed through my mind that he must be accustomed to wounds far worse than his recent one to be able to survive it without more than a show of discomfort.

I poured for the two of us, suddenly shy, and silently allowed him to tip a generous dollop of whiskey into my tea cup. He leaned back on the sofa, took a deep drink of his spiked tea, and stared at me for a long, uneasy moment out of those hypnotizing eyes.

I cleared my throat. "I suppose you're wondering why those two . . . two men tried to hurt me," I said in what I hoped was a casual tone of voice. "You said they were Austrian hirelings?"

"That's exactly what they were. Now what has a sweet, innocent young lady like yourself done to earn the enmity of the Imperial Army?"

His casual words brought the unpleasant truth home to me with full force. Someone, some fairly powerful member of the Austrian forces, knew why I was here in Venice. My chances for success had just dropped to a bare possibility. I fiddled with my teacup, playing for time. "I suppose it might be because of my parents," I offered. "My father was a Venetian patriot—he made a lot of enemies twenty-five years ago." I sighed. "But why don't they just deport me? Why try to hurt me?"

"They were trying to kidnap you, my dear Lucy," he contradicted flatly. "Obviously they are under the impression you know something you shouldn't. Is that true?"

I gave him my most innocent, amber gaze, willing him to believe me. "What could I know?" But Evan wasn't convinced. "That's for you to say. And they probably haven't got enough proof to deport you. Just suspicions, no doubt because of your family connections." His voice was lightly mocking. "When they can do nothing through normal channels it is a simple enough matter to dispatch two brigands to take care of things, no questions asked. I would suggest, my dear Lucy, that you keep away from dark alleys."

"Why do you call me Lucy?" I questioned out of the blue.

He raised an eyebrow. "Your name is Luciana, is it not? Lucy suits you better. Besides, I have no intention of trying to twist my tongue around your absurd name. I'll call you Lucy if I please."

"I wasn't objecting," I said evenly, meeting his gaze. "I'll do my best to keep out of solitary places from now on, I promise. Tell me," I hesitated a moment, "would you have killed them if they hadn't run away?" The thought had been preying on my mind for the last few minutes.

"Without a doubt." No remorse crossed his face, and I wondered at his callous attitude.

"You don't seem to mind the idea," I said crossly. "Have you killed men before?"

"I was a soldier, dear Lucy. I have killed a great many men in my life," he said wearily.

"And why are you no longer a soldier?"

He smiled, but it wasn't a pleasant smile. "I resigned my commission when I divorced my wife. Surely Lady Bute informed you of that juicy tidbit?"

"Why did you do that?" I asked with my usual subtlety and tact.

But Evan seemed disposed to enlighten me. "Why did I divorce my wife or why did I resign my commission?" There was a bleak, haunted look somewhere in the back of his eyes. "I divorced my wife rather than murder her. I resigned my commission rather than be cashiered. I was in a very old, very historic regiment that had no room for a divorced man in its noble ranks." His voice was flat and cold. "Which brings me back to you. I am waiting for your explanation."

"Explanation?" I echoed, confused. "I thought we agreed that they were two Austrian hirelings."

"Not about that, my angel," and the endearment was mocking. "I want to know why you've been following me. Falling at my feet, tossing tea trays over young ladies, dropping books right and left. You don't do this with every man you meet, do you?" His voice was cool and clipped and so offensive I wanted to throw my teacup at his dark gold head. Instead I took another deep gulp, feeling the whiskey warm my bones and relax my tight nerves.

Oh, my, but he was an unhappy man! I would have gladly given ten years off my life to be able to go up to him and smooth away that angry, bitter expression from his handsome face, to press my lips against that angry red scar. And as quickly as it had come all my fury evaporated. "Not every man," I replied lightly. "Only the most attractive."

"Hasn't that gotten you into a great deal of trouble?" he barked. "How many men has your fancy lighted upon?"

I smiled sweetly. "Only one."

A long silence ensued. "Well, then, my dear Lucy, I suggest you take yourself back to England as soon as possible and see if you can find some other young man to take your fancy. If I'm the first man you've been attracted to, then you can't be long out of the schoolroom. Go back to England, and your parents can introduce you to some likely young men."

I finished the tea, poured myself some more, and added a generous dose of whiskey. "I am twenty-three years old, Evan," I said calmly. "I have had a season, met scores of eligible young men, received three proposals of marriage, two of which were fairly suitable."

"Then why didn't you accept them?"

I took a deep breath and plunged right in there. "Because for the last twenty-three years I've been waiting for you."

The next pause was even longer. His teacup crashed down on the tray. "Jesus Christ!" he swore. "You must be completely out of your mind!"

To my relief I could recognize the strange blend of irritation, amusement, and fascination in his angry eyes, and I continued with more assurance. "Not at all. And you, my dearest Evan, have been waiting for me for the last . . . thirty-six years?"

"Thirty-seven," he corrected, distracted. "Which goes to prove that I'm too old for you anyway. I doubt my dear Amelia would have agreed that I'd been waiting for you."

"Well," I said with great practicality, "from what I hear of your late wife, you would have been a lot better off waiting for me, instead of getting involved with a monster like that."

He rose then and stalked across the room, looking more and more like the dangerous panther I had likened him to. He leaned over my chair, putting his hands on the arms and effectively imprisoning me. His face was very close, and his blue eyes blazed in a rage of noble proportions;

"My dear Lucy," he said softly, dangerously, "you are playing with fire. You cannot come to a man's apartment and tell him that you've been waiting for him all your life and then expect nothing to happen. Especially when you're absurdly lovely."

I met his gaze serenely. "What *is* going to happen?"

He stood up abruptly, yanking me to my feet with a jerk that left my arm throbbing more than ever. "Just this," he said in an undertone, and brought his mouth down on mine.

I had never been kissed like that before, either in love or in anger, and it was quite a devastating experience. He forced my mouth open with his, and his tongue plundered me ruthlessly, a cruel invader with no love, tenderness, or affection. Instinctively I resisted the harshness of his embrace, but it only served to increase his determination. My mouth was bruised, I could taste blood from my lip mixed with the whiskey on his breath, and still he kissed me, his hands like iron bars around me, so that I couldn't break free. And then suddenly I didn't want to escape. Twining my arms around his neck, I wove my fingers through his long, fair curls and answered his mouth as completely as my inexperience and infatuation allowed. And the violence left him, his lips softened on mine, moving to my eyes, my cheeks, my forehead in short, sweet, unhurried little kisses. A small sigh of pleasure escaped me as he brought his mouth to mine once more, and then suddenly I was thrust away, alone and lost, with the shelter of his arms brutally withdrawn.

Turning his back on me, he strode across to the chaise longue, retrieved my blood-stained shawl, and tossed it to me with an abrupt gesture. "Wrap this around you," he ordered coldly, "and I'll see you home."

I had had enough. "Coward," I said clearly and distinctly, and ran from the room, not bothering to shut the door behind me. A moment later I was lost in the crowded alleys, as all of Venice headed toward their afternoon promenade along St. Mark's Square, and, to my despair, there was no tall shadow behind me.

Chapter Eleven

THERE WAS NO way I could hide my damaged condition from my ever-faithful Maggie. With questions, shrieks of outrage, solicitous care, and stern scoldings she divested me of my blue flowered dress, which she swore she could salvage, brewed some strong, whiskey-less tea, and tucked me up in bed with a nice custard as a restorative and a box of rich, creamy chocolates.

"Where did the candy come from?" I demanded as I settled back among the feather pillows, my eyes devouring the luscious chocolates that my tea and whiskey-filled stomach rejected.

"They were delivered a short while before you got home," Maggie replied, distracted. "I couldn't find a note."

"Probably lost during delivery," I said easily.

"Maggie, dear, could I . . . ?" I held up my empty bowl appealingly, and a moment later I was alone.

The note wasn't too difficult to find, if you knew where to look. At this point I was getting used to Tonetti's flowery style, though the lilac scent ruined two perfectly good chocolates.

"Beloved Angel" it read, and mournfully I remembered who else had called me angel that day. "Words cannot describe my feelings of despair at missing you this afternoon! Only say that your poor, wretched servant may hope to see you tomorrow. Otherwise, all will be lost! Your slave, Enrico Tonetti."

I crumpled the note in my hand, wishing desperately that I had someone to turn to, to confide in, other than that scented fop. There was little doubt in my mind who I wanted that someone to be, and unbidden, the feel of his mouth on mine returned with shattering force. Wearily I crawled deeper under the covers, huddling against the damp, the loneliness, and the danger of the Venice night.

IT TOOK ALL my powers of persuasion and native guile to escape Maggie's almost fanatical surveillance the next afternoon. All morning she had clung to me like a limpet, devising the most absurdly obvious reasons for me not to leave the moldering palazzo. For the time being I was only too happy to stay within the ancient walls of the family home. Despite the centuries of violence that had abounded in and around the old palace, there was a curious aura of peace and serenity which I found most appealing. I knew full well that I hadn't much time for peace and serenity left to me in Venice. Obviously Tonetti's plans had been made. It was up to me to prepare myself, both physically and mentally, for the ordeal ahead. And the first thing I had to do was put Evan Fitzpatrick firmly out of my mind.

But that was easier said than done. Dutifully I sat in a small, hard chair in the west salon and stitched with careful little stitches on Maggie's newest creation, a muslin frock of butter yellow that would undoubtedly make me look like an overgrown daffodil. I could think of worse things to look like. And instead of Tonetti, all morning long my mind kept going back to Evan Fitzpatrick and the feel of his mouth on mine, his hard, clever hands caressing my love-starved body with a sureness that came from long and diligent practice.

It wasn't the first time I had ever been kissed. Various proper young gentlemen had pressed importunate, dry lips against mine during indiscreet evening walks. One had even gone so far as to tumble me into a sheltering clump of bushes. The poor young viscount had returned to the party with a blackened eye and severely impaired dignity, and I, my virtue still intact. But nothing had prepared me for this sudden upsurge of passion, the simple, immediate desire that had swept over me yesterday when Evan had touched me. And I remembered vaguely my thought then, that, this is how a kiss should be.

"Whatever it is you're thinking of," Maggie broke in caustically, "you'd better get down on your knees and pray for forgiveness. I've never seen so wanton a look on anyone's face in my life."

Quickly I pulled myself back together. "Then you've never looked in a mirror," I shot back, pleased with my sally. "I have no reason to pray for forgiveness, Maggie. I was just daydreaming."

"That was more than daydreaming, Miss Luciana. There's some practical knowledge in your eyes that wasn't there before, or I miss my guess. I don't know what your parents will say." She sighed gustily.

Carefully I knotted the thread. "They will say, Maggie, that it's about time." I put the froth of yellow material to one side. "And now I think I'll take a nap. I haven't been getting enough sleep since we've been in Venice." I yawned convincingly.

Suspicion flared in her hazel eyes. "You've never needed more than a few hours' sleep before, Miss Luciana. Why are you so tired all of the time?"

"I think all this heat enervates me," I replied guilelessly. "Why don't you take a nap yourself, Maggie? It's too hot to do anything else."

She looked torn, and the moment she spoke I realized her dilemma. Lust and duty had always been stern taskmasters, and she was leaning heavily in the former, having devoted her morning to her hapless charge. "There's a very nice young man who's offered to take me for a ride in his boat," she said with what in another person I might have called shyness. "If you really don't need me I might let him know that I'd be available this afternoon . . ."

"I'm sure he already knows that you're available, Maggie," I murmured, eyeing her low-cut dress that pulled across her straining bodice. In anyone else I might have thought the dress needed alteration, but with Maggie I knew it had been designed with that effect carefully in mind. "You go on ahead. I think I might explore some of the upper rooms, maybe nap up there. There might be more of a breeze up near the top floor." I waved a hand listlessly in front of my face, stirring the warm, humid air only slightly.

Poor Maggie still hesitated. "Well, if you're sure. I'd be glad to stay, Miss Luciana, if you thought it would be necessary. Pietro could come another day."

"Maggie, I shall be sound asleep in five minutes, and no doubt will sleep till dinnertime." I yawned again, hoping to hide the tense excitement that stirred beneath my uncorseted breast. "Don't waste another moment on me, for heaven's sake."

"Well, if you're sure . . ." she agreed doubtfully. "I only hope I can trust you to do as you say, and not leave the house."

I looked shocked and hurt. "Maggie, would I lie to you?" I protested. Maggie only shook her head.

IT TOOK ME FIVE minutes to change into the newly mended blue flow-ered dress with its shorter, modified sleeves, repin my long, thick hair, and find a fresh pair of gloves before I was out the door. I had no idea what time Tonetti planned to find me, but I knew I should make myself available for as long a time as possible. Maggie would come looking for me by five, but it was only half past two, and I could take my time.

By their own accord my feet started toward the Merceria and the Rialto Bridge. I wandered among the shops, most of them closed in the broiling early afternoon sun, and bought a few things: some bright yellow ribbons to match my dress, an ell of lace, which would look exquisite with my mother's light coloring, a string of millefiori beads that were far too expensive.

In Italy all roads lead to Rome. In Venice all streets and canals seem to lead inexorably to St. Mark's Square. It wasn't long before I found myself strolling along the pavement stones on the huge square, peering into shop windows, ignoring the milling Austrian soldiers in their gaudy uniforms and loud cheeriness.

St. Mark's Square seemed like an odd choice for a meeting, overflowing as it was with boisterous Austrians, curious Englishmen, superior Frenchmen, all of whom eyed me with embarrassing approval.

One ruddy-faced young soldier had just left his seat at one of the cafés and headed toward me when I saw Tonetti off to one side, resplendent in a pale lavender suit, beckoning me. When the Austrian looked again, I had disappeared under the New Procuratie, strolling along with seeming abandon as I chatted with my supposed Venetian lover.

"Signorina del Zaglia," he breathed, his spaniel's eyes moist with passion and a darting look of fear. "I have been half-crazy with worry." He seized my gloved hand and began slobbering over it, dampening the thin kid. I forced myself to bestow a flirtatious smile upon his oiled and thinning hair.

"For heaven's sake, control yourself," I hissed, snatching back my hand with a fond glance. "Don't overdo the whole thing."

He pressed one well-manicured hand to his breast. "Forgive me, Madonna," he said soulfully. "But the loveliness of your radiant graciousness makes me forget myself. Ah, if this were only a dream, the two of us could go off together, away from all this . . ."

"On whose money?" I questioned cruelly. "All English ladies are not heiresses, you know."

"But . . . but you are a del Zaglia!" he protested, momentarily disconcerted. "Of course you have money."

"Only if my parents approve," I informed him. "Besides, I don't think your wife and nine children would care for it."

"Soon to be ten," he corrected glumly. "My wife informed me of the happy news last evening." He sighed soulfully. "Surely there must be easier ways to make a living."

If there were, I had no doubt Signore Tonetti would find them. "This will only take one night, Tonetti," I said bracingly. "A few short hours, and you will be a rich man. And you aren't running any risks—you don't have to retrieve the paper."

"True enough," he agreed, brightening. "It is you they will catch, and I'll be long gone." His smile of satisfaction grated, and I put a lover-like hand on his lavender forearm and pinched him, hard.

"It would be best," I said icily, a sweet smile on my face, "if neither of us is caught. I'm counting on you to see to that. When are we going to do this?"

He pulled himself together. "He leaves tomorrow afternoon. Tomorrow night I will come and fetch you, sometime around nine. You'll get rid of the little bambina, yes?"

"Yes, I'll get rid of Maggie."

"We will stop first at a shop I know of, where you will change your clothes. Something a bit more suited to an Austrian whore. We'll continue on to the barracks, I'll escort you to the general's rooms, and from then on it is up to you. A few moments' search, a simple escape, and all will be well."

"And what if someone questions my presence?" I demanded, unmoved by this rosy picture.

"Signorina del Zaglia, with the dress and face paint I will provide, and the physical attributes nature so generously endowed you with, you will have no trouble at all lulling the suspicions of an entire platoon of Tedeschi. All you have to do is bat your eyes like this"—he demonstrated, and I had to stifle a burst of laughter—"and show some of your lovely . . . er . . . chest, and the Tedeschi will forget their questions. Trust me, Madonna."

I allowed him an overlong salute to my glove, and smiled benevolently. "Tomorrow night at nine, my pigeon," he announced thrillingly. "But now I must fly."

And fly he did, leaving me watching his mincing figure depart with mixed emotions. Irritation, amusement, and a very real fear warred within me for control. God help me if I failed tomorrow night! Tonetti certainly wouldn't.

As I turned I came face to face with that bastion of England, Florian's Café. I hardly even felt surprise as I recognized one dark gold head alone at a distant table, one pair of silver-blue eyes watching me with mingled curiosity and irritation before he buried himself once more in his paper.

I hesitated for only a moment. Tomorrow I could very well die—today I intended to seize every last moment of life that I could. With a graceful self-assurance I was far from feeling, I walked over and seated myself opposite Evan Fitzpatrick.

He lowered the newspaper slowly, those eyes meeting mine with an unreadable expression in their smoky depths. Before he could open his mouth to order me away, however, an eager waiter appeared at the table with the customary, "Behold me!"

Evan hesitated, but only for a moment. "Two coffees," he said tersely, and then flashed the smile that he seemed to reserve for everyone but me. The waiter responded, as he couldn't help but do, and ran off to do his bidding. And then the silver-blue eyes swung back to me, and of course the smile vanished.

"Your admirer desert you?" he questioned coldly. "He should have seen you home. I would have thought you learned your lesson yesterday. Venice is a dangerous place for an unescorted lady. I hadn't thought to see you again."

The thought didn't seem to faze him in the least. "Whereas I rather thought I would see you," I replied in a low voice. "So I had no need of another escort." I smiled brilliantly across the table. "Don't glower at me like that—it doesn't become you. You might as well accept your fate."

A look of reluctant amusement warmed the chilly depths of his eyes. "Now I'm sure you're about to tell me what that fate is, aren't you, my dove?"

I smiled serenely. "Indeed. Though you know it as well as I do."

The coffee arrived, and Evan stirred it absently, his eyes never leaving my face. For a moment he seemed lost in thought, and I leaned back and sipped the strong, bitter brew, happy just to be sitting in the sunshine in that glorious square, across from the man I knew I would love.

Finally he seemed to come to a decision, and his face was infinitely warm and beguiling as he spoke. So beguiling, in fact, that he only stiffened my resolve.

"My dear Lucy, you are being absurd. You've only just met me, we've never even been formally introduced, and yet you have cast maidenly decorum to the winds in a misguided fascination for me. I can't believe England is so lacking in young men that you would be desperate enough to have fancied a passion for an aging adventurer like me. A young lady with your very considerable physical charms could hardly have been lacking in admirers. Unless England has changed a great deal in the last two years."

"Two years?" I echoed, fastening on this last piece of information. "But what about your son? Haven't you seen him in that long?"

His face darkened, and I knew that once more I had overstepped the bounds of propriety. "My son is in the very capable hands of my brother Simon and his wife. They both adore him, and no doubt Jamie is far better off without me around."

The bitter expression was back around his mouth, and I wanted to kiss it away.

"Do you think he feels that way?" I asked in a low voice, wondering whether he would throw his coffee cup at me. I wouldn't have blamed him.

"No, Miss del Zaglia, he doesn't feel that way. But he will, sooner or later. He'll have no choice."

"And are you better off without him around?"

A bitter laugh escaped him. "No, I'm not. But I have enough sense to realize what is best for Jamie. I only wish you had the sense to keep your lovely little nose out of other people's business."

I met his gaze calmly, unabashed. "I am tactless," I admitted, "and indiscreet. You will have to work on curing me of it."

Another long silence. "Lucy," he said gently, "you know nothing about me."

I took another sip from my coffee, hoping it would take long, blissful hours to finish the tiny cup. "I know a great deal just from looking at you," I replied evenly.

"Such as?" he mocked. "You can tell that I'm scarred, bitter, and nasty to young girls. You are only lucky that I haven't given way to my baser instincts and become even nastier, and in more devastating ways."

I ignored him. "I can tell a great many things about you. You're obviously idealistic, or you wouldn't be so very cynical all the time. People are only cynical when their ideals have been betrayed." I leaned back in my chair, prepared to enjoy this, putting my fingertips together in a meditative fashion. "I would say, and this is sheer conjecture, mind you, that you would be the type to love the country rather than the city, fishing rather than hunting, old, smelly spaniels rather than beagles or bloodhounds."

I had caught his attention for sure this time. "You are surprisingly accurate," he said softly. "Continue."

"Well"—I thought for a moment, warming to my subject—"you would prefer Venice to Paris, Scotland to England, old ballads and sea chanteys to classical arias. You must have a lovely bass voice," I added absently.

"Not too bad," he admitted. "Go on."

"You prefer riding to driving even the most elegant curricle. You don't want to be tied to anyone or anything. You love the sea and the mountains. You read a lot. You're capable of killing, if necessary. And I think you're still capable of loving."

His eyes narrowed. "Very astute. And who have you been talking with?"

"No one. I just know you."

"You are astonishingly correct on almost every suit, but you forgot I like cats, too. You also neglected to mention my taste in women." There was a challenge there, and reluctantly I drained the last of my coffee.

I let my eyes wander over the long, lean length of him, the overlong dark blond hair, the tanned, scarred face with those fathomless blue eyes surrounded by tiny little lines, the broad shoulders, the long, slender hands that could snuff out a life so easily, that could bring me to life just as carelessly. I smiled, a small, sad, weary smile. "You probably have the execrable taste to prefer tiny, fragile, little blonde ladies."

One of those hands reached across the table and captured mine and held it lightly, so that it was hard to remember the steely strength in those long, thin fingers. "And that's where you're wrong," he said gently. "I much prefer tall, statuesque ladies with hair like the night, eyes like honey, warm and sweet, and soft, rounded bodies with just the right curves." He brought my hand to his mouth for a lingering moment, and I felt absurdly like crying. "But I also have enough sense never to seduce infatuated virgins, either highborn or otherwise. This will be the last time I warn you, Lucy. Go away. Go as far away and as fast as you can. The next time I might not let you leave." And he dropped my hand, stood up, and strode swiftly away from me through the rapidly increasing crowd, only the slightest trace of a limp reminding me of his wound. If he had turned back he would have seen a smile of wicked triumph light my face.

Chapter Twelve

THAT EVENING AND the next day passed far too swiftly, and yet the hours seemed to drag at a snail's pace. I had always thought I was so very brave, but the thought of dressing in some revealing evening dress and brazening my way into a gentleman's bedroom filled me with icy foreboding. That small, baser part of me wanted desperately to run back to Evan Fitzpatrick's small apartment by La Fenice, to fling myself against his broad chest and pour out the insane thing I was planning to do. He would never let me; he would go in my stead.

And be caught, and hanged, I thought wearily, knowing that I had no choice. Where the hell was Uncle Mark when I really needed him? Anyone with a small portion of brain would guess what I had planned and stop me. But not gullible Uncle Mark. He believed every word his devious goddaughter told him and was no doubt enjoying himself royally with the blue-haired widow.

Well, there was no hope for it. I would be waiting to meet Tonetti tonight, and if I failed to survive, well, nobler people than I had perished in the cause of a free Venice.

And if I did survive, and succeed, I wouldn't return to Edentide. I would have Tonetti take me straight to Evan's apartment, where I would pour out the whole reckless tale to him and receive whatever comfort I could manage to elicit from his cold, restricted soul. Remembering his last words to me, I had no doubt his response would be sufficient.

"Is something wrong with you, Miss Luciana?" Maggie asked the next evening when I had stalked the salon floor for the better part of an hour, each time ending up by the little balcony. "You haven't eaten a thing all day, you're nervous as a cat, and I know for sure you barely slept last night. I could hear you tossing and turning and muttering."

I managed a convincing laugh. "Something wrong, Maggie?" I echoed innocently. "Nothing's wrong. I suppose I'm just homesick. I don't think this Tonetti will ever contact me."

Maggie's eyes narrowed, and I wondered for a moment whether she was really fooled. "I was thinking of asking Mr. Ferland to stop by this evening after dinner and see if he's heard anything. We can't stay here forever, you know, miss. Your parents should be returning before long, and I'd hate to have to arrive after they did."

"No!" I protested wildly, and then managed to smile weakly. "Don't bother Uncle Mark. I'm sure he'll come by as soon as he hears anything. Perhaps you're right though. I *am* exhausted. I couldn't sleep a wink last night. I think I'll go to bed early tonight and try to make up for it." I yawned widely, my eyes taking in the ornate clock hands. A quarter to nine.

"It's early yet!" Maggie protested. "You'll just lie in bed and toss and turn."

"No, I won't," I yawned again. On impulse I moved across the room and gave her a brief, bone-cracking hug. "I'll sleep like the dead." A shiver passed over me at my unfortunate choice of words. "I love you, Maggie."

"Well, I love you, too," she replied, surprised. "Are you sure you're all right?"

"Positive! Good night." And I made my escape before she could ask another importunate question.

TONETTI WAS WAITING for me by the corner of the deserted side canal. I could smell his lilac scent long before I saw him, and once more he was in his gondolier's garb. He helped me down into the rocking boat, his damp hands betraying his nervousness, and for once I was spared his flowery compliments. The stop at the small, odorous tailor's shop was far too short, just long enough for me to don an ornate, somewhat tattered gold satin dress still reeking of cheap scent from its last wearer, the top of the dress practically nonexistent. In vain I tugged at the lace bertha in an attempt to restore some measure of modesty to my toilette. It was hopeless. It was also, I had to admit, outrageously flattering.

Tonetti himself painted my face, his eyes straying toward my décolletage at every other stroke. "Signorina," he breathed, when he had finished and was able to master his emotions, "if you should ever be in need of money, I know of any number of gentlemen . . . ," he swallowed. "God but you are lovely," he muttered in Italian. "Such amazing . . ."

The last word I didn't understand, but his meaning was inescapable. I considered slapping him, but thought better of it. I needed all the help I could get tonight, so I merely inclined my head graciously, the thick, black locks in their slatternly arrangement tumbling over my shoulders.

It was all deceptively simple. When we arrived at one of the side entrances of the imposing building that was housing the upper classes of the Austrian army, there was no one guarding the portal. Tonetti gestured proudly to his narrow chest. "A few bribes, Signorina, are worth the money." The long, cavernous hallway was practically deserted, and as we walked silently down the marble passageway, I could hear my heart pounding. It must be after ten, I reasoned, and then the pounding ceased. A very tall, very broad, slightly drunken Austrian officer was making his way toward us, a gleam in his glazed eye. I kept my gaze demurely lowered, trying not to panic as I heard Tonetti's desperate intake of breath.

"And where is this lovely creature going, eh?" he demanded when we came abreast of him. "She must be new around here. What is your price, villain?" This was all delivered in a very jovial tone of voice, and thankfully Tonetti was able to answer him in the same manner, albeit with just the right amount of subservience due the conquering army.

"She is for the General Eisenhopf, Captain." He spread his hands in a gesture of apology. "What can I say? When he has tired of her I will be sure to keep you in mind."

I could feel the man's hot eyes raking over me, my tumbled black hair, absurd height, and practically exposed breasts. He sighed gustily. "I doubt he'll tire of her for a long, long while. More's the pity." He stumbled on, and Tonetti and I breathed a sigh of relief, our eyes meeting in momentary accord.

We met only one more soldier, and the same tactics worked beautifully. Tonetti, in fact, was getting quite cocky, and I had to restrain him from bargaining for my future price. "For the general," he contented himself with muttering importantly. And then at last we were in the corridor outside his rooms, the long, tomb-like passageway dark and deserted.

"You're sure he's out of town?" I demanded in a whisper. "There's no chance he could suddenly return?"

"Signorina, trust me! He is gone, not to return till the day after tomorrow. No one else lives on this floor, and my brother-in-law is right now with my wife drinking chianti and getting very sleepy. All you have to do is search his rooms and then meet me down by the entranceway."

"You aren't going to wait for me?" I shrieked in a very loud whisper.

Tonetti looked suitably disheartened. "Much as I would like to, Madonna, I dare not. Someone must keep the gondola ready for our escape. If anyone questions you, reply as I have, that you are for General Eisenhopf. As you leave, simply say you grew tired of waiting."

"But what will the stupid paper look like?" I demanded desperately.

"According to my brother-in-law, it's on blue parchment with the seal of Franz Josef on it. And he hinted it might be somewhere near the bed. That is what made me think of using a woman for this."

"I'm sure that's not all that made you think of it, you coward," I muttered, panic making me rude. "Go away, then. I only hope to God I meet you when this is over."

He struck a pose. "I will await you as though my life depends on it."

"You'd better," I grumbled, opening the door and slipping inside the darkened room.

I leaned against the door for a moment, long enough to still the clamoring of my pounding heart. Now that the time had actually come, I couldn't afford to waste a second in needless panic. A few moments later I had a small lamp lit, and I surveyed the room in dismay.

There were a thousand places a paper could be hidden. The desk was littered with thick piles of official documents. More covered the chairs and tables, even the bedside stand had its share of reports and documents and such.

A long and desperate hour later I seemed to be no closer to finding it, and the panic began creeping back into my thoughts. All sorts of interesting information resided in General Eisenhopf's room, but not the piece I wanted.

I looked with distaste at the big, sagging featherbed, loaded with quilts and blankets. The first search had turned up nothing more than a tiny, pearl-handled pistol. On impulse I slid my hands under the heavy mattress and found the crackle of paper.

With shaking hands I drew it out into the fitful light. It was there in my hands, a thin scrap of official parchment that had caused me to risk my life, that could mean the difference between freedom and captivity for the ancient city of Venice. I stared at it in dumfounded bemusement for too long a moment and then tucked it down inside my bodice, letting it rest against my skin.

"Ah, and what is this?" A voice boomed out, and to my horror I came face to face with a burly, much-decorated, elderly Austrian soldier standing in the bedroom door. And I knew without a doubt that General Eisenhopf had returned.

Chapter Thirteen

HE MOVED CLOSER into the light, closing the heavy door behind him. "And where did you come from, my little pigeon?" he cooed in German.

I kept my face a perfect blank, aided by the overwhelming terror I felt. "I . . . I am a present for the General Eisenhopf," I stammered idiotically in deliberately terrible German.

The leer on the weathered old face broadened, and he moved so close I could see the tiny burst blood vessels in his large red nose. "But how delightful, Fraulein. How happy I am that I had to return early. And what a present, *mein Gott*! For the man who has everything, *hein*?" One meaty fist reached out and grabbed my breast, pinching hard. In another moment he had pulled my terrified, unresisting body against his large stomach, and greedy hands were pawing over my bodice, freeing my breasts from their meager confines. A wave of revulsion swept over me, causing me to shudder helplessly.

"Ah, you like that, *liebchen*?" The old lecher smiled, cheerfully misunderstanding my shiver. "And there will be a lot more for you, little one. I will . . ." I shut my eyes against the wave of nausea his filthy words were eliciting from me. I was helpless in his grasp, praying desperately for some form of deliverance. And then, knowing no deliverance would come, I trampled on his instep, eliciting a roar of pain. I then brought my knee up in his groin, my elbow in his throat, and ran, leaving the old lecher howling in pain and rage.

Down the deserted halls I ran, certain that pursuit was just barely behind me. But luck was with me, and I met no one. I was able to restore a small amount of modesty to my mauled attire, and at the end of the final corridor I saw the canal glistening in the moonlight, Tonetti pacing nervously back and forth.

"Did you find the general, little one?" A voice questioned close behind me, and I whirled to meet the gaze of the drunken young soldier.

I laughed convincingly. "I grew tired of waiting," I replied in my atrocious German. "He will have to wait for another night."

"But then you are free to spend the evening with me!" he said joyfully, and I shook my head with a great show of reluctance.

"Unfortunately not. I was promised to the general first. If he finds anyone has had me before him, I would hate to think of the consequences." Deliberately I bent over a bit, letting him ogle my cleavage. "For you as well as me."

"True enough," he agreed sadly, his eyes feasting on my frontage. "But be sure you look me up when he's finished, eh?"

"Of course," I said soothingly. He turned his back, and I ran the last few steps to the dubious haven of Tonetti s gondola.

"I have it!" I crowed in a triumphant whisper, fumbling with the front of my dress as I tried to dislodge the tricky paper. Finally catching hold of it, I thrust it proudly into his reluctant hands. "We've got to get out of here, fast! The general caught me. Everyone will be looking for us in a few moments. We'd better . . ."

"There she is!" A shout echoed through the building, and, looking up, I saw a pair of cold, evil eyes staring down at me from the overhanging balcony. Holger von Wolfram, accompanied by the two Venetian villains of the Doges' Palace. He pointed a beefy arm at me. "Get her!" he ordered roughly. "Kill her if you must, but get her."

Without waiting for Tonetti I took off into the night, my tattered satin dress waving behind me, my hair down around my bare shoulders, panic making my heart close to bursting. But one overlarge woman is a lot quieter than a platoon of Austrian soldiers. Each time I heard them gaining on me I would duck into one of the numerous alleyways and wait until the streets were silent once more. I knew I had a great deal more to fear from the two Italian henchmen, and even when the streets seemed deserted I moved warily, edging inexorably toward my goal. The apartment by the La Fenice.

Suddenly the theater loomed in front of me, and I broke into a run, up Evan's stairs like a terrified rabbit, banging on his door and calling his name. I looked back over my shoulder and saw the doorway darken, and I increased my pounding, desperation tearing at my vitals. What if he were out? Would I be murdered in this small, already blood-stained hallway?

And then the door opened, and I fell into the room, sobbing with relief and fright, and felt my trembling body enfolded into a strong, comforting embrace. I was safe. I was home.

For a moment all I could do was hold onto him like a lifeline. When at last I was able to stop the shuddering I moved away, reluctantly, and looked up into Evan's quizzical, concerned eyes. "Thank God you were here," I said simply.

The concern vanished, to be replaced by the blazing anger I saw so often in those silver-blue eyes. "What the hell," he began coldly, "are you doing out alone at this hour of the night? Why are you dressed like a strumpet? And what are you doing here? I thought you were safely asleep at Edentide."

"I was followed . . ." I began lamely.

"I don't doubt you were followed," he cut in. "Half the men in Venice were probably trailing you through the streets, what with you dressed like that! Have you no sense at all?"

"It wasn't like that!" I defended myself. "I . . . I . . ." I was about to pour out the terror of my night's adventures, the long, involved tale of my crazy mission to Venice, when I noticed for the first time my surroundings. Evan was dressed, or partially dressed, in a pair of soft gray pants and a hastily donned shirt unbuttoned to show the broad, tanned expanse of his chest. I noticed with distracted lust that it had a tracing of fine, golden hair. Beyond him was a candlelit table, the remains of a supper for two littered across the snowy cloth. A woman's evening cloak lay across the sofa, and from beyond the bedroom door I could hear furtive movements.

Evan must have heard them, too. "Excuse me a moment," he said roughly, and moved with a barely perceptible limp toward the bedroom door.

"Stay there!" he ordered over his shoulder, shutting the door behind his broad back.

The murmur of voices came to me, his deep and cool, and a light, laughing German voice. I thought back to the blonde at the embassy in dismay and began backing toward the door. This last was more than I could stand—the triumph of retrieving the paper was like ashes in my mouth.

In my confusion I bumped into the desk, knocking a sheaf of papers onto the floor. Picking them up, my eye caught only a line or two. Hastily I shoved them back on the desk and turned to run from the place, the contents branded into my mind. I knew from my sojourn in the general's rooms that they were official Austrian papers, and I knew without a doubt I was in the company of a spy. But a spy for whom?

"Where are you going?" The door shut behind him, and in the dim light I couldn't make out his face.

"I . . . I . . . ," I stammered witlessly, "I'm sorry to interrupt you. It was stupid of me. I thought . . ."

"You thought what?"

"I don't know," I floundered, smiling up at him, the tears brilliant in my eyes. "I am very gauche, I'm afraid. I didn't think." My hand reached the brass doorknob, and I turned it quickly.

"Wait a moment," he ordered, and I thought I could detect a softening in his voice. "Let me get my coat, and I'll see you home."

"No!" I cried in a strangled voice. The softening could only be brought on by pity, and pity was the last thing I wanted from Evan Fitzpatrick. "I'll be perfectly all right, I assure you." I kept the silly smile firmly affixed to my painted face as I felt the tears trickle down my cheeks. "I don't . . ." Words failed me, and on a choked sob I ran from the apartment into the dangerous streets of Venice, running once more from Evan Fitzpatrick.

As my thin leather slippers sped across the cobblestones, I thought I could hear a voice calling my name, loud, in almost desperation. A voice that sounded like Evan, but I couldn't be sure. Heedlessly I dodged into an alleyway, then into another, till I came slap up against a totally unfamiliar canal. I heard a soft footstep behind me, and as I whirled around I felt something hard come down behind my ear, and everything went black.

Chapter Fourteen

AS CONSCIOUSNESS slowly returned I became aware of a great many unpleasant things. An aching head was the first of my worries, followed by a cramped, stiff body, the stifling folds of a fish-scented tarpaulin preventing any fresh air from reaching me, and the steady rhythm of oars behind me. It didn't take the even rocking of the gondola to tell me I was in a boat; my riotous stomach, usually so sanguine about sea travel, was making it perfectly clear. Grimly I swallowed the bile that threatened to rise in my throat and kept my cramped, stiff limbs perfectly still.

Without moving more than a few pertinent muscles I could tell that I had been neither bound nor gagged. Apparently my captors considered the blow to my head enough to keep me immobile for hours. Indeed, it could have been hours since they clobbered me; I had no way of knowing.

"Durano is up ahead," one villain muttered in non-Venetian Italian. "Is she still out?"

A not-too-gentle foot prodded my posterior.

"Still dreaming like a babe," another answered, chuckling evilly. "The two of us might have a bit of trouble carrying a bambina like that, eh?" I knew with horror that it was the two Italian brigands from the Doges' Palace who'd finally caught up with me, and with a chill I remembered Holger's orders to them. "Kill her if you must, but get her." I should have stayed in Evan's apartment, no matter how *de trop* I was.

By amazing luck Evan had been able to rescue me before, but given the circumstances there was no way I could count on his help again, or even if he would want to. No doubt at this moment he was lost in the arms of his Austrian whore, far too involved in whatever deep game he was playing to spare a thought for me, on a boat ride to death.

I lay very, very still, tensing my muscles, and then in a sudden leap was over the side of the small boat, the fishy tarp following me like a cape. The water hit like a shock of ice, and I dove beneath the surface with more speed than care.

I was well paid for it. The water was only about four feet deep, and I hit my nose on an outcropping of rock. I surfaced briefly and found my shoulders caught in a punishing grip.

"Not so sleepy, eh?" the great hulking creature demanded with the travesty of a smile. "The signorina is far too eager to walk upon the shore,

Gianni. Shall we drag her behind the boat?"

"Pull her in, Ricci," the other replied in a bored tone of voice. "After we get to the house you can amuse yourself with her."

As I was unceremoniously pulled into the gondola I kept my limbs a dead weight, hoping against hope to tip the rocking craft. But Gianni, despite his non-Venetian accent, knew his way around a gondola, and I was dumped onto the seat with a casual cuff to the side of my head. I lay there in a mild stupor for another twenty minutes until the stars began to clear from in front of my eyes, listening with sick dread as they made their plans for my soon-to-be-departed virginity. I think I would have preferred that they murder me.

By the time we reached the shore a heavy, blinding fog had settled in, obscuring the land, the faces of my captors, and even a hand in front of my eyes. With stumbling, awkward feet I followed the first man, aided by a rough push every now and then from his trailing companion that would send me sprawling in the rough dirt.

I needed all my senses to keep me going. The island, or so I assumed it to be, appeared uninhabited; no lights or sound penetrated the thick fog that sank through my wet, clinging clothing and into the marrow of my bones.

"You want her first, Ricci?" the first man inquired courteously, and I could sense him turning in front of me. "It's all right with me if you do; I can always watch. Von Wolfram has said he no longer cares what we do with her."

"No, you go first," his companion replied with equal generosity. "Just leave something for me, eh?" His laugh chilled me more than the cold, dank fog. "Though there looks like more than enough for both of us in this one, my friend." He put one meaty paw in my back and once more I tripped.

It was miraculous that I was able to keep my balance, but my sudden equilibrium displeased Ricci, who was longing for the chance to kick my fallen body.

"Stupid slut," he muttered, crashing his heavy hand across my face. I stood there, still upright but swaying ever so slightly. I saw his hand upraised and numbly felt it connect with the other side of my face. I fell then, and lay on the rough dirt, every part of my body aching, knowing a good, hard kick was coming at any moment. I lay there immobile, determined not to cringe.

The kick never came. A sudden scuffle sounded behind me, a muffled oath, and the sound of a fist hitting flesh.

"Ricci?" Gianni spoke from up ahead, a worried note to his guttural voice. "Are you all right?"

Another thud, and then silence. Slowly, painfully, I struggled to a sitting position, my eyes trying to focus through the thick, gray fog. A seemingly huge, dark figure loomed ahead of me, with a horrendous humped back, hideously like something out of Victor Hugo. I stifled a small scream of terror as it came closer and then nearly fainted with astonishment and relief as I recognized it.

Evan had the body of the first bandit across his shoulders, giving him a nightmare quality in silhouette. "Stay there," he muttered tersely, moving around me with his burden. A few moments later he was back, picking up the second man and hauling him away with the same careless strength. And then finally there he was, his big, strong hands lifting me to my feet, his face through the mist no longer cold and angry but filled with concern.

I didn't even stop to question his miraculous appearance. I was still so stunned I merely accepted him as my *deus ex machina*. "Did you kill them?" I questioned, and was startled to hear my voice come out in a tiny croak.

He shook his head, the damp strands loose around his scarred face. "I dumped them in their gondola and pushed them out to sea. The tide should carry them to the mainland in a day or two."

"Won't they come back here?" The feel of his hands beneath my elbows was warm and comforting, and I barely stifled a protest as he withdrew them. Not for me, I reminded myself, thinking of the voice from his bedroom.

"I neglected to leave them with an oar. By the time they reach land and get back here, you'll be long gone. Out of Venice and halfway back to England."

It would be useless to question his arrogant assumption, so I said nothing. "How in the world did you get here?" My curiosity was reviving.

"By boat, of course. I've been only a short way behind you since you ran off into the night like a hysterical child. When the fog settled I was afraid I'd lost you for certain, but they'd just reached Durano. If they'd planned to go on I would have given up." His voice was flat and emotionless, but his eyes burned in the pale, fog-shrouded face, and deep within me I knew he would have followed us halfway across the Adriatic before he let them get away with me, no matter how many women he brought to his bed. Despite my chilled, wet garments I began to feel warmer.

"Can you take me back?"

"Not tonight. I was barely able to navigate following those two brigands. In this dense fog we wouldn't stand a chance. We'd reach the mainland just in time to welcome your energetic enemies." He turned around. "No, we'll have to find some sort of shelter and wait till the fog lifts. It should be clear by mid-morning, at the latest."

I viewed this last piece of news with surprising equanimity. "Does anyone live on this island? Someone who could take us in till morning?"

He shook his head, peering through the fog with narrowed eyes. "Entirely uninhabited. Why do you think they brought you here?"

"I have no idea, other than the obvious one," I lied. I could no longer trust him, much as I longed to. Apparently he wasn't much interested in my conjectures, for he moved off into the night, and I let out a small shriek that sent him rushing back to my side.

"What's wrong?" he demanded irritably.

"I would greatly appreciate it," I said in a stiff voice, "if you would control your distaste for me long enough to give me your arm while we wander around in the dark. I happen to be cold and wet and frightened. If it's too much for you, of course, please don't bother." My voice was frigid with rage and a barely controlled panic.

To my surprise a grin lit his face, and I felt my heart do a casual little leap within me. "My pleasure, Madame." He bowed, offering his arm like a courtier. "I will try to smother the normal disgust and repulsion I feel toward you for the time being, though it is very, very difficult."

Placing my hand on his forearm I could feel the steely strength of his muscles through the fine linen shirt. "Please do," I replied with distant courtesy. "And I will do my best not to compromise your tender sensibilities."

"You are too kind," he murmured, starting off at a slower pace through the impenetrable fog.

IT WAS A ROUGH journey. My slippers were in tatters, the satin dress completely destroyed by its sojourn in the sea. My head ached, my cheek throbbed, and it seemed to me I was colder than I had ever been in my life. Through it all the only comfort I had was the feel of Evan's arm beneath my hand, the certain knowledge that he would lead me to safety.

Instead he led me to a small, doorless, practically roofless cottage, sitting all alone in the midst of a damp and nasty-smelling swamp. His eyesight in the dark was far better than mine, and he steered my suddenly nerveless body to a narrow pallet on the floor. I collapsed in exhaustion and lay there, listening dazedly as he struggled with some damp lucifers. A moment later the meager light from a candle stub illuminated the hovel, and hovel it certainly was. The floor was dirt, the giant fireplace filled with wet, smelly ashes, and not a trace of food in the house. For the first time I realized how incredibly hungry I was, and a small groan escaped me.

"Don't you like it?" Evan demanded, and there was a curiously light note in his voice. One might almost have thought he was enjoying the whole miserable situation.

I summoned up my last ounce of courage. "Well, it's not quite as cozy as Edentide, but I suppose, given the circumstances, it will do." I watched in distrust as Evan disappeared into the next room.

"There's a bed in there," he said calmly, coming back into the room. "I suggest you get out of that absurd rag and try to get some sleep. I wouldn't dare attempt to get us out of here before daylight, even if the fog happens to lift sooner." He peered out the open door into the night. "I'll sleep here and keep watch."

For some reason I felt as if I'd been slapped in the face. "Keep watch for what?" I questioned stiffly.

He smiled an enigmatic smile. "There's always the chance your two admirers' paymaster might arrive. Durano is a perfect meeting place for people not wishing to be seen. Go on in and get some sleep. Tomorrow you can tell me what the hell you've been doing, wandering around Venice at all hours of the night dressed like that." His voice was like that of an indulgent parent, and I found myself with the curious urge to scream.

"Could we possibly have a fire?" I requested in a very small voice, trying to control my shivers.

"I'm afraid not." He sounded repulsively cheerful. "That would lead any-one who happened to be near the island straight to us. Once you get out of those wet clothes you'll feel warmer. Run along now."

I bit back the retort that rose to my lips as I struggled to my feet, the wet, horrible dress dragging around my ankles. If Evan Fitzpatrick felt safer treating me like an infant, that was his problem and not my own.

The inner room was pitch black, and I bumped into the bed, banging my knees painfully. I climbed into the sagging, creaking, no doubt flea-ridden mattress, and sat there, wet and miserable and cold and hungry. And alone. I sincerely doubted if I had ever been so unhappy in my entire life, and as my chilled, wet fingers fumbled with the myriad of tiny buttons, warm tears began sliding down my face. The buttons refused to yield to my clumsy fingers; the wet satin was too strong to rip, and I was about to throw myself down and cry my heart out when I felt, rather than heard, Evan behind me.

"You are a helpless one, aren't you?" he said softly, his voice and hands curiously gentle as he undid the buttons. It took him a long time, hampered as he was with my long curtain of sea-damp hair, the slippery satin, and the heavy, comforting blackness of the room. When he finished he moved away abruptly, before I had a chance to turn around, and his voice came from the doorway.

"Leave your dress at the foot of the bed and I'll hang it up later. There's a blanket beside your head . . . that should help. Good night." There was a great deal of finality in his voice, a finality I could scarcely argue with.

"Good night," I said in muffled misery, dumping my sodden dress on the dirt floor and tossing my cotton petticoats beside it. Some last vestige of modesty made me keep my chemise and pantalets on. He had seen me in them already, the time of my other abortive swim, and it hadn't seemed to arouse him then either. Sighing, I pulled the thin, thankfully clean-smelling blanket around my shivering body and tried to go to sleep.

Chapter Fifteen

IT WAS LATER, much later, when I awoke. My thin, cotton underclothing was sticking to my body like sheets of ice, my skin was covered with goose bumps, and my teeth chattered like castanets. I clamped hard on my jaw, biting my tongue in the process, and had to cope with the pain along with the dreadful, dreadful cold. I couldn't will my body to be still . . . the shivers that racked it made the bed squeak loudly in the silent cottage. I was trembling so hard I thought my bones would rattle loose in their sockets, and vainly I tried to find some warmth in the thin blanket I was huddled under. But there seemed to be no warmth there.

Suddenly I could stand it no longer. As surreptitiously as I could I crept from the bed, the thin blanket wrapped around my frigid body. The outer room was still pitch black, and silently I tiptoed past the pallet where I knew Evan would be sleeping, terrified that I should wake him. As I stepped outside I noticed with relief that the fog had lifted and a strong, clear moonlight was streaming through the clouds. The air was only slightly warmer, and even more damp, and I did the only thing possible. I dropped the blanket on the ground, and, barefoot, clad only in thin, damp, lace underclothing, I took off at a dead run across the now visible hill in front of the tiny house.

Ten minutes later I was back, panting, sweating, and gloriously warm and alive. The moonlight was very bright, and as I reached for my blanket I straightened up and looked straight into Evan's eyes.

"You must," he said slowly, "be entirely crazy."

The moonlight silvered his dark blond hair, gilded the planes of his face, and practically obscured the long, fascinating scar. With his linen shirt pulled from his breeches and unbuttoned I could see other, more recent scars on his broad, strong chest, and I wondered what kind of life he lived that would leave its mark so starkly on his fascinating body.

"Not entirely," I replied huskily. "I was very cold." A random shiver passed over my body, and belatedly I realized how very immodest my attire was, illuminated there in the moonlight. Not that that cold-hearted, god-damned man cared.

"You're going to be a lot colder in a few moments. A good case of pneumonia should keep you out of trouble for the next few months." His eyes were narrowed and unreadable, entirely unmoved by my overripe body in the thin scraps of cloth. I did my best to shrug off my disappointment.

Another shiver ran over me, and then another. "I suppose you're right," I said through chattering teeth, suddenly weak hands fumbling with the thin blanket that would provide me with scarcely any protection.

He moved quickly then, so quickly I scarcely saw him. In another moment the blanket was securely around me, and I was lifted in his arms as effortlessly as if I were one of those fragile blondes I was so envious of. For a moment I was blissfully, delightfully warm, and then he dumped me unceremoniously on the pallet.

As he towered over me I felt very small, very fragile, and very weak. It was a delicious feeling for a change.

He squatted down beside me, every line in his lean face visible in the soft moonlight streaming through the open door, and his strong hand reached out and gently touched my cheek. I winced, and his mouth tightened grimly.

"Perhaps I should have killed them," he said in a low voice, his fingers gentle on my bruised flesh. "Not that you don't deserve to be beaten."

Somewhere I found my voice. "I wish you wouldn't be so nasty. You really like me, you know you do. You wouldn't be following me around, pulling me out of scrapes, if you didn't."

He hesitated, about to say something, and then obviously thought better of it. "Perhaps I do," he conceded, "but I can't see much future in a friendship between us."

I swallowed. "I wasn't asking for friendship."

The beginnings of a wary smile appeared at the corners of his mouth, and his hand kept stroking my face. "And what were you asking for, Lucy?"

There was no way I could answer that, no way at all. I looked up at him mutely, but he wasn't the sort to let me weasel out of a situation.

"You don't really know, do you?" He was asking himself more than me. "I don't know if I've ever met such innocence before." Carelessly he pinched my other cheek and started to rise. "Go to sleep, my child, and dream of pirates."

I caught at his hand before he could move away. "Would you stay with me?" I asked, and my voice came out in a whispered croak.

His face was unreadable. "What did you say?"

"I said, Would you stay with me?" I repeated in a slightly louder voice that quavered only slightly. "I'm cold and frightened, and I don't want to be alone."

He stared at me for a long moment. "You're not making this easy, Lucy. Do you know what you're asking?"

Panic set in. "I . . . I thought it might be nice if we . . . if we just slept together. It would be comforting." I floundered helplessly before the amusement and something else in his silver-blue eyes. "I mean, without . . ."

"I know you mean without . . . ," he mocked me gently. "Unfortunately for you, life doesn't work out that way."

"What do you mean?" I whispered.

"I warned you that you would push me too far, and there would be no turning back." His hand slid behind my neck, under my damp, heavy hair, and I felt myself being lifted gently to him. His lips met mine in a kiss that brooked no refusals, no hesitation, no subterfuge. And without thinking I answered it, giving him all of myself with my mouth, opening for him, for the shocking invasion that I began to love.

His lips traveled along my neck, leaving a trail of burning kisses on my damp skin. He cupped my full breast, and involuntarily I stiffened, frightened.

He pulled away swiftly, as if burned, and I wanted to cry out in disappointment. "Change your mind?" he asked softly, his voice husky with desire.

I shook my head slowly, knowing I was mad, destroying any possible future for one night with the man I'd fallen in love with so precipitously. I was as reckless as my mother. "No," I said. I put my hands behind his neck, twining my fingers through the dark blond curls, and pressed my lips against the thin, angry line of his scar. "But Evan," I whispered shyly in his ear, "be careful with me. I'm not very brave."

He looked down at me, those strong, lean hands framing my face as he sought to read everything in my eyes. "My angel," he said, and this time the endearment was not mocking, "you are the bravest girl I know, so brave you drive me mad. And I will be very, very careful." And pulling me into his arms, he lay down on the pallet beside me, holding me gently, comfortably, until my trembling stopped, and I was no longer cold.

With deft, careful hands he removed the poor sodden scraps of my clothing before I was even aware of it. Turning in his arms I could feel his strong, rough-textured hands on my skin, stroking, warming me, setting me on fire. I should have been shocked, timid, shy, but it felt so good. More than good—he was exciting me in ways I had never even dared dream of. My head was pressed against his shoulder, my eyes tightly shut as his hands cupped my breasts, long fingers plucking at the tight buds of my nipples, sending shock waves through me, and if the core of fear within me had yet to be dissolved, why then I had perfect faith that no one but Evan would be able to do it.

He smelled like salt water and leather and sweat—an enticingly masculine scent that made me snuggle deeper against him. My brave, tentative hand crept out and touched his broad chest, and I heard an approving murmur from deep within his throat as his clever, clever hands kneaded away my terror. As they reached between my thighs I stiffened once more in fright, but this time he refused to back off. With gentle, inexorable strength he forced them apart, stroking gently, murmuring soft, comforting words until his hand found me, and I stiffened with something other than fear as he began a new sort of caress, one that made my hips arch in pleasure, and my hands gripped his shoulders tightly as I tried to stifle the gasp of joy that escaped my lips.

Pulling my head away from the comforting haven of his chest, I looked up and met his shadowy eyes. I kissed his mouth, opening mine beneath his probing tongue, and my body shivered with delight. Tentatively I ran my hands along the smooth, lean sides of him, over his firm, flat stomach. And then his hand grasped mine and brought it lower, so that I caught and held him. A groan of pleasure sounded in the back of his throat, and I felt a small surge of triumph wash over me, that I was able to give something back to him.

"God," he muttered softly, as his mouth moved along my skin, "you are so damned beautiful."

I squirmed beneath his hands, my breath coming in short, shallow gasps, longing for something I didn't recognize. "So are you," I said in a soft, breathless laugh, and found myself a victim once more of that fierce, gentle, demanding mouth.

And then his big, strong body covered mine, crushing any last protests I might have made. As one hand smoothed my tangled hair away from my forehead, the other parted my thighs. "This will hurt, my love, but only for a moment," but I was still too pleasure-dazed to worry. I felt first a gentle pressure, gradually increasing till there was a sharp moment of agonizing pain, and then it was past, and my body relaxed in the aftermath of the sharp, cruel hurt.

"I didn't like that," I said, disgruntled.

He was holding very still, and my body slowly relaxed around his invasion. "Sorry," he said in a breathless voice, not sounding very repentant.

"Is that all?" I whispered.

He looked down at me and smiled, a look of inexpressible tenderness in his usually cold eyes. "No, love," he murmured, and the endearment wiped away the last of my discomfort. "The best part is left."

With that he began to move, very slowly and gently at first, pulling out, almost all the way, and then pushing in again, gradually increasing the power of his thrusts as he could feel me respond. The heat surged through me, and I could feel the pressure building, building, until I thought I might explode. And then, to my amazement, I did, as I felt myself flooded with warmth, and the moonlit room swirled away into nothingness, and all I knew was Evan's lovely, strong body within mine, his rough voice gasping, "Now, now." And I heard a sharp cry of pleasure in the dimness and recognized it as my own.

After a long while, when our breathing had returned to normal, he moved off me, his arms still keeping me prisoner against his broad, strong chest. I could hear the racing of his heart, could feel my own beating a similar tattoo. "Christ," I said fervently, "I do love you." My only response was a tightening in his arms. But for the time being that was enough.

Chapter Sixteen

I WAS AN APT pupil. By the time the moon disappeared and the sun rose on that tiny, deserted island, I had had two more lessons in the ancient art of making love. My bones ached, my lips were bruised from kisses, and I was exceedingly tender in various strategic spots. I was also blissfully, idiotically happy as I lay wide awake in Evan's arms, listening to the sound of his heavy breathing, feeling the warmth of his body against mine. Never had I felt so in harmony with the world, and foolishly I envisioned nothing but more of such happiness in the future.

There was no reason under the sun, I decided, that Evan would have followed me, fought with me, rescued me, unless he was in love with me. It was only natural for him to fight the affliction; after a wife like his first one he was bound to be nervous of the whole idea of love and marriage. I felt nothing but a smug pride that I had overcome his scruples thus far, and I envisioned a small, lovely little wedding in the near future.

Mother would adore him at first sight, and Father—well, he'd be a good match for my intimidating father. I couldn't wait till they met.

As Evan's eyes opened and looked down on me lying sleepily in his arms, I had the very good sense to keep all these plans to myself. He would have to come to terms with it all in his own time. That he would, sooner or later, I had no doubt.

"How long have you been awake?" he asked gently, kissing me softly on the forehead. "Didn't I wear you out enough last night?"

I chuckled softly. "You did indeed." I ran a curious hand along his thigh, tracing the recent knife wound with careful fingers, and felt his reaction. "I still have some energy left, however." He smiled, and I was filled with such love I wanted to weep.

"Do you now? Well, you'll have to take pity on my declining years for a bit. *You* wore *me* out."

"Good!" I sat up abruptly, not in the slightest bit self-conscious of my nude body in the early morning sunlight. "Are you sure we have to go back to Venice?"

"I thought you loved Venice?" he questioned lazily, watching me out of narrowed eyes.

"Oh, I do. But I like this little island even better. There is only one problem with it."

"And that is?"

"No food. And I am absolutely starving!"

He laughed. "Nights like last night do build up an appetite," he agreed with false sobriety. "If you can somehow make yourself decent in that rag of a dress, I will take you back to Venice and treat you to the biggest breakfast you've ever eaten."

Jumping out of bed, I examined the pathetic rag that Tonetti had procured for me. "I doubt if it will be Florian's in this apparel." I searched around the dirt floor for my scraps of underclothing and began dressing with slow, deliberate reluctance, knowing he was watching my every movement.

"There's a trattoria not far from Edentide where no one will stare too badly," he promised, watching me out of hooded eyes. "And you may have fried eels, polenta, squassetto, pasta, and whatever else pleases your greedy little heart."

As I watched him dress quickly with his usual pantherish grace I would have almost foregone all that lovely food for the sake of another day on this enchanted island. I opened my mouth to say as much, then thought better of it. Instinctively I knew better than to push Evan too far, too fast. He needed time to come to terms with me, and that was the least I could give him. I was feeling a strange melange of emotions: triumph, smugness and the absurd desire to burst into tears. I planned to hide them all.

Therefore I was deliberately cheerful during the long ride back to Venice. We found a small shawl to drape around my low-cut shoulders and give me at least the appearance of decency. There was no way the dress could look like anything other than a rag, but with my hairpins lost and my long, thick, black hair trailing down my back, I looked rather slatternly anyway. With Evan to protect me, I had no fear that anyone would bother me.

True to his word, Evan fed me nobly in a small café only a few steps away from Edentide and surpassed me in appetite. The black-haired giantess with the ragged clothing did, however, create more than her share of confusion, but a glower from Evan's cold, angry eyes was enough to scare away the boldest admirer. Only one person failed to see the warning and came up with such an outrageous suggestion that my companion nearly strangled him on the spot. As it was, all Evan had to do was rise to his full, menacing height, which was almost a foot taller than the young macaroni, and the area around our table was quickly deserted.

As he sat back down again I chuckled, and his eyes met mine ruefully. "I don't suppose there's any chance you didn't understand him?"

"No chance at all. You should have named some colossal price for me . . . that would have scared him off faster than anything." I took another sip of the deliciously warm, strong coffee.

He reached out one strong hand and touched my face in a light, lingering gesture that was almost, but not quite, a caress. "He probably would have sold his mother to meet the price." The look in his eyes was inexpressibly tender, and I melted all over again. "Are you ready to go?"

It struck me then as very strange, that he had yet to ask me why I had been wandering out alone last night. However, I had enough sense not to initiate the conversation, so full of questions I didn't know yet whether I could answer. I had questions for him as well, remembering those damning papers in his room, the woman in his bedroom. Had he already serviced her before he followed me to the island? If so, he must have amazing . . . fortitude. Life was intruding into my idyllic interlude, but I could avoid it no longer.

Draining my coffee, I rose. "I suppose so. Would you rather I go back alone? We're only a short ways away."

He shook his head, and I noticed a slight grimness around his well-shaped mouth. "With your luck you would be grabbed within two yards of the palazzo. I'll see you to your door."

Flattered as I was by this concern, a certain uneasiness began to play beneath my ribs. I had no idea what excuse I would give Maggie, if I would bother to lie to her at all. If she got one good look at Evan she would know the truth anyway. But still no word of the future had come from his mouth, and patient though I was determined to be, I would have been much happier to have heard some expression of affection from his firmly shut lips.

Belatedly I remembered Tonetti. I had comfortably assumed that he had escaped safely last night with the all-important paper, but now doubts were beginning to cloud my assurance. As far as I could tell, the Austrians had been interested in me alone—a scented little fribble like Tonetti should have been counted as inconsequential. When I saw Uncle Mark I would have to pour out the details of the last few days of espionage and see if he could find out what happened.

We mounted the steps slowly, both of us reluctant. Before I had time to knock on the great oak door it was flung open, and a harassed and wild-eyed Maggie greeted me with a loud shriek.

"Miss Luciana!" she yelped, enfolding me into her exuberant embrace, dragging me into the darkened hallway. "Where the bloody hell have you been? We've been scared out of our minds!"

Carefully I detached her clinging hands as the door closed behind us, but to my amazement Evan was still there, his eyes unreadable, a cold, unsmiling expression on his scarred, handsome face.

"Who's we?" I questioned, foreboding settling in.

I heard a small crash ahead of me and knew before I looked up that Uncle Mark had taken up residence in the ancient walls of Edentide.

I was totally unprepared, however, for the look of recognition and respect on his face. "Fitzpatrick!" he greeted Evan, moving past me with barely a glance and clasping his hand in a hearty grip. "I should have known that you'd be here. Did Bones arrange to have you watch over Luciana?"

For the first time in my life I felt as if I had been given a crushing blow to my vitals. I stood stock still, motionless, waiting for Evan to answer.

Those silver-blue eyes came nowhere near me. "If you'd bothered to check before you came racing after her you would have known that, sir." His voice was both respectful and reproving. "Bones wouldn't have sent her off without arranging protection. Much as I disapprove of this whole insane scheme, the Old Man still has *that* much sense."

"You must have been the man she saw at the train station, then," Uncle Mark continued. "What an idiot I've been! All I can do is thank God you've been around to keep an eye on the little minx . . . At least this blasted Tonetti's never bothered to make contact. Damn it, it's no job for a lady! She could have been killed."

I kept my face averted, but I could feel Evan's eyes rest on me, and I waited for him to expose me. "Just so," he said briefly. "The entire idea of sending a young, inexperienced female into a dangerous situation like this is not only absurd but doomed to failure. I've been trying to scare Lucy out of Venice ever since she arrived, but with no luck. I'm handing her over to you, now, sir. I'm sure I can count on you to see that she leaves by the early evening train?" There was a note of steel in his cool voice. "I don't have time to look after her anymore, and we can't afford having her get in the way. Besides, I'm sure Bones would like her back in one piece."

I felt my body flinch slightly as if from a blow, and I caught Maggie's worried glance from out of the corner of my eye.

"You can count on me, Fitzpatrick," Uncle Mark said heartily. "I never wanted her to come in the first place. Well, all's well that ends well." He stroked his mustache, well pleased.

At Uncle Mark's words a bolt of cold, hard rage swept over me, mixing with my shame and mortification. I threw back my shoulders, tossed my still damp hair back, and met Evan's unreadable eyes with a brilliant, cheerful gaze.

"You tricky little thing," Uncle Mark chided me with a misguided attempt at playfulness. "It looks like your brief sojourn as a spy is over. You never let on that Fitzpatrick here was keeping an eye on you. I would have felt a lot easier about the whole thing. Evan's one of Lord Bateman's top men."

"Oh, he's very, very good," I said brightly in a high clear voice. "I had no idea, uncle, that he was working for Bones. You know how gullible I can be; I thought he had conceived a grand passion for me and that was why he was following me around Venice. Isn't that absurd?" If my brittle voice was close to tears Uncle Mark was too obtuse to notice.

"Well, well, when all's said and done, Evan's a very clever fellow," he remarked cheerfully. "And I'm sure you're delighted that he was just doing his job. You've never had any interest in young men; though damn me, it's about time you did. Well, we'll get you back to England and see what we can do about it. Wouldn't want her to end up on the shelf, would we?" he questioned Evan jovially, and I nearly screamed. Evan said nothing.

"Well, I've had a fascinating time," I said brightly, quick to fill the awkward silence. "But I'm quite exhausted. I think I'd like a bath, Maggie, and a rest, if we're to catch the train this evening." Turning my back on the three of them, I started off in the direction of the kitchen. The tears were beginning to come, and I wanted to be well out of the way as quickly as possible.

I paused by the door, counting on the dimness to shield my tear-streaked face from Evan's cold, prying, spying, damnable eyes. "Goodbye, Mr. Fitzpatrick. It's been most instructive." And before he had a chance to reply, if he even wanted to, I turned and continued with deliberate and unhurried grace into the kitchen, closing the door behind me with a soft click.

Maggie wasn't far behind me. One look at my stony, tear-streaked face, however, and she kept all her questions to herself. "It won't take long to get the bath ready, Miss Lucy. The gentlemen have left the house for a bit; you could go lie down for a bit."

"I'll bathe here," I said numbly, dragging the huge iron washtub into the middle of the room.

"Do you want to talk about it?" she questioned in a low voice.

"No, Maggie. Not now, and maybe not ever." Coldly, grimly, I turned my face away from her sympathy, or I might give way completely. This was my secret, my pain, and I wasn't about to share it. It would be mine alone.

At least I still believed one thing. No matter how shameful the eventual aftermath, it hadn't been a mistake.

I HAVE ALWAYS detested self-pity, but oh, my God, I did feel so damnably sorry for myself. I sat in the tub and soaked away the stains and traces of the last twenty-four hours and knew I had only myself to blame for it all. Only my absurd complacence that had me ready to believe a man like Evan Fitzpatrick would fall in love at first sight simply because I did. If I had left him alone he would have watched me from a distance, protecting me from Holger's brigands and leaving my pathetic virginity intact.

But no, I had had to chase, and flirt, and tease, and finally invite him into my bed, all under the mistaken notion that he had developed a grand passion for me and was too shy and cynical to do anything about it.

Shy! He was about as shy as an adder, and as honest and straightforward. Why hadn't he simply told me? I had certainly given him chances enough. All he'd had to do was look at me out of those aloof, beautiful silver-blue eyes and say, "Child, I am not following you for any reason other than espionage." But he'd allowed me to trick myself—no, even encouraged it.

"You're getting the floor wet with all that splashing," Maggie said dryly.

"And I won't have time to wash it before we catch the train, what with all the packing I have to do."

"Then it can mold and mildew with my blessings," I said bitterly. "And this whole house can tumble into the lagoon for all I care."

"Miss Lucy," Maggie said gently.

"Don't call me that!" I cried, splashing some more. "My name is Luciana. If some idiot of an English spy can't get my name straight that doesn't mean you have to forget after twenty-three years."

"I wish you wouldn't carry on so," she continued, as if I hadn't said anything. "It's not as black as you think. He does care for you. I'm sure he does. How could he help it?"

I took a deep, shuddering breath and met her troubled gaze with a weak semblance of a smile. "No, he doesn't care for me, Maggie. The sooner I accept that, the better. I suppose I'd better go home and marry Johnny Phillips after all." I rose, dripping from the tub, and caught the thick, clean towel she held for me. "And we'll simply have to hope our first child isn't as premature as Mama's."

"Well," she shrugged, "with any luck you won't have to worry about such things. I've finished with your yellow dress, Miss Lucy . . . Luciana, and you can wear that. You'll look a treat, I know you will."

I DIDN'T FEEL a treat. I stared at my reflection and saw a cold, sad, mournful face. No longer a Giorgione Madonna, but a Renaissance Magdalene instead. With only myself to blame for it.

My nose wrinkled in sudden distaste. There was a familiar, rather foul odor emanating from somewhere in the room. Staring around me, my eyes fell on something I'd missed before. A gaily wrapped package on my bed.

Tearing off the wrappings, I discovered a bottle of the nasty lilac scent Tonetti used so liberally about his person. There was no sign of a note anywhere around it, and with misgivings I unstoppered the filthy stuff. The bottle was empty except for the overwhelming traces of scent and a squashed-up note.

I spent a few futile minutes trying to dislodge the missive before smashing the bottle on the marble floor. The note this time was short and terse, unlike Tonetti's usual style. The spelling, however, was just as atrocious.

"Dear Lady," it read. "I am hiding in the Palazzo Carboni. The Tedeschi have followed me here and are watching all the time. Of your goodness, please come and rescue me and the paper. If you take the paper I will manage to escape myself. Deliver the paper to Signore Evan Fitzpatrick. Yours in dire need, Enrico Tonetti."

In a moment my mind was made up. I had spent far too much valuable time mooning after the so-clever Mr. Fitzpatrick. If I were to tell him and

Uncle Mark of Tonetti's predicament I had no doubt they would try to storm the place. A single woman had a much better chance of success, and I was that lone woman.

A knock sounded on my door, and I thanked heaven I had shoved the small, straight chair in front of it.

"It's only me, Miss Lucy," Maggie called. "Mr. Fitzpatrick asked if he might see you in private before he has to leave."

I bit my lip to stifle the protest. "Where is he going?" I asked casually.

"He's got to talk with the Austrian authorities before you can be allowed to leave Venice. He seems most disturbed, Miss Lucy. You really ought to see him." Her voice was wheedling, and my resolve stiffened.

"I don't think so, Maggie. Tell him I'm resting, and that I asked you to say goodbye for me." I kept my voice languid as I pinned up my still-damp hair with hasty fingers.

"I don't think he'll like that, miss."

"I don't give a damn," I said in the same sweet voice as I tied my best bonnet on, grabbed a pair of gloves, and headed for the balcony. "If he ever comes to England I will see him there. By the way, Maggie, who brought the package?"

"That nasty-smelling box? A very dirty little boy. He said it was from his father. What have you been doing while you've been in Venice, Miss Lucy?"

"Nothing, Maggie, nothing at all."

A loud, irritated sigh came from the other side of the door. "All right, Miss Lucy. You take a nap and we'll be ready to go in a few short hours."

"Fine," I yawned. And, tensing my muscles, I dropped over the balcony and onto the pavement five feet below.

Chapter Seventeen

THE PALAZZO CARBONI was not at all difficult to find. Uncle Mark had pointed it out to us on our first trip down the Grand Canal as an example of the foolishness of Venetians. A very rich Venetian noble had begun the grandiose structure, only to run out of funds by the time the first floor was completed. Despite the architect's screams of despair, a second, shorter story was added, giving the poor building an absurdly pinheaded appearance. It had been lived in by various families until it reached its present state of dereliction, the home, like some of the other great palazzos during this time of *dimostrazidne,* of rats and the large Venetian alley cats. When I thought of poor Tonetti living in those dank cellars my heart went out to him.

The palazzo, for obvious reasons, was uncomfortably close to the barracks. Tonetti hadn't gotten far last night, I thought unhappily, pulling my large, shielding bonnet closer around my face. I was counting on the light of day, the demureness of my dress, and the large, unflattering bonnet to protect me from the suspicions of any prowling Tedeschi. As I strolled along the fondamento I barely received my share of curious glances, and it took only a moment's inattention on the patrols' part to enable me to slip into the damp, deserted hallways of what had once been intended to be the showplace of Venice.

"Tonetti!" I whispered loudly, stepping gingerly over the littered passageway. "Where are you?" A dark, eerie silence answered me, and a rat scuttled across my foot.

Barely suppressing a scream, I turned to run out the way I had come. And then I remembered Evan Fitzpatrick, those cold, silver-blue eyes telling me I had outlived my usefulness in Venice, and my resolve stiffened. Gritting my teeth, I turned once more to those long, empty hallways with their lofty proportions and their sleeping bats, the cobwebs and filthy litter degrading the noble lines of the building. On silent feet I moved along, every now and then calling Tonetti's name in a loud whisper, with no answer but the scuffle of tiny paws.

I was almost finished with my swift, silent tour of the ground floor when another small, strange noise alerted me to the fact that I was not alone. I could feel the tiny hairs on the back of my neck rise, and I turned around with all the grace and calm I could muster to face Holger von Wolfram's glittering, pig-like eyes.

"Are you looking for something, Fraulein del Zaglia? Or should I say, looking for someone?"

I let out a silly little laugh. "Why, Colonel von Wolfram, fancy meeting you here of all places! I was just taking a tour of the old palazzo. My parents had told me of it when I was a child, and I've always taken a great interest in architecture. I thought before I left . . ."

"I am sure you have. The barracks that are nearby, for instance, I'm sure must have proved fascinating to a scholarly young lady like yourself."

"The barracks?" I echoed vaguely. "I don't believe I've seen them. Are they fairly ancient?"

"Old enough. You will be far more enthralled with the new prisons. They were built in the sixteenth century, but I think you might prefer them to the older ones."

"I don't think I'd care to see the prisons, thank you," I said with icy dignity.

"No?" he said politely. "Well, I doubt if you'll have much choice in the matter. Why do you suppose we allowed Tonetti's note to reach you? By arriving here you have incriminated yourself, Fraulein. As soon as we locate Tonetti and the very valuable document you stole from General Eisenhopf, there will be no question as to your guilt. I can deal with you through proper channels since my less-accepted methods didn't seem to work. I must congratulate you, Fraulein. There are not many women who could outwit the Ferrari brothers. Though I gather you had some assistance from Herr Fitzpatrick." He admired his highly polished nails. "Now if you will just tell me where Tonetti is, we can bring this entire thing to a pleasant conclusion. And do not worry, Fraulein. Hanging is a swift death, if the hangman knows his business. And our executioners are very knowledgeable."

"From lots of practice, no doubt," I snapped, my mind rushing ahead of him. Despite his interception of Tonetti's note, he obviously didn't know where he was right now. Obviously Tonetti found a way to escape safely rather than wait for me to rescue him, bless his cowardly hide. At least it meant the incriminating note was still safe.

"If you've lost Tonetti that's your problem. Obviously I expected him to be here, or I never would have come." There was no telling whether or not he'd been able to escape from this moldering wreck or was simply hidden so well the Austrians couldn't find him. Surreptitiously I slipped my reticule, which was heavily weighted with gold coins, from my wrist. "And what if I prefer not to die, Colonel?" I said conversationally. "When Venice is ceded to France I doubt they'd countenance the murder of a woman."

"You are forgetting the revolution," he said grimly. "A great many women lost their heads, some even as pretty as you, my dear. But once we regain the very important piece of paper Venice will never be returned to France," he smirked. "So you see . . ." The reticule hit him with full force, the weight of it knocking him off balance.

I didn't hesitate a second. I was off at a run before the purse left my hand, down the long, littered corridors, leaping over trash and garbage and cats, my heart about to burst, my lungs aching, running, running, running, with Holger's booted feet closer and closer behind me.

"It is useless, Fraulein," he shouted, tripping on a large black cat who proceeded to spit at him, "my men are waiting outside. You will never escape!"

I didn't waste my time answering his lies. I just kept running. For a moment it looked as if I might win, that Holger was so far behind me he'd never catch up. And then a large, evil-looking rodent ran in front of me, catching at my skirts, and I fell amid all the ruin, rolling over the disgusting rat and ending in a huddle by the dark, wet corner.

Before I had time to gather my dazed wits about me Holger was there, leaning over me with a grin of vile proportions, a hundred teeth seeming to shine in the dimly lit corridor.

"I will find Tonetti, never fear," he said, panting and disheveled. "But first I will take care of you, Fraulein." Two thick hands fastened around my throat and began pressing. The dark corridor became even darker, with tiny bursts of light in the back of my brain. "I will take the pleasure of finishing you myself. This"—and the hands tightened—"is for the trouble you have caused me. And this"—even tighter—"is for your damnable father who made a fool out of me. And this"—and the voice seemed to come from a long ways away—"is for your lovely mother."

Suddenly the pressure was gone, and I collapsed back into the corner, gasping for breath, the pain in my throat so horrid I thought I would prefer to die. As I lay there trying to pull myself together I could hear the sounds of a desperate fight, and the scent of overblown lilacs assailed my nostrils.

"Are you all right, dear lady?" Tonetti's voice came from somewhere near, and two soft hands began patting mine ineffectually. I straggled into a sitting position, my eyes trying to focus on the two men struggling. "Where were you?" I tried to demand, but my voice came out in a hoarse croak.

"I was watching all the time," he announced proudly. "Thank heaven Signore Fitzpatrick arrived in time. I thought you were done for,"

A horrid, rattling sigh suddenly issued forth from the enmeshed fighters, and one figure slowly detached itself, leaving the other limp on the blood-stained floor. I looked up to meet the cold, embittered silver-blue eyes of Evan Fitzpatrick.

"He's dead," he said briefly, not bothering to look at me. "Do you have the paper?"

Tonetti jumped up, all eagerness. "Enrico Tonetti, at your service, Signore Fitzpatrick. Let me tell you what a pleasure it has been to serve you, and to render my small assistance to the lovely Madonna del Zaglia. I can only . . ."

"Do you have the paper?" The voice was cold as ice, and Tonetti stammered to a halt. Searching through the somewhat tattered gondolier's outfit he still wore, he came up with the battered blue missive.

"Signore Fitzpatrick, my money . . . ?"

"Your money will be sent to you." Evan snatched the paper out of Tonetti's nerveless hands and tucked it into his pocket after no more than a cursory glance. Such an anticlimactic disposal of all that I had worked and risked my life for was almost more than I could bear. But Evan continued smoothly, ignoring my involuntary start of protest, "Do not think, Tonetti, that I didn't notice your heroic actions today. If it had been up to you she would have died."

Such concern warmed me, but only for a moment. He reached down and yanked me to my feet with such force I fell against him. He righted me instantly, and the rage on his handsome face was so formidable that a weaker woman would have quailed.

Holger's armed guards were, as I had guessed, a fabrication. We left the palazzo with no difficulty, Tonetti's sad, dark eyes following us speculatively. I wished I could say goodbye to him, but I didn't dare with the gimlet-eyed brute beside me.

Not a word did he speak to me during the gondola ride down the Grand Canal, not a glance did he give me. It was as if I were beneath his contempt. I sat there, huddled, angry and miserable, my throat aching, wondering what I could say to him, choosing not to say a word.

We were just pulling up to the railroad station when he spoke, and his words were like tiny daggers sinking into my flesh. "Ferland and your maid are waiting for you," he said coldly. "You'd best hurry."

"Evan . . ." I tried to speak, but the noise that came out of my damaged throat was barely recognizable.

No sympathy crossed his furious face. "With any luck you'll never talk again," he said in a low, bitter voice. "And if we had more time I'd beat you within an inch of your life for running off like that. Of all the wicked, stupid things . . ."

He jumped out of the docked gondola and pulled me onto the fondamento, his hands rough and painful. "We're only lucky someone didn't die because of your willful idiocy. Go back to England, Lucy."

And with that he turned and left me, striding off down the quay without a backward glance for the poor, lovesick, angry girl he left behind.

"Where the hell have you been?" Uncle Mark exploded from directly behind me. "We've looked everywhere for you! Fitzpatrick took off like a bat out of hell when he read that message you left in your room. I somehow don't think you've been very straightforward with me, my girl." He peered at me more closely, something in my face breaking through his outrage. "Are you all right?" he asked gently.

"Perfectly fine," I croaked, placing a shielding hand against my aching throat. "Mr. Fitzpatrick just dropped me off. We had a small contretemps, but everything is just fine."

"What in God's name happened to you, Lucy?" he demanded, and I winced at the appellation.

"Holger von Wolfram tried to kill me," I replied briefly. "I'll tell you all about it once we leave Venice. Shall we go?"

"I suppose Fitzpatrick saved you," he speculated. "It's a lucky thing he got you here in time. It would have been no more than you deserved if we'd gone off without you. You'd have had to rely on Fitzpatrick's good graces, and he never was much of a one for the ladies. Of a certain type, that is."

"Well, you've saved him from a fate worse than death," I croaked. "Shall we go?" I repeated, wanting to stay, wanting him to leave me behind, some rash, romantic part of me wanting to run back to the apartment by La Fenice and throw myself at Evan's feet.

"I suppose we'd better. I don't think he really would have minded, you know," he added enigmatically as he handed me into the private coach and the furious recriminations of Maggie.

"Who?" I asked, wearied at Uncle Mark's irritating habit of harking back to ancient conversations. "Who wouldn't have minded what?"

"I don't think Evan Fitzpatrick would have minded having you left on his doorstep," Uncle chuckled.

"Well, we'll never know, will we?" I said bitterly.

"You can ask him when he comes to England."

"He never comes to England. He prefers to abandon his son to his brother and run around Europe playing spy."

Uncle Mark looked unconvinced. "Well, I wouldn't be surprised if he found an excuse in the very near future to arrive in Somerset. Thanks to you and Tonetti he won't be needed in Venice much longer. As a matter of fact I'll wager you ten pounds that he does."

"And I'll lay you a fiver," Maggie piped up.

I looked at the two of them through tear-filled eyes, both of them so very dear to me. The train started with a jerk, and we pulled slowly out of the Venice station. "You are both trying to cheer me up," I said damply. "And I appreciate it. And I'll also take your money, and double you!"

Chapter Eighteen

"LUCIANA, MY DOVE, would you do me a favor?" My lovely, small, delicate mother interrupted my thoughts as I sat disconsolately on the terrace, staring out over the rolling hills of Somerset. "Your brother Paolo's little friend has disappeared. He's quite unhappy, and I wondered if you might be persuaded to look for him."

Belatedly I roused myself from my torpor. I had been very lucky indeed to have suffered no more than a gentle scold from Mama and not a word of reproach from my father. One look at my stricken face when we arrived back in England had silenced my parents' natural rage, and during the last two weeks I had been both cosseted and blessedly left alone, to get over my broken heart as best I could. I had no doubt Maggie and Uncle Mark had filled them in on all the gruesome details of our sojourn in Venice, down to my night spent on Durano in the company of Evan Fitzpatrick, but apart from a few more reassuring hugs than normal, my parents behaved as if nothing had happened. I couldn't have been more grateful.

"Which one?" I questioned idly. The hot English sun added to my lassitude, draining me of my usual energy, so that all I had done for the past two weeks was sit on the terrace and stare off into the distance.

"Oh, you haven't met this one yet. Paolo's been off visiting with his people, and the two of them arrived last night after you'd retired," Mama said blithely, a surprisingly mischievous expression in her china-blue eyes. "The boy is quite lonely and unhappy, and apparently wandered off while Paolo was talking with his brothers."

"Well, Paolo's brothers can be a bit overwhelming," I said caustically. There were five of them, ranging from my oldest brother, Lucifero, who was twenty-four and surprisingly sedate, down to Marco, age one and a half, who was already horrifyingly demonic. Paolo, at age ten, was right in between and had friends wandering in and out so frequently I barely noticed them among our massive brood.

"But you will be a dear and go look for him, won't you?" she entreated, knowing full well that I would. "You are so good with children."

"You mean you're tired of me moping around all the time?" I said, and Mama smiled her charming smile.

"That, too, darling. A walk will do you good before lunch."

AS I STROLLED aimlessly across the lawns I thought back to that curiously naughty expression on my mother's pretty face. She had never been terribly adept in the art of prevarication, and briefly I wondered what was going on in her active mind. Before I had time to work it out, however, I came to my favorite old oak tree, my ancient refuge from a hoard of brothers, all eager to tease me about my height or pull my long, black hair.

Tilting back my head, I looked up in the leafy branches and immediately espied a small figure perched halfway up.

"Hallooo," I said in a soft, friendly voice so as not to frighten him. "What are you doing in my tree?"

"Is this your tree?" A young voice floated down, and I could hear the traces of tears in it. "I'll come down."

"Oh, no, don't bother," I waved him back. "Do you mind if I come up?"

A disbelieving laugh floated down. "Ladies can't climb trees," he scoffed.

"This one can," I replied, plopping down on the grass and stripping off my shoes and stockings. I rolled up my sleeves, tucked my voluminous skirts into my waistband, exposing an indecent amount of calf and ankle and snowy white pantalets, and began the climb.

By the time I reached the boy I was more than slightly out of breath, but game as ever. For the first time since I had left Venice I felt a small trace of happiness. And then I looked at the boy, and my triumph faded.

"My, that was splendid," he said with great enthusiasm, his silver-blue eyes meeting mine and his young mouth curving into a grin. "I didn't think anyone your age could do that."

Quickly I put a rein on my emotions. "Oh, I'm not so very old," I said casually. "And I bet both my mother and father could climb up here even faster than I did."

"I like your mother," he confided. "I don't have one anymore, and I didn't like her very much when I did. But yours seems just the sort of mother one should have."

"And what do you think of my father?"

"He's a little frightening at first, but I think he doesn't really mean it. He seems like a pretty good father, too, but I like mine better."

"You still have a father then?" I questioned artlessly, holding my breath for his answer.

The shadow came down over his plain, earnest young face. "Yes, I do. And he's the best man in the world, and it's not his fault that he can't be with me right now."

"I'm sure it's not," I soothed him.

"Sooner or later he'll come for me, and we can go back to Penstow. That's our house in Cornwall. It's by the sea, and it's very beautiful and very old. It's made of stone, and the roof leaks a little, but we have a barn with cows and baby kittens, and houses for the men who work there, and a beach to swim from."

"You're very homesick, aren't you?" I questioned gently.

He nodded his bright gold curls, and I wanted to press his little head against me. Instead I gripped the thick branch tightly and swung my legs in an aimless fashion.

"It's all right with Uncle Simon and Aunt Sophie," he continued stoutly. "They live in Somerset, too, you know. But it's not the same as having your very own father, is it?"

"No, it's not the same," I agreed quietly. "Listen, Jamie . . . your name is Jamie, isn't it?" He nodded, and I felt a queer little feeling rush through me. Not that I had needed that last confirmation; the eyes had been proof enough. "There's nothing we can do about your father. He's off in Venice, and we can't make him come and get you any sooner than he wants to. But why don't you and I just spend the day out here, away from the house and all those people. Paolo's a very good sort of fellow, but he hasn't seen his brothers in a long time, and they get awfully rowdy. I know of an excellent fishing hole . . . you do like to fish, don't you?"

"Rather," he exclaimed, his eyes lighting up. "I used to go fishing with my father, after my mother left. But ladies don't fish."

"And ladies don't climb trees or go barefoot," I mimicked. "I don't know where you've gotten your ideas about ladies, Jamie, me lad, but this lady does all those things and more. Are you game?"

A big grin split his face. "I bet I catch more fish than you."

"You're on." I paused. "By the way," I said deliberately, words that I never thought I'd say. "My name is Lucy."

IT WAS A LOVELY day. I cajoled some simple fishing tackle out of Muggs, one of our tenant farmers, and very tactfully allowed Jamie to catch two more fish than I did. We threw them all back but had great fun wading in the brook, splashing each other and shrieking with inordinate merriment. I showed him my secret cave and the ancient raven's nest that had long since been deserted. We wandered through my favorite blackberry patch and ate so much we felt sick. My hair came unpinned as always and tangled down my back, my arms were scratched from the blackberry bushes, and my dress was ripped in a dozen places.

Jamie looked a trifle better, but then, he was dressed for an excursion in the woods. Even so, it was an odd pair of ragamuffins that made their way across the lawn in the late afternoon sunset, and I wondered a trifle guiltily whether anyone had gotten the wind up after our long disappearance. We had just reached the steps when Maddelena appeared, jabbering noisily in Italian and throwing up her hands in excitement.

"You'd better go with her," I advised Jamie, who looked uneasy at the sight of Maddelena's witch-like appearance. "She wants to clean you up." I gave him an encouraging little nudge, and he followed her dutifully enough. The sight of his small, compact little body and the soft nape of his neck beneath the gold curls made me want to snatch him back from my old nurse and hug him fiercely. I controlled the impulse, but just barely.

"You're wanted on the terrace, Miss Lucy," Maggie popped out of the door, bustling with excitement. "Best hurry up and change."

"If I'm wanted they'll have to take me as I am," I said calmly, wiggling my toes in the long grass. "Can you have someone go down to the giant oak tree and get my shoes, Maggie? I'm afraid I left them there."

"Certainly, Miss Lucy. And you owe me ten pounds." She whisked herself back into the house, and I stared after her in perplexity. Mentally shrugging, I wandered around to the terrace, taking my time about it. I could see my parents' backs, my mother's with her small waist, my father tall and lean and elegant still. And then, just as they turned and saw me, I remembered what Maggie had said. And with a horrid sinking feeling I looked across the terrace, and my eyes met the silver-blue gaze of Jamie's father.

"Ah, there she is at last," my father said silkily. "One thing I've always admired about my only daughter is her elegance in matters of dress."

And the one thing I've always hated about my father is his nasty, sarcastic tongue.

"Luc," my mother reproved him softly. "Don't be wicked." She turned to me, and the mischievous look was out in full force. "Luciana, darling, Jamie's father has come to fetch him. Did you find him in the woods?"

"Yes." My voice came out in a strangled croak, and I could hear my father's damnable laugh.

"Come, Carlotta." He held out an elegant arm, and my mother took it, giving him her usual adoring smile, a smile he returned, before raising a satanic eyebrow at his erring daughter. "We will leave these two alone to make their own mistakes. Don't be stubborn, child," he warned, and the two of them glided into the house before I could open my mouth to protest.

As they went I heard my mother's soft, clear voice say to Luc, "I think we should go back to Edentide, my love. The Austrians will be gone soon, and I have a longing for the old place. It still seems to work its magic on people." She sighed happily.

"Whatever you say, little one. Though I think we make our own magic . . ."

Evan stared at me for a long moment. "You look very fierce."

"Do I?"

"You shouldn't blame me, you know."

"I don't blame you for anything. Except for not telling me the truth," I accused him bitterly.

"Lucy, when you willfully involved yourself in the dangerous game of spying, you gave up any right to, or acquaintance with, honesty. It's not a truthful profession, and you should have damned well known it."

"I know it now." If this sounded sulky I couldn't help it.

He moved closer with that pantherish grace I had tried so hard to forget, and the night on Durano came rushing back to my senses with stunning force. "Do you realize," he said softly, "how silly you're being? With that dignified manner and your appearance? Your dress is torn, your bare feet are muddy, you've got freckles across your nose, and blackberry stains on your mouth. I wonder . . ."

Before I could guess his intention he had pulled me into his arms and his mouth was on mine, draining any attempt at resistance I might have shown. He raised his head and looked down at me with teasing laughter in his sunlit eyes. "You do taste of blackberries." And then he kissed me again.

"Father!" A shrill voice sounded from inside the house, and thankfully I felt myself put to one side as a small dynamo came hurtling through the French doors and into Evan's arms. As I watched father and son greet each other an uncomfortable knot formed in my throat, so that I had to swallow a few times and blink back tears.

"Have you met Lucy?" Jamie demanded when the initial welcome was past. "I've just met her, but she's my dearest friend. I want her to come to Penstow and visit sometime. Are we going to Penstow, Father? How long can you stay this time? Isn't Lucy pretty? Do I have to go back to Uncle Simon's? Couldn't you possibly stay a bit longer this time?" The small face was wistful.

Evan laughed, his eyes lighting up his dark, scarred face and making him look almost carefree. "Yes, I've met Lucy. Yes, she's very pretty. Yes, we're going to Penstow, and yes, I'm staying a long, long time. And no, you don't have to go back to Uncle Simon's."

"I don't?" he shrieked, his face suffused with joy. "Not ever? Are you going to stay with me forever and ever?"

He smiled. "Forever and ever. So, for that matter, is Lucy."

"What?" It was my turn to shriek in disbelief, only to have Jamie's strong, little arms crush the general area of my knees. "I most certainly am not!" I was torn between tears and laughter. "You don't want me at all. It was I who seduced you, and now you feel you have to be a gentleman."

"Don't be absurd. I've never behaved like a gentleman toward you, and I'm certainly not about to start."

"But you don't love me!" I wailed.

"You foolish woman, I loved you from the moment you fell at my feet in the Merceria. Or maybe it was when you went swimming in those tiny scraps of clothing in the broad daylight. It was definitely by the time you tossed the tea tray on General Eisenhopf's mistress."

"That was General Eisenhopf's mistress?" I questioned, momentarily diverted. "How nice."

"They didn't think so," he grinned. "Are you coming with us?"

"No."

"Lucy"—and his tone of voice was low and dangerous—"I am too old for all these romantic misunderstandings. If you are too stubborn I'm sure I can persuade your father to help me club you on the head and carry you off to Cornwall. You are alarmingly easy to kidnap."

"You wouldn't!"

"I would, and he would."

I had no doubt of it. Much as the idea appealed to me, it might have its share of discomfort. I looked down at the child clinging to me like a limpet and met those trusting, silver-blue eyes, so like his father's. He smiled up at me, and I smiled back.

"Father," Jamie said confidently, detaching his crushing grip, "she'll come. But you have to be nicer to her if you want her to be my new mother. You practice," he ordered his formidable father, "and I'll say goodbye to Paolo."

He disappeared into the house, past the amused and curious figures of my eavesdropping parents, and Evan turned back to me with a dangerously tender expression on his tired, scarred, handsome face. "Very wise, is my young son." He proceeded to obey Jamie's instructions, and not much practice was needed at all.

The End

About the Author

Anne Stuart is currently celebrating forty years as a published novelist. She has won every major award in the romance field and appeared on the NYT Bestseller List, Publisher's Weekly, and USA Today. Anne Stuart currently lives in northern Vermont.

Made in the USA
Middletown, DE
18 April 2022

64434169R00154